A More Perfect Human

CJ Powell

Copyright © 2021 by C J Powell

All rights reserved.

No portion of this book may be reproduced in any form without written permission from the publisher or author, except as permitted by U.S. copyright law.

Nige

London. An unfamiliar skyline. It has changed. It will always change.

Towers of glass and metal stretch up like the hands of the devoted praying to an unseen God. Holographic billboards blink neon from a clouded sky. Hover taxis buzz past like slow, fat flies. Everywhere is light, everywhere is sound, unrelenting.

A perfect distraction from other things that might occupy the night sky.

In a quiet corner of the docks, Nige Davies stands over the worktop in the boat shed he rents, and slathers peanut butter on white bread. He tucks his phone between his ear and shoulder with his free hand.

"Did you want to meet up Friday?" he says. "A few beers and a burger with your dad?"

The silence answers his question. That jarring sensation in the pit of his stomach.

"I can't, Dad. I've got dinner with clients, then straight back to the hotel. We've got an early flight. I didn't tell you because it's not like I'm even stopping."

"You could stay at mine and I'll drop you off at the airport in the morning?" He doesn't want to sound desperate.

"I wouldn't want to put you out. The flight's at 4. I'll just want to get a few hour's kip before I head back. Work's a nightmare at the moment, what with Kenneth's birthday Saturday."

Nige knows when to stop. Pushing just makes it awkward so he changes the flow hoping to keep Lewis on a little longer. "They doing a big party again this year?" He knows they are. They do it every year.

"Uh huh, we're introducing a whole bunch of new influencers on the show. It's a pretty big deal."

"I take it business is good."

Lewis laughs. To Nige the sound is golden.

"When's it not?" There's a brief pause on the other end. Muffled words. "Look, I gotta go. We'll chat another time."

"No problem, matey," he says, hoping he sounds less disappointed than he feels. "Let me know next time you're in town. It'd be great to see you, even if I'm just taxiing you from the airport to your meeting or something."

"Sure Dad. Will do." Lewis hangs up.

Nige was the same at his age. Making hay while the sun shone. But you missed a lot working nights. More than you might think. And those early years were irreplaceable. One day your little man becomes a real man, a beautiful butterfly. And when he does, that boy you used to play cars with, that little mate who tugged on your hand pulling you around on garden adventures looking for caterpillars, finally discovers you aren't this infallible guardian; he sees through the perfect facade you hold up to protect him, and then disappears for good.

When your boy grows up, a friend dies.

Nige flicks a fleck of sawdust from his sandwich - the stuff covers the worktop, the floor, even his single bed in the corner - and wraps it in clingfilm. He places them in his bag and checks his watch. Nearly time to pick up Aidan.

He turns off the mains gas and puts his freezer dinner packet in the bin.

What would Lewis do if he found out his old man was living in a boat shed? Would he come then? Would it be worth the trouble, the worried looks, just to see him and the kids? Sometimes Nige finds himself resenting the man Lewis had grown up to be, how that man had erased his little boy. He never thought it would happen despite how many times his own dad had told him, "they grow up too fast."

The old man had spoken from experience. He'd missed a lot of Nige's childhood.

Nige looks to the boat that dominates the centre of the room. The twenty-foot yacht rests on two large wooden stands. It had once been his father's.

His phone pings with a text. It's Korrigan, his business partner. *Change of plan. You and Aidan aren't working the club tonight. Had a private enquiry. I'll explain in person. Grab him and get here asap.*

Nige takes one last look over the shed, pulls his windbreaker up over his head, and steps out into the rain.

The Investigation

In a noisy corner of Camden, Trent Macadamia PI sits on the corner of his mahogany veneer desk in the fifth-floor room he rents. The building is old. It shows.

He keeps the office gloomy. It gives him an air of mystery. It also hides the dark patch of growing damp on the wall behind him. It does not hide the smell of musty old books, which gives him an air of mouldy librarian.

It's not possible to stay in the room longer than a few hours without developing a hacking cough.

He clears his throat. "Why don't you go to the police?"

"I did. Our insurance has been downgraded. He has to be missing for two weeks before it kicks in."

The day has been rainy, but hot. Stifling. Almost tropical. One of those autumnal anomalies that makes you think summer is back for one more stab and gets the papers frothing at the headlines about another 'Hottest September On Record'. Where you can't tell if you're covered in sweat or condensation from the thick, heavy air.

Though it's not yet dark, the overcast sky means the streets below are lit with an orange glow. Shredded by dusty blinds, the lights cast diagonal amber slits across the ceiling.

"And you don't want to wait because…?"

"Because he's my husband, and he's been gone a week."

Mac's new client sits watching him, waiting. If this were a classic detective movie, Suzy Wheeler would be a dangerously attractive blonde bombshell with legs up to her armpits and hair that smells like wild orchids on a soft desert breeze. But it's not. And she's not.

Despite the question of where such a long-legged woman could possibly keep her internal organs, and the worrying amount of time he'd have to spend following her while she shopped for trousers, Mac had always hoped that his line of work would bring him in to the proximity of – and furthermore a complicated but highly sexual relationship with – a blonde bombshell with legs up to her armpits. Someone to spend those long, lonesome nights with after working one of the grislier cases involving a particularly errant pet or dastardly cheating husband. A relationship only enhanced by his stoic lack of commitment and rogue-like independence.

Alas, not this time.

Suzy Wheeler, like all women not airbrushed by some bastard trying to sell leg lengthening lozenges, has legs that end around waist height. And though Mac doesn't know what a wild orchid smells like, least of all one on a desert breeze, he knows this woman does not carry that particular scent. Instead, it is the faint soapy hint of Head and Shoulders he catches as he leans forward. To top it off, she's a former school friend of his older sister and knows that he was once admitted to hospital, aged ten, with five raisins stuck up his nose and one in his ear.

So, you know… probably not his type, anyway.

"Do you think you can find Harry or not?" Her eyes are red rimmed. She fidgets with the strap of the mock leather bag that is draped over her shoulder.

Harry's her husband. A bodyguard working for a 133-year-old man called Terrence, one of the Di Blasio corporation's influencers. Harry didn't return home after his last shift a few nights ago.

She called his mobile. No longer in service.

She called Di Blasio. They told her Harry was working overtime, and that she shouldn't expect him back this week.

And when she asked to speak to him directly, they told her it wouldn't be possible.

With an index finger, Mac pokes around inside one of his ears and screws up his nose hoping to hide his uncertainty with nonchalance. He's not quoted a missing persons case before, but she doesn't know that. Does she? "Well, it's going to be expensive."

"I don't have much. Amanda said you might do mates' rates." She looks hopeful.

He tucks the short stub of a pencil behind his ear then rubs the week-old stubble on his chin. Mates' rates? Bloody Amanda. Not the best footing to start a negotiation. His stomach rumbles as if to remind him that he's only got one bag of rice and several frozen peas back home for the next week. He coughs to cover the sound.

"I've only ever heard of one other investigator taking a case against Di Blasio," he says. "I think she's still in prison. So I'm afraid mates' rates is still expensive. There are just no cracks you can get inside." He turns his hands back-to-back and wiggles his fingers as if easing something apart. Suzy frowns at the motion. He quickly stops. "And if you do find a way in, they close around you like a Venus flytrap. If I'm going to risk it, I have to make it worth my while."

He makes a show of looking over his notepad. The page is blank save a few doodles and the words 'Di Blasio' in large blobby bubble letters which he has drawn a line through. After Suzy mentioned the company name, he didn't feel the need to write any more.

He tucks the pad into the chest pocket of his once white shirt. (Not yellowed by age, just a lack of skill with a washing machine.)

"Amanda said this might cover it," she says and places a cheque on the desk. His lamp – the one with the green plastic hood, one that Mac thought looked particularly "detective-y", and cost less than a fiver from a nearby charity shop – illuminates the dog-eared paper starkly on the dark wood. It's about half of his base rate, but his bank balance is currently balls deep in the red, and he hasn't picked up a case in over a month.

His eyes flit between the cheque and her face. "What you've given me is thin at best." He shifts uncomfortably on the corner of his desk. His leg is going dead but this is his position of power, and he's not going to shift until he's got the case at his price.

She sniffs, and for a moment Mac thinks that she might cry. What would he do then? She clears her throat and her jaw hardens.

"Everyone I speak to tells me Di Blasio is impenetrable, but your sister said you'd at least try." She moves her bag to her lap and holds it firm. "She said you were good."

Mac drags his hungry eyes from the cheque on the table. There's enough on there to cover this month's rent, and he is already behind by two.

"Don't get me wrong, I don't like to say no to a challenge, believe me, but there aren't many PIs in London that would risk a case involving Di Blasio."

If he doesn't take the job, he'll just be bumming around in his lung-destroying office until either consumption or starvation take him to the other side. But maybe, with some expert negotiating, she can pay a little more.

Suzy screws up her face in frustration. "There must be something. Harry can't have just disappeared. I just want to talk to him. Make sure he's ok."

Mac moves his head from side to side, weighing up the options.

"He's never been gone longer than a day or two," she continues, "and never without a quick call."

"Hm." Mac untucks his pencil and taps it against his lips in thought. He spins off the desk and sits in his wheelie chair across from Suzy. "Have you thought that maybe his phone just ran out of battery?" He takes his notepad from his pocket. Feels more confident behind it, like a mask. He peeks over the top the way a psychiatrist might after asking a particularly oedipal question which could turn out to be the key to all of their patient's trauma. "You know what us boys are like."

"It's been nearly a week." She doesn't look happy.

"I'm just going over all the options before I give you a proper quote. Maybe he…" Mac looks around his tiny office for inspiration. His eyes fall on a vertically skewed blind, which in his mind looks like teeth. "Broke his mouth?"

"What?"

"Yeah, you know." Mac squares and stiffens his jaw as if it's immobilised by wire. "Cn't steek."

"This was a waste of time." She stands. Snatches up the cheque and stuffs it into her bag. "Amanda didn't say her *little* brother was good." Mac doesn't like the emphasis on little, nor the look. "She said you were desperate. But I guess if you're happy to mock potential customers—"

"Woah." Mac pings forward from his chair and moves to the other side of the desk holding out a hand. "Wait. I guess I could have a look around. I have um… some numbers I could ring."

She turns, having already made it halfway through the door. "So the cheque will cover it?" She leans her head to one side, face passive.

Bugger. He's only gone and fallen for the classic walkaway. The oldest trick in the haggler's handbook.

"Well, I know a guy whose brother works for Di Blasio. He could point me towards someone on the security team. Help me get my fingers under some metaphorical paving slabs and see what's wriggling beneath." He wriggles his fingers again.

She doesn't move.

"It's better than what you've got, which is nothing." He leans his head to one side and pouts, hoping it makes him look a little more friendly, in the way a small puppy might in order to get close enough to steal your burger.

Suzy takes a step back towards the desk. "I'm just so worried." She lets out a heavy sigh.

"Look, I'm sorry. I wasn't making fun. Just take a seat." He holds the back of her chair and turns it invitingly "Would you like a cup of tea? I have chamomile." When he says he has chamomile, he means he has one mystery bag left in his desk drawer. It could be anything.

She plops down. "I'm ok, thanks."

Phew, the bag lives to brew another day.

He flicks through the roller calendar on his desk. It's positioned so that she can't see it, hiding the lack of entries. Not a single mark until his own birthday in three months, and then his mum's in five.

"Now," he says to himself, flattening his nose with one finger in concentration. "If I move that to there, and that to there, I think I can get started tomorrow afternoon." He looks up at her. "I could have something to you by the end of the week. Now, about my fee…"

Suzy's mouth tightens into a reluctant half smile. She takes the cheque from her bag. Mac loosens his tie.

"I'm afraid that's all I've got. With Harry gone, and our justice insurance downgraded, I can't access anything more at the moment." She looks at the cheque as if it were a dead pet.

He feels bad. There really isn't anything he'll be able to get out of The Di Blasio Corporation. But if she's going to pour her money down the drain, then it might as well be his drain.

Then he has a thought. Maybe he can feed two birds with one scone.

A glance at the clock. Early evening. It's about the right time.

He stands, rolling his sleeves to his elbows, and walks towards the window as if pacing the room in thought. He looks out. Scans both sides of the street near the cashpoint across the road, which shines like a beacon in the grim London night. The hard spatter of rain on the windowpane makes it difficult to see anyone on the road, but the park has a lot of places to hide.

He sucks air through his teeth and looks at her. "Look, Suze, I could maybe do you a bit of a cash in hand discount? I'd need half now though."

"Are you sure?"

He winks and clicks his tongue showing a confidence he doesn't feel. "I am!" He pushes a button on the intercom on his desk. "Wendy, start writing up a contract for Mrs Wheeler. I'll be down with details in a second."

The intercom isn't actually connected to anything. In fact, it is an ancient answer machine bought from the same charity shop as his green desk lamp. Its wire disappears into his desk drawer, coming to a frayed stop next to the sole teabag. Despite the astronomical rent price, and a year or two of trying to build up a Moneypenny/Bond style relationship with Wendy, his package doesn't stretch to use of the in-house receptionist.

He isn't even sure her name is Wendy. But looking like you have a receptionist makes you seem a little more *luxuriant* – a word Mac often says whilst rubbing his thumb and first fingers together. And also a word he thinks means something it doesn't.

"Thank you, Trent. I really appreciate it."

"Don't worry about it. A friend of Amanda's…" He lets the sentence run off. She gets it.

"Is there an ATM nearby? I don't have much cash on me."

"Who does these days?" Mac looks to the side and smoulders. Thinks, does this look cool? "There's one across the street." He stands and moves towards the door. "If you go now, I'll watch you from the window there."

"Watch me? Why?"

"Oh, no reason. Get the money and run back here." He waggles two fingers like little walking legs. "I'm sure you'll be fine."

Suzy seems to shrink inward, clutching her bag to her chest as she moves through the door. "Run?"

"You know, cus it's raining. I'll make a few phone calls right now. Get the investigation moving as soon as poss. Hurry back. You'll be ok." He smiles. His hand twitches; he almost pats her on the head. Doesn't know why. Restrains himself just in time.

She sighs and hurries down the corridor.

Mac picks up the phone.

"Mikey," he says after a few rings. "Macadamia. How the bloody hell are you?"

Mikey Mansfield runs a bar a little way off the main stretch in Camden. It's a perfect spot for meeting various informants. Dark, and full of lonely old drunks who can't even look up from their drinks, let alone remember what they see when they do.

"What is it?" says Mikey, charming as always.

"Straight to business - love it. Your brother? He still work for Di Blasio?" Mac pulls his trench coat and wide-brimmed hat from the stand by the door. Puts them on.

"Cousin and yeah." What little brightness Mikey had in his voice when he picked up the phone has disappeared completely. "Why?"

"Could you give me his number? I'd love to have a chat with him about a case I'm working on." Mac leans closer to the window and uses one finger to pull down the blind, sending a cascade of dust to the sill below. He can see Suzy hurrying across the road towards the cash point, like a moth to a flame. She pulls her hood down tight over her head against the downpour.

"I don't really want you bothering my family. You're alright Mac, but you're a massive ache in the nuts when it comes to your cases. I've got customers who don't come in anymore if they think you're gonna be around. What's it all about?"

"Client confidentiality. My lips are sealed."

Mikey grumbles.

"Come on mate." Mac adopts Mikey's half Essex, half cockney lilt, pronouncing it more like 'caaahm' with roughly thirty more a's. While Mac's accent is usually that of a rather chipper Englishman, he often employs the tone of those he speaks to in an effort to fit in. "I gotta earn a crust." Something he's heard Mikey say when referring to money. He hopes the context is right.

As if by magic, Mikey's tone lifts. "Oh mate, don't get me wrong - we all gotta do what we gotta do. For the life of me, I ain't gonna stand in the way of someone earnin' a crust. But come on, I need a little info or you ain't gettin' the number."

Outside, Suzy reaches the cash machine. Rain lashes down. Ominous shadows move behind the trees across the road. A huge puddle takes up half the crossroads that separate the bank and the park.

"How about if you give me the number, I never question another one of your regulars again?"

"That a promise?"

Two hooded figures emerge from the bushes by the park and stalk towards Suzy.

"Yep, yep. I promise," says Mac. It's not a promise.

He rifles through the drawer of his desk, keeping his eye on the road. Inside are several plastic straps, much like those slap-on bracelets that were so popular in the 90s. The ones your Mum never let you have because rumour had it that apparently, after an over-eager slap, someone from another school lost an arm.

He grabs three. Stuffs them in the pocket of his trench. Then takes a cheap knock off Go-pro from atop his desk and fixes it to the lapel of his trench coat.

"Got a pen?" says Mikey. "Just need to find my mobile."

He glances once more out of the window. The two men are circling around the big puddle, one clockwise, the other anti. They converge on Suzy's position.

"Can you text it, Mikey? I need to dash." On his way out, he passes an old umbrella stand and grabs a cricket bat signed by the Surrey County Cricket team of 2009. The year of Mac's birth. A present from his father, given shortly before the old man fled the nest never to be heard from again. Mac hated cricket. But the wood was solid enough.

"His name's Phillip. I'll send it…"

Mac doesn't hear any more. He's already running down the stairs, hand planting his hat on his head, coat winging behind him.

The Bounty

By the time Mac reaches ground level, he is breathless. He pants his way across the reception, breath reverberating off the tacky faux-marble walls, and steps out into heavy rain.

Wendy – or whatever her name is – doesn't even look up from her phone. It's not uncommon for her to see him fly across the reception out of breath.

At the end of the street, the two hooded men already have Suzy pinned against the cash machine. One has his hand on the back of her neck. The other stands a few paces behind with a knife in his hand.

Mac doubles his stride, and with the harsh white noise of the hissing rain, they don't hear him approach. He lifts his bat and cracks the one with the knife across the back of the head. The man stumbles and Mac kicks him in the knee, sending him off the curb and into the puddle. The murky brown water swallows him whole.

Suzy screams as the other guy pushes her to the concrete. He turns to face Mac. His pointed, rat-like features screw up when he sees the bat Mac is holding.

Just as he opens his mouth to speak, a pair of women sprint out of the park and through the puddle towards them. They wear matching black catsuits. One has a bright blue shock of hair pulled tight in a ponytail; the other has the same style in red.

Mac's eyes widen and he fumbles for the bracelets in his pocket. "Oh no. Stop. Not again." He shouts at the newcomers. "I'm filming it. I'm filming it. I'll appeal if you get him."

"You know only bracelets count, Macadamia," the red-haired woman shouts. "We've been trailing this guy for weeks. He's ours."

Mac grabs the nearest mugger and snaps the bracelet around his forearm. It clicks together, then whirrs and tightens around his bony wrist.

"Bollocks," says the guy as the bracelet flashes a bright green; the beacon is active and the police will be closing in on him soon. Forgetting his accomplice, he turns and runs into the park.

The other man stumbles out of the puddle in the opposite direction. "Leave me alone," he whines, but the two women are on him like seagulls on a chip packet.

"Yeah, leave him alone," shouts Mac, jumping into the puddle and sloshing towards the fray.

Red grabs the man, and with impressive athleticism, throws him to the tarmac. Blue snaps a bracelet of her own around his wrist.

"Oh, come on," Mac huffs. "I stopped the mugging. I should get the bounty."

"You snooze you lose Macadamia," Blue says, and shoves the man away as his bracelet starts to flash. He runs too.

"Peace out bitch!" says Red as she throws him the V's with both hands before running back into the park with Blue in tow.

Mac looks down to check his camera is still on. If it caught everything maybe he could appeal, but that's doubtful. Like Red said, only bracelets counted when it came to the bounty.

And if you snoozed, you most certainly always 'losed'.

"What just happened?" says Suzy, now stood out of the rain under the porch of the bank. Her arms folded across her chest. Weight shifted to one side. Eyebrows raised.

"Are you ok?" he says and moves to join her.

"I'm drenched, but I'm fine. Answer my question."

"Bounty hunting," he says. Surely she's heard of it.

Suzy shakes her head.

"The police don't have time to look out for petty muggers so people like me, and those two women, get a small bounty for whacking one of these on their wrists." He pulls out one of the bracelets and hands it to her. "Once that's on, it's not coming off. The police home in on the location and pick up the suspect. It works well for petty crimes like muggings. Crimes where it's more preferable to do the time than chop off your arm."

"How much do you get?"

"Depends on their place in the London's Most Wanted charts." He takes out and holds up his phone. "There's an app. That guy was probably about a hundred quid. It works out cheaper than the police doing the work to track them down." He stares off into the park. Grimaces. "So I just lost a hundred pounds to those gits. Again!" He stamps his foot and slips off the kerb.

"Hm." She turns the bracelet over in her hands. "So looks like you can probably give me fifty off my balance then."

"What?" says Mac as he rejoins her on the pavement.

"Don't play stupid. You sent me out here as bait. The least you can do is give me money off." She hands the bracelet back. "Or I'll tell your sister you sent me down here to get mugged. What would your mum say?"

Mac gulps. He knows exactly what his mum would say. "You wouldn't."

Suzy steps to the cash machine and takes out a thick wedge. "Half now. Half when you find my Harry." She holds it out to him. "Minus fifty."

Jesus Christ, where did she learn to negotiate? The FBI? Mac takes the money and stuffs it into his pocket.

"Bye Mac."

She pulls the hood of her coat over her head and steps out into the rain, leaving Mac alone under the porch of the bank.

He runs a thumb along the edge of the cash in his pocket, then takes out his phone. Mikey has sent through his cousin's number. Mac calls it.

The Job

Nige drives his Ford Focus through the rolling gate of his security firm's small warehouse. He ducks his six-foot six frame out of the car and sucks in the warm night air, which is fragrant with the swampy odour of the Thames and the exhaust fumes of passing trucks.

The docks are quiet aside from the continual hum of throbbing industry and the sound of sea gulls on night patrol inspecting bins. Powerful lights shine from the tops of cranes which loom on the horizon like alien war mechs, protecting the unfinished skyscrapers that seem to rise from nowhere, crushing London's last bands of green. Starlike coronas in the constant downpour give the underside of the absolute cloud cover an orange-purple hue.

Nige approaches the front door and turns the handle out of habit. It no longer works. It just goes round and round ever since Spoony Phil kicked his way in after forgetting his keys, again. He'd fix it tomorrow, because he knew no one else would, and because it would niggle in his mind until he did.

He readjusts the sign on the door - 'Korrigan and Davies Security' - and buzzes the intercom.

His firm hires doormen to 'almost one percent of London's most welcoming pubs and clubs'. Or at least that's what it proudly states on their website.

"Who is it?" His business partner's voice chimes through the little speaker box by the door. He sounds uncharacteristically and alarmingly chipper.

"It's us, Korrigan," shouts Aidan, before slamming the passenger door of Nige's car, causing the whole thing to rock violently on its suspension.

Nige winces.

"I know." Korrigan laughs. "Get in here you two."

There's a click and a buzz, and the door cracks open.

They climb the stairs and, without sticking the kettle on for their usual pre-gig cup of tea, cross the kitchen to the office where the big man dwells. They are already late for this evening's job at a well-known under 18's club night in Camden.

As Nige enters, he checks his watch.

"Boys, boys, boys. How is it going?" Korrigan grins at them from the other side of his desk. He looks as if he's trying to keep a swarm of bees in his mouth, and his shoulders wiggle in some form of strange happy dance causing his stomach to jiggle in time.

He's always been heavy, but a lifetime's habit of overeating to muscle up, followed by a move to a desk job – without redefining his calorie surplus – has done him no favours.

He plonks his black boots up by his keyboard, kicking an old crisp packet stuffed with protein bar wrappers to the floor. As he leans back and places his hands behind his head, his swivel chair groans like a bow-legged beach donkey carrying one too many children.

For a moment it looks like the chair might shoot right out from under him and spill him onto his back. By some miracle, and despite the chair's undeserved lifetime in chair hell, it maintains its structural integrity for the good of its owner.

The office is a classic 'manspace' with empty food wrappers, unfinished mugs of murky brown tea, and a smell reminiscent of an expensive cheese buffet confined to a badly ventilated room on a summer's day.

"Come on, mate." Nige taps his watch. "We're late. It's those twin Di Blasio influencers tonight. I should really get in early to show their security around."

Next to him, Aidan buzzes with excitement. His youth predisposes him to hold celebrities in higher esteem than his more experienced colleagues. "I've been looking forward to this *all* week."

"Well, have I got some news for you!" Korrigan slides a neatly bound file across his desk with his index finger. He gets a kick out of binding, even if it's just two pages. His eyes linger on the cover for a moment before darting from Aidan to Nige. Eyebrows dancing in what *could* be described as a sensual way, but definitely shouldn't. His hands shake ever so slightly, face red, fighting to keep his lips sealed. He's clearly excited about something.

Nige takes the file and opens it to the side so Aidan can also read it. His jaw tightens as he recognises the smiling face in the photo.

Kenneth Bailey, at one hundred and thirty-four, is the oldest of the five Di Blasio influencers and the biggest celebrity on the planet.

Aidan titters.

"Are you serious? This is a joke, right?" He turns the page to find a list of dos and don'ts, then again to find a schedule which goes in to far too much detail. "Tonight? Bit last minute."

Korrigan's eyebrows continue to waggle with maddening enthusiasm. He pushes his tongue into his cheek and shakes his head, rocking back again on his chair. It lets out a protesting squeak as if to say "Kill me!"

Nige glances back at Aidan. The young lad is beaming like the sun, but his eyes are glazed, not really focused on anything. He remains silent, though his mouth works slowly. An odd expression for someone who usually resembles a marauding viking.

"Aidan." He clicks his fingers in front of his face. "He's joking." He shakes the job spec at Korrigan. "You're just doing this because you know I can't stand these bloody influencers. There's no way we get hired to look after three of them on the same day."

"I'm not joking," says Korrigan. "They want you up at his apartment tonight."

"But we're already booked to look after the twins at the club. Seems a bit of a coincidence, doesn't it?"

Korrigan shrugs, then frowns. "I spoke to Kenneth's manager on the phone. She said it was an in-house recommendation. Your boy works for them, right?"

Nige thinks back to the earlier conversation with Lewis. "He hasn't mentioned putting us forward for anything. Either way, we haven't got anyone to spare."

"I've already made the call to the club. Those two new guys we interviewed last week are going to fill in for you." He pauses. "Spoony Phil is going to take charge over there."

"Hm." Nige rubs the back of his bald head. He isn't so sure about Spoony Phil. The man's too much of a 'head butt first, ask questions later' kind of guy. He drops the binder on the desk. "You're trying to tell me the biggest company in the world has hired us –" he points at himself, Korrigan, and then at gawpy Aidan "– to look after the biggest celebrity in the world, one on one? Like proper bodyguards?" He glances around the office. Raises his hands to indicate the mess. "That's deranged. Why the hell would they hire us?"

Korrigan clutches his chest and gasps in mock offence. "Are you saying we're not up to the task?"

"That's exactly what I'm saying. Don't Di Blasio have their own security to take care of the influencers?" He frowns and taps the assignment on the desk. "This guy is—"

"He's Kenneth Bailey." Aidan's words come out in a dreamy monotone. "He's my hero. A national treasure. First The Twins and now this…"

The kid still has that glazed look on his face. Nige waves a hand in front of his eyes with no response.

"Hero? What has he ever done except look pretty and do a thousand bloody sit-ups every hour for the last one hundred years? What good are sit-ups if you can't even throw a punch?"

Aidan doesn't answer; instead he continues to gaze at nothing.

Nige gives Korrigan an accusatory glare. "You've broken Aidan. He's gone into an idiot fanboy trance. I thought you were bloody joking when you said we were looking after those twins, but this…" He shoves the binder back across the desk. "We can't do this."

"You keep saying things like that Nigel, and sooner or later you'll die and prove yourself right." Korrigan presses his knuckles on the table and pushes himself up to stand. "This is our chance to hop into the big leagues." He stabs the binder with a thick, hairy finger.

Nige sighs. He did not become a doorman to hop into the big leagues. He became a doorman because he was tall, could take a knock or two, and desperately needed the money. Plus, he liked the idea of protecting people out for a good time from those out for a bad one. Thirty-five years later you don't start having dreams of security superstardom.

"And besides, I've already taken half the payment." Korrigan continues. "It's way more than the bonus they're paying to look after The Twins at the club." He opens the binder to the last page. "See for yourself."

Nige pulls the binder closer so he can read it better. "Christ on a bike." He picks his eyes up off the paper and pops them back into his head. He looks at Korrigan again. "Jesus Christ on a bloody bike." He looks back at the figure on the bottom of the page. "Jesus flippin' Christ on a bloody bike."

"And that's just the 50% they paid up front," Korrigan says. "I've signed an NDA. You'll need to do it too before you head off. They want you there at eight. No earlier. No later. It's all pretty hush-hush. Apparently they're a bit short staffed or something."

"Short staffed?"

"Some bug going around with the usual bodyguards. They don't want the influencers to catch it."

"Fair enough." Nige shrugs, then wrinkles his nose. He moves his head from side to side, weighing it up. He doesn't like it. They've never looked after someone so famous, and with Aidan barely into his twenties, it would be up to Nige to come up with a plan if something went wrong. "I'm still not sure. This is kind of big."

"Well, if Lew suggested us then he must think we can handle it. Oh, and look at this." Korrigan spins his desk computer around to reveal an image of an immaculate kitchen.

Nige raises an eyebrow. "What's that?"

"It's a kitchen refurb for Debs's birthday. She's always wanted one, and now we can afford it."

Nige stares at him, knowing full well his angle, knowing how it feels to not be able to provide for your family. The room is silent. A wordless battleground of wills, fought with minute facial expressions and gleaming granite worktops.

Korrigan smiles and Nige knows he's lost. "You know I love Debs," he says trying not to give in straight away.

"She'd love it. And this is our big chance to get our company out there! Just imagine how many other high-profile celebs will want us looking after them after they find out we've worked with Kenneth Bailey!"

"Go on, Nige," says Aidan, pressing his palms together. "Please."

"All you need to do is stay in his suite. Watch over him." Korrigan's eyes are pleading. "Make sure he doesn't trip over his yoga mat. It'll be a doddle, like babysitting. There'll be armed Di Blasio guys downstairs the whole time. The job's only for tonight and a bit of tomorrow, but you never know, it might lead to more."

Nige holds up the billing page. "This much for a day's work?"

"That's only fifty percent remember."

Nige looks at the paper again. The corners of his mouth lift. He lets the smile cross his face.

"It is quite a lot of money."

Religious Nut Bags

Roughly an hour after saving Suzy Wheeler from muggers, Mac pulls open the door at Mikey's. He descends the three steps from street level into the dark interior of the bar.

His dissipating adrenalin rush from the earlier fight has left him all warm and fuzzy. It's nice to be working a proper case. Nicer to know he has a hunk of cash back at the office and another pending bounty out there to claim.

The white noise of metal guitars hisses in the background as he crosses the sticky floor. Compared to the grinding, honking traffic of the streets outside, the bar is an oasis.

The place has remained relatively clean despite the years of alcohol abuse that have gone on inside. The faint odour of burning wood emanates from out back where Mikey regularly smokes all sorts of succulent meat substitutes, nuts, and salty cheeses to serve to his customers.

It is rumoured that Mikey keeps a sword on the wall behind the bar. The story says he once used its blunt edge to bash a man unconscious. Mac doesn't know all of the details but apparently the man had been a little too handsy with Mikey's daughter while she waited tables.

The regulars are all withered, leather-faced working men out for a quiet drink.

Mac likes it here. Since leaving home and heading for the big city it's been a safe space for him. Somewhere he can scratch a social itch without actually having to speak to anyone. Somewhere he can feel less lonely.

The only light in the room comes from a handful of vintage neon beer signs on the wall behind the bar. A dull blue-pink glow radiates throughout, gently warming the corners and casting faint shadows into some of the more discreet booths. A muted wall-mounted TV is the only other source of light. It currently glows the green of a football match. The broken-down men on barstools, draped over their drinks like aged crows perched high in dying, leafless trees, watch it with keen interest.

Mikey himself stands at one end of the bar, dressed all in black, with large hands resting on the smooth wooden surface as he speaks to a skinny man in a loose, worn suit. Though they've never actually met, Mac knows it's Mikey's cousin. He recognises him from family photographs that are taped to the mirror behind the bar.

Mikey nods as Mac approaches and then speaks to the man. "Phillip, this is Trent Macadamia." He eyes Mac for a moment, his lips firm. "I don't want you getting him in any trouble."

"Hey." Mac raises his hands. "I just need a little help with a case." He gestures to an empty booth with an upturned palm. "After you, Phillip."

Mikey reaches across the bar and rests a hand on his cousin's shoulder. "Come back and talk to me when you're done. And don't tell him anything you wouldn't want to say in court."

"That doesn't leave a lot." Phillip picks up his coffee. His shoulders slump as if a great weight has been tied to each hand. Large grey bags hang beneath his eyes. He looks about as tired as anyone Mac has ever seen. He crosses the room. Mac smiles at Mikey, then follows.

The corner booth is situated in a little cave of its own. Pasted posters of pin-ups and old punk bands, worn as thin as tracing paper, do little to hide the chipped black paint of the walls beneath.

"Thanks for agreeing to meet me," says Mac when they are both seated.

Phillip's eyes dart around the interior of the bar. He leans forward and speaks in a hushed whisper.

"I shouldn't really." Even though they are close enough for Mac to smell his coffee breath, he has to focus on Phillip's lips to see what he's saying. "They don't like us talking to anyone outside the company about corporate matters."

"You've nothing to worry about here." Mac points at the others in the bar. "These old birds aren't interested in what you have to say. And even if they heard every word that came out of your mouth, they wouldn't remember a syllable in the morning. You can sing Di Blasio's deepest, darkest secrets at the top of your lungs here without fear of any repercussions." One thing that excites Mac most about this case is the possibility of getting some backstage gossip on Di Blasio's influencers. He's been a fan ever since he can remember.

"That's the thing. I'm just a low-level marketer. I don't know any secrets."

"Well, can you tell me about Terrence's movements over the last week?" Even if Phillip didn't know any secrets, he must know something about the ageing influencer, and Mac felt that would be the best place to start looking for Suzy's husband. "A guard looking after him has gone missing."

"Terrence?" Phillip asks, his Adam's apple bouncing above his closely bound tie as he speaks. He drains the last of his coffee. "Not much. I don't really deal with him." His eyes flick from side to side as he scans his memory. They stop and look up to Mac's own. "Last Thursday we were supposed to have a meeting about Kenneth's birthday show, but my manager and Stefan Di Blasio pulled out last minute for something else. We had to postpone it to the next day."

"Is that unusual? Cancelling meetings."

"One so important, yes. Everything around Kenneth's birthday show is scheduled months in advance, so it's a little strange to postpone so last minute."

Mac taps his pencil on his lips and jots a few notes in his pad. Suzy mentioned the last time she'd spoken to her husband was on Wednesday before he left for work.

"And what of Terrence? Any filming? Any promos?"

"One thing, but it got cancelled. Not sure why. Like I said, I don't work with him. But his department has been quiet this week."

"So, the day after my client's husband goes missing, the CEO of the Di Blasio corporation and your manager pull out of an important meeting for something else, and since then Terrence hasn't attended any of his previously booked engagements."

Phillip glances around the bar. "That's a bit of a leap."

"It's my job to take leaps."

Philip taps his fingers on the table, then leans closer. "If you put it like that it sounds weird, but Terrence keeps himself to himself when he's not working. And anyway, all the influencers have had less on these last two weeks to make sure they are fit for Kenneth's show. The Twins have something tonight, and that's it. We've got to have them in top condition. The world is watching."

"Kenneth's birthday show, it's Saturday, right?" Mac already knows this. He has a food delivery arriving in the morning with a multitude of salty and sweet snacks ready for the four-hour long yearly show that celebrates the birthday of the oldest living man on the planet. And this year it's something special - Di Blasio are introducing the world to their five new influencers. He loves them all already, and he's only seen their body shots on the billboards.

"That's right."

"So, the guard I'm looking for would have been at Terrence's home last week?"

Phillip nods. "If he was looking after Terrence, yeah."

"Could they all still be there?"

"Maybe."

From the centre of the room, someone groans. Mac glances over. One of the men propping up the bar flops an arm at the television. The screen is strobing between dark crimson and bright white. Mikey moves over to fiddle with the cables at the back.

"So three of the five influencers, Kenneth, Dawn, and Terrence, are all home this week," Mac continues. "What about The Twins? What are they doing tonight?"

"Some drinks promotion. It's totally beneath them."

Several more annoyed mumbles come from around the bar. "Jesus Christ Mikey. Can't you sort that?" Shouts one of the punters as the screen continues to flash. "I'm about to have a fit in a minute."

"Quiet you." Mikey emerges from behind the TV and points a rigid finger at the man, who quickly disappears back into his pint. "I haven't a clue what's going on with this thing."

Mac keeps an eye on the room as he continues speaking to Phillip. "I guess they'll have security if they're going out in public. Do you think my client's husband could be there?"

"He could." Phillip shrugs.

"Where is it?"

"Other side of Camden. The Electric Ballroom. They're on around 10ish."

A few dull cheers go up around the bar as the TV starts working again. Mikey bows, then frowns as a new image on the TV screen forms: two robed figures standing in front of a large white circle with a picture of an angel on it.

"Where's the footy?" says one of the men at the bar.

"Another peep out of you and you'll be out," shouts Mikey. He moves next to the TV and taps the remote. The channel number changes, but the two figures remain. They seem to be on every one. They begin to talk to the camera, but it's still muted.

"What is that?" Mac stands. Moves towards the bar.

"No idea." Mikey continues to thumb through the channels.

"Turn it up."

The figure on the right is speaking as the other stares menacingly into the camera with his arms folded, a little like a hype man on a hip hop album cover. Though their crimson robes are hooded, their faces are visible. In their early twenties. They look similar. Brothers perhaps?

"...in league with demons. And if Stefan Di Blasio and his health guru influencers, Kenneth, Dawn, Terrence, Dominic and Martha are not silenced before the televisual event this Saturday then the angel will strike down from the heavens, wiping the world of their filth, and punish those who follow so blindly."

The figure stops talking. A slight nod of his head suggests he's counting as if waiting the perfect length for a dramatic pause. Who are these guys?

"Their great age has nought to do with the poison that the vile corporation peddles, but a pact made with the devil himself. Mark our words, if we do not stop them a great plague will ravish this land. For too long they have done as they please unpunished."

The hype man is frozen in a menacing grimace, eyes vacant, as if he's just holding it for effect. Is this for real?

"The Church of Fallen Angels will knock them from their pedestal and we urge you, the people of this world, to rise up, take up arms, and stand with us in putting an end to this abomination. If it is not dealt with by this Saturday, when their new disciples are revealed, then the world will plunge further down the rabbit hole than it can ever return, and that cannot be allowed. Brothers and sisters, join us. Kind regards, The Church of The Fallen Angels."

Then, both of the men onscreen turn. Their robes part to reveal something which looks a lot like a large green warhead. They rest their hands on it and hold position for an awkwardly long amount of time.

Then the one on the left, the silent hype man, looks above the camera, presumably at the person filming, and says, "Was that alright, Dad?"

A brief hiss of static, and the screen resumes it's regular programming with a shot of some gleaming sticky buns.

"...I just love the way the warm cream spurts out when you take a nibble," says a sultry female voice.

Mikey mutes the TV. The bar is silent save the noise of the rain and traffic humming outside.

"Football," drones one of the regulars, and Mikey turns the channel back.

Mac turns to face Phillip. "What the hell was that?"

Phillip shakes his head, still staring towards the television. "I have no idea. That's not a marketing thing."

"No. I thought that would be a bit much, even for you guys. It looks like some religious nut bags are calling a hit on the influencers. And was that a bomb?"

"It looked like it."

Mac returns to the table and sits. "Do you think they'd pull Saturday's show?" He's been looking forward to it all month. The influencer's were a big part of everyone's lives. They were role models. They were teachers. You'd be hard-pushed to find someone who didn't have a crush on at least one of them. Mac felt a threat on them was like a threat on society.

"No way. It's not just Kenneth's birthday. Mr Di Blasio has the next few years hinging on the new influencer's reveal. It kicks off a marketing campaign that'll span the next decade. The show goes on no matter what."

Phillip's phone buzzes on the table. He picks it up quickly, as if his life depends on it. His face sinks a shade greyer.

"I have to go," he says, and wiggles out of the booth in that awkward half-squat, half-shuffle used to exit badly designed restaurant seating.

"Wait. I still have a few questions." Mac hurries to stand but is kneecapped by the table leg.

"They are calling everyone in...," Phillip says and then indicates to the TV. "...because of that."

"But it's gone eight. Isn't that outside of working hours?"

Phillip lets out a short sharp bark that ends in a cough, probably a seldom practiced laugh. "Working hours? Good one. They can call us in any time they want." He waves to Mikey as he heads for the door. "See ya cuz."

Mikey hurries down the bar towards him. "It's been ages. I thought we could have a catch up over a pint."

"Sorry, maybe Christmas?" Phillip is gone before Mikey can reply.

Mikey shakes his head. "This year or next?" he mumbles.

"Is he always like that?" Mac says.

"Ever since he started working for Di Blasio, no one sees him. He's on one of those unlimited hour contracts."

"And we thought the zero-hour ones were bad." He looks towards the door. "At least he's got a job, I suppose".

Mikey returns to the bar and resumes polishing a pint glass. "Job's got him mate. Job's got him."

In Da Club

The rain continues to slam down as Mac leaves Mikey's bar, so he takes brief refuge beneath a nearby bus stop.

A holographic ad for a Di Blasio brand soft drink repeats, making it look as if Kenneth himself waits for a bus. In the ad, he takes a sip from a lemon coloured can. Tanned, toned, and grinning from ear to ear, the glow makes him look like a Greek god.

If Mac didn't know better, he'd think Kenneth was in his forties at most, and a hot forties at that. A forties that has never smoked, never missed a night's sleep, never done a day of hard labour, and never missed a yoga session.

Mac looks down at himself and sighs. It wasn't half depressing seeing a man five times your age looking fitter than you've ever been in your whole entire life. But also, oddly inspiring.

Suddenly, he has the desire for a citrusy soft drink.

He'd hoped to get a little more out of Phillip, but now he has a lead on Harry, or at least someone who might know where he is.

He hitches his collar and begins trudging towards The Electric Ballroom. He has an hour or two before The Twins are on so treats himself with a hot dog and can of lemonade from a cart on the corner.

"D'you see those guys with the bomb?" the vendor asks him as he dishes out some crispy fried onions from a sizzling hot plate. The salty-savoury smell makes Mac's mouth water.

"Yeah. Do you think they'll actually do anything?"

"Couldn't care less, mate. Don't get me wrong. I wouldn't wish death on anyone, but those influencers have had their day. It's all a bit boring now." He grabs a can out of the fridge on his wheeled cart and passes it over. Droplets of condensation cover it.

Mac pulls the top and takes a swig. Doesn't respond. Doesn't know how. Guesses the older generation, the ones who've had the influencers in their lives longer, may have grown tired of them.

He pays and continues through the throngs of people that spill off the pavements onto the gridlocked streets.

It might be fun to hit a club. He hasn't been clubbing for ages. Not since uni. He has good memories of him and his mates drinking, dancing, and trying to chat to girls who were completely out of their league.

When he breezes up to the door there is no queue. Makes sense. It's still early. But with The Twins going on at ten, he expected it to be heaving already.

"Sorry mate. Wednesday is under 18's night," says a wall-like bouncer barring the entrance. He wears a brown moleskin coat that makes him look as wide as he is tall. A long scar on one cheek gives off a comic book villain vibe. He has a tattoo of a spoon across his throat.

"What?"

"You're too old." The bouncer folds his arms.

"That's never been a problem before." Mac looks around. "I need to talk to one of the Di Blasio security guards. It's official PI business." He takes out his wallet and quickly flashes a silver plastic police badge he picked up from a Poundland 'my first policeman' kit.

Sometimes it gets him in places.

"Let's have a look at that." The bouncer holds out a hand.

"Actually, I'll just wait for them to come out."

He turns and walks away. There's an alley which runs along the side of the building. Maybe he can sneak in that way.

Ten minutes later, having climbed through a small horizontal window in the side of the building, and fallen onto the head of a very confused and sweaty teenage boy doing a poo, Mac stands above a swollen dance floor with absolute realisation as to why he hasn't been clubbing in years.

Despite the fact that he's not even into his thirties, Mac gave up on modern music a while back. To him the bloops, buzzes, and bleeps that fill the air sound like a jackhammer and a phone double-teaming a chainsaw. Double-teaming in the violent sense, but also, in the bit he believes is called 'the drop', double-teaming in the sexy, sexy sense.

It makes him a little queasy.

The place stinks of stale alcohol and sickly-sweet spillages. The dance floor below, with its colourful intermittent lighting, looks like someone has dropped a bucket of luminescent worms. Sweaty gyrators sweat on other sweaty gyrators at every turn. Almost every nook or cranny has at least one snogging underage couple hidden within its shadowy depths, like an underground crypt packed with vampires.

And there's nowhere to sit.

Since when were teenagers so horny? He was never like that. When he was a boy, teenagers stayed in and played computer games.

From his vantage point on the top level, he can make out a door next to the stage labelled security. He presumes The Twins will enter through it for their 'whatever it is they are going to do'.

If he can get backstage during the show, then maybe he'll find Harry. Or at least someone to talk to about where he might be.

He just needs to find something that might justify what Suzy is paying him. He can imagine the earful he'll get from his sister at Christmas if he takes the money and doesn't get anything.

Plus, you know, Suzy won't find out what happened to her missing husband, which would be a bit sad.

A momentary squeal of feedback signals a pause in the music. The DJ screams. "How are we all doing tonight, you ceeeeeerazy kids?"

To which the crazy kids roar their approval.

"Who's looking forward to The Twins coming on stage?" he continues.

Those crazy kids roar again. This time louder.

"I can't hear you."

More roaring. If possible, louder.

"Oh yeah! That's what I like to hear. They are back stage ready for you guys and in less than five minutes they'll be coming out here to party with you all."

"Roar," roar the crowd and the jackhammer-phone-chainsaw-fight-club-sex festival continues with renewed vigour.

Another momentary fade. "And this is a shout out to Melissa Grady. Your dad is outside ready to pick you up. Ohhh yeah."

"Jesus wept," says Mac to himself, although he has to shout as he can't hear his own voice over the din.

He moves back to the lower floor and eases his way towards the security door through the raving mass of bodies.

A short and sharp toothed bouncer stands in front of the stage with his hands clasped by his groin. He watches the crowd with crabby little eyes that skip like flies. He's not a Di Blasio appointed guard. Mac can tell. Although he looks tough as nails, his danger level is that of a deranged ferret as opposed to the cool, great white presence that The Di Blasio bodyguards emanate.

He has seen them in the news and on social media. They know what they're doing. Considering they look after the five biggest celebrities in the world, they should.

It surprises him that The Twins are here at all. An under 18's night in the middle of Camden? They'd be more at home filling a stadium. He can see what Phillip meant when he said this was beneath them. It does seem a little below their pay grade.

Still, a great opportunity had come along at the right moment, and he wasn't going to waste it.

Head up, he strides over to the ferret-like bouncer, and in the internationally recognised greeting of an absolute geezer, rubs a thumb under his nose, sniffs, then nods upwards.

"Alright mate. Trent Macadamia. Private law enforcer and bounty hunter. Can I get in there?" He points to the security door.

The bouncer doesn't look convinced. Mac considers that perhaps to him, it looks like a man with a cold and a stiff neck is just trying to get backstage. He shakes his head.

"No?" Mac leans closer. "I need to talk to one of the DB bodyguards. I'm working a case. It's kind of a big deal." He takes out his wallet and taps the plastic badge.

The bouncer raises a hand and takes a long moment to look at Mac's ID. The intermittent flash of the strobe reveals a tattoo on his forearm. A candy cane crossed over some sort of triangle. It reminds him of Junior School lessons on Ancient Egypt. The bouncer angles his mouth to speak into a radio on his lapel. He says something inaudible, then glances over Mac's shoulder and nods.

That look is familiar, though Mac has not seen it lately. He recalls a hazy flashback of his university years, being smashed in a club and bothering a bouncer. It is the look one makes to another carefully concealed bouncer that says, 'get this guy out of here'.

He braces for impact.

A firm, and rather large hand grips his bicep. Moist stubble, which reminds him of horrific uncles, brushes past the top of his ear. "Come on, mate. You're a bit old to be in here, don't you think?"

He jerks his head around, pretty much grating half his cheek away on the bouncer's unshaven face and points towards the door on stage. "No. Wait. I just need to get backstage. Official PI business."

He pulls away and tries to scramble over the barrier to the stage, which is probably not the brightest of ideas. The ferret bouncer lurches forward, pulling him into a headlock. The second doorman forces Mac's arm up behind his back.

"Ow! There's no need for— Ow…" They drag him away, his feet barely scraping the ground. "Excuse me."

His cries go unheard under the din of the absolute bangers pumping out of the club's more than adequate sound system. He is hauled past the speakers towards a door illuminated by a fire exit sign. "Gosh, that's loud."

Another bouncer, poised like an animatronic on a ghost train, pushes the door open. Beyond, a rain sodden alleyway beckons, and before Mac can dig his heels in, he is flying horizontally through the door and out into a pile of soggy cardboard boxes and bin bags.

"I told you on the door, it's an under 18's night, you bloody nonce!"

Before he can rise from the foul-smelling landing pad, the doors slam and the thumping music settles to a low thud.

Tinted by the security light above the door, the rain beats down in whacking great orange globules. He wrestles his way out of the seeping rubbish and brushes his coat down, finding himself at the dead end of the same alleyway he'd first snuck in through.

Looking back, he can see a large black Bentley parked roughly halfway between him and the main road. Steam billows up from a grate below, but even through the mist he can see the car is occupied by two hulking sets of shoulders in the front seats. He ducks down behind a set of large wheelie bins and tries to read the plate. It looks like The Twins' escape vehicle.

He weighs up his options.

Behind him, just before the filthy brick wall of another building cuts off the alley, there is another door into the club. If his calculations are correct, it doesn't connect to the main club interior, so maybe it's an entrance to the backstage area.

If he hides in the bin, then maybe when someone next exits he can block the door before it shuts and get backstage.

Hoping the DB bodyguards in the car don't spot him, he hops in.

He removes a couple of bags, keeping a small throwable one nearby which he hopes to use to swing and block the door once it opens. Then, like something of an expert, he wedges a plastic bottle under the lid so he can see out, and tucks himself in for the wait.

At least it's warmer and drier than outside.

It's been some time since he's hit a nightclub, but not since he's hidden in a bin. The trick to sitting in one is not to move. You think it smells bad now? Just wait. If you get to wriggling, and end up disturbing a stagnant air pocket buried below like a leviathan in the darkest depths of the ocean, you can easily awaken a stench so deadly that even the hardiest of refuse collectors would run screaming and vomiting.

The worst part is when someone comes and puts a bag in. Either they aren't looking and you get hit in the face. Or they see you and you have to pretend you're looking for something to eat, which on one or two occasions Mac has been asked to prove.

He checks his phone. 9:30pm. What time do under 18's nights kick out? Eleven? He expects The Twins will leave right after their promo. So maybe he has an hour?

The pump of the music vibrates through the wall behind him. A low rumbling throb growing gradually louder. Something small and metallic in the bin's lid begins to rattle in time with it.

Mac rolls his eyes. Those kids are going to come out deaf by the end of the night.

The Influencer

The foyer of Kenneth's apartment building is huge. A large crystal chandelier, suspended from the ceiling three floors above, casts a warm glow around the room. It sparkles like a galaxy of stars, illuminating cosy corners enclosed with bookshelves and comfy seating.

While Aidan stands in the centre of the room enthralled by the splendour, Nige talks to the receptionist. It's been nearly twenty minutes of frustrating back and forth. Apparently, there's no mention of an externally contracted security team in his records. This is clearly a wind up.

Just as Nige takes out his phone ready to give Korrigan an earful, a woman exits the elevator next to the reception desk.

"You must be my two new bodyguards." She smiles. Her heels clack on the tiled marble floor, and shoulder-length corkscrews of brown hair bounce as she approaches.

"What gave it away?" says Aidan with a confident charm. He moves closer and points to the word "security" embroidered on his chest.

Nige knows the lad does this to bring attention to his pecs whenever women are present. "Probably not that because you were facing the other way." He says and holds a hand out. "Nige Davies."

"Maggie Greaves. Kenneth Bailey's manager." She shakes his hand, and her brown eyes linger on his face for a moment. "It's a pleasure to meet you. Under usual circumstances the head of security would see you in, but as I'm just getting in myself, I'll take you up. Do you both have ID?"

He takes out a battered black wallet and hands over his licence. Aidan does the same.

"No problem, Ms Greaves."

"Call me Maggie." She uses her phone to scan the IDs.

She waits a moment for it to process, then smiles. Her umber skin is flawless. He guesses that when you work for the biggest health food company in the world, you can't have anything but. The pressure must be tremendous.

"Looks good to me," she says. "Let's head up."

She leads them to an elevator, runs her ID over a reader and hits a button labelled simply as 'K'. "Did the security stop you as you came in?" she asks as the lift takes them up.

"Didn't see anyone. Only the guy on the reception. He didn't seem to have us down."

Once at the top, the elevator opens onto a short corridor that leads towards a single door.

Maggie brushes the door with one knuckle, as if knocking was once but is no longer required, then opens it a finger's width. "Kenny. It's me. I'm with your new bodyguards."

The room beyond isn't dark as such. Nige might describe it as 'romantic restaurant gloomy'.

A cheerful yet slightly muffled voice comes from within. "I'll just be a moment."

She pushes the door open and leads them into a spacious kitchen. The apartment is the size of the entire top floor of the building. For the most part, it is open plan. The kitchen leads on to a sitting room, and to their right, from a cracked doorway, steam billows.

The living area is dotted with dim orange globes, placed in small clusters with feng shui precision. Each casts a warm glow. One wall is made entirely of glass. Blinds cast slits of shadow across the living area floor against the bright white glow from the city beyond. Outside is a balcony with a swimming pool and seating area.

"Welcome. Welcome," comes a voice from within the room.

Nige, who's eyes aren't as good as they used to be, has to squint to see through the dark. Hidden in shadow and standing on his head with his legs crossed in a gravity defying and impossibly yogic way, is the oldest man on the planet. He wears that content Mona Lisa smile that has always grated on Nige. It's a smile that in his youth Nige would like to have removed with a slap.

"Great to meet you, Mr Bailey," he says, in contradiction to his thoughts.

Aidan gawps, and does not say anything. Nige elbows him in the ribs. He gulps. "Huh? Oh. Hi... um Mr K..." The letter trails off becoming a sound like a skateboard on tarmac.

"This is Nigel and Aidan." Maggie taps them both on the shoulder as she says their names. "They'll be looking after you tonight."

"My friends call me Nige." He raises a hand. "It's a funny coincidence, us being here. We were supposed to be helping your guys with The Twins tonight at a club we work at, but I heard you were short staffed. The flu or something?"

Kenneth chuckles without commitment. "Yes, this damned little flu outbreak. It's done in some of our best chaps. Right before my birthday too. What a bind. Still, it's always nice to see a new face. Come on in. Do make yourselves at home." Like a transformer, his wiry form uncurls, and with hand outstretched, he approaches them.

Maggie moves between them and makes a show of checking her watch. "Kenneth, it's nearly time for you to go to bed, have you eaten your evening snack?"

The man's smile falters briefly, then returns with full force. "As always, Maggie. But thank you indeed for the reminder. I'll go and get prepped for nap time. Boyos, there's food in the fridge. Do help yourselves."

"I brought my own," says Aidan, pulling a bent and crumpled box of Frosties out of the satchel he has slung over his shoulder, and placing it on the kitchen worktop.

"Aidan!" hisses Nige.

"Oooh." Kenneth's eyes widen. "They used to be one of my favourites when I was a... well, when I was a younger man. Can't have them anymore though, can I Mags?" He gives his manager a stern look, his mouth a thin line. There's a moment's awkward pause. Then he laughs. "Oh, I'm having you on. Who needs Frosties when you've got strawberry flavoured paste direct from the tube?" He claps Aidan on the shoulder. "Better hide them away from me, though. Just in case I'm for the turning." He makes a veracious chomping motion towards the box, like a raptor snapping at a fleeing palaeontologist. "Yum-yum-yum." He chuckles.

Aidan gives a giddy high-pitched giggle.

"Righto gentlemen." Kenneth claps his hands and rubs them together. "Don't let me stop you doing whatever you need to do. Off to the land of nod for me."

Nige had no idea the extent to which the influencer's lives were dictated. This wasn't living.

"I'll be back at nine tomorrow morning," says Maggie. "The chef will send up your steamed veg and blueberry smoothie at seven. The masseuse will be in at eight."

"Sounds like my perfect morning," says Kenneth. "I'll be sure to have my aerobics and shower done before they arrive." He pauses and cocks his head. "Maybe me and the boys could have a little coffee?" He holds an imaginary cup up, little finger erect, and tips it towards his lips.

Maggie's nose crinkles. "I'm not sure. You had one on Friday."

"It's not every day I have the pleasure of guests." He points at his two new bodyguards. "I'm right in thinking you two upstanding gentlemen like a little coffee?"

Aidan nods, eyes wide. "Oh yes please."

Nige gets the impression Aidan would have reacted in the same way if Kenneth had said, 'I'm right in thinking you two upstanding gentlemen like getting kicked in the dick?'

"Don't break any rules on our account." He says, and holds his hands up. "I've got a flask."

"Shouldn't be a problem. Our chef does the best coconut flat whites." He points at Nige. "Coconut flat white." Then Aidan. "Coconut flat white." Then looks to Maggie with a pleading eye, "go on Mags."

She deflates. "I'll ask the chef to send three up tomorrow. But yours is a decaf."

"Yes." Kenneth pumps a fist, then puts a hand next to his mouth as if he's sharing a secret with them. "There's a two in three chance I'll get the wrong one. It's like caffeine Russian roulette." He shoots them some finger guns. "You have to take the victories where you can, my boys. Anyway, with that little treat set up, I'll bid you all adieu." He doffs an invisible cap, then heads through the steaming doorway that leads out of the kitchen. A billow of rolling mist wafts out as the door opens and closes.

"They'll all be decaf," whispers Maggie. She taps her long acrylic nails on the kitchen's dark granite worktop. "I've left schedules on the coffee table in the other room, and there's another one tacked to the fridge over there. I want you to call me first if there are any problems, ok?" She looks Nige in the eyes to make sure he's heard.

He nods.

"Do help yourself to food. Oh, and you might have heard something on TV earlier."

Nige squints. "I don't really watch TV."

"You mean those guys who took over every channel?" Aidan puts a hand next to his mouth before continuing in a whisper, "and threatened death on 'you know who'." He jerks a thumb towards the door Kenneth just disappeared through.

"What?" Nige looks between them wide eyed. Grinds his teeth. "A death threat? When did you hear that? You've been with me the whole evening."

Aidan holds up his phone. "Jeez, Nige. Phones. Ever heard of them?" He gives Maggie a conspiratorial wink. Nige knows it's intended to say something about his age, but it only highlights Aidan's.

"Don't worry Nigel," says Maggie. "We don't think the threat is that severe. Kenneth knows."

"Then why is he so, you know, chipper?" says Aidan. "I'd be terrified if a bunch of religious nutters wanted me dead." He glances at Nige. "Well, not terrified. You know, just a bit annoyed." Puffs out his chest. "Probably not that bothered, actually."

"We don't worry about that sort of thing." She waves a hand.

"How can you not if he's getting death threats?" says Nige. He's trying to keep his cool in front of her. There's no way he would have agreed to come if he'd known.

"They get threats all the time. It comes with the job. You can't go on the internet without finding hundreds of people wanting to kill them. That's just the world we live in."

"Should we be worried?"

Maggie closes her eyes and shakes her head quickly. "No, no. You'll be as right as rain. We have company guards on all the doors downstairs, then another four in a control room on the fourth floor. We have cameras in all the corridors. You two are basically here just to keep a closer eye on

Kenneth." She chews at the corner of her mouth. "You won't even need to bother the guys downstairs. Just call me if there are any problems." She picks up her bag from the kitchen island. "I must be off. I've a meeting to get to."

Nige checks his watch. Nearly 9pm. "They work you hard, don't they? Meetings this late!"

She smiles, swinging her bag on to her shoulder. "You don't know the half of it. I'll hopefully see you guys in the morning. Night."

Nige's smile drops as soon as she leaves, and he turns on Aidan. "Death threats?"

Aidan looks at the floor with his hands in his pockets. He digs his toe into the hardwood flooring. "I was scared you wouldn't want to come."

"Hm." Nige releases a frustrated sigh. "She better be right that it's nothing to worry about. I don't want to deal with any crazies tonight."

For a moment Aidan holds his chastised dog expression before dropping it. A smile lights up his face. "Can you believe it?" His eyes dart around the apartment. "He touched my actual shoulder."

"You weren't this excited about The Twins."

Aidan waves a hand and leans towards Nige. "They don't really count. They're like meeting the bass player in your favourite band. You know everyone only cares about the vocalist." He reaches for his box of Frosties with fidgety hands, then puts it back down again. "And we're getting paid. I'd do this job for *free*."

"Looks to me like you need to calm down so I'm giving you hallway duty."

"But… what if he comes back out?" Aidan points towards Kenneth's door.

Nige removes one of Maggie's schedules from the fridge and passes it to him. "Sit out there and read this. I'll come out in about an hour. If you've calmed down sufficiently by then, maybe we can swap."

Aidan takes the schedule reluctantly.

"It's for your own good," Nige continues. "You don't want Lord Kenneth seeing you all gushy and fan girly, do you?"

Aidan grunts, and like a grounded teenager sent to his room, huffs away and out through the front door.

Nige watches him go, then turns his attention to the apartment. In the centre of the living room sits an ornate coffee table. To him, it looks more like something you'd find in an art gallery. Cushions positioned around it suggest you sit on the floor rather than the sofa. He moves to sit. His bad knee shakes causing him to freeze midway. With a wobble he pulls himself back up using a wooden cabinet as support. A photo in a heavy frame on its surface clunks down onto its face. He lifts it. An old photograph, an early picture of the Di Blasio influencers.

Kenneth is in the front centre; behind stand Terrence and Dawn; to his left are The Twins, Dominic and Martha. They are all smiling. For a moment he marvels at how old they all look. They seem to have grown younger since this picture was taken.

Stefan Di Blasio Sr - the current CEO's father - stands in a long white lab coat slightly separated from the group. On Kenneth's right is another woman. The pair stand closer than the rest, but Nige doesn't recognise her.

He replaces the photo carefully, and instead of finding somewhere else to sit, moves to stand at the balcony window where he looks out over the London skyline.

Two hidden pairs of eyes, one inside the apartment, the other out, watch him closely.

The Mark

Through the gap in the bathroom door, Kenneth watches the bodyguard as he stands silhouetted in the window against the bright lights of the city.

He must be at least six foot six. What a lump! And with his forehead slopped right up against the glass. Kenneth rolls his eyes - there's sure to be greasy marks all over it come the morning.

He doesn't want more security. This apartment is supposed to be his own personal sanctuary. But in the last few weeks things have changed. And for the worse. Di Blasio's minions are closing in.

Maggie even has her own key now and comes and goes as she pleases.

When did that happen?

All he has is this bathroom and his bedroom for himself. But he knows sooner or later some drone with a screwdriver will come and remove his bathroom lock, and then his last little piece of privacy will be lost.

He closes the door, holding the handle down so that it doesn't click when it shuts.

His bathroom is sparse: sink, toilet, rolled matt for his meditation, open rainfall shower, several large potted plants including spider, aloe vera, and a few choice shrubs flown in from what remains of the rainforests of Brazil - nothing too extravagant - jade incense holder smoking sensually and wafting the scent of cinnamon throughout the apartment, roll top bath with to-die-for gold-plated clawed feet, cabinet carved from the darkest jet containing some of the most arousing aromas and perfumes known to man. The essentials.

He touches his stomach absentmindedly. He doesn't like the idea that someone could just walk in at any moment, especially considering his condition.

He loosens his kimono, and lets it fall to the ground. Gazes at himself in the mirror. The dried dark patch of skin on his stomach grows steadily by the day. It wouldn't be a big deal to any normal person, but Kenneth is far from normal. He is the oldest man on the planet yet he has a chin like a young Rob Lowe, glowing skin to match, and a body to die for. Blemishes just aren't permissible.

He is perfect inside and out. Or at least he was until last week.

The patch branches out gradually, like an oil slick on water. It now covers his chiselled abs – which have won several awards – fans up past his chest, stroking the fringes of his throat, and down past his waist. He runs a trembling hand over it. It has the texture of wood. The peeling, split bark of a silver birch.

Upon first notice, he'd scrubbed the mark vigorously with a sponge, but scales of skin just kept on flaking until his belly was red raw.

The thought of it itches in his mind night and day. He hasn't had a skin condition in almost seventy years. Not since the start of the programme, at least. He's usually baby soft all over.

He dreads the fortnightly check-up on Friday. There'll be a big fuss. He's more worried about that than the blemish itself.

They'll make him go over every little thing he did, every little thing he ate over the last month, trying to pick out an alteration from his set schedule that could have caused it. They'll find nothing. He's never deviated from the life plan that Stefan Di Blasio Sr. set out when they started working together.

He cranes his neck to check his back in the mirror. Thick webs of dryness stretch across it, linking all the way from his shoulder blades down to his waist.

Every day it's worse. He should really tell someone, but he knows what Stefan Jr would say. "Kenneth's past it. Take him out and shoot him."

He opens the medicine cabinet, takes out a bottle of the Di Blasio appointed moisturiser, and applies a palm sized dollop to the mark. The cracks and crags gleam in the bathroom light. If anything, it looks worse.

He retrieves his kimono, and wraps it around himself. If it continues like this, the mark will soon cover his face. And what will happen on the show on Saturday if it does? It's not like they really need him any more now they've got these new hot-shots coming in.

Maybe it'll get him out of having to go. You get to one hundred and thirty-five and birthdays start to lose their meaning.

Hell, they're meaningless by ninety.

All the yearly celebration does is remind him of how many things he's outlived. Things he lost long, long ago.

Another year since his mother died. She's now been dead longer than she was alive.

Another year since he rode bikes with his brother down the road by the terraces in Liverpool.

Another year since he last saw the love of his life, Victoria.

He looks at himself in the mirror. Riches, fame, health - he'd give it all up just to see her again. He rubs his face with both hands. No point dwelling.

And then there's the whole hoo ha of the party. The TV show, the screaming audience, the glistening hosts with their overly gelled hair and inhumanely white teeth.

Horrible.

The worst part of the night-long special is when the new pop band wishes him a happy birthday with a specifically written song. What they play is not music. If someone were to play him a recording of last year's band and another of a rotating cement mixer filled with parrots, he'd be hard pressed to tell the difference.

They were no Vera Lynn.

"Ah Vera," he breathes, and lets his mind wander to the time they'd met in the seventies back when he'd just started with Di Blasio. It doesn't seem as long as the sixty-plus years it is.

Following the band, there's the non-stop interviews, each one full of loaded questions planted by the Di Blasio press team. It's incessant.

"You are looking amazingly well. Do you really just eat what Di Blasio tell you to or is there another secret?"

"How do you feel about being voted abs of the year yet again?"

"My grandad's fifty years younger than you and he's nearly dead - how do you do it?"

To which he'd always answer the carefully scripted responses drilled into him over weeks of rehearsals.

It had to be perfect. In the week after, everyone would go crazy on Di Blasio merchandise and products. It was like Christmas for Di Blasio, and as ever, Kenneth had his part to play.

To top it off, he's not even the star attraction anymore. It's the new influencers everyone's banging on about. Those entitled little buggers.

He carefully brushes the kimono aside and touches the mark once more with his fingertips. A flake of skin roughly the size of a thumbnail breaks away and floats lazily to the floor. He gasps and picks it up. Quickly washes it away down the sink.

Perhaps it's a sign. Perhaps this will be his last birthday. Maybe the human body is only designed to live so long. Maybe, just maybe, despite all of Di Blasio's efforts, he is finally starting to age again.

He half hopes, half dreads.

He pulls a match from the medicine cabinet and lights a fresh incense stick. Then he sits cross-legged, eyes closed, and begins to clear his head ready for sleep, which – with the mosquito-like thoughts buzzing around his brain – might take some time.

In Da Bin

After an uncomfortable while, Mac watches that same ferret like bouncer emerge from the backstage door. From his vantage point in the bin, he can only see his head and shoulders.

The bouncer looks up and holds his hand over his face to shield his eyes from the rain. He waits for a moment then seems to nod towards the sky, before backing through the door and closing it.

Mac doesn't move. Maybe next time.

It doesn't take long for the doors to open again. Two burly men in well-fitted suits step out into the rain. They move past the bin and out of sight, followed by another bodyguard holding a large white umbrella over a slim and attractive woman. She is wearing a long white coat.

Mac knows who she is instantly. Martha. One of The Twins. He tries to tell himself that she's old enough to be his grandmother's grandmother, but he still gets a little hot under the collar.

At the sight of her, Mac's willingness to question the security regarding Harry's disappearance dissipates. He is frozen. Starstruck.

"I cannot believe Stefan's got us doing a club gig like this three days before Kenneth's birthday," she says over her shoulder to a man dressed in a black trench coat, also accompanied by a bodyguard, this one holding a black umbrella.

Dominic, her brother, wears a black pinstripe suit and fedora like a 1920s gangster.

"I know Marti. What can they possibly stand to gain from sticking us in front of a couple of hundred kids?" It sounds as if he's heard this complaint before. "You should have a word with Ian."

Mac counts seven bodyguards. Harry is not among them.

"I will. We shouldn't be up this late."

Mac checks his phone. It's only 10:30.

Martha continues. "I'm going to have bags under my eyes. I can just see the papers now. 'Has Martha lost it?' 'Shock horror! Martha has bags under eyes at the Kenneth birthday show!'" She stops and turns to face her brother. "You're a man. You'll be fine. But for me, it'll be tabloid carnage."

The guard holding her umbrella ushers her along.

Mac spins slowly as they head past, tracking them through the crack.

Why not snap a quick pic? This is a once in a lifetime opportunity. And it'll be evidence for Suzy that he was here, and Harry wasn't.

He lifts his phone with a shaky arm. A bright light flares as he takes the picture and his heart falters in panic. He's forgotten the flash.

"What the hell was that?" says one bodyguard.

"I can't see," says Martha.

Wait? Can't see? His phone isn't that powerful. The flash must have come from outside.

Above him, he feels something land lightly on the bin lid. The bottle he'd been using to wedge it open shoots away, closing the bin completely. There are several light splashes on the tarmac outside.

"Get them back inside now!" says a bodyguard from right outside, but it's difficult to hear much with the pounding bass and pouring rain.

Something whips through the air, followed by a heavy thud against the front of the bin. It jerks on its wheels. The sound of footsteps splash past. Someone bangs hard on the back door of the club. The music inside pounds so loudly that it almost drowns out the panicked knocking. Maybe that's the intention.

"Let me in." More hard knocks on the wooden door. "Please. No. Wait."

The pounding at the door stops.

Holding his breath, Mac squeezes himself down under the bags as the bin lid slowly bends in from above. Someone is once again standing on top.

A few more light splashes of feet on tarmac. Then nothing. No voices. No life in the alley. Just the patter of rain and the humming bass from inside the club.

He takes baby breaths, waiting, listening, wondering what he'll see if he ever musters the courage to open the lid.

He doesn't want to. Not yet. Whatever is outside doesn't have to be there until he looks. He is the cat in that physics problem. Or is the whole of the world outside the cat? Either way, he never really concentrated much at school, which is probably one reason why he is now sitting in a bin outside a nightclub in Camden.

His heart beats in his dry throat. His temples pulse in time. The stench is stifling, sickeningly warm. It's getting harder and harder to breathe.

He taps the lid. It jumps slightly. Sees nothing. Realises his eyes are closed. With another harder tap, he chances a look but there is still nothing save the brown brick of the opposite wall.

He waits a moment, anticipating the light splash of deft footsteps in the puddles outside.

Nothing.

He inches the lid open and rises. The first thing he notices is the darkness. The security light above the door is out. His eyes have grown accustomed inside the bin, and he can just make out something across from him that at first he mistakes for a bag of rubbish.

The lid slams shut as he falls back with the realisation that what he's just seen is not the white drawstring of a bin bag. It is in fact a spine sticking up through the neck of a decapitated body.

He breathes inward in rapid, uncontrolled succession, unable to exhale. His chest is fit to burst. "Oh-God-oh-God-oh-God." His head swims as the vision repeats. Spines. Blood and spines and neck holes.

He pinches himself on the cheek hard and forces out a breath. Come on, Macadamia. Get it together. You need to move, now.

He eases the lid up once again, this time looking anywhere but at the headless body. And therein lies another problem. The alley is an abattoir.

To the left, one bodyguard lies slumped, his face pressed against the closed door of the club. To the right, Dominic lies face down next to Martha. The front of her white coat stained a deep red that blossoms ever wider in the rain.

Mac eases himself out of the bin, careful not to touch anything.

What should he do? Knock on the back door of the club? Get help?

He should leave. Pretend he was never here. But he can't move.

He looks towards the Bentley. The doors are open, its engine still running.

Exhaust and the steam from the nearby grate make the street at the far end seem a thousand miles away. A different world. Streams of pedestrians flood past. The noise of the heavy traffic dulled.

He still grips his phone. Maybe he should take a picture. This is huge. World changing. Newspapers would pay big money for pictures of this.

His head spins as he sees Martha's upturned face. The rain drips into her open eyes. No, it wouldn't be right.

But he can't stop himself. He snaps several photos of Dominic and Martha. He doesn't have to sell them, but if he doesn't take them, he won't have the choice later.

"Hey, what the—"

Mac turns. The ferret bouncer is standing in the furthest doorway.

"Gimme that phone." He steps forward with hands outstretched. His fingers are claws.

Mac holds the phone to his chest and backs away.

The bouncer slows and drops his hands as well as his tone. "You've seen something shocking. Let me help."

Mac trips on the leg of a bodyguard. Almost falls.

"You knew this was going to happen," he says as realisation hits. He glances up, though the tops of the buildings hide in the thick downpour. "You signalled them."

He looks again. A fire escape rises to the top of the building just above his bin. The assassins came from up there.

He takes a picture of the bouncer.

"Don't do that." The bouncer lurches forward. "Come here."

"No, no, nope." Mac shakes his head back and forth as it dawns on him. "You're one of them off the television, aren't you? With the bomb."

The bouncer touches his radio. "There's a guy here. He has pictures. Kill him."

Mac turns to run. He puts his head down and races towards the end of the alley. Something flutters above him as he reaches the Bentley. With the doors open, he has to inch his way around. Inside, the bodyguards are dead in their seats. Their throats slit.

For a moment he can't feel any rain at all. He glances up. Something large and bat-like falls towards him from the sky above. And ahead a second shape, half hidden in the mist, and silhouetted in the bright, neon, beckoning light of the street descends through the air to cut him off.

He grabs a lid from a barrel-sized metal bin as something splashes down behind him and gives rapid chase.

He holds the lid above his head and passes beneath the second shape as it continues to drop from above. Metal crashes on metal. He almost falls under the weight as the dark shadow surrounds him, hiding all view of the street ahead. He fights to stay upright, shoving his way past some sort of leathery fabric that pulls in tight around him. Then he's out in the neon and hustle and white noise of the busy street.

Pedestrians curl their lips as he barrels out of the alley, holding a dustbin lid above his head and panting. The crowd parts around him like a river around a boulder. A man in a suit jumps back so as not to touch him.

"Murder!" Mac shouts. "There's been a murder in the alley."

He looks back. The alley is dark. He lurches to the edge of the pavement. With one hand he grabs the man in the suit by his lapel. "Why aren't you listening to me? There's been a murder!"

"Please. I have children." The man yelps and hurries away.

Mac looks down at himself, covered in bin juice and carrying a dustbin lid like a shield. People are ignoring him now. They start to cross the street, leaving him vulnerable and exposed out in the open.

The alleyway is now empty. Whatever had dropped from above is no longer there, and he can't see anything at the far end past the full beams of the Bentley. As his eyes try to pierce the darkness, the headlights flicker and die, leaving the cavernous alley dark and open, like the hungry mouth of some gigantic beast.

He can sense eyes on him from within. It's a bad idea to stay. Pulls his collar up. Hat down.

Whoever it was, whoever murdered The Twins and their entourage, would be after him now.

He crosses the road through the gridlock and disappears into the crowds.

My Money's On Clone

From the window, Nige watches the elevated train meandering between skyscrapers like a glowing white snake. The little circles of faces are visible within the carriages. Hundreds of different stories, hundreds of different lives, all travelling together.

Though he has ridden the train dozens of times, from up here, in Kenneth's plush apartment, with its aroma of sandalwood and incense, it's difficult to remember what it's like. The rank smell of warm, tired bodies pressed together. The slow plod home after a day's work. The worn unsmiling faces of teachers, nurses, factory workers, shop assistants. Underpaid and overworked. People who would stand closer to you than you could get to your own children without first making an appointment. All living the same hardships, with the same uncertainties, but too British to open their mouths and seek comfort.

The train disappears into a station.

He presses his forehead to the cool glass and looks towards the streets below. The tiny tops of umbrellas are pulled along like iron filings drawn toward a magnet. It's almost impossible to concentrate on one before it becomes lost in the crowd. Hundreds more people going about their nightly lives.

Streams of rain running down the windows are veins of starlight refracting the spectrum of pinks, blues, whites, and greens which radiate from the screens and signs that light up the city. Each of which battles tooth and claw for the only thing worth fighting for, attention.

He spins his phone between his fingers and takes a picture of the rain on the glass. He adds a filter, then deletes it completely. There are a million like it out there - his view is nothing special.

No one looks anymore. It's just likes for likes.

Across the road from Kenneth's apartment the Di Blasio building stands tall. The structure looks to be made from one solid piece of glass, the joins between the panes so fine that they are barely visible. The illusion broken only by the occasional lit square where someone is still working.

He thinks of Lewis. His son lives in Manchester with his wife and children – two of the sweetest little kids he has ever known – but regularly travels down to the city and works at that very building. He hopes he's now at home with his family. Lewis hates the job, but it pays the bills.

In one window, a young woman types at a laptop, her face a pale blue from the light of her screen. Nige checks his watch. What tyrannical boss expects someone to answer emails at this time?

His gaze tracks up the building. More lit windows. More sad-looking, young employees working late into the night.

At the top of the Di Blasio skyscraper, higher than Kenneth's apartment building goes, a huge billboard glows like a miniature sun. The clouded sky beyond is almost invisible through the haze of light pollution. On the screen, a gigantic image of Kenneth beams down at him, a glass of green liquid in his hand, his skin radiant and perfect. He has looked this way for as long as Nige can remember. The face of Di Blasio takes a sip and winks.

Kenneth's getting ready for his 135th birthday. Join us in celebration. 29th September. Reads the slogan.

Behind the sign, lightning forks across the sky. Nige glimpses his own scowling reflection in the glass. He rubs a hand across his face.

Thunder rolls, and another flash strikes, hitting the billboard and causing it to cut out momentarily. Nige blinks away the afterimage of the bright LED screen. A figure stands atop the billboard. A long strip of fabric flows from their back and lifts in the wind like two large wings.

Inside Nige's head, a thousand whispering voices well up.

His in-ear radio fuzzes.

"Everything ok in there?" says Aidan. "Wanna swap? I've calmed down now, and I might need a pee."

Nige looks across the apartment, towards the front door, then back to the top of the billboard. Whatever was there is gone. Maybe he should think about getting some glasses. "Coming."

He awkwardly scoops up Maggie's schedule and notes from the coffee table, bending at the waist as he does so. His knee still quite stiff.

As he crosses the apartment - it's bigger than his house - he passes a large mirror framed by mahogany carvings of extinct animals and catches himself still scowling.

He doesn't like it here. It's too... over the top.

"Quiiick!" Aidan hisses through the open front door.

"How old are you?" He holds himself stiffly to hide his hobble as he crosses the kitchen.

"I'm desperate."

Nige wags a finger. "You told me you'd calmed down."

"I have. I promise I have," Aidan shouts back as he jogs away down the corridor. "This is just too exciting."

Nige shakes his head and sits on the folding chair outside of Kenneth's door. Leaning to one side, he fishes his car keys out his back pocket and drops them to the floor. He pulls a battered paperback from his jacket.

The book belonged to his wife Fiona. He was never much into reading whilst she was alive, but he uses it now as a way to connect with her. See the things she saw. Live the moments she lived. Almost in tribute. He wishes he had read more with her so they could have talked about it.

It's a bonus that the works of Maeve Binchy turned out to be pretty bloody riveting.

There's a lot of waiting around in security. And since she passed, Nige has realised a good book is second only to a lunch box of thick peanut butter sandwiches.

He finds his page and removes the bookmark - a picture of a small yacht silhouetted by an orange sunset. He smiles, thinking back on the summers he and Fiona spent dreaming in each other's arms, weightless on his father's boat, gazing up at the stars as it swayed, laced to the wooden pier down in Port Isaac.

The water twinkled like the sky above, and the light of the full moon would glint off the head of each tiny ripple. Gentler, calmer nights.

She would lay her head lightly on his chest as he told her his goals and dreams. He was going to make something of himself. They would escape together on exotic adventures. Just the two of them. Sail the forgotten coastlines of Europe. And when they grew tired of that, they'd journey to the Caribbean, get married and have a whole tribe of kids.

He looks up and down the short corridor, and tucks the picture into his front jacket pocket. How plans change.

"Those coastlines aren't going anywhere," she'd said when they found out she was pregnant with Lewis the following autumn.

She was right, of course. The coastlines hadn't gone anywhere.

But she had.

"Do you think he's still awake?" Aidan waddles back down the hallway, still zipping himself up.

"Have you been through this?" Nige holds up Kenneth's schedule.

"I had a quick glance. Have you seen it includes the time he needs to go for a…" Aidan widens his eyes as if to explain, "and the assigned weight and colour of the resultant…" He raises his eyebrows.

"Mm."

"Can I take watch inside now, please?"

"Sure, but don't bother him. You can get him to sign your moobs in the morning over a –" Nige takes on an exaggerated posh English accent "– delightful coconut flat white."

Aidan tuts. "He was being nice."

"He was," Nige says and adopts the accent again: "It'll be nicer than that muck you have in your thermos, I assure you."

Aidan brushes the shoulders of his puffa jacket. Stands a little straighter. "Do I look ok?"

"For a security guard."

Aidan's face falls, then it lights up again. "You don't really think he's a shapeshifting lizard, do you?"

Nige frowns, affronted. "Korrigan said that. Not me."

Korrigan thinks the Di Blasio influencers are lizard-people. He regularly regales Nige with his ridiculous theory that they continue to look so young because they aren't human at all, even going so far as to say that these '*shapeshifting reptiloids*', who come from the '*centre of the earth*', are in fact the '*tyrannical dictators of all humanity*'.

Nige goes so far as to say that Korrigan is full of '*a load of old shit*'.

"Ah yeah," Aidan squints and points an unsure finger. "You said clone, didn't you? We should place bets. I'm gonna go for genuine super old man that looks like he's a hot sixty."

"I'm sixty. He looks forty at most. Put me down for a tenner on clone."

"OK. I'll go in and check on him." Aidan eases the front door. "If I see a tail, I'll try and get a picture." He disappears inside.

Nige places his book face down on his lap and opens up Maggie's schedule again. Tomorrow looks full on. Meditation, yoga, an interview, six meals, more exercise, a meeting about the birthday show. Aidan was right: all toilet breaks are scheduled too. Each section of the day is planned to the minute. No wonder Maggie was rushing off to a nine o'clock meeting. Keeping to this must be a nightmare.

On the next page is a long list of dos and don'ts. This job is more like looking after an exotic fish than a man.

If this is the secret fountain of youth, how are normal people supposed to attain it? Where did it all go so wrong?

The first Don't reads: 'Do not feed him after eight pm. Intermittent fasting begins for twelve hours.'

The second: 'Do not disturb him while he sleeps.'

"Oh God," Nige sighs. He stands, and places the papers and his book on his chair, hoping Aidan hasn't done anything to wake Kenneth.

He taps his lapel radio. "Aidan, we're not supposed to disturb him if he's asleep."

No reply.

He trains his ears through the door. A strange pressure pulses at his temples. He presses his eyes with his fingertips and shakes his head. Now is not a good time for a migraine.

Opening the door, he steps into the darkened apartment. He squints to help his eyes adjust to the dim lighting. A cold draft blows through the room.

Nige's blood freezes. On the floor of the living area the handle to the balcony door lies broken. The door is wide open.

His hand falls to his taser.

Droplets of windswept rain are spattered across the floor, mixed with tiny shards of black plastic and glass from the door handle. They glint in the prism of light bleeding in from the billboard across the street.

"Aidan?"

The lad is nowhere to be seen.

Aside from the door, nothing is different. He takes another step forward. Grinds his teeth. Did Aidan break the door? No one could have come in from outside. They are on the top floor of a forty-four-storey building.

His heart beats fast. "Aidan," he whispers into the silence. The hissing rain from outside, and low hum of the air conditioning, almost drown him out.

One step further and he feels a sharp tug on his trouser leg. Aidan is crouched behind the kitchen island, his hand deep inside the box of Frosties. Several sugar-coated flakes rest in his bushy, viking-like beard. His eyes are wide.

He motions frantically to duck down, and so, with two audible pops from his knees, and a stifled groan, Nige does.

Date Night

As soon as she steps through the front door of the restaurant, Maggie realises why Ian booked this particular place. It's dark, and the booth the waiter leads her to is away from the main dining area.

Hopefully no one will recognise her. It's risky to be out together - especially now - but they can only meet like this away from the office. Stefan Di Blasio has spies everywhere.

Ian isn't there when she arrives, so she orders a glass of water and looks over the menu. There's not a lot she can have, but perhaps a salad without the dressing would be ok.

Just after the waiter brings her glass, she feels a hand on her shoulder. Looks up. "Ian."

He smiles. "Sorry I'm late. It's been a busy day." He sits and calls over a waiter. Orders a beer.

She looks at her water. She'd prefer a wine. It's different for execs.

"Did the hand off go ok?" he says, stretching his arms out along the back of the booth. He looks at her. Those eyes. Blue and piercing. Is he handsome? She can't decide. But there's something there.

"Are you sure now is the best time for this? What with that cult?" She taps a nail on the rim of her glass. She doesn't want to appear nervous, but can't help it. This is all so new. So exciting.

He smiles again. "You booked the bodyguards I sent through to your email, right?"

"Yes, and I managed to get them in without our security seeing." With all the lying and sneaking around, she feels guilt too, but knows she shouldn't.

"Well then, let's just enjoy ourselves."

She smiles. She doesn't know if she remembers how.

Falling Through The Cracks

The rain is relentless. Mac can't remember the last sunny day. It's almost as if God has decided his children are so dehydrated he needs to water them until they are better. Either that or he's going for another annihilation, Noah's ark flood style, but this time slowly, so it hurts more.

He lurks beneath the shelter of a pay phone. Above, the London monorail shrieks past on sparking wheels.

The bouncer from the club had taken a good hard look at his ID. His name, his address, his date of birth. It was all there. They would know how to find him, to silence him.

He contemplates ringing his mum and Amanda. But they'll likely be asleep. Unlike him, they are both early to bed, early to rise types.

He watches the busy streets around him, scanning for anyone that stares a little too long, or stands a little too close. Right now, with his jangling nerves, anyone throwing him a moment's glance lights up his radar.

At least he's safe if he's out in the open.

His phone, with the pictures of the bloodied bodies, weighs like a hot brick in his pocket. As he wandered aimlessly away from The Electric Ballroom, trying to figure out what to do, he'd considered deleting them, as if that would somehow remove the memories from his head. Erase that he was ever there.

He tries to straighten his thoughts. Had those same feather footed assassins killed Terrence? Did that mean they'd killed Harry Wheeler? A story like that should have dominated the news for the last week, which meant Di Blasio were keeping it from the media. But why?

Would they also hide the deaths of The Twins? It wouldn't be good for business if the public found out that one – let alone three – of their prized social influencers were murdered. And in the lead up to one of their most profitable weekends, too.

He doesn't stand much of a chance if Di Blasio wants him silenced. That means no going to the police.

A tremendous weight presses on his shoulders, and on the fringes of his mind he can hear a blaring horn. Some unseen juggernaut racing towards him, aiming to flatten him into paste.

He wants to run, hide, but there's nowhere to go.

Nearby, sheltered under the lip of a doorway, he can see three homeless men sleeping beneath cardboard boxes. He could just join them. Leave the world, leave it behind, with its rents and responsibilities and celebrity butchering assassins.

He thinks of the cash from Suzy tucked away in his desk drawer. Would it get him very far?

Poor Suzy, he can't imagine how she must feel. If he were to run, she would never know what happened to her husband. Just another missing person gone. A life dissolved to nothing.

Like so many others, Suzy can't afford the police. Justice would never be served.

Harry was dead. The Twins, dead. Terrence, probably dead. And, if Mac doesn't come up with a plan, a way to reveal the killers, then he was dead, too.

He's up against a brick wall with nowhere to go except through. He would have to stand in the path of that oncoming juggernaut and Hulk-smash it to bits. And by God, he likes to think he is a good, or at least desperate, enough private investigator for the job.

Despite what he told Suzy about the impregnable nature of The Di Blasio Corporation, every company has cracks. You just have to know where to stick your fingers in.

He has a little more invested in the investigation now.

Death is a great motivator.

But where to start.

The bouncer. The ferret faced, grabby, murdering, 'don't take a picture of me', git bouncer.

He takes out his phone and finds the picture he took in the alley. It's dark and rain blurs the lens. Only part of the bouncer's face is visible, so there's not much to go on. He can remember something written on his jacket, and there had been an ID badge looped around the belt on his trousers. Neither are visible in the picture.

Something blinks red in his periphery. A little light on his lapel. His camera. He forgot to take it off. It would still be transmitting back to his office. Full footage of the night, including both altercations with the bouncer, should be on his hard drive. It wouldn't show the murder, but it might help him find out who the bouncer worked for.

The perfect crack, he thinks metaphorically, in which to insert a finger.

He steps off the pavement in the direction of his office. Then sniggers.

The Intruder

"Did you see it?" Aidan is so close Nige can feel his breath on his cheek.

He moves to stand, but Aidan pulls him back down. Caught off balance, he falls back to the hardwood floor with a thud.

"Shhhh!" Aidan flaps his hand – the one not in a cereal box – with mild hysteria. "Don't stand up. Is it- Is it still in the room?" There is a tremble in his voice that Nige has never heard before.

"Is what—?"

"It came through the window while I was getting a snack." The box of Frosties rustles.

"Who was it? Someone from the cult?"

"Not a who. An it."

"Well, where did it go?" He eases himself up, hoping Aidan won't notice, and pull him back down again.

"It came through the door and I ducked. Sounded like it headed for the bathroom. I don't think it saw me. It was weird. It rustled like paper."

"Jesus Christ Aidan. Why didn't you take him out? We've been paid to do a job." He moves towards the bathroom door and unholsters his taser.

Aidan pulls himself up on the breakfast bar, pouring a noisy puddle of frosted flakes all over the kitchen floor. "Oh balls," he moans. "That's all I brought with me."

Nige pinches the bridge of his nose and squeezes his eyes shut. "Well, that's the element of surprise gone."

He scans the living room one last time. A trail of droplets leads from the open door across the hardwood floor. He chastises himself for not noticing them when he came in.

He follows them towards the bathroom door and eases it open. It's misty with steam. Hot and humid and dim, save for the light of several flickering candles around the mirror. Cinnamon scented incense clings to the steam, taking him straight back to his own kitchen and Fiona's home-baked cakes.

Strange tracks trail across the wet tiled floor towards a door on the other side of the bathroom. Small footprints with two wide strokes on each side, as if someone has walked through dragging a garden broom in each hand.

He strides through the door into a dark hallway. There's no time for caution. Aidan follows a reluctant step behind. The thick carpet silences their footsteps. That pressure behind his eyes again. He shakes his head. Aidan has a pained indentation between his eyebrows.

At the end of the hall, he gives Aidan a quick nod, then kicks the door. They both launch through making as much noise as possible, hoping to startle the intruder.

"Come out now."

"We're tough guys!"

In his bed, Kenneth jerks upright like a whack-a-mole.

"What's all this?"

In the shadows on the far side of the room, a stick thin figure in a long shawl stands hunched over him. It turns to them, face hidden.

"Get him," Nige shouts. The pressure behind his eyes has built to a roaring hiss.

Aidan leaps across the bed with a growl, and rugby tackles the intruder to the ground.

"Come with me, Mr Bailey," Nige says as he grabs Kenneth out of bed and drags him across the room into the hallway. "Aidan," he calls back as he marches Kenneth through the bathroom, "dump him, we're out of here."

There is a short *whumph*, and a heavy pressure shoves Nige forward, almost knocking him to the ground. He glances back as Aidan shoots through the door backwards. He lands on his back in the middle of the hall.

"Go!" Nige gives Kenneth a not particularly gentle shove in the direction of the living room and runs back to drag Aidan up.

"It… It…" is all Aidan can say as Nige half carries, half drags him through the bathroom.

He slams the door behind them.

"What's happening?" Kenneth asks.

"Wait there," Nige tells him, then looks back. "Aidan, block off the bathroom door."

"With what?"

"With anything. I don't know." He points to a chest next to the door. "That massive bloody chest."

"Not the chest. It's from a Buddhist monastery. I brought it back from an excursion in the Himalayas. Its value is unparalleled." Kenneth visibly wilts.

"I don't care if the Dalai Lama built it with his own bare hands using wood from Noah's Ark. Aidan chuck it in front of the door."

Aidan does, just as something crashes on the other side.

"Into the lift," says Nige, pointing Kenneth down the corridor.

"How did they get in to my chambers?" says Kenneth as the doors open and Nige manhandles him in.

"Through the window." He mashes the button for the fourth floor. Shouts back, "Hurry up, Aidan. I *will* leave you." He won't but he knows that FOMO is about the only thing that will get the younger generation moving.

Aidan appears and dives into the lift just as the doors begin to close. One catches his foot so they open again.

Nige flares his eyes. He bashes the close button. He watches the apartment door, but nothing emerges. The lift doors eventually shut with the mind numbingly casual ease of a lift whose occupants are in a hurry.

"Are you hurt?" Nige looks Kenneth over as the elevator descends.

"I'm fine," says Aidan.

Nige gives him the look.

"I don't think so," says Kenneth. He is wearing white linen trousers and a black oriental style kimono covered in colourful butterflies. His feet are bare. He closes his eyes and blows out a long, steady breath. "Who was it? Not those robed chaps from the TV?"

"Aidan?"

"Tall. And slim. Taller than you even, Nige. I saw it outside first. It flew up to the window from nowhere. It had wings."

"You mean like a hang glider, or one of those wing suits idiots wear to jump out of planes?" Nige is very aware that at some point in the past Kenneth has done this, and glances at him for a reaction. There is none.

"No, like actual wings. But I didn't get a good look. I had it one minute, and then the next..." He makes a whistling noise and moves his hand through the air like a plane. "I was flying through the doorway." He touches the back of his head. "Did it throw me?" His nostril twitches in disbelief. "Me?" He indicates his size by lowering his upturned palms from his chest to his waist.

"I don't want to start playing the blame game, but are you sure you didn't trip?" Kenneth raises a single eyebrow.

"The boy's sure," Nige says cooly. "Mr Bailey, we'll get you down to the safe room and then maybe some of your security can go back up and investigate."

"But…" Kenneth hesitates. "I don't think they're supposed to know you're here." He winces as he says it.

"What?" Nige looks at Aidan for some sort of confirmation but sees the same blank face staring back at him. He turns bulging eyes back to Kenneth. Draws his lips over his teeth in a snarl. "You what?"

"Mags didn't tell them about you. She hired you privately."

"Oh, this just gets worse by the minute." He rubs a hand across the top of his head. What is he supposed to do here? "I knew this was a bad idea."

"She mentioned she had made your manager aware."

"Korrigan?" Nige's jaw tightens. He can't tell if Kenneth is lying. It wouldn't be like Korrigan to hide things.

"What does she think will happen if Di Blasio knows?" Aidan asks.

"I think she just wanted a couple of extra hands on deck. What with the death threats and the flu."

"So she does think the threats are something to worry about." Nige grumbles.

"Takeshi should be working security tonight. He's a good friend. He'll help us."

Nige shakes his head in frustration. "What do you think they'll do if they see us two with you not knowing who we are? We'll head down to the carpark and call her from my car."

The numbers on the lift screen descend. No one speaks for a moment.

"I hope no one else gets in before we get down there," says Aidan, with a little jerk of the eyebrows. "That'd be a bit awkward, wouldn't it?"

The lift stops at the fourth floor. Nige looks accusingly at him.

He makes a guilty face. "Jinxed it."

Nige moves between Kenneth and the door, pushing him back into the corner of the lift. "Be ready for anything," he whispers to Aidan.

He readies his taser.

Reluctantly, the doors chunk open. In the hall, as solid as marble pillars and dressed in all-in-one black combat suits, stand four Di Blasio security guards.

Kenneth's First Ever Televised Interview

1976

"Today we have with us Kenneth Bailey, former world war 2 veteran turned Health Guru," says the interviewer. "To start, Kenneth, may I say your skin is radiant. Who is your dermatologist?"

Kenneth smiles. His cheeks redden slightly. "My dermatologist? Water, fresh fruit, clean air, and yoga. Hydration is the name of the game."

The interviewer laughs. "Tell us, what exactly is a Health Guru?"

The woman made him feel very at ease before they went on the air, but Kenneth is still a little nervous. And despite the rigorous media training he's been through over the last few weeks, he doesn't know what to do with his hands. Wherever he puts them feels unnatural and he is horribly aware of the cameras catching his every move, broadcasting it live to the thousands, if not millions, of people watching the news this evening.

"It's a new term really, hard to describe unless I give you some context." His hands finally settle on his lap.

He was told that the interview was going to be more about him and less about the Di Blasio products. "Let the people get to know the real Kenneth," Frank, his manager at the time, said. "We'll move on to selling when the people like you. And once the documentary has aired."

Kenneth can see Frank now standing behind the camera. He twirls his hands in a 'go on' gesture. The interviewer smiles revealing unnaturally white and straight teeth. Kenneth blows air from his cheeks. It's hot under the lights, and he is on the verge of breaking out in a sweat. How bad would that look?

"There are five of us. Myself, Dawn, Terrence, Martha and Dominic." He pauses a moment, suppressing the sadness that wells up whenever he thinks about the fact that there used to be a sixth member of their group.

"Stefan Di Blasio wants to debunk the myths surrounding the optimum human lifestyle, and he's chosen us to do it. We're more guinea pig than guru."

"How exciting! And what exactly is Mr Di Blasio's main aim?"

Kenneth holds up three fingers. "Increase the quality of human life, increase the length, and eradicate certain ailments like heart disease, type two diabetes, and some forms of cancer through proper diet and exercise."

"A very noble cause." The interviewer cocks her head. Her hair hardly moves despite gravity's best efforts. "And what steps is Mr Di Blasio taking to achieve these aims?"

Kenneth smiles. "You'll just have to wait and see. The documentary is showing on BBC 1 on Monday at 8pm."

"That's right." She shuffles some pieces of paper on her desk – though Kenneth can see they are blank. "'Lifestyle of Our Future' is a documentary focusing on this last year of your life."

"Mine and the other influencers'."

"And what do you say to the people who think Stefan Di Blasio is faking results just to sell more of his own products?"

Heat rises from beneath his collar and his shirt is suddenly too tight. He glances at Frank, whose hand has gone to his brow. She's not supposed to ask questions like this. He squeezes his knees and closes his eyes for a moment, trying to clear his head the way they'd taught him.

"Well, I can tell those people that it works. Look at my face." He points to himself and leans closer to the interviewer. "How old would you say I am, Maria?"

"I don't know. You've got one of those faces. You could be 35, you could be 55."

"I'm 76. I was born in the year 1900." He leans back, satisfied by the look on her face. She believes him. "I've never had any work done, and I've only been with the programme for five and a half years. I've never felt better in all my life and it's all down to Stefan Di Blasio." He smiles, feeling increasingly confident. He pats her hand lightly, then stands. "Maria. Have you ever seen a 76-year-old do a back flip?"

She smiles and shakes her head.

Kenneth spreads his arms wide like a gymnast. "Which camera has me?" he points to the one Frank is standing by. Frank beams back, his hands balled into fists of excitement. "Have you got me?"

The camera man nods.

Kenneth does a backward somersault, landing neatly on his feet. He straightens his tie. "Now Maria, that wasn't fake, was it?"

She shakes her head again. "I can't see any wires."

The Security

"What are you doing up, Kenneth?" says one of the security team, clearly the leader, speaking as a parent might to a small child who's snuck out of his room after bedtime.

"There was someone in my room, Jeff. These two gents got me out quick as a shot."

"Interesting. We'll be sure to check that out, but first, if you don't mind me asking, who are these two gentlemen?"

Nige doesn't like the look on the security chief's face. He has a gleam in his eye that he can't quite place.

Kenneth looks down for a moment then back at Jeff. "Maggie hired them to look after me."

"But we look after you?" The security chief tips his head, and folds his arms.

It is at this point that Nige catches on. He looks like a jealous girlfriend who has just caught someone chatting up her man.

Kenneth opens his mouth, but closes it again and looks down.

Nige steps forward. "Ms Greaves knows you guys are spread thin right now, what with the flu thing. She wanted to get two close bodyguards in as backup."

"Hm. Flu. Right." Jeff chews the words as if tasting them, then takes a step closer. "Surely you know how reckless this is." He is only a few inches taller than Kenneth but he seems to tower over him.

"Maggie won't be in for it, will she?" Kenneth says, fumbling with the tie of his kimono.

The elevator doors begin to close between them. Jeff kicks his foot in the way. "It's not up to me. It's up to Mr Di Blasio." He points upwards, then lays a hand on Kenneth's shoulder, gently guiding him into the corridor. "Let's get you to the safe room. Dom, take Kenneth along will you."

"Is Takeshi here?" asks Kenneth as he follows one of the other guards along the corridor. "I thought he was on tonight."

"He's taking care of The Twins this evening. They were a bit short staffed, you know, with this flu."

Kenneth's tanned face shifts a shade paler. "I see. Are you coming, Nigel?"

"Sure." Nige moves to leave the lift, but Jeff steps across the doors.

"Dom," Jeff calls back over his shoulder, "you get Kenneth settled. We'll be in shortly."

The guard leads Kenneth further up the corridor.

"So Nigel. It is Nigel?"

"My friends call me Nige. And this is Aidan."

"I tackled the tall thin guy." Aidan beams.

Jeff raises an eyebrow. "Good for you."

Nige doesn't like this guy at all. He looks past him to Kenneth being led away.

"Nigel." Jeff clicks his fingers in his face. And for a moment, with the adrenalin still pumping from their escape, Nige almost bats the hand away. "Talk me through what happened up there."

Nige takes a breath and tells him what they saw.

"It happened quick. I'm sure whoever it was must have flown in on a hang glider or something, then they broke in."

"Or a wing suit," adds Aidan, waving a knowing finger. "You know the ones idiots jump from planes with."

Jeff frowns. "Well, I'm sure it's nothing Jay and Esther can't handle." He turns to the other guards, presumably Jay and Esther. "Upstairs. See if you can find whoever it was."

They step into the lift and the female guard bobs her head to suggest Nige and Aidan get out. They do, and the lift doors shut. It rises.

"We'd like to stay with Mr Bailey, if that's ok?" says Nige.

Jeff nods slowly. He looks back further up the corridor, where Dom is opening a door and steering Kenneth inside. Once Kenneth is out of sight the faux friendly gleam in his eye drops.

"That won't be necessary. You two did a fine job getting the old boy out. Thanks for that, but you should leave now." He leans across them and presses the call button for the second lift.

"But—"

The elevator doors open.

"But what?" Jeff stares, unblinking. "I think it would be better for you and I if you both left. This isn't the sort of job for you two." He shakes his head and holds out a hand, gesturing to the lift. "Kenneth will be taken care of. Esther and Jay will find nothing. We have CCTV all over the roof. Nothing came in or out."

How can that be? Is he hiding something, or was Aidan mistaken?

"I'll do you a favour," he continues. "I'll tell Maggie I let you go. I'll make sure you're paid in full. And I won't tell Kenneth you lied to him about the break in."

Nige tries to think. Everything is happening so quickly. "What? We didn't—"

Jeff's face is severe. "If you don't leave right now Mr Di Blasio will find out that his most prized asset," he points back down the corridor, "that stupid old man in the other room, has been compromised by a pair of bungling idiots. You've messed with a schedule honed to perfection and implemented flawlessly for over sixty years. Do you know what that could do to Kenneth?" He pauses, looking them both up and down like vagrants. "Who knows what pathogens you've brought in off the streets."

"Look—"

"If anything happens over the next few days. If Kenneth gets a spot, bags under his eyes, or even yawns at his birthday bash, people are going to start asking questions. And if people are asking questions, people aren't buying products. And who do you think Mr Di Blasio is going to look at to recoup his lost earnings? Your children's children will work their whole, long, miserable lives paying for it just because their stupid Grandaddy couldn't leave when he was told to."

Nige clenches his jaw to keep from snarling. A threat on his family isn't the sort of thing he'd usually take lightly. Perhaps they should leave before he does something stupid.

"But we saved him." The worry is plain on Aidan's face.

"Esther and Jay won't find anything up there and you know it," says Jeff. "You two are just a couple of fakes. Playing the heroes. I bet that daft old fool fell for it hook, line, and sinker."

Nige's hands clench. The muscles in his forearms pop.

Jeff looks down at Nige's fists, clearly unimpressed. "What are you going to do with them?"

Nige relaxes his fingers. It's best for them both if they just leave. He couldn't live with himself if his anger got them both in trouble.

"You know what, Aidan." He doesn't take his eyes from Jeff. "To be honest, I was really nervous about this from the start. This is probably the best outcome we could have hoped for." Aidan opens his mouth to say something, but Nige cuts him off. "As long as we get paid, why wouldn't we leave early?" He steps into the lift.

"I knew you'd get there." Jeff holds his stare. "A good night's work for you two, I bet." The corners of his mouth twitch. Nige just wants to hit him. "Hell, a good month." He flicks his fingers dismissively at Aidan. "You too."

Aidan backs into the lift. Nige hits the button for the carpark. Jeff watches them as the doors close.

"Wh—" starts Aidan.

"Don't." Nige's voice is low. "There's nothing we can do."

Aidan falls silent and looks away. "You're doing this because you don't like Kenneth, aren't you?"

"No." Nige grits his teeth and pushes his fist hard against the metal just above the buttons until his arm shakes.

"It's Lewis, isn't it? You don't want him to get fired?"

Nige bursts. He can't keep it in. "Who the hell does that guy think he is?" His face is purple, he breathes like a bull about to charge. "Who the hell…" Too angry to speak. He pulls his fist back, wanting to smash the lift buttons to bits. Squashes the rage deep down. It'd only cost him.

Aidan takes a cautious step back, almost as if Nige is a ticking bomb.

"You can't just talk to people like that. Throw money and threats in their faces and hope they go away. It's not right."

"What are you saying?" says Aidan.

The doors open on the carpark. Nige hits the close button.

He looks at Aidan with gritted teeth. His face slowly regains its normal colour. "I'm tired of being treated like I have no importance. We were hired to do a job and we're gonna bloody do it."

Aidan's face lights with excitement. Then it falls just as quickly. "But there's four of them, with guns."

Nige shakes his hands out and bobs his head from side to side like a boxer warming up. "We just go in there. Get Kenneth. Grab him. Go. Figure the rest out later."

"Yeeeah." Aidan copies his head bobbing. "Ok!"

Nige's thumb hovers over the fourth-floor button. He hesitates, then presses.

During the brief journey to the fourth floor Nige could have sworn Aidan repeated the word "ok" upwards of one hundred times as he paced backwards and forwards, throwing uppercuts in the air as he did so.

When the doors open, Nige leans forward to check the corridor. Empty.

The door to the control room is closed. The cushioned carpet silences their steps as they move towards it. They stop outside, leaning in to listen. Though dulled by the thick security door, Jeff's baritone reverberates through.

"…he ordered the younger guy and they both left."

Kenneth sounds small in comparison. "A couple of rough, tough guys like that? They didn't seem frightened."

"They were practically shaking when I said they should go. I would have asked them to man up, but you're not allowed to do that anymore without getting sued to buggery. Not everyone is cut out for this line of work, Kenneth. Probably best if they stick with bouncing night clubs and taking care of Z-list celebs. You're above their pay grade."

"Cheeky bugger," Aidan mouths at him.

"But they made such fast work of the assailant," says Kenneth.

"Esther and Jay messaged down. The only thing out of the ordinary was a broken window. Did you actually see anyone, or was it just them in your room?"

Nige looks at Aidan who shakes his head. Could it be that the intruder had broken free from the bathroom and escaped? Or something else? Was someone lying?

"I was asleep then Nigel pulled me out of bed."

"My theory - they broke the window themselves and made the rest up. It's quite a big deal to say you've saved Kenneth Bailey from an intruder in his own home, and with the death threats I expect they saw the opportunity to make a quick buck from your misfortune."

Nige bristles. His stomach tightens like a drawstring bag. But what is he going to do? He steps back from the door. What's his plan here?

"Bloody leeches," Jeff continues. "Do anything for a quick buck." A silence broken by a sniff, then a loud thump from inside the room. "Oh, it just makes me so mad."

Nige and Aidan exchange identical scowls. Is Jeff just jealous?

Back down the hall, the lift dings and the doors open. Nige spies a maintenance cupboard opposite the safe room and shoves Aidan into it as Esther and Jay step into the hallway. He leaves the door open a crack, allowing a sliver of light to brighten the otherwise pitch-black closet.

The two whisper as they approach. "Believe which bit?" says Esther.

"The bit about it not being the food. About it being something that could happen to any of us if we get that old."

"Nah. It's gotta be the food. You eat that much paste out of a tube and you're bound to get all freaky. Dawn's been an influencer the longest out of all of them, so it's obvious she was the first to go. My money's on Kenneth next. That's why they want him over there."

"I'm just glad they locked her away in the lab. That thing was weird."

The pair go quiet as they approach the safe room and enter.

Something else was happening here.

"Did you hear them?" Nige whispers. He can't quite see Aidan's face, just the tip of his beard and nose.

"Something about food?"

"No! Dawn. They've got her somewhere. They've locked her away and they're getting Kenneth now."

Were the security kidnapping the influencers? Why? Maybe something to do with the new ones that Lewis had mentioned.

"We have to help him." There's a swish and a click as Aidan extends his baton. He leans forward, the corner of his mouth curls into a snarl. "They've got guns right, and there's four of them. We'll have to be quick, but at least there's more of 'em to hit."

Nige pats his belt - taser, torch, cuffs, pepper spray - and takes a deep breath.

Aidan's forearm clicks as he squeezes the grip of his nightstick. "Plan?"

Nige uncaps the mace and checks the battery on his taser. He shakes his head. "No time for plans."

He springs out of the cupboard. The door across the hall is closed so he shoulder-barges through.

Raising the pepper spray, he unleashes a full blast into the nearest person's face. Luckily, it's not Kenneth.

Jeff cries out.

To his left Dom rises from a swivel chair, but Nige tases him in the chest. He falls to the floor like a slinky rolling down the stairs.

At the back of the room, Jay and Esther are standing with Kenneth.

"Nigel? What are you doing?"

"We're here to rescue you," he shouts over the sound of Dom writhing, and Jeff's obscenities. "We didn't choose to leave. Jeff threatened us. He lied. They've got Dawn locked up somewhere and now they're coming for you."

With frantic hands, Jeff makes a grab at Nige, but being half blind, he trips over Dom's flailing legs. Aidan clonks him over the head with his baton, and he falls.

A look of understanding curls across Kenneth's face, and for a moment, he closes his eyes, moving his concentration inwards. He takes a deep breath.

"Um, Kenneth, we gotta go. No time for meditation."

Kenneth nods.

Jay and Esther move forwards, unholstering their weapons as they do so. Nige blasts pepper spray at them, but they are too far away.

"I believe you." Kenneth speaks slowly as if nothing else is going on in the room. "Don't ask me how I know, but I—"

"Kenneth, we've got to go."

"Oh, sorry."

In one fluid motion, Kenneth shoots out his left hand and grabs Esther by the pistol arm, jamming the gun in its holster. He kicks Jay, driving his right foot into the back of his leg, forcing him to his knees. He then pulls the pistol from Esther's holster and knocks Jay over the back of the head with it. Jay falls face first into the desk.

"Kenneth. Stop!" Esther shouts through clenched teeth. She turns to grab him. She catches him by the throat, but Kenneth is lightning quick. He side-steps and swings his arm up through hers, sweeping down and breaking her hold on his neck. He takes one of her hands and twists it into a goose neck before spinning her around.

"Excuse me, gentlemen," he says to Nige and Aidan as he guides her through the room and out into the hall. "My mother said a man must never hit a woman, so we'll just pop her in the cupboard." With his free hand, Kenneth opens the janitor closet and pushes her inside. "Be a sport and hand me that desk chair, would you?"

Nige can't speak. Where did he learn to fight like that?

Esther bangs on the other side of the door. Kenneth clicks his fingers. "Spit spot."

Nige rolls the chair out through the door and slides it up under the handle, locking it in place.

Aidan's mouth twitches. Nige can see he's thinking the same thing. "Where did you... That was... You're amazing." His big glossy eyes gaze at Kenneth in awe.

Kenneth nods knowingly. He hasn't even broken a sweat. "Don't just stand there lollygagging. Away!" He sprints down the hall towards the elevators.

"Where did you learn that?" Nige says as he and Aidan follow.

"I'm the only remaining man on the planet who fought in a world war. Plus, it doesn't take a lot to master two or three different martial arts if you've got the time and money." He grins.

'But I—"

"Most think this physique is purely aesthetic. That is as I intend. It's good to be a strong, tenacious warrior Nigel, but it's even better to be an underestimated one." He stops at the lift.

Nige rushes after him. His knee quietly protests, but he's not about to show it.

Kenneth hits the lift button but Nige passes, continuing to run. "No lift. Jeff could stop them. Stairs down to the carpark."

Kenneth overtakes him halfway down the first flight. Nige has to stop to pause for a breath after three storeys, bent double with hands on his thighs. Despite the slight ache in his knee, he thought himself fit, but Kenneth is another level. He shakes his head, catching himself before he becomes too impressed.

"He's amazing." Aidan floats past in a daze, unable to take his eyes off his idol.

"Marry him then," Nige says bitterly.

Aidan looks back with a face that suggests he is considering it.

The door at the bottom of the stairwell opens into the small underground carpark where Nige had left his old Ford. Gleaming sports cars charge from wall mounted plugs. Rolls Royce, Tesla, Bentley, even one metallic green Lamborghini. Nige's car stands out like an ordinary thumb surrounded by sore ones.

"Is that your automobile?" Kenneth points.

"How did you guess?"

Nige pats himself down for the keys. They aren't there. He slaps his forehead.

"Balls on parade! Aidan, did you pick up the keys by the chair upstairs?"

Aidan looks puzzled. "Should I have?"

"Yes. Yes you should." He looks over the cars that fill the garage. "Jeff and the others will be here soon. Which one's yours?"

"The red Ferrari…" Kenneth points to the car in the corner, and then proceeds to point at others throughout the space. "That Lamborghini. That Lamborghini. The yellow Ferrari. The Rolls. The Bentley. That's one of my fav—"

Nige rolls his eyes. "Have you got keys for any of them?"

"Oh no, I don't drive." Kenneth looks down and lightly kicks at a loose piece of tarmac. "They took my licence."

Suddenly, the light goes off. His eyes, having been accustomed to the dazzling fluorescents, are suddenly useless. He can't see a thing.

Rubber squeals, and a splintering crash punctures the calm quiet. Three black Jeeps smash through the entrance barriers at the top half of the car park and speed towards their level, stopping at the lifts and barring the only exit.

The Tall Ninjas

Nige pulls Kenneth down behind his car. "Who the hell is that now?" he hisses.

Just as the three of them duck behind his boot, the doors of the Jeeps fly open. Around ten figures emerge and move stealthily towards the lifts and stairs.

Nige peeks. They all wear tight fitting black wraps, like ninjas, or goth mummies. Their faces covered. He can't quite see that well, but one figure from each Jeep looks to be over eight feet tall. They move with a strange fluidity, like water snakes carving through the ocean. The rest are all of normal height.

The thing that stands out most about the tall ones is their body shape beneath their clothes. They are angular and thin though their stature doesn't appear weak or hunched. Similar to the intruder in Kenneth's room, they are tall and upright and strong. Unusual humps jut from each of their backs as if they have something rolled up and stuffed beneath their clothes.

One of the tall ones leads a group into the lift. The rest run for the stairs. Each carries a uniquely curved blade.

When the last disappears out of sight, Aidan stands up. "They looked cool. Who were they?"

"Not the foggiest," says Kenneth. "Do you think they were after yours truly?"

"Isn't everyone? And was it me, or were three of them super tall?" Nige tries the handle of his car door, keeping both eyes on the Jeeps at the end of the car park. It is locked.

"Yeah, like eight foot," Aidan says, holding a hand high above his own head. "Stretched out like they'd been on a rack."

"Were they members of that cult?" Nige pats himself down just in case he has his keys on him.

"Don't know. In the video they have purpley robes on." Aidan motions towards the car. "Can't you smash the window and hot wire it?"

"You've been hanging around with Spoony Phil too much. I haven't got a clue how to hot wire a car. Besides, they're blocking the up ramp." He points to the Jeeps, then cocks his head. "Aidan, come with me."

Gripping his taser tightly, he jogs to the Jeeps. The doors have been left open. He leans inside the driver's side of the first.

The dashboard is smooth, completely featureless. He checks under the steering wheel and in the centre console for a key or ignition point, but there isn't one. Nor are there any glove or storage compartments. He glances in the back - just seats, no belts.

He bangs his hands on the dashboard, hoping something might spring open.

"What the hell's this?" He looks at Aidan who is now sitting comfortably in the back seat. "Is this some new trendy thing that I know nothing about? Some sort of minimalist fashion?"

"I don't think so. It's usually the more gadgets the better. The windows in mine are AR screens so you can make it look like you're driving underwater or on Mars."

"Sounds safe." He gestures back at his crumpled Ford. "I can barely cover that hunk of junk and I own the business. How the hell do you afford it?"

"Easy!" Aidan rubs his thumb and first two fingers together. "I'm neck deep in crippling debt. I've never seen anything like this though." He raises an eyebrow, leans forward between the front seats, and strokes the matt black dashboard. "I want one."

"We can't drive this."

They return to Kenneth, who is still crouching behind Nige's car.

"We'll move out on foot."

"Oh lovely, a quick stroll through the showery streets of London," says Kenneth.

Ignoring him, Nige points to a sign indicating the exit, and marches towards it, hoping the others follow.

The Nuts

Mac is too late.

It didn't take long to get back to his office, but there is already someone waiting outside for him.

The guy is clearly not supposed to be here. Two or so years working as a bounty hunter in Camden quickly gives you your bearings on the local thugs. If Mac is anything he is judgemental, and judging by this guy's thick set jaw and jutting brow, he's definitely a thug. Just not a local one.

The thug hides well. Skulking in the shadows behind the bins by the Chinese. The perfect place to see every approach on the way to the office door. But this is Mac's manor. He knows where to look for those trying to remain inconspicuous.

He approaches his office building from the dark of the nearby park.

"I see you," Mac whispers under his breath, feeling quietly pleased with himself for spotting him.

He squints in a way that he knows would look really cool if anyone was watching. He is strangely exhilarated. This is proper PI work. None of that grunt work taking creepy pictures of cheating lovers, or finding lost pets. This is action, albeit scary and life threatening, but good solid action.

He stretches his head from side to side, hoping maybe his neck will crack.

It doesn't.

Of course, what the guy behind the bins probably doesn't know is there is a back entrance to the office. The route is a little technical. It involves a shimmy up a drain, followed by another shorter but more perilous shimmy across two slim window ledges.

Mac has done it twice before. Once last month whilst escaping the landlord who had come for the rent, and once last year when a gang of little hoodlums had come after him because he'd snapped a bounty bracelet on their drug dealing mate.

He holds his hands out, palms up, and lets a few fat drops of rain fall onto his skin from the large oak above. He'd never risked the double shimmy in wet weather.

From the deep shadow behind the bins, steps another man: the ferret faced bouncer. He says something to his friend, then slinks back into the darkness.

That settles it. Drain pipe it is. He will only crack this by finding out who ferret face is. And to do that he needs to see what the camera caught in the club.

Maybe he could sell Di Blasio the information. That'd be worth a mint.

Five minutes later Mac is standing at the base of the slippery drain pipe with his belt in his hands, wondering if it could be of any use in his ascent. In the end he decides no, throws it over his shoulder, and pulls himself up to the small flat roof one storey above the ground.

In one corner of the roof, jammed under a rusted pipe, a depressed-looking football watches him as he edges along to the first of the two window ledges.

He looks down. When you are safe and dry inside a building, and not being battered by what he is sure must be a force eleven gale, the first storey doesn't seem so high. But out here, with a cold slap of rainy wind beating him across the face every five seconds, it is as if he is atop the white cliffs of Dover staring into an unforgiving and bleakly grey English Channel.

He shakes his head and tentatively steps on to the first ledge. His white-knuckled fingers grip the crumbling brick that borders the window. Through the glass, he can see the first storey landing and the top of the stairs that lead up from reception. But this window doesn't even open from inside. Sealed shut with decades of rust and grime.

A car splashes by on the street below.

The next ledge is a bit of a jump. Relatively easy in dry conditions despite the way you have to stoop to fit.

Mac doesn't like the idea of a jump from slim wet concrete to even slimmer wet concrete, so he slides down to his belly. The cold ledge eats through his shirt and within seconds he's soaked. He eases across the gap like a slug.

Through the next window is a solicitor's office. Ellen is never in after six o'clock and picking the lock of her door is easy. He pulls a tab of plastic he wedged in the window for events just like this and it pops ajar. He eases his fingers in and opens it.

He does his best to shake the water from his coat before entering, then closes the window, and crosses the office. A neat little room with a small desk and several bowed shelves packed with thick law hardbacks. One mug, one chair, one desk. Lonely.

It reminds him of his own office.

Though he bets Ellen has more teabags.

After picking the lock, he climbs the four storeys to his office, always on constant alert for anyone lying in wait. No one is.

Surprisingly, his door remains locked. He'd half expected it to be forced open, office in bits, but everything is how he left it.

He hurries across the room, pushes the wheelie chair out of the way, and kneels at his computer.

He checks the footage. The camera feed paused when he turned the go-pro off in the phone booth on Camden high street. His monitor shows a close-up of his own down-turned face looking a little saggy and worse for wear.

Perhaps he should buy some of that Di Blasio anti-ageing cream *"bio-engineered specifically for 20 to 30-year-olds who want to prevent rather than cure."*

He skips the video back to the moment just before he was ejected from the club. It is dark, and the bouncer is in black, but for a few frames, caught in the flash of a strobe, his entire jacket is visible.

An embroidered badge on his chest reads 'Korrigan and Davies'. Mac saves the picture to his phone. He spots that weird tattoo again on the bouncer's hand. The candy cane and triangle. He sends that to his phone as well, just in case.

Before he leaves, he takes a few extra bounty bracelets from his draw as well as the cash from Suzy. He puts both in his jacket pocket. Then to the hat stand behind the door to change and get his cricket bat.

But the bat's not there.

"Looking for this?" A greasy voice rasps like fish and chip paper in the silent office. A shadow unfurls from the darkness over by the damp patch.

"Nooooope." Without turning, Mac steps from the room. Closes the door behind him then sprints to the stairs. "Nope, nope-iddy nooope."

His feet hardly touch the ground as he flies down. His hand a monorail tracking the time smoothed wooden bannister. Behind he hears his office door slam against the wall, followed by the patter of light footsteps giving chase.

This is no longer exciting action. He is no longer exhilarated.

Someone shouts up from downstairs and he can hear distinctly heavier footfalls gallump up from the ground floor below. Without thinking, he opens the first window on the landing and steps out onto the ledge of the third floor.

Almost as soon as he presses the window closed behind him, his foot skids on the smooth concrete. His heart punches hot and hard in his throat as his fingers fight for grip on the wet brick.

There is no way down.

Two storeys below is the drain pipe he climbed to get in. But for some incredibly stupid and infuriatingly practical reason, it angles away from this particular window ledge and off on a merry jaunt around the corner of the building, as if it has something better to do than saving PIs in peril. He'd have to jump to reach it hoping it didn't come away from the wall. And even then, that was if he managed to catch it with his wet and slowly freezing hands.

A dark shape passes by the window, and he tries his best to look small. Once again he lies down on the ledge and slugs his way over to the next.

A blind covers the window there. It's not possible to see inside. He pulls at the edges with numb fingers, only managing to rip a nail to the bed.

What's the opposite of exhilarated? Because that is how he is now feeling.

Just above his head to his left, a set of thick telephone cables stretch down and across the road to a wooden pole by the park. If he stretches on tiptoes, and gives a short but fully committed hop, he could just about reach them. If he missed - game over.

But what would he do once he was holding them? Shimmy down? He's had about enough of wet shimmies tonight to last him a lifetime.

Returning to the window, he cups his hands over his eyes and tries to pierce the darkness behind the blind. Even if there were a three-storey ladder inside, he can't get in.

Something clinks against the brick by his head. His belt still slung over his shoulder. He removes it and holds one end in each hand.

"Oh god," he says to the belt, then looks up at the slick wires that angle downward across the road. "Are you thinking what I'm thinking?"

The belt does not respond.

He motions throwing it over the wires, catching the other end, and whispers, "Aaah," as he imagines zip-lining down to the street Indiana Jones style. It won't be fun, but it could work.

He spots a few pegs sticking out of the pole. He could probably use those to climb down. Probably.

"This isn't a good plan," he says as he whips the belt up in the air and over the wire. He stretches to his full height. His rubber soled hi tops slip just as he grabs the other end of the belt.

There's a moment of heart jolting panic as both feet leave the ledge and the wire dips, and then he is sailing through the night towards the telephone pole.

Uncontrollably fast towards the telephone pole.

Uncontrollably fast, face first towards the telephone pole with no hands to slow his fall.

He closes his eyes and puts his feet out, hoping they will cushion the impending blow.

With it being rainy, and the pole being as slippery as everything else, naturally his feet slide either side, and Trent Macadamia comes crashing surnames first into the thick and unforgiving wood.

Groaning, he clutches the telephone pole in a fierce hug, and waits for everything to slot back in to place. Then, with as much speed as he can muster, clambers down the pegs and drops to the pavement.

He checks his phone to make sure it is still intact and has another quick look at the picture of the bouncer. Korrigan and Davies Security. If he can find the company, he'll at least be one step further along the chain to finding who did this.

Without a look backwards, he limps into the shadows of the park.

The Streets

Nige peers through a crack in the door down the alley that runs alongside Kenneth's building. The weather is still miserable.

Just to the right of the door, a legion of large green wheelie bins stand chained to posts. One of them is open, and brown water chugs out of a crack in the bottom. Soggy boxes and other assorted rubbish litter the wet concrete.

At the opposite end of the alley, the neon glow of the high street reflects in black rippling puddles. People holding umbrellas stream past.

"You have no idea who those guys in the Jeeps were?" he asks.

Sweat beads on Kenneth's brow, his lips are slightly parted. He looks pale and tired. "The Tall Ninjas?" he says. Nige can tell he isn't trying to be funny, but stifles a laugh in spite of this.

"Why's everyone after you?"

Kenneth waves a hand. "I'm the personification of corporate greed. I'm a desecration of God's will. I'm the Devil. An airy fairy liberal. A raging right winger. I'm a feminist, a misogynist. I'm all these things and more to those who are the opposite." He shrugs. "I can never win."

"But people love you." Aidan keeps watch at the door they've just come through.

"Which is another reason for people to hate me, my good fellow." Kenneth steadies himself on the wall. "My life's the same. Day in, day out. I've never harmed a soul, yet they all seem to want to give me the old heave ho." He pauses and scratches his stomach. He looks down at his midriff, then pulls his kimono tighter. "But, it's never come this far. I've always felt safe up there on the 44th floor." He looks to Nige. "Why did you come back?"

"Something Jeff said just got to me." He gives Kenneth a tight smile. "While we were waiting outside the security door, those other two came past. We overheard something about the food and Dawn turning all freaky. I didn't really understand it. Do you know what they meant?"

Kenneth quickly shakes his head. His hand rests on his abdomen. "Can't say I do."

Nige pushes the door fully open to get a better look at the alley, then turns back. "But why all of them tonight? Do you think Jeff, the intruder in your room, and those um... tall ninjas are together?"

"I'd be more worried if they weren't. Maybe because my birthday's approaching they are all coming at once? Perhaps it symbolises something."

Nige rubs his ears. They itch when he is stressed. "How do you not know your own security can't be trusted?" He is sorry to hear his own voice come out so gruff, and even more so when Kenneth steps back warily. He doesn't mean to scare him.

"I rarely converse with the security team. With anyone, actually. They just keep me up there in my box until they need me, like some old priceless silverware. They take me out, dust me off, stick me on the telly, then pop me back away again when they're done." He puts a hand to his head. "I'm feeling a little giddy. I think from all the excitement. This is the most fun I've had in months."

"I wouldn't call this *fun*. Once those guys from the Jeeps find out you're not in your apartment, they'll be back. Hopefully, your security will slow them down. Unless they are together, in which case we're doubly screwed."

"I should call Maggie. She should have returned from her meeting by now." Kenneth raises his arm and taps a slim, black device on his wrist.

Nige slaps his arm back down. "No, no. They might be listening in or tracking the call. Give that here." He takes Kenneth's bracelet, drops it on the floor, and stamps on it.

"What are you doing?" says Kenneth, stepping away from the wall, wobbling on his feet.

"They could track you with that. You talk to no one except me or Aidan until we're sure who we can trust." He steps out into the rain, then back in again. "And that includes Maggie. A whole bunch of knife wielding ninjas invading your home on the same night they hire us does not seem like a coincidence."

"Mags has been with me for nearly a decade."

Nige looks to Aidan. "How are we going to move him out of here? That street is rammed."

"I'm not scared," says Kenneth. "When you've charged down machine gun turrets with little more than a horse and a sword, a walk down a busy street rather loses its ability to intimidate."

"I'm more worried about people mobbing us when they spot you."

"Nothing I haven't handled before. But there is one minor problem we will need to deal with before I can go out." He looks down. "I'm not wearing the right footwear for a jaunt in the rain." He lifts a naked foot and wiggles his toes.

Nige pecks at his forehead with bunched fingers. "Aren't you the fittest man on the planet? A quick run through some puddles won't hurt. Worried you'll get a cold or something?"

"It nullifies my privileges if I go outside wearing inappropriate clothing for the weather conditions." It sounds as if he's reciting from a contract. He pauses for a moment, then speaks half to himself. "But I suppose what good are privileges if I've been knifed to death by a bunch of mummified goliaths?"

"You've got a point. Here." Nige unzips his windbreaker and wraps it around Kenneth's shoulders. "Pull it up over your head."

Kenneth pulls the back of the jacket up so that his face is half hidden in shadow.

"If you bend low and keep this up, no one will see you." Nige then places his own foot parallel to Kenneth's to compare. "Nothing we can do about the shoes. Those dainty little princess feet'll get lost in either of ours."

Nige holds the door to the alley open and Kenneth steps out slowly. Raindrops catch on his long eyelashes.

"It'll be like British bulldog back on the playground," he says. "A short but perilous nip across the road to the Di Blasio building."

"We're not going there," says Nige. "One of the lads on our books lives not too far from here. We should be safe there while Korrigan comes to get us. It's about a twenty-minute walk."

Nige takes a thin strap from his utility belt and holds it out to Kenneth. "Put this on your wrist."

Kenneth does. "It doesn't quite fit my aesthetic as well as my phone, but I suppose now is not the time for fashion statements."

"It's a tracking bracelet. Both Aidan and I have apps on our phones. If we get split up in the crowd, it'll help us find you."

"Good thinking." As the rain falls on the three of them, Kenneth's attention is on the far end of the alleyway, where people speed past at a frenzied pace. Cars lurch and honk. It's manic. "I've not been outside like this in a long time." He shakes his head slightly. He suddenly looks quite ill. His breathing shallow and quick. "Once more unto the breach."

They head down the alley, hugging close to the shadow cast by one of the walls. A bittersweet industrial scent of tarmac kicked up by the rain fills the air, mixed with rotted garbage and exhaust fumes. Despite the wet weather, the air is warm with bodies and combustion.

"Me at the back. Kenneth in the middle. Aidan up front. We're going left, straight along the road until I say. Aidan, keep an eye out. I'll make sure no one follows us."

Together they fall in step with the crowd, caught up like leaves in a fast-flowing river.

Nige glances at the people around them. To his right, a stiff jawed woman in a knee-length black coat, eyes focused ahead of her and umbrella clamped in hand, doesn't even notice them appear from the alleyway. To their left, a businessman gives them the slightest glance but doesn't stop talking into his phone. Clearly too busy to see that he is stepping shoulder to shoulder with the most famous man on Earth.

It's funny how sometimes when you really don't expect to see something, it can become almost invisible.

Nige keeps a hand on Kenneth's back, guiding him through the crowd as fast as he can.

Ahead, a group waits by a crossing. They stop just behind. Kenneth stands stock still, his elbows out like wings, holding the jacket firmly overhead.

Nige scans those around them. The man to their right takes a second glance. His eyes widen. He pokes his friend's arm. Says something inaudible over the din of the traffic.

Not one hundred metres in and they've already been spotted.

This is going to get out of control fast. The red figure on the traffic pole turns green just as the man reaches out to touch Kenneth's arm. As people begin to cross the street, Nige steps forward, and with one hand on the man's back, gives a sharp push.

The man falls, clawing at those around him to catch himself. Another person trips over him. The full attention of the little crowd turns to the fallen pair instead.

Nige hurries Kenneth across the road without a glance back. He bends close and speaks out of the side of his mouth. "We need to get you a better disguise."

Kenneth's teeth chatter in response. He is soaked already. Nige too. Behind them someone shouts. "Hey, Kenneth?! It's Kenneth."

Kenneth turns back, about to bolt, but Nige holds him firm. To run would be too obvious.

Nige feigns looking around, as if searching the crowd for the famous Kenneth Bailey, as the three of them turn left down the street towards a line of tourist shops, glowing bright and still open despite the hour.

He ducks under the awning of the first shop they come to. Picks up two London hats and two pairs of sunglasses from the racks. Leads Kenneth inside and all the way to the back.

"Stand there and face the wall." He points to the furthest corner. "Look like you're interested in something."

"Can I get some shoes?" Kenneth wiggles his toes. They are white with cold.

"Sure, whatever."

Kenneth moves to the back of the room.

"Let me know if anyone comes in." Nige says to Aidan.

Nige's shirt is almost see through, stuck to his skin. He picks up two 'I love London' T-shirts and takes them to the counter, along with the hats and glasses. Glances back at Kenneth standing by the knock off trainers. Wonders whether his client can tell that he is making this all up as he goes along.

The shopkeeper, with a mobile fused to his ear, doesn't even look up as he scans the barcodes.

"You got any ponchos, mate?"

The man, continuing his conversation, points over Nige's shoulder to where a stack of bright yellow ponchos are neatly wrapped in plastic.

Nige grabs two, hands them to the man to scan, then pays.

"Is there somewhere to put these on?"

The man rolls his eyes, and with a significant amount of huffing, tucks his phone into the crook of his neck, then points towards the back of the shop. "Quieter around the corner."

Nige takes his purchases, then hands Kenneth the T-shirt and poncho. "Stick this on." He strips off his own white T-shirt and drops it to the floor with a wet splat.

Kenneth removes Nige's jacket and hands it back to him. He starts to unwrap his kimono, then hesitates.

"What's up? Not scared about getting your nips out in public, are you?" says Nige, pulling his new T-shirt over his head. It's tight around his shoulders and stomach.

Kenneth glances around. The shop is empty. The entrance, and main street beyond, are out of sight around the corner. "Don't look."

"You're literally the fittest guy in the world," says Nige turning to face away. Maybe he's old-fashioned, but he's not that keen on watching Mr Abs 2030 and 2031 getting changed. "What have you got to be embarrassed about?"

"Oh gosh," Kenneth says from behind.

"Everything ok?"

"Don't turn around."

There's a loud gastric grumble.

"Was that you?"

"My stomach is squirming. I'm famished. I'm not really feeling too good."

Nige pulls the large yellow poncho out of its packet and over his head, then puts on the sunglasses and cap. "Probably just nerves." He catches himself in a mirror. He looks like a rubber duck.

Behind him, he can see Kenneth inspecting his stomach. He glimpses something that looks like scales.

"Perhaps," says Kenneth.

"Ready?"

"Wait," he squeaks. In the mirror, Nige watches as he hurriedly pulls the T-shirt down over his stomach. "Ok."

The tight fabric makes Kenneth's muscular torso stand out even more. Somewhere inside Nige, a familiar jealousy rises.

"Arms up."

Kenneth obliges. His stomach rumbles again as Nige pulls the other poncho down over his head.

"I think I'm going to faint." Kenneth blinks slowly and sways on his feet. His face has lost its trademark glow.

"Jesus, one little walk in the rain and you're nearly passing out. I knew you guys weren't as fit as they make out. It's twenty minutes to the flat. You can wait that long, right?"

Kenneth's eyelids flutter. "There's a restaurant up the way," he says. "Maggie has taken me before." His posture has become stooped. He looks almost lost in the floppy yellow poncho. "They are considerate of my position. Very discrete." His eyes plead.

"I'd prefer to take you somewhere I know."

Kenneth leans on a rack filled with postcards depicting red London buses, black taxis, and the odd union jack painted boob. "If I've learnt anything, it's to trust my body. I'm afraid I don't have a twenty-minute walk in me. It's like I've been on a weeklong fast. But I ate not three hours ago."

It's risky, but the streets might become less crowded as the night goes on. A brief pause somewhere safe to go over their options might be a good plan.

"What's the place called?"

"Marco's. Just up the street from here."

Kenneth seems to gain some energy from the thought that food is near, but he still looks weak. He starts to slope back to the front of the shop.

Nige's ear-piece clicks and he hears Aidan's voice over the radio. "There are two guys here. They look pretty shady. They've been staring at a 3D puzzle of Buckingham Palace for at least five minutes. They don't look like the sort of guys who'd be allowed near kids." There's a pause. "But maybe they look weird enough to actually want to build a puzzle."

"I've told you before, people like puzzles. I like puzzles. It's not weird." Nige leans forward to get a better look at the front of the shop, but can't get a good angle without stepping out completely. "What do they look like?"

"Like two rejects off the set of The Matrix. Oh, they're going back there."

As Aidan finishes speaking, two men, barely into their twenties, charge around the corner. They stop and stare for a moment at Kenneth. The youngest of the two, gangly like a baby giraffe, openly gawps, his chin falling to somewhere between his knees. He is wearing a long leather trench coat. A pair of rain splashed goggles sit atop his head. His wild brown hair sticks up in spikes.

The other, shorter, but just as thin, is wearing a black waterproof cagoule over what looks like a crimson dress.

Original Cultist Material

"Er, Kenneth Bailey?" says the one in the dress.

Kenneth leans into Nige and slurs. "Fans. They'll leave faster if I talk to them, believe me." He wobbles forward. "I'd love to give out autographs boys, but you see I'm in a bit of a hurry." His head starts to droop to one side. He sounds drunk. "Maybe a quick selfie for the road?"

The lad in the dress quickly composes himself and unzips his rain mac to reveal a large wooden symbol of an angel that hangs from his neck on a silver chain. It is roughly carved, obviously homemade.

He holds it out in a shaking hand and slaps his friend on the arm. "Pete, stop gawking."

Kenneth steps back. "Uh, Nigel?"

The other throws his trench coat open, whipping it behind him like a cape. Beneath he is also wearing a crimson dress, but more importantly, he carries a pump-action shotgun. He takes aim at Kenneth.

In that moment, Nige realises it isn't dresses they are wearing, but long flowing robes. He dives forward, flattening Kenneth to the ground as the shelf of jackets behind them explodes into denim confetti. Then pulls him out of the way behind a row of tourist knick-knacks.

"Wait a minute. Wait a minute!" shouts the unarmed one. "Dad says you aren't supposed to shoot him until I've told him why. Flip. Ping. Heck. Peter. What if you'd got him and he ended up in hell with no judgement? The devil wouldn't know where to send him."

"Oh, sorry." Pete's voice is lower, slower, the voice you might expect a slug the size of a double-decker bus to have. "I'm sorry, Kenneth." He raises his voice. "Kenneth Bailey. You have made a pact with demons.

You are an abomination to nature. The great angel sentences you to die." He turns back to his friend. "That alright Dave?"

"Um... sure. Go for it."

There's a moment's pause. And in it Nige contemplates the interesting fact that, of all the assailants they've run into tonight, it's these two wackos that have come the closest to actually killing Kenneth.

"Can you stand back up, please? It'd be much easier if you were stood up," Pete says politely.

"I don't think so," shouts Kenneth.

Nige puts a finger to his lips. "Don't talk to them. They're cultists." He hisses into his radio. "Aidan!!" Where is the lad? Why isn't he helping?

"Cultists?" says Dave. "Who are you calling cultists? We're The Church of Fallen Angels, Followers of the New Way. Saviours of Earth's People." He comes closer. "Destroyers of Corporate Greed. We seek vengeance for the fallen angels."

Nige looks back, but they still haven't emerged around the edge of the shelving unit where he and Kenneth now hide. If having a long list of made up names for your weird religious sect doesn't scream cult, he's not sure what does. "Sorry, I must have mistaken you for someone else," he shouts, as he scans the aisle for an exit.

Pete takes over. "Slam Dunk Record Holders of the Seventh Level of Heaven..."

At the back of the store is a staff only door. Nige points towards it and gives Kenneth a little push. While the cultists are preoccupied with introducing themselves fully, they might be able to get to safety.

"... The Righter of Wrongs, Eliminator of Pongs..." Pete's voice builds to a crescendo.

"Eliminator of Pongs?" Nige mouths at Kenneth with a frown.

Kenneth doesn't seem to register what's going on. His eyes are half lidded. He's not hurt. But something is wrong. Nige shuffles ahead, keeping low behind the shelves, and pulls Kenneth towards the back door. The cultists continue to spout their nonsense, and it is indeed that. He even thinks he hears one of them say "Pot Noodle Devouring Messengers of the Lord" whatever that means.

There's a slap followed by an "ow!"

"Dad said to stop making up your own sacred names."

"The pot noodle one is one," says Pete, in a low whine.

"Shut up and shoot him."

Chik-chuk goes the shotgun as Pete cocks it. Nige glances back, the cultists are now at the end of the aisle. Something *whumphs* from behind the shelves and both of them look back as, for the second time that night, Aidan flies into view. The two are seemingly picked up in a gust of hurricane force wind and dashed against what is left of the wall of jackets in a tangle of limbs.

"Aidan." Nige stands, and moves to head back, but the inside of his head starts to buzz like it did in the apartment. He shakes it. What the hell is going on?

Aidan pushes himself up on to all fours and waves a hand. "Get Kenneth out. I'll catch up."

Nige looks back to Kenneth who is now crawling towards the door on his own. He chases after him, helps him to his feet, and shoves him headlong through the back door.

The room beyond is a dark kitchen. A half-eaten pizza sits on a grease-stained box on a small wooden table. Like a zombie sensing living flesh, Kenneth lunges for it but Nige rushes him on. They pass through a beaded curtain which leads to the back way out of the building.

Kenneth flops, almost unable to hold himself up.

Nige puts an arm around him as they move down a road that runs parallel to the main street. "Come on, old man. What's the matter with you?" He hauls him further up the alley. Looks back. Aidan hasn't yet emerged from the back of the shop. He'll be ok. The kid's tougher than anyone.

"Food," Kenneth's voice falters. His eyes flutter. "My abs… low body fat… no reserves… too perfect…"

Nige pulls out his phone as he drags his charge along. Types 'Marco's restaurant' into maps. It isn't far. They just need to get back on the main strip.

He pulls Kenneth's poncho hood over his head and pushes him through the nearest open door.

The kitchen beyond is a stark white contrast to the darkness in the alley. The air boils with heat and steam, and the sounds and smells of sizzling food. Sweet aniseed, pungent garlic, and the tang of chilli hit them like a force field. An old woman, face as wrinkled as an accordion, filthy apron draped around her neck, sits on a chair in the corner one-handedly chopping onions. She shouts orders, waving her free hand at three young men who are slaving over pots and grills. Nige can't understand a word when she directs her shouts – and her knife – at him.

He hurries Kenneth through the kitchen and out behind the counter of a small Chinese takeaway. A queue of roughly ten people are staring blankly at a television screen as they wait for their orders. On the screen, a newsreader is sitting in front of a picture of the two men they had just encountered. On the bottom it reads 'Bomb scare: Truth or Hoax?'

"I really should pay more attention to the news," he mumbles.

He doesn't stop but picks up a can of coke from the counter and bustles Kenneth out through the front door before anyone can so much as look at them.

As they battle along the busy pavement, he thumbs the can open and holds it up to Kenneth's lips.

"Drink this. It'll perk you up a bit." He's not sure if Kenneth is even allowed coke, but it has to be better than him passing out on the high street.

"Top's a bit dusty." Kenneth takes a huge, sleepy gulp. Then his eyes light up and he grabs the can out of Nige's hands. "My God." He takes another swig and his eyes roll back with pleasure. "I'd forgotten."

"Is it up here?"

Kenneth, already more awake, nods and points at a large neon 'Taxi' sign about a hundred metres up the road. "Opposite that."

There's a tightness in Nige's chest. This wasn't anything like manning the door outside a club. Here, he wasn't just looking out for the drunks that might want to glass him. Here, anybody could be a threat.

He glances back to see if he can spot Aidan. The lad should be able to find them thanks to Kenneth's tracker.

He also checks to make sure no one else is following. It's impossible to tell. In the human river that flows down the pavement, blank staring faces stream past, and he can't stop for long without causing a disturbance.

Aidan will be ok, he tells himself. Getting Kenneth somewhere safe, somewhere for them to take a short breath, is the priority. Then he'll try to call.

He wraps an arm around Kenneth's slender waist and pulls him on towards Marco's.

Do Not Feed Him After Eight PM

If you aren't looking for it, the charcoal sign outside the restaurant is easily missed. The only indication that something special hides within the walls of the black building is a string of well-dressed couples queuing beneath a crimson canopy.

Two security guards stand at one end in charcoal suits and crimson shirts. They match the sign and the canopy perfectly. One turns out to be an old friend whom Nige worked some nights with back when Lewis was still at home.

"Wait here." He motions for Kenneth to step into a darkened doorway. "I know one of the doormen. I'll have a word. Make sure we aren't hanging about outside too long."

Kenneth nods and leans against the frame of the door. He takes another swig from the coke he clutches in both hands. He is hunched and shaky. Something is very clearly wrong.

Nige strides to the front of the queue, takes off his glasses, and pulls his poncho hood down. "Alright Deano."

Dean is short and wiry, with tight, frog-like features. Bulbous, staring eyes suggest he's seen some unpleasant things.

He smiles and throws a mock punch into Nige's shoulder. "Mate! Long time, no see. What you doing here? Looking…" He looks Nige up and down, taking in the poncho and cap. He cocks his head, "… good?"

"Yeah - funny. No time for catch ups, mate. Need a favour." He leans in. Whispers into his old friend's ear.

Dean looks past him, and spots the shadowy figure in the doorway. Without a word he nods, then communicates something to his colleague.

Nige helps Kenneth to the front of the queue. Dean disconnects the velvet rope that blocks the way. The other guard opens the large black door.

The men in the queue groan as they duck inside.

"That's why you gotta book early gents," says Dean.

Their reply is lost as the door shuts, cutting all sound from the noisy street outside.

The reception is small. A slender maitre d' stands behind a black plinth. Behind him, through an open doorway, the restaurant opens out into a dusky, candlelit dining room. Plush velvet and soft silk wash the room in a sea of burgundy and black. Diners chat in a mix of expensive suits and sparkling evening wear. Softly, somewhere out of sight, a soprano sings 'Night and Day' over a trio of sax, piano, and double bass.

The maitre d' smiles and stretches his arms. His black jacket is extravagantly detailed with crimson roses that are hardly visible in the dim light. "Good evening, gentlemen. May I take your..." he pauses, looking slightly perturbed, before settling on the word he wants and adjusting his demeanour, "... ponchos."

Kenneth pulls his over his head and holds it out. "Julian, it's me."

He has perked up a little – from either the coke or the familiar territory - but is still quite pale.

Julian smiles brightly and takes the poncho. He gives it a firm shake to one side, flicking droplets of water on to the varnished mahogany floor, then folds it over one arm.

"Sir, such a pleasure to have you with us." He traces a white gloved finger down a reservation book, which sits before him on the plinth. He frowns slightly. "I don't seem to have you down tonight. Did Miss Greaves make a reservation?"

"An unexpected outing. Can you seat my friend and I? Somewhere private. We're looking to eat in record time."

"Of course, sir."

"We wish not to be disturbed." Kenneth leans forward pressing his point.

"Of course, sir." Julian bows ever so slightly, then looks at Nige, who gives his best smile. He picks up a menu. "This way."

"I will also be dining from the menu this time, Julian." Kenneth places a hand on the plinth. His knuckles whiten as he struggles to hold himself up.

"Are you sure, sir?" Julian's professional mask slips for the briefest of moments. He looks at Nige as if he's an alien.

"Quite sure." Kenneth closes one eye like he's fighting to stay awake.

"Right you are. This way gentlemen please." Julian picks up another menu and leads them along a corridor away from the main restaurant and the sound of diners.

Nige takes Kenneth's elbow. "Are you ok?" He whispers as they follow.

Kenneth doesn't reply. Just leans heavily on him as they walk.

"Will Miss Greaves be joining us tonight?" says Julian as he ushers them through a door and into a private dining room.

A long mahogany table stands in the middle of the room with a chair at either end. The walls, panelled with the same dark wood as the floor, are home to several large paintings, each depicting a raging sea battle. White foaming oceans rage over burning ships, and open-mouthed sailors are captured mid-scream as they fight.

"She won't," Nige says as he helps Kenneth to a chair.

"Your waiter will be in shortly. If you need anything else, please ask for me," he says and closes the door behind him.

Kenneth slumps down in his seat. "I don't know what's come over me." He looks exhausted.

"It could be shock. You've had quite a night."

Kenneth rubs his face with one hand. His appearance is a long way from the man on the billboard.

"Order something." Nige takes out his phone. "I'm going to try and get a hold of Aidan, and then I'll arrange a lift out of here."

He steps out of the room and into the hallway. On his phone is a missed call and a text from Aidan.

Followed you out back. You'd gone. Don't know what happened. Meet you at warehouse unless you say otherwise.

When Nige rings him it goes straight to answer phone so he texts back. *Are you safe? Call me when you get this.*

He calls Korrigan. The phone rings only twice before he answers.

"Nige, how is it? You still there?"

"I need you down here with a car. We were hit from every angle. I have no idea where Aidan is." His voice waivers. He clears his throat.

"What happened exactly?"

Nige fills him in. Starting with the intruder in Kenneth's room, then the Di Blasio security, then the Tall Ninjas, and finally the cultists. "I told you we weren't cut out for this."

"Where are you now?"

He glances up towards the reception where the maitre d' is seeing to another couple. He catches Nige's eye as he leads them to the dining room.

"At a restaurant on the same street as the apartments. Marco's." Nige has to hug the wall to let a waiter rush past, balancing a tray of champagne flutes precariously on one hand. "How fast do you think you can get here?"

"I'm on the other side of town. It'll be quicker if I send someone. I'll meet you at the office."

"Don't tell the driver it's Kenneth he's coming for. Send me his number in case our plans change."

He hangs up just as two more waiters pass by with a fully loaded tray each. The food smells amazing. This time the waiters push through into Kenneth's room. He follows them in. They buzz around the table, expertly offloading their trays, and as quick as they came, they leave.

Almost every inch of the table around Kenneth is covered. Two large pizzas, a bowl of fries, two tall glasses of coke fizzing quietly over ice, and two sets of gooey brownie steam by melting blobs of vanilla ice cream.

"I got them to bring everything at once." Kenneth grins and rubs his hands together.

Nige's nostrils flare. "I thought this place was posh?"

"Not really, but it's all real sugar. Most people can't afford the tax on it."

"We're not going to get through half of this. A car's gonna be here in five minutes to pick us up."

Kenneth already has several fries in one hand and a slice of pizza in the other. With little decorum, he squashes them into his face. "Oh. My. God." He says and takes a large gulp of coke. He purses his lips and blows out a breath. "Why did I ever give this up?" He shakes his head and just stares at the food, taking it in.

"Aidan's going to meet us at the office."

"I'm glad he's safe." Kenneth looks him in the eyes. "Thank you Nigel. I appreciate all you've done for me today."

Nige smiles, tight-lipped. "Just doing me job."

"I know, but you didn't have to. You could have nipped off when Jeff took me." He looks down. "Such betrayal. I thought…" His shoulders slump, and for a moment he looks utterly miserable. "Those were the people I thought I was safest with, and now I have nothing."

Nige leans against the wall. "Now, you know what it's like to be a real human being." He tries not to sound bitter.

"I suppose. Still –" Kenneth sits a little straighter "– there's nothing like eating yourself out of a funk." He holds a piece of pizza aloft. "I'd completely forgotten what this tasted like. Seventy years of eating Di Blasio garbage, and I tell you now with my face full of potato and cheese, long-life is not worth it. This is damn near orgasmic."

He continues to stuff his face.

"You really haven't eaten any proper food this whole time? I just thought that was a load of marketing rubbish."

Kenneth shakes his head. "Last time I dined like this was in my sixties. Since I signed my contract, I've eaten Di Blasio fare exclusively: shakes, pastes, and meals with a few steamed vegetables to perk them up." He twirls a chip between his fingers and pops it in his mouth. "What did you think they did to make us look like this?" He indicates his perfect face with an upturned hand before lopping off a hunk of brownie and forking it in with some more fries. His eyes roll back in his head.

"I had a theory they cloned you every year and just replaced the old one."

Kenneth snort-laughs a blob of chewed chocolate across the table. "You mean they've got some massive bin somewhere filled with dead Kenneths? I think I'd know about that." His smile waivers for a second and for a moment he squints as if searching through his memories. He shakes his head and wrinkles his nose. "Nah. I'd definitely know. Points for originality, though. It's better than the one where we're all shape shifting lizard overlords."

"It's hard to believe anything Di Blasio says is true." Nige scratches his head and looks at the food. "Are you sure you should be eating this? It's all junk."

"Are you sure I shouldn't be?" Kenneth waves a fork over the feast. "It's just fats, carbs, and protein. The body needs it all to survive. Who told you pizza and brownies were bad for me?"

Nige raises an eyebrow. "You did, actually. You're the influencer. You influence."

"You're supposed to take it with a pinch of salt."

"My mum never let us have salt." He looks at Kenneth in mock accusation, then picks up a slice of pizza. Regards it in his hand. "You're right. I haven't got a clue. One week chips'll give you cancer, the next they're a healthy source of energy."

Kenneth nods and folds his pizza into a cone. "It's fear mongering. They want to keep you confused so you have no choice but to buy what they have on surplus that week." He pushes the cone into his mouth.

"I know that."

Kenneth waves the crust and speaks through a mouthful of food. "No offence, but you're smarter than you look."

"You know, saying 'no offence' at the start of a sentence doesn't make it any less offensive."

Kenneth drops the crust on his plate and looks at the glistening food in front of him. "So what if it's not healthy. What harm can it do? At least three different groups have tried to kidnap or kill me tonight. If I'm going out, I'm going out bloated and munching on something I enjoy, not sucking some pink paste from a tube."

"Good point." Nige takes a bite of his slice. "You really have no idea why all these people are out to get you?"

Kenneth chews in thought. "Other than the usual million and one reasons given by the religious nutters, right-wing militants, left wing fundamentalists, and disgruntled ex-Di Blasio employees?" He shakes his head. "This is the first time anyone's come this close." He rests both elbows on the table and leans his head on his hands. "And this is the first time anyone other than Di Blasio security has been watching over me. A little suspicious, don't you think?"

"A minute ago you were thanking me."

"I don't mean to say you're to blame. I just mean it's not a coincidence."

Kenneth's right. Why had they been hired tonight of all nights? He'd like to ask Maggie. Perhaps she suspected something of the Di Blasio security. "Do you think Maggie knew this was going to happen?"

"There was a commotion a few nights back. She won't tell me what. I don't think she knows exactly. They've not let anyone else come up to my apartment since. Security bring up my meals. The cleaner hasn't been in at all. I was beside myself when you arrived. The place is a dive." He looks at his hands, then around at the food on the table. His lip curls as if he's only just realising how big a binge he's just had. He wipes the grease from his fingers with a napkin and drops it on top of the half-finished bowl of chips.

"They say it's so I look my best for my little party," he continues. "They think I don't know something's up, that I'm in my own little ignorant bubble, but you don't get to be my age without being able to read people. Maggie's hiding something."

Someone knocks on the door. Nige stands, his hand reaching for his taser.

Kenneth draws a pistol from his waistband.

Nige takes a small step back. "Where did you get that?"

"Took it from Esther," he whispers, then raises his voice hiding the pistol beneath the table. "Enter."

The door opens. Maggie enters.

Her curls are up in a messy bun atop her head. She wears high heels and a long rain coat drawn up with a belt. She is panting, out of breath. "Kenneth, what are you doing here?"

She steps further into the room and takes in the table loaded with food. She picks up a chip, examines it for a second as if she's never seen one before, then drops it. "You haven't been eating this, have you? You know what's going to happen to me if they find out?" She turns and notices Nige crouched behind the door ready to pounce. Her eyes become slits. "You. I knew I shouldn't have trusted outside security. What do you think you're doing here? Sneaking out for a late night snack." She removes her rain coat revealing a sequinned playsuit beneath.

With her facing away from him, Kenneth tucks the pistol back into his trousers. "This isn't Nigel's doing. I mean, getting me here safely is all him, but—"

"Why are you here?" Nige looks Maggie up and down suspiciously. "Lookin' a little snazzy for a meeting?"

"What are you talking about?" She bends and pulls off her heels, then replaces them with a pair of foldable flats she retrieves from her bag. She glances at Kenneth and chews at the corner of her mouth. "It wasn't a meeting. It was a date."

Kenneth's mouth tweaks up in a saucy half smile. "You devil. Why didn't you tell me?"

"Yeah right, and risk Stefan finding out? He'd flip out." She looks down and fiddles with the tie of her playsuit. "Plus, he's kind of a big deal."

"Ooo." Kenneth waggles his eyebrows. "Who is it? Do dish."

"You promise not to tell anyone?"

Nige looks between them. Letting them talk while he thinks. If she was on a date then him being hired to look after Kenneth tonight must just be a coincidence. Unless someone else knew about it?

"Scout's honour." Kenneth holds up three fingers.

"Ian Stockwell."

Kenneth's eyes widen. "Oh Maggie, you hound."

"Who's Ian Stockwell?" Nige realises he still has his taser pointed at her and lowers it.

"Stefan Di Blasio's number two. Owns about thirty percent of the company."

She blows air through her lips. "He probably won't call me again now the way I ran out on him." She plonks her shoes on the table. "Julian rang me. Told me you were here eating from the menu and I just freaked out."

"Little traitor." Kenneth's mouth tightens and he shakes his head. "We were besieged, Maggie. From all sides. Nige saved me."

"Are you saying the only reason you hired us was because you were on a date with your boss?" Nige presses the door closed.

"I was only going to be out a few hours." She loosens her hair and shakes it out. Droplets flick to the floor. "What happened?"

"What didn't happen? Someone came into his bedroom like something out of Nosferatu. Then *your* own security –" Nige points at her sharply "– tried to kidnap him. Then some crazy Tall Ninjas came running out of nowhere. And then those same bloody cultists that you told us not to worry about followed us through town and tried to blow our heads off with a shotgun. We were lucky to get away. Aidan's still out there somewhere."

Maggie puts a hand to her lips, shocked. Her eyes rise to the ceiling as if she's trying to remember something. She looks at Kenneth for confirmation.

He nods. "If it weren't for Nige I'd be hung, drawn, quartered, shot, stabbed and impaled by now."

"I was told they would have even more security tonight because of the death threats. Ian said no one would get anywhere near you. How did they all get in?"

"For all we know that extra security opened the door," says Nige.

"I don't know what to say. I was told—"

Nige cuts her off. "Whatever you were told, you were lied to."

She rubs her arms as if she is cold. She glances up at Kenneth, not really meeting his eye. "I was told they would get you tomorrow. Not tonight."

"What do you mean, get me? Who?"

"Jeff and the others. They were supposed to pick you up and take you over to the labs in the morning for tests, but they must have brought it forward. You see, something's happened to Dawn."

"Dawny?" He frowns, worried. "Is Dawn alright?"

"All I know is that she fell ill Monday night, and they brought her to the main building where they are treating her now. She's stable as far as I'm aware."

This doesn't sit right. Esther and Jay had said they'd locked her up.

"What's up with her?" Kenneth touches his stomach. Something he's done a few times that evening.

"They won't tell me."

"That at least clears up what Jeff and his team were doing. They were just getting me over there early." Kenneth gives Nige a look. "I feel a bit sorry about fighting with them now." He puts a hand to his forehead. "And I pistol whipped poor old Jay on the noggin. Maggie, call them up and get them to come grab us post-haste."

Nige shakes his head. He can't have made such a bad call, could he?

Maggie takes her phone from her bag, but he puts a hand out. "Let's think about this. Either your security are on our side, in which case they'll have had a run in with those Tall Ninjas. They were outnumbered so will be in no fit state to come and get us. Or, they're not and will come straight here with the ninjas in tow. We're safest here, just us three, and we'll be safer still when we're back at the warehouse. If you didn't tell anyone you were hiring us to babysit," Nige raises an eyebrow at Maggie, "then we'll be untraceable there."

"It was Ian who found you. I gather from our conversation tonight that he works with your son. He has as much reason to hide this as I do."

Nige brightens. "Did Lewis put us forward?" A warmth grows inside - Lewis thought of him.

"Maybe." She shrugs.

He glances at his watch. Korrigan's driver should be arriving soon.

"Is there anyone at Di Blasio you can trust?"

"Only Ian," Maggie's forehead wrinkles. She shakes her head. "There's not much socialising outside of work. It's not really encouraged. Another reason I had to be so quiet about tonight."

There's a knock at the door. They all jump. Julian enters. "Ah Miss Greaves, good to see you."

"You sneaky little snitch." Kenneth wags a finger.

Defiantly, the maitre d' stands straighter. "I wasn't sure who this man was and thought it best to make sure you were safe. You looked terrible, sir. I was quite sure you had been drugged."

"What did you think was happening? My kidnapper was taking me to dinner?"

"I've heard of stranger things," Julian says, his nose pointing proudly upward.

"You didn't call anyone else, did you?" asks Nige.

Julian bows his head. "I took the liberty of calling the Di Blasio switch board. They are sending over a few members of Mr Bailey's entourage now to pick him up. I also have a message that another car is waiting for you outside."

Nige lets out a frustrated groan. "We better move. We don't want to get caught up with your boys again."

"But—" tries Kenneth.

"No buts. If we decide they are ok, then we'll call them from my office, but now is not the time to make that decision. We need to get to a safe place, gather evidence, then we'll make the call."

Kenneth stands and spirals his hand in a little helicopter motion. "Julian, box this up. I shall partake of this little feast on the road."

Julian is halfway through another "Of course," when Nige interrupts.

"Not happening!" He pulls open the door and ushers them all out.

"They'll be here any minute," says Maggie.

"Julian, is there a back way out?"

He squints in thought. "There's a fire exit that leads on to Basinghall Street; it's not very customer facing."

Nige takes out his phone and calls the number Korrigan sent for the driver. Tells him to meet them round the back.

"Can do," comes the reply, "and you better watch out, whoever you're running from is coming in."

From back towards the reception, a waiter is heading their way with a large tray of food. Further back, Nige spots three large men in Di Blasio tactical uniforms.

"There," shouts the closest. They give chase down the slim corridor only to get lodged behind the waiter with his tray.

"Fire exit, now," shouts Nige.

"This way. This way." Julian sidesteps quickly down the hall, leading them away.

"Move," shouts the guard and the waiter quails into a ball on the floor, having dropped his tray with a resounding clatter. The guards jump over him and give chase.

They follow Julian as he launches through a door into a brightly lit kitchen. Nige squints to allow his eyes to adjust. He can feel the heat on his skin, and smell the scents of baking dough and garlic.

"Everybody out of the way. A-list coming through," shouts Julian.

The chefs move aside as they clatter through the kitchen. Nige looks back and in his haste knocks a large pan of boiling pasta to the floor.

One chef shouts. The others join in an explosion of European expletives.

Behind them, the lead guard hits the pasta and slips. His feet fly higher than his head. The others move clumsily to catch him, but only manage to trip and stumble themselves.

Julian holds the back door open as Nige and the others pass him.

"Good luck, sir," he says, and without another word slams the kitchen door shut. They hear it bolt on the other side.

The street is quiet. With no shops or business fronts, it is a stark contrast to the road on the other side. The rain has slowed, but not given up entirely.

And right on the kerb is a long silver Mercedes Benz. The car is polished and shiny, though the paint is thin, almost yellow. The headlamps are the only lights on the street. A man waits, hands folded behind his back, by the open passenger door. He looks as if he's just come straight from a funeral. Protruding, tired eyes with loose bags beneath. He wears an ill-fitting black suit, faded and scruffy around the collar and cuffs.

"Nige?" he says, his face gives an involuntary twitch. Jerky insect-like movements and the chemically sweet smell of artificial fruit suggest he is buzzing off several energy drinks.

"We're in a hurry."

They climb in.

The interior of the car smells sweetly of old treated leather. The driver guns the engine, and they fly down the quiet side street without looking back.

The Bouncer's Hideout

People stand as far from Mac as possible as he rides the hot, overcrowded tube. His coat, drying in the warmth, is covered in greasy stains from the bins. Thin yellow shirt appearing pink against his wet skin. Knees caked in sludge from the shimmy up the drain pipe. He knows he smells, but the chill has blessed him with an impenetrably blocked nose. He feels dirty all over. It makes his entire body itch.

It's not been a good night.

He can't take his eyes from a suspicious dark swipe of brownish red on the toe of his sneaker. It's clearly blood. He tries to hide it with his other foot.

He doesn't meet anyone's gaze, too embarrassed to look up. But he wants to talk. Wants to tell his fellow commuters that The Twins are dead. That he was there when it happened. That's why he looks like this. It is the biggest story in the world, and he's the only one who knows. It's bursting to come out. But he keeps his mouth shut.

He glances up. The sense of apprehension from the others in the tube car hangs thick in the air. Though no-one looks at him, he can sense their attention. Spots it in sideways glances and hushed whispers. He's just another crazy guy, stinking of stale alcohol and rubbish, and occasionally rubbing his testicles which still ache from their meeting with the telephone pole. If he saw someone like that he would avoid looking directly at them too. Just in case they did something unwanted, like ask for a helping hand.

Getting off at his station, he hurries up the escalator to the surface, moving towards the river with the dwindling crowds.

When he reaches the industrial estate, he checks the large map outside. Korrigan and Davies operate from a warehouse labelled D2.

The whole world is a pallid orange, illuminated by the streetlights. The only sound, a low hum and grind of large but distant machinery, seems to come from beyond the horizon. The quiet is almost unreal in its contrast to the city streets he has just left behind. He drifts. Feet barely touch the pavement as he succumbs to his adrenaline-charged tiredness.

He jumps as an old silver Mercedes sails past, splattering dirty water up his legs. It disappears around the bend in the road.

"Oh bloody hell," he says, but his voice comes out muted. He looks at his trousers but can't tell which dirt is new or old.

Rows of warehouses stand before him like cards laid out for a game of solitaire. He checks his phone for guidance. Korrigan and Davies' building is just around the corner.

The same Mercedes turns out of the row he's looking for and drives back up the slight incline towards him. He squints but can't make out the driver through the rain-soaked windshield. The headlights dazzle him. The car accelerates as it approaches. His nerves jangle. It's going to plough straight into him.

The car flies past. He turns to give the driver the finger. They either don't see or don't care because they don't stop. He isn't really sure what he would have done if they had. Probably legged it.

He is exposed. Wandering up the open road, with bright light all around him and no crowd to disappear into. What if ferret features and the back alley killers are lying in wait just around the bend?

This is dangerous. Stupid.

A crumbling brick wall caked with years of spattered mud stands just over head height on his right. He clambers up and over, and drops into the shadows behind a line of lorry trailers. Beyond, men are working hard in the rain, their voices echoing softly across the tarmac as they load active trucks from a large warehouse. Bright light shines from the open bays, but not enough to reveal his position between the trailers and the wall.

Feeling a little more confident now that he's hidden, he creeps along until he reaches the compound exit.

Directly across from where he stands is their warehouse. A similar walled compound to the one he is in, but less than half the size. Two strong metal gates cover the entrance. Beyond those, parked by a tall roller door, is an old Renault Clio. Above a smaller door is a window to the first floor. A light is on up there, but from this low angle he sees nothing inside except ceiling.

He doesn't fancy breaking in if someone's there. There's no rush, and he has nowhere else to be, so he looks for somewhere to get out of the rain.

He glances up at the nearest lorry cab. Its blank windscreen faces Korrigan and Davies' building. He tries the door handle. Locked. But it's an old model and one he's seen before. He quickly picks it, and stealing a look back to the men loading crates at the warehouse, climbs inside and out of the rain.

He rubs his hands together. They are frozen. Whips out his phone. Like all good PI's, he has a plethora of highly illegal apps that allow him to really get under those metaphorical paving slabs and dig up the real dirt.

Access medical or criminal records by facial recognition? He's got 'em.

Hack an ATM to get the bank details of the most recent user? No problem.

Hotwire a keyless DAF truck? Hey presto. The engine smoulders into life and he turns the heat up full whack. Toasty.

His body aches and after a short, snuggly while his eyelids begin to weigh down.

The loud whine of a motorbike wrenches him from the brink of a particularly terrifying dream riddled with large bat-like creatures falling from the sky to devour him.

A vintage motorbike and sidecar pull into D row and stop outside the gates. The driver wears a black cagoule over a long flapping dress. He blocks Mac's view of the passenger.

The engine cuts out, and without getting off, the driver toddles the bike up to the wall by the gate, takes off his helmet, and drops it into the passenger's lap.

The passenger's eyes are hidden behind a pair of goggles. Large orange circles that reflect the street lights above. Neither step from the bike. They exchange words. Mac wishes he could hear them.

Then it hits him. It's not a dress. It's a robe. These are the same two from the television in Mikey's bar.

After a brief discussion they climb from the bike and, using it as a boost, jump over the wall.

As they creep towards the warehouse, something else catches Mac's eye. A shadowy shape dropping from the sky. The light pollution makes it difficult to see as it lands on the roof. The cultists don't notice it as they approach the main door, but it reminds Mac of something.

Something bad.

Wanted

Nige leans his forehead against the car window and watches the city pass. No one has spoken since they left Marco's.

The driver stares ahead, unblinking, silent, eyes always on the road.

The interior of the Mercedes is dirty and old. The grooves in the leather seats filled with crumbs. Something sticky covers the radio button where the driver must have changed channels while eating. A sweaty itch irritates Nige's neck, and he tries not to let his skin touch the seat.

Stuffed into a little compartment on the left of the wheel is a brown paper bag, darkened with grease. Smells like donuts or a pastry.

The driver catches him looking and picks up the bag. "I've still got half left if you want it. It's a sausage roll."

"I'll have a little nibble." Kenneth leans forward, reaching out.

The driver passes it back.

"Merci beaucoup. No clue why, but I'm absolutely ravenous." He peels back the brown paper like a banana and takes a bite.

"You shouldn't really be eating that, Kenneth." Maggie presses into the corner of the back seat, as if putting more distance between herself and the offending sausage roll will somehow give her plausible deniability.

"Oh Maggie, they'll never know." Kenneth takes another bite, and through a mouthful of pastry, says, "Need to keep my sugars up. Doesn't look like we're going to get much shut eye tonight."

Nige continues to gaze out of the window as they argue about what exactly counts as a breach of his contract.

They pass the flashing neon signs and towering office buildings that dominate Canary Wharf as they head towards the Thames. Huge LED screens flanking the roads show footage of Kenneth and the other influencers peddling the many Di Blasio wares. Running gear, protein shakes, breakfast cereals.

They pass a video of Dawn selling Di Blasio toothpaste. "I hope she's ok," says Kenneth. No one offers a reply.

The billboards all flick off as the ad changes, momentarily leaving the road dark. A different, more unsettling image appears in their place.

Nige recognises himself clutching his taser and can of mace. He looks crazed. Aidan is visible behind. Another image shows a guy that Nige doesn't recognise in a trench coat. Beneath both photos bold type reads, 'Wanted in connection with the kidnapping of Kenneth Bailey.'

There is a sizeable reward.

Big and bright, the pictures line the road for as far as he can see.

He turns to the back seat and raises an eyebrow.

Maggie sucks air through her teeth and wrinkles her nose. "I thought that might happen. Di Blasio owns hundreds of billboards around London."

"Well, thanks for warning me. Aidan's still out there somewhere!"

Kenneth grips the back of Nige's chair and pulls himself forward. "I can call Stefan. Tell him I'm safe."

"No. Not yet." He rubs his ear between finger and thumb.

What should he do? What's the right call? Leave Aidan out there on his own, wanted by the police, or call Di Blasio and put them all at risk?

The driver glances at him. His face deadpan behind his polarising driving glasses, as if he hasn't noticed Nige's face ten feet high on the billboards flanking the road.

"How do you feel about that?" Nige asks him, nodding to the ads, and more specifically, the reward.

"I've been paid by Korrigan to drop you off. I ain't a grass." The driver squints and shakes his head as if the very thought offends him.

Nige smiles. "If only there were more people like you." He glances at his phone. No message from Aidan. Tries his number. No answer.

As the car slips off the overpass, the phone lights up in his hand. It's Lewis. Nige knows why he's calling. At any other time he wouldn't hesitate to pick up, but what would he say now? Frozen in place, he stares at the phone until it stops ringing.

As they near the river, the industrial estate's orange glow guides them towards the warehouse.

Nige calls Korrigan as they approach along the main road.

"I've seen you," Korrigan says. "Just letting you in now."

The gate trundles open and they pull in to the courtyard. "Good luck," says the driver as they get out. And with a squeal of rubber, he reverses out of the gate and away.

Nige hurries Kenneth and Maggie inside and follows the sound of a singing kettle up to the first floor. Korrigan's in the kitchen. The room's different, but he can't quite put his finger on why.

Korrigan sets down the mugs he's holding and moves in for a hug. "Mate, am I glad to see you. I was so worried." He throws his arms around Nige's waist and lifts him so high his head displaces a ceiling tile.

"It's Aidan we should worry about." He looks around the room again, finally realising what is different. Korrigan has cleaned. It's not spotless, not even close, but it no longer looks like the dwelling place of large, hungry men who work late and eat fast.

"The boy called me. He'll be here any minute," he says.

"Why hasn't he been answering my calls? I've been worried sick." Nige is more relieved than annoyed.

"Maybe out of battery? You know what he's like. Says he won't be long. Says he's got something to tell us." He picks up the mugs again. "Why don't we all have a nice cuppa?" He turns towards Kenneth and bows slightly at the waist.

"And might I say what a pleasure it is to have you here, uh-Mr Bailey." Nige winces, expecting with sickening dread that his partner may refer to their client as 'your lordship' or something equally vomit inducing.

Like a bard in the court of a king, Korrigan flutters a hand.

Nige inwardly gags.

"An absolute pleasure," he continues. "Thank you once again for using our, uh-humble services." He bows again.

Kenneth is holding his hands behind his back. He looks like he's chewing something very small between his front teeth, his concentration elsewhere. "Have you a bathroom? I need to… post-haste."

"Not surprised." Maggie folds her arms and moves her weight to one hip.

"Just there." Korrigan points.

Without another word, Kenneth ambles across the room. His movements are stiff, his arms glued to his sides. He disappears inside and shuts the door behind him without stopping to turn on the light.

Nige lets his shoulders drop. For now they are safe, at least. He nods at the mugs in Korrigan's hands. "If you're making a cup, I'll have one."

"Sure. Young lady?" Korrigan smiles at Maggie. "Tea?"

"No. Thank you."

"Chocolate hob nobs do ya, Nige?"

"Bring the packet." He sits at the small dining table where he and the lads have had many a microwaved lasagne. "How long did Aidan say he'd be?"

Before Korrigan can answer, a tearing sound comes from behind the bathroom door, followed by a groan.

Korrigan chuckles. "Sounds like he's having a tough time in there."

Suddenly, a boom shakes the floor and something large thumps hard on the stairs. As Nige's ringing ears readjust, he hears familiar voices. "Flip. Ping. Heck. Peter. Why couldn't you have just used the knob?"

"Dad says it's a good idea to let people know you mean business by making an entrance."

"He doesn't mean physically create one."

"Well, what does he mean?"

"He means enter with pizzazz. Now the door's on the stairs and we can't get up."

"Well, what's more pizzazzarous than blowing a door off with a shotgun."

Korrigan looks at Nige, then raises an eyebrow. "Who's that?" he mouths.

"Cover for us," Nige whispers back, not answering the question. Jerking his head, he indicates for Maggie to follow him into the office. He looks back at Korrigan. "They probably won't hurt you."

Korrigan's eyes widen. "Probably?"

Nige nods in an attempt to be reassuring and closes the door.

"Who's there?" Korrigan shouts, deep and imposing.

"Sorry, is Kenneth in?" Footsteps creak upward.

"Don't know who that is. What you done to my bloody door?"

"We know he's here. We tracked him." In the kitchen, something beeps faint and rapid.

"No, no, no. Stay there please, Mr Korrigan," says Pete with his slow slug like voice.

Nige motions for Maggie to hide behind the desk, then rests his ear on the door to listen.

"How do you know my name? Look, you're going to have to leave," says Korrigan. "There's nothing in there except my office."

The beeping becomes louder, followed by the faint click of the door handle. They're right outside.

Nige tenses. He's going to have to do something. Hopes Korrigan is ready to lend a hand on the other side.

"Korrigan... NOW!" he shouts and pushes with all his strength through the door. It crunches into a soft body, then cracks off its hinges beneath his weight.

"Ow. Ow. Ow," comes a voice from beneath the door.

"Um... Nige, I'm very sorry to say I haven't done anything," says Korrigan, holding his hands in the air. He shrugs causing the three mugs still dangling from his fingers to clink together.

The taller cultist holds the shotgun covering them both.

"Did you not hear me?" Nige keeps his eyes on the two black barrels inches from his face. "I said Korrigan now."

"Yes, but he does have a ruddy great shotgun, and what does now mean, anyway?"

"I don't know. Jump him when he's distracted. Anything."

"Ah. Ok. Next time."

Nige puts his hands up and rolls sideways off the door.

"Don't get up," says Pete keeping the shotgun aimed.

"Urgh," the cultist beneath the door says. He pushes it off and eases himself to a seated position next to Nige. Gives him a withering look and rubs his ribs.

How do these two cretins keep getting the better of him?

"You alright, Dave?" Pete tuts. "It's as if these guys don't want to be saved."

The one named Dave ducks his head inside his robe like a snail disappearing into its shell.

"I'm going to have a knob shaped bruise," he says from within.

Pete giggles.

"Door knob!" Dave pops back out and admonishes him, then looks into the office room. "Is that Kenneth's manager in there? Come out."

Maggie hurries out with her hands above her head and stands close to Nige.

"Tracker is suggesting the next room over." Dave stands up and holds a small black box out towards the bathroom door.

"He's not here," says Nige.

"Oh, can you just not? You're making this very difficult for us. We're just trying to save the world." Dave looks at Pete and shrugs. From a holster under his cagoule he removes a hi-tech looking pistol that's all LEDs and tubes. "Did you guys not see our broadcast?" He glances at Korrigan, who still has his hands up. His brow knots into a frown and he rubs his chin as if trying to think of how to explain something simple, something adults take for granted, to a child who just can't understand. "Kenneth is in league with the devil, the embodiment of corporate greed. If we don't stop him, we're all doomed."

He moves towards the bathroom door and takes a hold of the handle. "Come out, Kenneth," he calls through the door. There is silence from inside. "Peter, go in and get him." He moves to the centre of the room and covers Nige and Korrigan.

"Are you decent?" Pete pushes the door slightly. "I'm coming in." He steps in, utters a questioning hum, then pokes his head back out.

"He's not there, Dave, but you should have a look at this thing. It's proper weird." He studies Nige and Korrigan. "I think these guys are a bunch of Di Blasio cultists."

"What are you talking about?" Nige shakes his head. "You're the bloody cultists."

Pete and Dave gasp simultaneously.

"How dare you?" Clearly offended, Pete puts a hand to the breast of his crimson robe. Then wags a finger in circles pointing at Nige. "We're trying to put a stop to all your flipping hell stuff. Cultists indeed? If you think we're cultists, then why have you got a demon sausage in your bathroom." He raises an eyebrow and wobbles his head as if he has all the answers.

Demon sausage? Nige looks towards the bathroom door.

Maggie looks at Nige, worried. "What have you got in there?"

Nige crosses the room. "You sure Korrigan didn't just forget to flush?"

Pete backs up to let him through, still tracking him with the shotgun.

As he approaches the open door, there's a scent he doesn't recognise. Not chemical, more earthy. Something like iron, like when you have a nasty nose bleed.

There's a figure on the floor. Nige rushes in thinking Kenneth has fallen and is lying unconscious by the toilet. He slows as he realises it can't be Kenneth. But the figure is wearing the 'I Love London' T-shirt, which is now torn and stretched out of shape.

He covers his mouth. Makes an involuntary noise, holding back the sudden urge to throw up.

It looks as if Kenneth has been wrapped up like a spider's dinner and then painted with a red brown varnish. His arms are fused to his sides. His head, now as smooth as a pink flib of bubble gum stuck beneath a school desk, flows into his shoulders as one solid piece. Strands of the same red brown substance stretch out from his body like resin, fastening him securely to the floor, toilet, and wall.

The overall shape is not a lot wider than Kenneth's slender frame, but somehow Nige knows he's in there.

Kenneth's 105th Birthday Show

2005

"We're going to have a little break from all the fun for a moment. It's that time in the show, Kenneth, where we talk about the causes that you've been helping with this year."

The interviewer's hair is tall and springy, with several lines carved into the side. He is less than a fifth of Kenneth's age, but has a lot more confidence than Kenneth did when he was that old.

He'd have made a great influencer.

"How has the last year been?" he says. "And what issues are affecting you at the moment?" He leans forward on the armchair where he sits. "I understand you've been working hard in some of the poorer parts of the UK to teach kids how they can achieve what you have."

"We do a little of that every year Jason," says Kenneth. "It is very important for me to set aside two or three days every month to visit with children and get a notion of what they, and their families, are doing to improve their lives."

Kenneth would probably like it more if it wasn't scheduled and enforced by Stefan's marketing team. It's just a way to push expensive Di Blasio products on the kids who then go home and whine to their parents.

"It's nice to offer a little insight and advice," he continues on script. "I'm living proof that it is possible to create a healthier, longer living population. But for some reason our government refuses to teach our findings in schools. I take it upon myself to help the boys and girls from the poorest parts of the country with the education they deserve. Pass it on to future generations like small seeds from which mighty oaks may grow."

"What a noble cause. I can't think of anything better than helping the kids of tomorrow live better and fuller lives."

"Well, that's what it's all about, isn't it? Making sure we all improve together. It's about discovery, learning, and implementation. Any hardships we face, be it climate change, health, hatred, it's not a problem for the individual." Kenneth looks into the camera as if talking to the people at home. Di Blasio don't like it when he goes off piste, but this is going out live and they can't stop him. He's tired of being their puppet and he's got something to say. "It's not just those people affected directly that suffer. A problem in the microcosm is a problem in the macrocosm. All effects all. If the general health of a populace goes down, it effects the economy. We pay more taxes to cover the NHS and fewer people are able to work. If there's more hatred on the streets, people get scared." The interviewer touches his ear piece. He smiles nervously. "Hatred builds. If I've gleaned anything in my one hundred and five years on this glorious planet, it is this - we all have to look out for one another. There's no one else out there that's going to do it."

The Intermediate Phase Of Transmogrification

Nige taps the soft resin with his toe. It curves around the cap of his boot like stiff cloth. He kneels. The bathroom is small. It's a squeeze. With one finger, he strokes the strange material through a rip in Kenneth's T-shirt. It's smooth and dry and reflective, like silk. But strong.

Looking back, he tries to gauge whether the cultist can see his hands from the doorway. He broadens his shoulders to hide them and deftly retrieves the gun from Kenneth's shredded waistband.

"What is it?" says Pete. "Is Kenneth becoming his final demonic form?"

"I'll show you." He says hoping to draw Pete in.

Pete steps closer.

"Don't go in there," shouts Dave from outside, but it's too late.

Nige spins around, and kicks the bathroom door closed, trapping the cultist inside with him. He moves inside the range of the shotgun, pushes the pistol into Pete's skinny ribs, and says, "Drop it."

Pete looks down. "Oh, bugger." He places the shotgun on the sink.

"What's going on in there?" Dave shouts. "Peter, come out."

"Don't say a word." Nige turns Pete around to face the wall, then pats him down quickly to check he has no other weapons. It's impossible to tell. His robe seems to have hundreds of pockets stuffed with all manner of gadgets and gizmos.

Nige picks up the shotgun and wraps the strap over his shoulder. "Open the door."

He stoops low to hide himself behind Pete, who although taller than average, is at least six inches too short to hide behind successfully. He keeps the pistol pointed at his neck as Pete opens the door. Through it he can see Dave behind Korrigan, and as he and Pete re-enter the kitchen, he spots Maggie stood to the side with her hands up.

Without missing a beat Dave grabs Korrigan and with some difficulty wrestles him into a similar position.

"Let him go or I'll blow his brains out." Dave's hands shake as he cowers behind Korrigan, who is somewhat more of a shield than Pete is for Nige.

"Maggie, come take this." Nige holds out the shotgun.

"Stop it," says Dave. He aims his gun at Maggie then back at Korrigan. "Can't you see I've got a gun? You're supposed to not be moving."

"Oh, this is great." Korrigan rolls his eyes.

"What's happened to Kenneth?" Maggie takes the gun. Surprisingly, she looks quite at home with it. She points it at Dave – and Korrigan.

"He's gone all weird. Like a gelatinous sausage. Go in there and tell me if that's normal influencer behaviour."

"Oh my God, really?" Korrigan looks unusually gleeful despite the situation.

"Hey." Dave tries unsuccessfully to shake him. "I'm holding you hostage. Stop being so cheerful."

Maggie steps into the bathroom. Judging by the way she abruptly backs out and paints the wall with the contents of her stomach, what has happened to Kenneth isn't normal influencer behaviour.

Korrigan beams. "Is it like all his skin has melted into itself?"

Maggie nods. She wipes a hand across her mouth.

"I was right. I was bloody right. Shape-shifting lizard. Aidan owes me a tenner."

"He's not a shape-shifting bloody lizard." Nige moves around the room to get a better angle.

"No? Well how come Ultradox94 on YouTube says he's one then." If anyone could look smug with a pistol held to the side of his head, it's Korrigan. "Sounds like he's gone into the intermediate phase of transmogrification to me."

"What the hell's an intermediate phase of transmogrification?"

Maggie spits and regains her composure aiming the gun at Dave. "What the hell's a shape-shifting lizard?"

"He *could* be a shape-shifting lizard," pipes in Pete.

"He's not a shape-shifting lizard," Nige huffs and gives Pete a violent shake.

"Oh, shut up the lot of you," shouts Dave. "Let Pete go or your friend's brains are going to be splattered so far up the wall even you, you lanky demon worshipping brute, won't be able to reach to wash them off."

Korrigan laughs and shakes his head, buffing the pistol back and forth. "Looks like we have ourselves a Chieveley standoff, boys."

"Don't you mean Mexican?" Maggie frowns over the barrel of the shotgun.

"Nah Chieveley services. Along the M4. Half way between London and Bristol. Spoony Phil says that's where all the standoffs happen. Drug deals in the carpark are always going south. Plus, there's a Marks 'n' Sparks for a quality snack on the way home."

"Spoony Phil is a liability," says Nige.

Korrigan shrugs. "He's an acquired taste. You know, like olives. Some people think they are just gross, salty grapes, but I—"

"Right, that's it," Dave says, shaking with anger. "I'm counting to three and then I'm going to shoot someone."

"Oh chill out, mate." Korrigan makes a calm down motion with his hands.

"One."

"If you shoot him. I'll just shoot this guy." Nige grips the back of Pete's robe tighter.

Maggie sidesteps to get a better shot but Dave is tucked in behind Korrigan.

"Two." Dave's eyes are wide. Nige can see that the hand holding the gun is shaking.

"Dave. Stop." Pete wriggles in Nige's grip.

Dave looks desperate. "We can't. You know what we have to do." He grips Korrigan's shoulder more firmly. "Two and a half."

Korrigan starts to look worried. "Nige?"

"Is everything ok up there?" calls a familiar voice from downstairs.

In that moment Dave makes the crucial mistake of taking the gun off Korrigan and pointing it towards the door. With perfectly trained precision, Korrigan launches himself backwards, flattening the cultist against the wall like a pancake. The gun clatters to the floor, behind the fridge.

Aidan pokes his head around the door just as Korrigan is pinning Dave to the ground in an armlock. "I heard shouting. Are you guys going to Marks 'n' Sparks? I could nail a bag of mini poppadoms and a Fanta." He pauses, reading the room. "Can I get a twirl too?"

He's soaked through. Even his beard is dripping. Long hair stuck to his cheeks. He spots his bosses with their respective captives, then frowns. "Lads?"

With little resistance, Nige pulls Pete's arms behind his back and cuffs him to a kitchen chair. "Chuck Korrigan your cuffs, boy."

Aidan does, and after a fair amount of struggling, Korrigan manages to secure Dave to another chair next to Pete.

"Let us go. We are on a mission of utmost importance." Dave stamps his foot.

"Shut it you." Korrigan grabs a stained tea towel and ties it around Dave's mouth. His eyes twitch, no doubt horrified at the taste.

Nige walks over to Aidan and gives him a hearty slap on the back. "Boy, am I glad to see you!" He shakes his head. "I'm so sorry I left—"

"It's fine. You had to get out." The lad's kind eyes beam. "But mate…" He glances up as if in fervent prayer and pinches his thumbs and forefingers together. "You would not believe how much of a bloody nightmare it's been getting across town." He blows through pursed lips. "Anyway, where's Kenneth? Is he safe?"

Strangely, with the action of the last few moments, Nige had almost forgotten about Kenneth. His mind having written it off as something perfectly normal like the fact that planes full of people can soar through the air, or huge, heavy cargo ships can just float happily on water. He glances at Maggie, who shrugs. "He's all in one piece at least. But that's as far as I can say." He points to the bathroom. "Have a look."

Aidan enters the bathroom. There's a moment's pause before a short "hm" of epiphany. He comes back into the kitchen shaking his head, then looks at Korrigan. "I can't believe I owe you a tenner."

"What?" Maggie places the shotgun down on the kitchen side.

Aidan jerks a thumb back towards the bathroom. "Intermediate phase of transmogrification, right?"

Korrigan grins. His eyebrows dance. "The boy knows."

Nige slaps his forehead. "Where have you been? Korrigan said you had something to tell us."

"I've just been trying to get here without using my card. Did you know we're wanted men? It's all over town. Every TV station. Every Di Blasio billboard has got you and me on there."

"I know. We can't stay here." He doesn't want to admit how worried he is. This has gone from bad to worse very quickly and if Kenneth doesn't wake up, what then?

"It'll be fine. We were helping him." Aidan waves a nonchalant hand. "Kenneth'll vouch for us once he's transmogrificated."

Nige closes his eyes and rubs his temples. It's not often that he thinks of his friends as idiots, but they do have their moments. "I don't think we can count on that. What if what's happened to Kenneth is permanent? He may be dead."

"Couldn't you tell Di Blasio?" Aidan looks at Maggie hopefully. "Tell them that this has all been a big misunderstanding."

"I can speak to Ian." She opens her bag and takes out her phone. "We'd have to get Kenneth back to the main building, though."

Nige steps between them. "We still don't know if we can trust Di Blasio. For all we know they might want to hush up the fact that he's turned into a big pink hotdog sausage. And that might mean…" He sweeps a finger across his neck.

"We can trust Stefan." Maggie holds her phone up. "He's not a bad guy. More of a playboy. Likes yachts, women, a bit of a drink. He's not some evil genius that might go kidnapping his top influencer and offing anyone who finds out."

Nige scratches his chin. Can they trust Di Blasio based on Maggie's word? He could protect them. "You know him better than us. And it does seem like those Tall Ninjas, with their creepy big knives, are the real ones to watch out for. But let's not put all our eggs in one basket just yet." He moves to the bathroom. "Aidan, help me drag the old boy out."

The bathroom is too small for them both, so Aidan waits at the door as Nige kneels by Kenneth's side.

"You don't really think Korrigan's right, do you?" Nige whispers.

Aidan leans forward. "How else do you describe that? You didn't feed him after eight, did you? That was one of the rules."

Nige gives the lad a withering look. "He's not a gremlin." He takes hold of what are probably Kenneth's feet with both hands. The fleshy mass pulses gently like a wriggling caterpillar. It's soft but firm, like a stiff crust of bread.

"I didn't want to say anything in front of everyone," says Aidan. "But I saw something in the shop. Before I hit the deck and everything exploded."

"What?" Nige thinks back to that buzzing behind his eyes just before Aidan came flying in from the front of the shop. He'd had the same feeling in Kenneth's apartment.

"It came through the front door. I think it was the thing from Kenneth's bedroom." Aidan looks a little embarrassed. "The one I tackled. It threw me just the same, but this time I wasn't standing anywhere near it."

So the thing from Kenneth's apartment was following them, and it had managed to throw an eighteen stone man without even touching him. How? Maybe Stefan Di Blasio could help them. But it would be stupid for them all to turn up at the Di Blasio tower.

Nige pulls. The resin securing Kenneth to the floor catches for a moment, then creaks and comes away with a dry crack. He lays the feet down, then steps over Kenneth's prone form and picks up the head end.

"It held up its hands," continues Aidan. "Then it was like a gale force wind just came out of nowhere, and I was flying into those muppets in the other room. Then they were flying too. By the time I knew what had happened, it was gone and so were you."

Nige swallows. Leaving the boy behind had been hard. Heat rises in his cheeks. He knows that this isn't the point of Aidan's story, but he still feels ashamed for ditching him. "Did you get a good look at it?"

Aidan shrugs. "Not really. It was wearing a big black sort of rain mac. You know, like the long ones we sometimes wear outside the clubs." He rubs his head and Nige notices a bruise coming in just above his right eyebrow. "It gets weirder, though. Nothing else in the store moved. Not even a postcard. Just me and the cultists, flying like a tornado hit the shop."

"Hm. All the more reason I suppose to get Di Blasio on side. We're clearly out of our depth." He lifts up Kenneth's head. His fingers sink as if he's holding a thick balloon filled with jelly. He holds back a gag. "Get the feet."

Aidan grimaces as he does, and backs out. As the body slides on the ground between them it rustles like paper. They place him in the middle of the kitchen, causing Pete and Dave to squirm in their seats.

"What are we going to do with him then?" says Korrigan.

"Uh." Nige looks at the others. Everyone has their eyes on him. Even the cultists. Why? He doesn't know what to do any more than the rest of them. But it's his fault they are here. He searches in his wallet and takes out a business card. Hands it to Maggie. "I don't like the idea of anyone phoning from here. I've seen the movies, I know they can triangulate a position from a phone call. Go to DB HQ and speak to Ian. Tell him we weren't trying to hurt anyone. Tell him we were just doing our job. And tell him that Kenneth is safe, but don't mention…" Nige points to Kenneth the Fleshy Cylinder.

"And what are you going to do?" she says as she prepares to leave, hooking her bag over her shoulder.

"We're taking him somewhere else until we know your boss is on side. If he is, you can send someone to pick us up."

"And if he's not?" Korrigan grabs his car keys from the counter.

Nige clears his throat and looks around the kitchen. No suggestions are forthcoming. "Then I guess I'll think of something else."

The Watchers on the Roof

The lorry is warming up nicely, but Mac is frozen in his seat. There has been no movement from the roof. His eyes bounce around the top of the building. He hopes that what he saw earlier was just a trick of the light against the rain.

But when the cultists blow the door to shreds, he sits up. Maybe they aren't with Korrigan and Davies after all.

He waits, and soon another man with a large bushy beard arrives. There is still no movement from the roof. Perhaps he imagined the shape. A remnant of his earlier dream.

After some time, three men and a woman exit the building. One of them is Korrigan. Mac has seen his picture on the about us page of the firm's website. Davies follows with what appears to be a rolled up rug on his shoulder.

At the sight of their black windbreakers, ferret face's words repeat in his mind.

Kill him.

Words that make your breath catch in your throat. Words that could suck the life from an anxious body with the sound alone.

The cultists are missing.

He reaches for his notepad. Jots this latest development down in a spider diagram he's been busy populating. The plot continues to thicken like a good soup.

Looking back up, he watches as Davies opens the boot of the clio and folds the rug into the back.

The woman has a brief discussion with Korrigan, while he takes an extra-large rain mac from the back of his car and gives it to her. She leaves through a side entrance and heads back up the main thoroughfare.

He taps his pencil against his lips and watches the three men as they squeeze into the tiny car. It sinks on its suspension. Davies has to stoop quite significantly to fit in the front seat, and the bearded man takes up most of the back.

Mac looks at his notes. The events are clear but something doesn't add up. The cultists shot their way into the bouncer's warehouse. Something went on inside. Then the bouncers came out with no sign of the cultists. And what's with the rug?

Oh! It suddenly hits him. But it could only be holding one corpse, so if it were a cultist, then where is the other?

Maybe he's stumbled on some sort of gang war, but how are the influencers involved?

He takes another moment to check the roof, but he can't see through the sheets of rain.

The clio's headlights illuminate the side of the building as the engine starts up.

And that's when Mac sees them.

Several black-clad figures leering down at the car like terrible gargoyles. Fierce blades shimmer in the flashing light.

And Mac hears those words again in his mind.

Kill him.

The Dibber

The dibber is the bane of Korrigan's life. His wife always laughs when he rings her up to say he's coming back from the office because he's forgotten it again.

"Why haven't you got it on the keyring with the garage dibber," she often said.

She has cute names for things like that. The TV remote is "the 'mote", cleaning your teeth is "doing your peggle weggle doodles", and when you went a bit mad you were "going doolally tap". Once you'd heard her say the things a few times, it all made sense. It was like cockney rhyming slang, except it didn't rhyme and Debs wasn't a cockney. The sort of thing only someone who's been married for nearly forty years could understand.

Debs is his angel.

He smiles as he reaches the top of the stairs and enters the kitchen having once more forgotten the remote that opens the warehouse gates.

She's stuck with him through thick and thin, and money had been pretty thin when he started the business. Now that he's a little thicker, she's still around.

If you were to ask him honestly, he would say she's gotten a little thicker around the edges too, but he hardly notices, and when he does, he couldn't care less - if anything, he likes it. She's always been that gorgeous coat check girl he fell for all those years ago. No changing that. She'd given him two amazing daughters who drove him doolally tap, and he loves her for those gifts.

He starts by the kettle where he usually leaves his keys. He mimes pushing the button with his thumb in the international sign of 'I've lost my dibber', as if will alone could manifest it.

Not by the mugs. Not on the table. Not in any of the cupboards. Although there's no reason to believe it'll be there.

The cultists, still handcuffed to their chairs, watch as he scuttles about.

The one called Dave groans through his gag and struggles at his cuffs, but only manages to make the chair hop.

"Shut it you," Korrigan says, raising the back of his hand.

Outside, the horn honks.

"I'm going as fast as I can," he calls, knowing Nige can't hear him. "Honking the bloody horn's not going to help."

He shakes his head and climbs down on to all fours, groaning as he does so - it isn't as easy as it used to be.

It's not under the table and chairs. He beats his fists on the thin carpet, sending a few dried specs of old food hopping across the threads. "Oh, where is it?"

Debs' eagle eyes would have spotted it immediately.

"Mr Korrigan, are you just going to leave us here?" says the other cultist, Pete.

"What else would we do with you?"

"Let us go home, maybe? We promise not to bother you again. I expect we're probably too late now if Kenneth has gone into the first stages of his demon form. I suppose the world is already doomed."

"Seriously, what do you think is going to happen?" Korrigan climbs out from beneath the dining table and stands with his hands on his hips, facing them and the window.

Pete opens his mouth to speak, but before he can start, Korrigan spots something outside.

"Oh, the gates are open. Nige must have found it." For a nanosecond, he grins, until his eyes focus on the two vans speeding up the main road. "Shit on a shovel."

The vans are gleaming white, each decked out like police riot vans with a grill that could cover the windscreen if the occasion called for it. They are clearly heading this way.

Pete jumps around on his chair like a child on a space hopper. He cranes his neck to see through the window. "Di Blasio security vans. I expect they're tracking Kenneth too. The tracker you gave him wasn't very secure."

"What tracker?"

"A tracker registered to the Korrigan and Davies security company. It's how we found you. We hacked it, so they must have too."

"Shit on a shovel. Sorry boys, but you're on your own."

Korrigan hurries from the kitchen. Dave grumbles loudly and Pete responds in a soothing tone, but he doesn't hear what he says.

At the bottom of the stairs, he turns away from the front door and heads along the hall toward their lockup. He has just the thing for an occasion such as this. Illegal times call for illegal measures.

Thumbing in the code to open it – Debs' birthday – he pulls open the door and hits the light.

They don't have much gear. Not many opportunities to use cool gadgets as a doorman. A couple of stab vests, a handful of pepper sprays, and some cuffs. But he's proud of what they have.

He throws his stab vest over his sweat saturated shirt, tightening the elastic bungees. Though Aidan made some modifications when Korrigan outgrew it, it still rides high on his belly. At least it covers his chest. He squeezes into his utility belt and checks that the taser, pepper spray, and extendable baton are still in their holsters. A little dusty maybe, but they'll work.

He opens a green footlocker which stands beneath the vest hooks and lifts the bottom out revealing the secret compartment he dug beneath it years ago. Inside is another lock box.

Butterflies dance in his stomach.

Spoony Phil gave him the four objects within the lock box as a start-up present. It was never really made clear how he got them, or why he felt a company that booked doormen into pubs and clubs would need two smoke and two fragmentation grenades. But Korrigan didn't have the heart to turn the gift down when he'd opened the Tesco's shopping bag Spoony had used to wrap them.

At least he'd wrapped them.

Two black canisters, and another two like large green blackberries. He expects they won't need the blackberries. They might not even work. God knows how old they were, or what state they'd been in when he was given them all those years ago, but at least the sight of them might act as a deterrent.

As he stuffs all four into his pockets, he realises his hands are shaking. He closes his eyes for a moment and takes a deep breath. Di Blasio were always harping on about mindfulness as a way of life, and while he'd be the first to admit it was all a load of mumbo jumbo bollocks, there had to be something to it judging by the way Kenneth looked pre-transmogrification.

But then again, Kenneth was a lizard person.

Feeling somewhat centred, he returns to the corridor. "Let's smoke these turkeys," he says to himself with a squint and a mouthful of grit. He wishes Debs could see him now.

That's when the darkened corridor in front of him shifts.

The walls have now become theatre curtains of the deepest black, twitching before a shadowy reveal. But the curtain isn't a curtain at all. Two sets of leathery wings block the doorway that leads out into the courtyard. Suddenly, they snap inward.

Standing between him and the front door, stooped like hooked tent pegs, are two tall, thin silhouettes.

The Enemy of My Enemy

Two large white vans squeal to a stop, blocking off the gate.

"Who's that?" says Aidan as he leans forward in his seat. "Give 'em a honk. Let them know they're blocking us in." He reaches forward to press the horn.

Nige swats his hand away. "Don't. It's Di Blasio."

"Uh oh," he says and falls back into his seat.

"Out the car. We'll try to get round the back of the warehouse and sneak out that way. We'll leave Kenneth in the boot. There's no way we're sneaking anywhere with him." He hopes the Di Blasio team won't bother to look in the car for Kenneth, and won't recognise what they see if they do.

"But—"

We'll come back for him when they've gone."

"What about Korrigan?"

"We'll head through the front and go out the back. Pick him up on the way." He opens his door carefully. The interior light of the car flicks on.

"We can see you." The voice is tinny, but recognisable over the megaphone. "Come out slowly."

Jeff stands between the gateposts. His face is sombre and a large wound covers his right eye. Behind him, more members of the Di Blasio security force point automatic rifles at them. Nige can't see Esther, Dom, or Jay.

For a fleeting moment, he wonders what need a food company has for automatic rifles.

"We don't want to do this the hard way. But we will," Jeff continues.

Aidan jumps toward the front seats, points through the windscreen, and with an enthusiastic snarl shouts, "Let's ram 'em! Punch it Nige."

Nige doesn't move. "In a clio?"

"Right. No. Silly idea."

Aidan lowers the back window. It only goes halfway, so he has to angle his chin up over the glass. "I think we got our wires crossed a bit back there, Jeff. Maybe we can talk about this. We weren't trying to kidnap Kenneth."

Jeff turns his head downwards. It's hard to tell if he's angry or just thinking. He lifts the megaphone to his lips slowly. His voice doesn't crack, but it waivers slightly. Not through anger, but sadness. He sounds like he's just about ready to give up. "Come out of the car."

Nige unwinds his window too, as he realises why the other security from Kenneth's apartment aren't there. "Did they get your guys, Jeff?"

Jeff drops the megaphone to his side and glares at him. The muscles of his jaw stand out. "No thanks to you," he shouts. "I couldn't see. Dom couldn't even stand after you tased him. We were sitting ducks." The bloodshot whites of his eyes stand out like twin blood moons in the night. "Come out now." He hisses through gritted teeth.

"I'm sorry. I am. We were just doing the job we were paid for." Despite what has happened, getting Kenneth out had been the best choice. Otherwise he'd be dead like Jeff's men. "You have to admit you weren't going to do what was best for Kenneth."

Jeff rubs his forehead.

Behind him, one of the riflemen jumps. "They're here."

"Open fire." Jeff turns and they break for cover. His men begin firing at the roof.

Nige ducks down, anticipating the swarm of bullets about to turn the car into a cheese grater. From this angle, in the mirror's reflection, he sees several dark shapes leap from the roof. They land amidst Jeff and his squad. Swift hand to hand combat begins.

"Oh balls," says Nige.

"Who is it?" Aidan asks.

"Tall Ninjas."

"What do we do?" Aidan winds his window back up frantically as if that'll protect him.

The fight outside has drawn the attention away from them. "They all look pretty distracted, so I suggest we continue with the sneak out the back plan." He takes Kenneth's gun from his pocket. "Have you ever fired one of these?"

Aidan shakes his head.

"Neither have I." He looks at it. Is there a safety catch? Is it even loaded? He doesn't know. Holding it feels worse than not, so he puts it away again. "Out the car. Through the warehouse. On three." A deep breath. "Three."

The pair of them exit the car and sprint for the front door.

"Kenneth!" Aidan turns back to the car.

"No. Wait." Nige reaches out to stop him, but he's already gone.

His eyes shift frantically between Aidan and the fight. They are going to be seen. Aidan grabs the boot and pulls it open just as something drops from above, landing delicately on the car's roof. At first it looks like a giant bat. Two black sail like wings extend from its back. And then, with a loud whip-like crack, they roll in as if on elastic bands. The figure stands, a rake thin silhouette. A blade the shape of a treble cleft glints in its hand.

It jumps from the car and kicks Aidan in the stomach, knocking him against the tall metal door of the warehouse. The creature advances, blade held aloft.

"Leave him alone." Nige rushes forward, reaching for the gun. Gets in close. He can't afford to miss.

He aims. Though facing the other way, the figure ducks, spins and catches his wrist, sending the pistol skittering across the broken tarmac.

Shiny, beetle like eyes peer from beneath the wraps covering its dark face. They regard Nige for a moment with what appears to be malicious humour. Then the figure whirls, twisting Nige's arm and crashing him face first into the ground.

Before it has a chance to advance, Aidan is up. He lunges in for a full nelson. But the creature is too fast. It skips under his groping hands, as graceful as a ballet dancer, and stabs with the knife. The blade cuts deep under Aidan's ribs. The boy cups his hands together on open air. He falls. His head cracks as it hits the curb.

Nige struggles forward, but his knee has twisted in the fall. It won't take his weight.

"Nige, I can't see," Aidan says, with wide, frightened eyes. He reaches out towards Nige.

The creature steps back and raises the blade again.

"No!" Nige heaves himself to his feet. "Wait." His body is heavy and slow. He curses the day he grew old without knowing it. Drags himself forward as if against a strong current.

The figure slashes down. Aidan tenses, then, as the life leaves him, gives one last shudder.

No. Not Aidan.

Nige throws his full weight into a tackle and slams the attacker into the wall, all care for himself discarded. Pulls out his pepper spray and unleashes a full can into the thing's face. With his other hand, he wrestles the blade away. It skids under the car.

The creature is fast, but Nige is fuelled by white-hot rage. Blood red covers his vision. He draws his fist back and lands a punch on the masked face. Then another. The thing claws at his forearms, arching bloody gouges into his skin with long pointed nails. But submerged in his fury, Nige does not notice.

He forces its chin up and slams his fist into its exposed throat, again and again until something pops and it begins to gurgle. He pulls himself up on the slatted metal warehouse door, and stomps down on its head. By now it isn't moving.

He hobbles to Aidan's side.

"Aidan." He kneels, then lifts the boy's head. "Come on, mate." Aidan's neck is loose. His eyes open to the rain. He shakes him, but nothing changes. The sounds around him pale into insignificance. No. This can't be. They were supposed to be working a club. This was supposed to be a normal night. "Aidan."

A scream drags him back to the moment. He lays Aidan down and crouches behind the Clio. The creatures are making light work of Jeff's squad. Only one of the things lies prone, but it's already rising again as two more lay waste to the armed security. Three of Jeff's crew lie dead on the tarmac.

He reaches under the car and picks up the creature's strange knife. It is light and perfectly balanced, and on the hilt is the image of a hook crossed over a flail. He wipes it on his leg, transferring Aidan's blood to his jeans. He wants to run in and cut the monsters to shreds, but knows that would only result in his own quick end.

He glances at the doorway that leads into the office. Korrigan may need him. Plus, there is a shotgun upstairs.

Taking one last look at the dying fight, he stumbles across the small expanse and into the unlit corridor.

He lurches up the stairs.

"Korrigan," he whispers as he enters the kitchen, but instead of seeing his business partner, Nige is greeted by the twin barrels of a shotgun poking up over their overturned kitchen table.

"He went downstairs and we haven't seen him since," says Pete, who is crouched in cover with the shotgun trained on Nige, not necessarily threateningly, more in defence of what ever might come through the kitchen door.

"Who the hell let you out?" says Nige, for the moment frozen to the spot.

Dave's head pops up. He looks very proud of himself. "There is no knot nor bond that can restrain The Church of The Fallen Angels."

"Who is it? Who's outside?" says Pete.

Nige raises the blade, more as a show of stubbornness than a hopeless bid at defence. "Di Blasio and those Tall Ninjas from Kenneth's apartment building. Are they not with you?"

"The Church of The Fallen Angels currently only has four members." Pete jerks his head to one side in thought. "So probably not."

"Quiet you." Dave prods him in the ribs.

Using their bickering as a distraction, Nige ducks down into the corner by the fridge and out of the range of the shotgun. "Well, if they aren't with you, and they aren't with Di Blasio, then we could probably do worse than stop fighting ourselves and start fighting them."

"Sounds like a plan," says Pete. He stands and cocks his gun.

"He's tricking us." Dave pulls him back down. "Vile demon, we will not fall for your despicable lies."

Nige sighs as he settles into a seated position against the wall. "Aidan is dead." He leans his head back, too tired to hold it up. "Sooner or later they'll be in here, and we'll be next. You can either blindly believe that I'm against you, stay there and die alone, or put that thought aside and we might stand a chance of getting out of here." He stands and moves towards the door.

"Wait," calls Pete. He holds out a hand. Then he counts on his fingers. "If you're not with them, and they're against Kenneth, and Kenneth is a demonic sausage, and—"

"Peter, only you could make a death-defying escape sound so dull," says Dave. Then, with a striking similarity to a teacher who once caught Nige throwing eggs out of the bus on a school trip, he looks at him and wags a finger. "Mr Davies, we will come with you, but I will be keeping my eye on you. I don't want to see any hellish nonsense. If you so much as utter a... a demonic prayer or unleash a fiery spasm of brimstone from your fingertips, then so—"

Nige leaves the room. The cultists give chase.

At the bottom of the stairs, Nige looks through the open front door. Pete and Dave creep down the steps behind him. The sound of fighting has ceased. A man wails in pain followed by hushed conversation. From this angle, he can't see the gates where the vans are parked.

To his left, the hall leads to the lockup and the back entrance.

At the far end of the corridor something catches his eye. A pin glinting in the streetlight coming through the glazed window of the back door. He knows where it's from.

"I have to find Korrigan." He moves to pick up the pin. "Watch the front door."

The cultists turn and aim their weapons.

Nige taps in the pass code and opens the lock-up. Inside is Korrigan, pale as a ghost, standing with his back against the wall. Cuddled in one arm are his grenades. His other hand is raised above his head, ready to launch one of what he calls "the green blackberries".

At the sight of Nige, he relaxes.

"Thank God." He lowers his arm. "Are they still in the corridor?"

"No, everyone's outside. We're leaving."

Korrigan holds out his hand. The grenade is wrapped almost fully in his melon sized palm. His sweaty knuckles white with the strain of gripping it. "You didn't happen to see a grenade pin did you? I may have got a bit over excited."

Nige holds the pin up. "I've got it here."

"Oh good. My hand is cramping up. I was shaking so much when those things came out of the walls, I dropped it."

Nige checks the grenade for a hole but can't see one. "I don't think it'll go. Can't you hold it?"

"I'm pretty sure a grenade is like a shit, Nige. If you hold it too long, sooner or later it's gonna blow." Korrigan steps forward and looks over Nige's shoulder. "Where's Aidan?"

"Look…" Nige pauses, not sure how to go on. "He's been hurt."

Korrigan's lip shakes. "Is he ok?"

He swallows and shakes his head.

Korrigan closes his eyes and leans back against the wall. He takes a deep breath. "When did this get so out of hand?"

He clears his throat and straightens. His jaw sets like concrete. Eyes hard as stone. Nige is reminded of the Korrigan that he grew up with working the doors. A lad that took no lip from anyone. A lad that grew up fighting on the playground when the sporty kids picked on him, fighting on the streets to protect the innocent club goers when rowdy pubs would kick out, fighting for everything he ever got.

"We can't let them get away with this," Korrigan says. "You keep that pin, and take these." He angles his arm forward and Nige takes a smoke grenade and the other frag. "I think the fuses are six seconds."

"You think or you know?"

"I think I know."

Nige leads him out of the lockup.

"Who let them out?" says Korrigan when he sees the cultists standing either side of the front door.

"We're helping each other," says Nige.

Dave holds a finger over his lips. He whispers. "They've got the Di Blasio security chief. They're questioning him."

"The ones who killed Aidan?" Korrigan strides forward, grenade aloft. "Who are they? I'm gonna fuck them up."

Nige catches his arm, holding him firm. "The Tall Ninjas from Kenneth's apartment. This may sound stupid, but I think they can fly."

Nige leans out of the front door between the two cultists. The centre of the parking area is now the floor of an abattoir. Members of the security team lie in bits on the tarmac. Jeff is on his back in the centre. Two dark figures stand over him on either side like druids at a pagan sacrifice.

Another kneels beside him, talking in a hushed, slithering voice. From where he is propped up on his elbows, Jeff spits into its face.

"I have no idea where Kenneth is, and I wouldn't tell you even if I did," he says.

The creature presses down on a wound on his chest. Jeff growls and falls back.

"We can get them all," whispers Korrigan. He holds his fist forward. "With this."

Nige pushes his hand down. "Jeff's just doing his job. Is there any way to get him out of this?"

Korrigan shakes his head. "Can't see one."

"We could distract them," says Pete. "Get them all in here, sneak out the back, and throw that in." He nods to the grenade. "Give him time to get away."

"That might work," says Nige.

"OK. What should I say to get them over here?" Korrigan says as he mops his brow with the back of the hand holding the grenade.

"Give that to me and go wait down the other end." Nige holds out a hand for Korrigan's grenade. "Even with my knee we stand more of a chance if I throw it and leg it than if you do."

Out on the tarmac, Jeff growls again. "I came here looking for him. Why do you think I have any idea where he is?"

The lead creature stands and looks at the others. "He's telling the truth. He knows nothing. Kill him."

"Quick," says Nige, holding his hand out for the grenade.

Korrigan's fist shakes with the strain of keeping it so tightly gripped for so long.

Nige places his hand over the grenade. "Nice and slow. Don't let the lever pop out." He waits a moment. Korrigan's hand shakes, but not much else. "That's too slow."

"I can't let go. My hand is spasming." He grips his wrist and narrows his eyes. Then lets out a sigh. "I'm just going to drop it. Let me do it."

Nige looks his friend up and down. Shakes his head. "No. Get up the other end. I'll use one of mine as the distraction, then we'll use yours in the hall." He pats Korrigan's hand down.

Korrigan nods and backs away.

One of the creatures steps toward Jeff. It draws its knife.

Nige steps out through the front door. "Oi, you lanky pricks," he shouts. "Cop some of this." He pulls the pin.

The three dark shapes turn toward him as one and he can sense two more converging on his position from the side. It's enough to panic him and the grenade slips out of his sweating hand.

Nige's eyes go wide and he sprints back in past the cultists. "One, two."

The cultists give chase.

"Three, F—"

The grenade detonates. A rush of hot air knocks the three of them to the hallway floor.

Nige hobbles back to his feet, struggling to catch his breath. "You told me six seconds." His knee flares white with pain as he limps towards where Korrigan is waiting at the end of the corridor.

Korrigan gives a thumbs up. "Lucky it wasn't three. Are they coming?"

"Yes they are," shouts Pete as he ducks under Nige's arm to help him along.

To Nige, the next series of events happens in slow motion, and after the knock he is about to suffer, he will only remember it as a series of disconnected frames.

Korrigan stands in the open doorway, beckoning with his free hand and holding the grenade aloft, ready to throw.

A flicker like a pitch-black flame drops beside him.

A glint at its centre flashes out, slashing Korrigan's side.

Korrigan, more surprised than hurt, snarls at his attacker.

A head squashing thud of a shotgun blast.

The flash of a blade striking Korrigan again, and a long red wound seeming to appear across his stomach just below his stab vest.

Korrigan's roar. His fist, gripping the grenade, rises and strikes his assailant.

"Get back Nige," he shouts as he stuffs the grenade into the black cloth of the figure's robes. He pulls the door shut, closing himself and his attacker outside.

Nige dives back the way he came. The world flashes. Pete's shotgun fires again. Then darkness.

The Other Enemy of My Enemy

A scratch of needle nails on Nige's cheek. Someone slapping him awake. He is outside. The rain has almost stopped, but the wet cold of the tarmac eats through his T-shirt, bringing him quickly to his senses. The warm night air smells of fire and blood and rain-soaked concrete. Someone holds him up by his lapel. He blinks away unconsciousness.

"Pathetic," says a sibilant voice.

The hand holding his jacket lets go and he falls to the floor. He only just catches himself on his elbows before his head hits the tarmac.

Day hasn't yet broken, but the courtyard is lit with the flicker of flames from the warehouse. A cloud of smoke rolls over him, bringing with it the suffocating stench of melting tarmac, and the painful memory of Korrigan's sacrifice.

"Seeing as your little distraction allowed Di Blasio's security chief to escape, I'm going to have to interrogate you instead," says the voice.

The mix of smoke and his dizziness make it difficult to see the black-clad figure in the dark. Four similar shapes shimmer into view behind it, as if appearing out of thin air.

The creature turns to them. "What of his partner, Korrigan?"

"It appears he detonated a grenade. He and Madok are dead."

"The bodies burned?"

"They are alight."

The taste of rage fills Nige's mouth like a battery to the tongue. He holds it back for now. Lets it build. Waits for his moment.

The creature turns back to him. "By now I'm sure you know at least part of what is going on here, which is why I'm afraid, whatever you tell me, I can't let you live. But perhaps the threat of violence against your son and grandchildren will loosen your lips."

Nige pushes himself upright - in his earlier years he would have sprung to his feet, fists swinging. "Don't you touch them or I'll—"

"We do as we please, Davies." The figure shrugs. "We always have and always will."

From the way the cloth moves over the figure's face, Nige can tell he's smiling.

"Who are you? How do you know who I am?"

"Wouldn't it be a bit cliched if I were to tell you now? No Nigel, I'm afraid you will go to your grave without the knowledge of why. All we need to know is where Kenneth and Victoria are hiding, and we'll be on our way." He leans his head to one side. Nige feels a deeper unease as if he is being studied. "I will say this though, you do look a lot like him. You have the same 'I'm about to die' look." He looks back at his comrades and laughs. It's an awful sneering sound that has the same effect as a fork scratching across a plate. Why are they comparing him to Kenneth? He looks nothing like him. "But that's all the clues you're getting."

Nige hears a scream from above and Jeff falls to the ground, landing hard on the tarmac by his side. He groans and rolls over, curling into a foetal position.

"Ah, you found him," the figure says, looking up.

With a powerful rush of air, and the thick whisper of wings, another creature lands. Its wings fold neatly into its silhouette.

"We have no need for the security chief. He clearly has no idea where Kenneth is," says the creature standing over Nige. It flicks indifferent fingers.

The other creature that brought Jeff nods and draws its knife. It grabs him by the head. With little ceremony, it slits his throat, and pushes him face first to the ground.

"Put him with the other bodies in the warehouse. Make sure it burns quickly." It turns back to Nige. "Now, don't make me repeat myself."

"I don't know." Nige can't take his eyes from where Jeff is lying face down. Blood pools on the filthy ground around his head. "I don't know where Kenneth is, and I don't know a Victoria."

From within the fabric that wraps around its waist, the figure slides out a sickle-like blade. "Your granddaughter is Katy, five, your grandson Charlie, three. I wonder which would win in a race for their lives once I'd sliced off their feet?" He ponders for a moment before becoming serious again. "Where is Kenneth? Victoria is the one who came to you this evening at his apartment."

Nige glares. It takes everything to stop himself from getting up. His fists ache to beat this thing to a pulp. But sometimes the best action is no action.

"You have my word we will not harm your family, if you tell me."

"And what's that worth?"

"A man is nothing save his word."

"You're not a man." Nige snarls.

The creature throws its head back and laughs. A harsh cackle that reverberates into the night sky, bouncing off the hard brick walls of the compound. "You ridiculous little ant." He raises his arms, and gestures to the other figures around him. "We are the pinnacle of men. We are just and true and good, and we do what we need to do so that humanity can continue with its ignorant little existence." He spits each word out with rising fury. "Not a man? I've never heard something so foolish in all my many years. Now, waste another minute of my time and I will personally pluck your granddaughter from her home, and drop her from the top of the Di Blasio building. Two minutes, and I'll take little Charlie along to watch."

Nige wants to throw up. "I don't know anyone called Victoria. I thought that was you in the apartment." His insides are ice. He glances at the car. "Kenneth's in the boot." He looks down, ashamed. Defeated. But his family means too much. He's trapped.

"Oh? So close. How did we miss him?"

The creature raises its head to command the others to investigate, but the growl of an approaching engine drowns him out. He looks towards the Di Blasio vans which still block the gate, but they remain silent and dark. The roar intensifies, and blinding light shines through the space between them. With an ear-splitting crunch, and the grind of metal, the cab of a lorry smashes its way through, throwing the vehicles out of the way like toys.

Its destructive path continues into the courtyard. With a whine of shredding rubber, it swerves towards the three dark figures standing behind the main one. With no time to move, they are cut down like grass beneath a mower.

Distracted by his fallen comrades, the leader turns. Nige doesn't miss a beat. Pushing himself stiffly to his feet, he prepares to charge. Shoulder down, he hurls himself towards the stick thin figure. But with a crack like a whip and a swish of air, a pair of wings spring from the creature's back and it takes to the sky. Nige falls heavily to the tarmac.

He rolls, but the creature is gone.

Under the cab of the truck, from where the three creatures lie crushed, something pops like the strike of a match and smoke starts to billow out. Embers appear and grow as their bodies erupt into flame. The door to the lorry cab flies open and a grubby man in a trench coat staggers out.

"Did I get them?" he shouts over the sound of the grumbling truck engine. He looks to the sky. "Did I get them all?" He sniffs. "Jesus, what's on fire?"

A light grey smoke buffets him, and he steps away, fanning his face.

"Everything." Nige holds out a hand and the newcomer pulls him to his feet. "You missed one, but he's gone. Who are you?"

"Trent Macadamia PI. Or Mac. We should go. That thing might still be up there."

Nige limps towards Aidan's body. Glances to the figure that killed him who still lies prone by the warehouse door. He kneels down and rests a hand on the lad's arm. Blinks stinging eyes. "I'm sorry." Doesn't know what else to say.

Mac watches him in silence.

Nige pulls open the boot of the clio and drags Kenneth out. Throws him over his shoulder.

"Is that one of those cultists?" says Mac. "I saw them come in. Did you kill them?"

This guy is the other one from the wanted poster. He looks about as used up as Nige feels. Can he trust him? He hasn't the energy not to, and there's no one else to side with.

"No. No idea where they've got to." He pats Kenneth. "I'll explain this when we're somewhere safe. I've got a place nearby."

There's a scuffle of movement. The thing that hurt Aidan stands up, though it looks hunched. It rolls its neck, then strokes its throat.

"Look out." Nige steps back.

Mac does a forward roll and the creature slashes at open air.

"You killed Aidan," Nige growls. "I decked you once. I'll do it again."

"I don't think so." It holds its knife out at chest height. Its long, thin limbs move like black spider legs as it creeps softly forwards.

A flash of movement from above and the lead creature lands on the clio. "Do you know how many years of life you just wasted, boy?" It glares at Mac.

"I literally have no idea what any of you are talking about." Mac has his fists up as a 1920s boxer might. Judging by his stance, Nige assumes he's never had any coaching. "Smashing your mates with a truck just seemed like the right thing to do at the time." He glares through his fists at the lead creature. "Who are you? I've had a rubbish night and if it's going to end with me riddled with knife holes, at least give me a bit of the backstory."

The creature on the car considers this. "Alright, we are—"

"Demons!" Pete hangs out of the office window above with his shotgun aimed at the creature.

Dave is with him. He fires his pistol, flipping the creature on the car. It lands hard on the ground. Pete blasts the other against the wall. In an instant they are both smoking like the ones under the van. Glowing embers erupt under their wraps, and their bodies quickly and unceremoniously fizzle away to dust.

"Are you ok Mr Davies?" Pete waves. "Did the demons hurt you?"

"I'm fine."

"I like what you did with the truck." Dave shouts down to Mac.

The PI shrugs nonchalantly. "Thanks. I just kind of improvised." He looks at Nige with a raised eyebrow. "Aren't they…?"

"Yep." Nige looks up. "Lads, we're going. You can come with us, or you can stay here."

"We will keep a close watch on you and Kenneth Bailey until our task is complete," says Dave.

"Kenneth Bailey?" Mac's eyes are wide.

Nige shrugs Kenneth into a more comfortable position on his shoulder. "Yeah, when we're somewhere safe. I'll tell you everything."

Kenneth's 120th Birthday Party Build Up

2020

Stefan sits with one leg crossed over the other, his hands together on his stomach. "As you can see, Jenny," he holds a hand out towards Kenneth, who sits next to him, "the Health Influencer programme is going from strength to strength. Kenneth, Dawn and the others are looking younger and healthier than ever. And it's all thanks to Di Blasio products and our pre-planned exercise and eating schedule, which, if you don't mind me plugging, you can buy directly from our website." He laughs to himself. "Sorry, shameless, I know. But we're just so darn proud of it."

"Don't worry. I'm using it myself and I can tell you I feel better than ever." She smiles.

Stefan opens his palms and beams. "And you look great."

They laugh.

"Thank you."

The hilarity peters quickly.

"So, you have exciting news?"

"Yes." Stefan rubs his hands together. "We've just started taking on applicants for our next batch of influencers," continues Stefan. "We're starting them quite young this time. All consenting adults mind you."

Kenneth can't wait. Maybe now he'll get some privacy. Maybe now he'll get out of doing these stupid interviews. Some time off. Wouldn't that be something.

"My goodness - where do I sign up?" Jenny leans back in her chair in feigned surprise and excitement. As if she didn't know exactly what this interview was going to be about.

Stefan laughs.

"Sorry, Jenny, but we're only accepting applicants between the ages of eighteen and twenty. But all details are on our website. We've had applications from across the board. Young adults from all walks of life. This time we're looking for people who really have something special about them."

Kenneth lets out an unintentional snort. This time? Thanks.

"Thirty people," continues Stefan, "will get through the first stage, and from there they'll have access to a three-month diet and exercise programme crafted by my very own right-hand man, Ian Stockwell. We're then going to narrow it down to a final five."

"Sounds great." Jenny nods. "And Kenneth, how do you feel about these new influencers? Not worried that they'll move in on your turf?"

She laughs.

Stefan laughs.

It's all so fucking hilarious this interview business, isn't it? Kenneth has to smile to stop himself from murdering everyone present. "No," he says, hoping his expression atones for the flatness of his voice. "I've been around for a good while. People know me—"

Stefan cuts in. "Kenneth and the others are national treasures."

Kenneth closes his mouth and resumes what he was doing before he was brought into the conversation: counting the hairs on the interviewer's head. Something he does to keep himself looking interested. Every thirty hairs or so he nods or agrees. He's up to 449. Someone just said something about 'national treasures' which usually refers to him. He gives an enthusiastic thumbs up.

Stefan continues. "The new influencers aren't going to be replacing them. We're still keen to find out what happens to the human body as it ages past one hundred. We're just looking for the next generation."

"Well, it's definitely true that Britain, and indeed the world, has been seeing more and more people reach their centenary year," Jenny says. "Did you know in the last ten years alone the age of retirement in this country has been pushed back fifteen years? People are healthier and happier to work long into their eighties."

Kenneth snorts again. He's recently had a death threat from a man that very age, furious that his retirement had been pushed back another five years.

Ignoring his interjection, Jenny continues. "And that is thanks to the work Di Blasio has done over the last fifty years."

"Thank you Jenny. We are proud of what we've achieved. My father and I have always wanted something more from life. We strive to push the boundaries of human existence and endeavour. To find that thing we all feel we're missing, and we think we're coming close."

"That sounds important. What do you mean?"

"We've noticed chemical triggers in our influencers that have never before been recorded in a human being. It points to some sort of clock. And we believe it's counting down."

Jenny leans forward, clearly interested, and not just professionally. "To what?"

"Probably my death," says Kenneth without a smile.

"Oh Kenneth." Stefan laughs again. "We don't know. I'm as excited to find out as you are. I promise as soon as we know we'll come back on the show and tell you all about it."

The Dream

It's like a dream, but different, bigger. Kenneth can see everything he's ever done in his long life stretching in front of him. His memories flow together, reduced to a mixture of feelings and sensory information, concentrated and archived like a defragmented hard drive.

All around him bright pinks, oranges, and blues explode and implode like supernovas containing hundreds of stars. Each star a memory, a moment.

He is suspended in the void, but it's more than that. The void is him, and all that lies beyond, also him. He is everything, omnipresent, the universe. It's not an unpleasant sensation. Warm. Comfortable. No thought of danger. All is calm inside.

Inside what though?

There's something he can't quite remember. A reason he is here. But every time he tries to concentrate, something else takes his focus, and the thought flits away like blurs and trails of colour within vision that has glimpsed the sun.

He can't move. He has nothing to move. His body simply isn't there. He knows if he concentrates on the feeling for too long, that his shoulders – phantoms that may have never existed – will begin to itch, and his legs will want to wriggle and move. The sensation threatens to drive him mad. But it's easy to move on and forget.

Forget what?

Memories distill:

The sound of his mother's voice calling him home for dinner after a day's play on the old road where he'd lived as a boy.

The songs she sang with her own made-up verses and lines because she was too preoccupied with the joy of singing, to learn the real words.

His time in the trenches, caked in mud, wet, cold. Tired. Stinking. Never being able to close his eyes for fear that the Nazis could come over the top at any moment.

The start of his life with Di Blasio. The TV shows, the flashing cameras, the crowds. The exercise, the food, the glamorous celebrity he became. Someone he never wanted to be.

Victoria. Her beautiful smile.

The desperate loss he felt when she left without a word and never returned.

His life spreads out in front of him like a meal, and he knows he can take a bite of any moment he chooses. But he is reluctant to.

The two parts of his life are opposite ends of a magnet. One repels. The other attracts. It surprises him to find which is which. His childhood was so interesting, filled with ups and downs, new experiences and learning. His later life, a steady straight of joyless preservation.

What good was it to live if all you did was prolong your existence?

As quickly as the question comes it is drawn away, replaced by clear, mindful energy. He half expects to see a God or some other form of supernatural intelligence, but in the end there is only him.

Kenneth sees himself, the way he has been for the last sixty years.

Alone.

The Dawn

Maggie heads home before she goes to the office. She just needs five minutes of peace to get her story straight. Also, she knows that if she turns up in Korrigan's rain mac, which makes her look like a giant black packet of crisps, no one will take her story about a secret kidnap plot, shape-shifting lizards, and eight-foot ninjas seriously.

She hopes Nige and the guys can find somewhere safe to go while she talks to Stefan Di Blasio. She calls his assistant to check he's in.

"He came back about an hour after we found out Kenneth had been kidnapped," Duncan says. His voice as near to a dry croak as it can be whilst still being able to enunciate words. "If he had hair, he'd have pulled it all out by now. I must have made him eight cappuccinos already. Where have you been? I've been trying to reach you all night." He lowers his voice. Maggie pictures him bent over the phone with a hand covering his mouth. "I think he's a little suspicious of you to be honest."

"I had a family emergency," she says. An unquestionable excuse. "Give me a couple of hours and I'll be in."

Though she doesn't want to admit it, she's worried about what Stefan will say. Will he believe her? Will he want to help them? What will happen to her if he doesn't? What if he already knows what's happened to Kenneth? She wants to put off going in for as long as possible, at least until a few extra bodies are in the building to witness her enter.

Nige and the others will be ok holding out for an extra hour or two. It wasn't like anyone else even knew she'd hired them.

When she rocks up at eight, the building is much busier than it usually would be. The tired eyes of all-nighters watch her with envy as she crosses the reception and heads into an elevator.

Stefan's office is on the top floor. When the lift opens, Duncan is behind the reception desk. Despite the pallor of his face, which is a graveyard grey, he is, as always, dressed impeccably. Hair combed into a neat side parting. Tie fit snug under his chin and a slim fitting light grey suit.

"Thank God you're here." Duncan looks at her with tired, sagging eyes.

"Jeez Duncs. How long have you been here?" she leans on the desk.

"I haven't been home since I got in yesterday morning at seven. A new record." He taps the intercom. "Mr Di Blasio, Maggie's arrived. Shall I send her in?"

The little speaker hisses. "About bloody time. Where the hell has she be—"

He releases his finger. His mouth tightens at the edges. "Good luck."

She smiles nervously and makes her way inside.

Stefan's office is roughly the size of a tennis court and decorated more like a bachelor's man cave than a place of work. A large mahogany desk stands in the middle of the room, backed by an antique green leather chair. The leather is real and the chair alone costs tens of thousands. The walls are black painted mock brick, and the light fittings are all a fancy shade of tarnished bronze.

A door in the corner of the room, decorated with the same bronze and matt black scheme, leads to an elevator, which Stefan uses to travel to the basement level of the building where the research facilities and labs are situated.

Behind the desk, a fire roars. It's not real. A one-of-a-kind procedurally generated fireplace that can be turned up and down with a dial. The heat from the screen perfectly matches the direction and intensity of the computer-generated flames.

Standing before it, with one arm resting on the solid dark wood mantle, his features glowing orange, is Stefan Di Blasio. In his hand he holds a mug that reads, 'World's Best Boss'. A bit of a stretch. She expects he bought it for himself, or at least asked Duncan to get it.

He's fifty-five but doesn't look a day over thirty. He's been taking his own medicine since before Maggie started working for the company.

Above the fireplace is a television. A muted newsreader speaks. Behind her is the picture of Nige and Aidan from the wanted ads that she expects still cover the capital. Scrolling text at the bottom reads 'Kenneth Kidnapped'.

He spots her looking at it. "Why is it never good news?"

She shrugs and crosses the room towards him.

"I've had Duncan trying to reach you all night."

"I'm sorry, Stefan." How should she begin? Her date with Ian? It's against company policy to date other employees. But as Ian is Stefan's second in command it might mean less trouble. Equally, it might mean more. "I was on a date and then I—"

"A date?" He raises his eyebrows and purses his lips. Doesn't look at her. He doesn't seem angry, just disappointed. Which is always worse. His eyes lift to her face. "Three nights before Kenneth's birthday show, three nights before we show our brand-new influencers off to the world. Not the best time to go on a date, is it?" He wags a finger. "You know sales are starting to slow and public opinion of the influencers is dropping. The future of this company is riding on this weekend."

Funny, he says that a lot, as if somehow a billion-pound company will suddenly go bust if they don't maintain astronomical sales. As if preserving the status quo can only be seen as a failure.

She bites her lip. How will he take the news that she's been with Kenneth the whole time?

Before she can speak again, he opens a desk drawer and pulls out an unopened bottle of whiskey. "You look like you could do with a drink."

She expects she does. "It's a bit early f—"

"I insist."

He cracks the seal and pours some into the empty water glass on his desk. He holds it out to her. She takes it.

He adds some to his own mug. Downs it. Pours another. Looks at her. He's holding something back. Why hasn't he asked about Kenneth yet? Does he know?

She takes a tentative sip. The whiskey tastes of smoke and fire. The drop of amber liquid bites. She coughs, garnering a disappointed look from her boss.

She clears her throat, then takes a bigger gulp for courage. He maintains his silence making it impossible for her not to fill the gap in the conversation.

"I need to tell you something." She hesitates. The bottom of her stomach feels like it's going to drop out. "I know where Kenneth is."

He holds up a hand. "Let me stop you before you get yourself in to a tizzy," he says, cutting in. She hates that word. Tizzy. It's so condescending. "I've spoken to Ian," he continues. "He's told me all about your romantic evening and the extra security you hired in to watch Kenneth." He pauses. "But how do you know where Kenneth is now?"

"I've been with him. They have him safe in a warehouse by the docks." She hopes she's not making a mistake by telling him. "We didn't call because we didn't know who we could trust. I wanted to come straight to you personally."

Stefan nods to himself. "That's a smart move. But you see, that's not what Jeff told Ian. He said your boys beat them up and kidnapped Kenneth right from under their noses. Then, when they got away, they sent in assassins to take care of anyone left alive. Jeff was lucky to escape. I think he may be on the warpath. Ian's trying to keep a handle on it."

She shakes here head. "They thought Jeff was kidnapping Kenneth. The assassins aren't with them."

He raises his eyebrows. "That's what they told you." She can't tell if it's a statement or a question.

"Nige and Aidan were just trying to look after Kenneth."

"Nige and Aidan…" he says, slipping a piece of paper from a tray beneath his desk, "… of Korrigan and Davies Security? The same Korrigan and Davies security that organised the bouncers at the club where The Twins were working tonight." His eyebrow twitches, and he looks nonchalantly into his mug. Gives the whiskey a swirl. "Have you heard what happened there?"

Her heart starts to race. And it's either the drink or her nerves, but her stomach rolls. "No."

He looks back up at her. "Murdered in some back alley in Camden. Stabbed to death with their entire team." He says it with the cold indifference he's known for.

Maggie puts a hand to her lips. How could something like this happen? And why is she only finding out now? It should have been all over the news. "Why isn't anyone talking about it?"

"The press don't know. Just us, and the police, and they'll keep it under wraps for as long as we need them to. Heaven knows we pay them enough. I don't want it getting out unless we can control the spin. And The Twins weren't the first. We had some trouble at Terrence's home last week. He's dead too. His security team, wiped out." He places his mug on the desk. "It's spooked some of the security guys."

At first she can't speak. She doesn't know how to take it. She'd had no idea. How can he be so calm? So cold? "Spooked? Your influencers are dead."

He holds up a hand once more. "We have new influencers. The main problem has been the loss of security. Those people have families and those families have been asking questions." He looks at her suspiciously. "It seems a little coincidental that the guys you hired were working with both The Twins and Kenneth, don't you think? Ian has looked into whether they have any connections within the company and he's come back with a name. Lewis Davies."

Nige had mentioned his son Lewis at the restaurant. "That's Nigel Davies's son." But it doesn't make sense. Nige and the others were so genuine.

She's lost for words. Had they been tricking her the entire time? But why had they let her go? Unless Nigel and the others didn't know. She puts a hand to her head. Trying to puzzle it out.

Either way Kenneth is in danger where he is. Maggie fumbles her phone. "They are at a warehouse at the docks. I can give you the location. They are all together now. And those cultists are there too. The ones from the TV."

"That confirms Ian's suspicions. They're all working together."

She shakes her head. The confrontation earlier can't have just been for her benefit. "I don't think so."

He shrugs. "Either way, Jeff left hours ago following a tracker they attached to Kenneth's wrist. It's being dealt with. They'll be back with Kenny shortly. But you really should have come forward sooner."

She lets herself fall into the chair opposite. The seat is a few inches shorter than his. "I know. I know. I'm sorry. But Stefan, Kenneth's kidnap isn't the only thing that's happened to him tonight."

Stefan leans his head to one side, his gaze suddenly more intent on her. "Go on."

"I don't know how to describe it. He's changed..."

With those words he appears to stop listening to her. His eyes glaze as if he's coming to a decision. His lips twitch. He forces back a smile. "I want to show you something."

He heads towards his elevator.

"But what about Kenneth?" She follows. "He's in danger."

He touches a hand to his chest as he enters the lift. "There's nothing I can do about it. When you've been in high stakes business as long as I have, you learn to let go of the things you can't control and embrace those you can." She steps in to stand behind him. "It's not all bad news. What better way to kick off the careers of the new influencers than with a memorial show for the last ones. It shouldn't affect it too much if Kenneth is there or not."

She tries to hide her disgust as the lift descends, but knows if he turned to look at her, then he'd see how horrified she is at what he's saying.

"You have to work with what you've got," he continues. "PR has already got the ball rolling to replace Saturday's show if it comes to it. It'll be a little rushed, but I'm sure the public will forgive us considering the circumstances and the timescale."

"These were your friends. Your dad's life's work." She shakes her head.

"We all deal with grief in our own way, Maggie. Some like to sulk, some like to break down. I build. And that's exactly what I'm doing. We've got another major announcement to make. It's going to knock anything we've ever done out of the park."

"And what's that?" He knows. He knows what's happened to Kenneth. She looks around the elevator as if for an escape route. What's he taking her to see?

"You'll see." He smiles, clearly excited.

She shrinks to the back of the lift. "What's happened to Kenneth?"

He turns to her, an unnerving grin on his face. "It's better if I show you," he says.

The elevator comes to a stop and the doors open. A corridor runs to the left and right. Ahead, through large oval-shaped windows, are the labs where the influencers are tested and their schedules and dietary regimes perfected. She doesn't come down here much. It seems darker than the last time. More oppressive.

"We hoped it would happen to Kenneth sooner or later," he says, stepping out and turning left.

"What do you mean?" she has to jog to keep up with his stride. "You already know?"

"What do you think we've got down here? We've known for a while something was going to happen to all the influencers."

Nige had said something about Dawn being taken to the labs. "Is it Dawn?"

Without stopping, he glances back, that smile having crept higher. "Just wait."

Despite the early morning hour, the labs they pass are all empty. Usually techs and scientists would be flitting around, busy with tablets and experiments. But not today. It's as if the scientists just upped and left in the middle of their work. There's only one lit window at the end of the confined corridor.

She suddenly feels very alone.

"It's amazing, really." Stefan stops at the window, his face illuminated by the light. "I don't think in all his years of experiments my father would have ever imagined something like this."

When she catches up with him and sees what he's looking at she gasps.

Though she has never before seen anything like what lies beyond, somehow she knows exactly what it is. It is like a puzzle piece, that at anything other than the perfect rotation makes absolutely no sense, but when slotted in correctly, perfects an artwork in a way never before imagined.

Inside the lab, several scientists crowd around a human form beneath an array of UV lamps in the middle of the room,

It is Dawn.

But then it isn't.

She lounges like Cleopatra fanned by palm leaves. Her dark skin has a metallic sheen like a beetle back or petrol on water. Her face has changed too. Her features are sharpened, elf-like. Her limbs slim, angular, and strong. At nearly eight feet tall, she dwarfs the scientists that work around her.

But that's not what takes Maggie's breath away.

That's not what makes her drop her phone, causing it to crack on the grated metal flooring. Or the reason that she is hesitant to enter as Stefan beckons her to follow him inside to see more closely.

What stops Maggie in her tracks, are Dawn's wings.

The Boat Shed

Nige takes them to his safe space. A boat shed on the same estate. It's a secret even to Korrigan.

He hasn't moved in officially. Still keeps his and Fiona's old house to maintain appearances with Lewis. Rents it out sometimes on Airbnb to cover the boat shed costs. Since she passed, he hasn't spent much time there. He can get breakfast and lunch from the estate cafe, has a small stove and a cupboard of cans for dinner, and a foldout bed. It's not comfortable, but he doesn't seem to sleep much anymore, anyway.

He has a fridge, a chair where he keeps most of his clothes, and an old grey sofa from home. The room smells of sweet sawdust with an underlying bite of adhesive. Wood shavings and splotches of brown varnish cover the concrete floor.

He lays Kenneth on the sofa. It's stained and the cushions are floppy and useless, beaten to death by Lewis jumping all over them, but Nige likes it. You can read a happy home in the wear and tear of a good sofa. He tries a smile. It doesn't catch.

Mac follows him inside, while the cultists remain by the door on lookout.

"Is this your yacht?" Mac inspects Nige father's boat which takes up almost the entirety of the space.

The smooth white hull glows faintly in the pale light from the skylights above. A long silver mast hangs fixed to one wall and the rigging fills rows of hooks below.

"It's not a yacht." Nige is quick to correct him. "It's basically just a seaworthy caravan."

"Sam's Pathfinder," says Mac, reading the words painted along the side. "That's a cool name."

"My Granddad was Sam. It was my dad's boat. Bit of a wreck when the boys at his old sailing club found it adrift, so I've been doing it up." Nige flicks on the three hooded halogen lamps that hang from the ceiling pushing the shadows to the corners of the room.

"Adrift?"

"Uh huh. Dad went out one day and never came back. They found the boat. Never found him. Overboard they reckon."

"I'm sorry."

Nige shrugs. "That was nearly five years ago. I had planned to sail it one day."

"*Had* planned?" Mac rests a hand on the hull. It shines under the lights.

"Until my wife died."

"I'm going to stop asking questions about the boat now." Mac tightens his mouth into a sympathetic smile.

Nige fills a kettle. "You're the other guy from the wanted poster, aren't you?" He studies Mac carefully. He doesn't look dangerous.

"The what?" Mac's eyes widen. He fumbles through his pockets, taking out his phone. Scrolls for a moment, then slaps a hand to his brow. "Oh, that's ruddy brilliant." He turns the screen around to show Nige.

Nige squints. "I can't see what that is. Some sort of list?"

"I'm number one on the bounty app. Every hunter in the city is going to be after me." He pauses a moment. "I wonder if they'd pay me if I stuck a bracelet on myself." Shakes his head. "Nope. Ridiculous. Oh, and you're number two, and those two," he points at the cultists, "are in tonight's top ten. We're officially London's most wanted." For a moment he nods to himself proudly, before the realisation of what that means slaps him across the face.

"What did you do?"

"Broke into an under 18s night. Witnessed a murder. Almost got killed. You?"

"Saved Kenneth Bailey. Lost some friends. Almost got killed." Nige's grits his teeth. "That under 18s night wasn't The Electric Ballroom in Camden, was it? I was supposed to be working there tonight."

Mac nods. "Looks like we have a few things in common." He looks towards the sofa. "You said that was Kenneth Bailey. Do you mean *the*

Kenneth Bailey?"

"I do."

"Maybe you should explain. We might know something that could help each other."

They trade stories as Nige makes the tea. Mac tells of his dealings with Suzy Wheeler, the murder of The Twins, and the chase from his office. Nige covers his booking to look after Kenneth, then the influencer's subsequent binge and transformation.

"Well, I've never seen anything like it." Mac hovers over the sofa, inspecting the... well, the *thing*. "Do you have any idea what's happened to him?"

"I overheard some Di Blasio security talking. They said something weird happened to Dawn. Maybe this is similar. Maybe it's happening to all the Di Blasio influencers."

"It didn't happen to The Twins. The Twins were chopped to bits. And Terrence," he nods to Kenneth, "maybe, but I think probably chopped to bits too."

"But why?" Nige remembers what Lewis had said on the phone regarding the new influencers. "Pretty convenient that it's all happening a few days before the new Di Blasio influencers are introduced, don't you think?"

Mac taps his chin for a moment in careful thought. "I can't see why Di Blasio would murder their old influencers just to clear them out of the way for the new ones. No. I think that the timing is a coincidence. This..." he says reaching out to touch Kenneth, then recoiling, "...this is the reason they are killing the influencers."

"You think someone is trying to stop this from happening?"

Mac nods. "Probably to hide it from the public."

Nige thinks back to what Esther and Dom had said in the corridor. "The guards I overheard said that what had happened to Dawn might have been the food."

"I eat Di Blasio food all the time and I've never turned into a giant flaccid penis." Mac looks serious. "But it's strange. I get this weird feeling in my gut that this happening to Kenneth is right, you know? Like it's right that I have a beating heart and a thinking brain. Right, like I was born and I will die. That thing is exactly what is supposed to happen. I can almost smell it."

Nige passes him a steaming mug of tea then looks at Kenneth. From the moment he'd seen him in the bathroom, he'd felt there was nothing wrong with what had happened to the influencer. Like he'd forgotten that this sort of thing happened all the time. It was a strange feeling, almost as if a memory had been implanted in his head. Or alternatively, some mental barrier had been stripped away.

"I think I know what you mean." He lifts his clothes from the small wooden dining chair placed against the wall and drops them on the rough concrete floor. He sits.

"And what about them?" Mac jerks his head toward the door where the cultists are engaging in a whispery skulk.

"They wanted to kill Kenneth. Think he's some kind of demon. Had us all at gunpoint."

"Do they really have a bomb?"

"They haven't mentioned it. They seem to have some cool gadgets…" He leans forward and raises a hand to his mouth. "But I don't think they are the sharpest knives in the drawer. They seem a little young."

Nige studies the pair. There's a family resemblance. They could be brothers. Dave notices his gaze and hushes Pete. They stiffen like challenged gorillas.

He raises an eyebrow and leans closer to Mac. "They seem to have calmed down a bit since those winged devils arrived. With everything else gone to hell, I guess they know now they were right. It's just the demons didn't turn out to be the ones they suspected." He rubs his eyes with the heels of his hands. His migraine is returning.

Mac nods. "Demons is a good word."

"If your story is accurate, those demons must be the ones that killed The Twins. But what are they?"

"At first I thought they were with you." Mac nods at Nige. "The bouncer at the club had a Korrigan and Davies top on. That's why I'm here. But now I have no idea."

"Those doormen at the club were new. We only interviewed them last week. Aidan and I were set to do the gig, but then we got the job working for Kenneth so they were our only options. Could that mean something? They infiltrated our firm so they could get to The Twins?"

"And you said Kenneth's manager hired you but didn't let the Di Blasio security know?"

A little light comes on in Nige's brain. "You don't think she booked us to get us out the way so the new guys could take our place? She said she was going on a date."

"Sounds fishy to me. And you said she buggered off before it all kicked off. If you were to ask me, and you should because I'm a professional –" Mac takes a deep breath. "– I'd say Maggie hired you so that there would be available slots at the club for her guys to get in there and make sure The Twins were in the perfect position to be assassinated, further putting you and your colleague in a position to become scapegoats for the attack on Kenneth, negating any blame herself and allowing her to have an alibi. I doubt very much that she was even on a date."

Nige scrunches up his nose and takes a sip of his tea. "It definitely sounds right. But why did she come and find us at the restaurant if she wanted an alibi?"

"Beats me. Maybe to delay you while the Di Blasio team showed up?"

"Uh. All this is hurting my head." Nige blinks several times. His head feels fuzzy, like hundreds of flies are trapped inside. "We'll put the idea that Maggie's in on it out there, but it still doesn't answer who or what those tall ninjas are. Or why what's happened to Kenneth might make them want to kill him and the other biggest celebrities on the planet."

Mac squishes his nose down with a finger. He touches his face a lot which Nige knows is a sign of anxiety. Fair enough considering what he's been through. "If they aren't with the cultists, and they aren't with Di Blasio, then... um."

"You have a bigger player to worry about."

The voice comes from high in the rafters. At the sudden sound, the cultists spring their weapons in the direction of the ceiling.

Golden, early morning light trickles through an open skylight. It sparsely illuminates a tall figure crouched on one of the thick iron beams that support the roof.

Nige snarls. "Who are you?" He stands and points. "Come down here and face me."

"Please. I mean you no harm." The voice is female. Something flickers behind her. The tips of translucent wings highlighted silver by the slowly rising sun. "I assume you think of me like the others. I'm not one of them." Most of her body remains in shadow.

"Who are you then?"

"I'll come down. Maybe that will help explain." With the graceful precision of a trained dancer, she steps off the beam and floats to the deck of the boat.

When she descends into view, Nige isn't sure what he's looking at. Somehow it looks familiar, but if you had described it to him before tonight, without a picture, then he would have imagined something entirely alien.

Instead, she seems to be the most natural thing in the world. Something he's seen a thousand times, somewhere in the moment between being asleep and awake. That second where the room comes into focus, but you're still living in your subconscious.

She is the answer to a riddle asked long ago. One you've given up on ever solving that still nags at you when you are alone and life is quiet. She radiates an almost holy aura.

If the cultists are right about the existence of angels, then she is surely one.

Large, graceful wings, decorated with intricate swirls and shapes of green, gold, and black, flick noiselessly behind her as she lands. Ringed circles at each peak stare like unblinking eyes.

The majesty entrances him and Nige suddenly feels heavy, hypnotised.

Pete splutters and drops his gun. "An Angel, Dave. An Angel."

The cultists fall to their knees.

The angel's eyes sparkle golden green. A face, so very nearly human, though angular and rigid. Her chin comes almost to a point. Her skin gleams like her eyes, with a metallic green that shimmers as she moves her head from side to side, taking in the room.

She locks her gaze on Nige. He realises he's pouring tea all over his boot. She wears a red polka-dot dress, like those worn by women in the 50s. Her long white hair is tied up with a matching bow.

She is so delicate, elegant, poised.

"She's come to save us." Dave's voice rings high.

At this, the angel's eyes flash like magnesium on fire. "You," she says and raises an open hand towards the cultists.

Nige can feel that strange sizzle behind his eyes again. The same thing he'd felt in the shop and back at Kenneth's apartment before Aidan had been thrown. A pressure like the air itself is taking a breath. He can see her body tensing. He thinks he knows what's about to happen.

"Wait," he shouts, waving his hands in the air. "They're with us."

She lowers her hand, and the heavy weight in the room lightens.

"That was you in Kenneth's apartment," he says. "And you in the shop. You're Victoria."

"They were pointing guns at Kenneth," she says. She wags a finger at Dave and Pete, who grovel like worms before her. "Who do you think you are, hm? If you've harmed so much as a hair on his head, I will beat you both to within an inch of your lives."

The two of them whimper and whither, their noses practically buried in the sawdust covered concrete.

She turns her attention back to Nige.

"You're correct," she says. "Victoria Desdemona at your service." She nods towards the sofa. "Is that him? Is that my Kenneth?" Her face softens.

Nige stares back. He doesn't know what to say. Mac stares, equally dumbstruck.

"I'd hoped to have been here before it started so I could tell him it would be ok, but I was too late. At least I got to see him in his room one last time before his change began."

"What's happened to him?" Nige's voice is hoarse, low. He moves to Kenneth's side, just in case. "What are you?" A part of him thinks he already knows the answer.

She hops down from the deck of the boat to ground level. Her dress billows ever so slightly. The tips of her wings flick and fold against her back.

"He's entered his chrysalis."

"Chrysalis?" say Nige and Mac simultaneously.

"What's a chrysalis?" Pete looks up from the floor.

"Did he get enough to eat before he went in?" she says, ignoring the cultist. "You were with him."

"I'll say. He smashed a whole pizza buffet."

She moves to stroke the thick skin covering Kenneth's body. Nige steps forward protectively.

"It's ok. I won't harm him." She smiles, which for a moment, seems to push back the gloom in the old boat shed. "You know my name. How do you know who I am?"

Nige shakes his hands loose, realising he's balled them into fists. "Those things that attacked us were asking after you."

"So they know I'm here too?"

"Who are they?" Mac cuts in, approaching her.

"I'll start with me. Then we'll move on to them. You may want to take a seat."

Nige returns to his chair and Mac climbs up to the deck of the boat, sitting so that his legs dangle over the side. The cultists remain on the floor, and continue their woeful grovelling.

"I was one of the first Di Blasio influencers," Victoria begins. "Back when they didn't really know what they were doing. There were others before me. The failed experiments. Few survived the earlier processes."

"What processes?" Nige leans forward, resting his elbows on his knees.

"Cryogenics. DNA correction. The organ scrubbing. They used to cut men and women open for maintenance and cleaning. Most died, the rest went insane. Once you'd signed your life away, they could do what they wanted with you. They preyed on the suicidal, the homeless, those who had nothing to lose, and promised them everything. That was me and Kenneth."

Nige looks down at Kenneth's form. He'd known nothing of his past.

"I was one of the lucky ones. I managed to get away. I settled in Tibet, and once there I just tried to survive on my own. Sixty years out there alone then – poof – this happens." She ruffles her wings. They make the sound of leaves blowing in an autumn wind. "I thought all those procedures had somehow mutated me, but I'm told this is perfectly normal."

Nige looks at the chrysalis. At some point it has begun pulsating slowly. "Is that what's happening to him?"

She nods. "It's another stage of human development."

Nige frowns, unable to get over how unsurprised he is. "I thought as much. I don't know how I know, but it seems completely natural." He looks at Mac hoping for a sign that he's not going mad, but the PI can't take his eyes off her.

"It is." Victoria holds out her arms, letting her wings extend out and up. "This is what all of us are meant to become. But we were made to forget."

Nige sniffs. "Are you telling me I could become a giant butterfly if I just ate right?"

"Just look at her." Mac's voice comes out in an awed whisper. "Is it so hard to believe?"

Nige strokes his stubble. It should be, it really should be, but it's not. He doesn't understand what's going on inside his brain, but seeing Victoria, and knowing what is happening to Kenneth, makes him feel like his mind has been opened. He shakes his head. "But why doesn't this happen to everyone?"

"It could, but for some people it's easier." Victoria puts a hand to her breast. "For me, due to what Di Blasio put me through, my life span was extended to way beyond the average, and as I was the eldest of the influencers, I was the first to change."

"And what are the other ways?" Mac stands on the boat hull inspecting an old lamp attached to the underside of the boom. Nige has always thought it strange. There's no way of turning it on inside the boat, and the bulb inside is blue. There's a sensor attached, which suggests it comes on remotely.

"Some are just lucky."

"Lucky how?"

"Genetics. There are a few bloodlines that are predisposed to reach the stage earlier, at around one hundred years old. There aren't so many of these families left. They are hunted by another group."

"Those guys in black?" says Mac.

She nods.

Nige clears his throat. "Who are they? We killed a few at the warehouse, but we saw others at Kenneth's apartment."

Victoria's eyes widen. "You killed some? I'm impressed."

"We had our own losses." He toes the ground with his foot.

"I'm sorry." She looks at him with a maternal care that surprises him. "But if you came into contact with The Guardians, the fact that any of you lived is quite something."

"Who are they?" Mac says and hops down from the boat.

"An ancient group, thousands of years old." She responds quickly. "They believe only the chosen should reach the Age of Emergence. They are cruel, and ruthless. They've been here since the dawn of man. They are the ones who helped us forget this was possible. Scrubbed entire societies off the face of the planet to hide this secret. And now they are after you because you know."

"What makes them different? Are they born this way?" says Mac.

"No one is born this way." Her face tenses as she pauses. "They frighten and hurt children. Use their blood to extend their lives." She shakes her head.

Mac's mouth hangs open. "And this goes on all over the world?"

She nods. "But it takes its toll. Their transformation doesn't work the same way as others do. I guess it's a chemical thing. They have to continue to feed even after they've changed. They knew the influencers were coming close to the change. Maybe someone clued them in on it. That's why they killed them. If they are the only ones with this power, then they have the control."

Nige says nothing. All he can think about are his grandchildren, Charlie and Katy. He needs to phone Lewis, check they are safe.

"They've designed the world we live in so no one can change by accident," Victoria continues. "They control the production of food so it poisons us. They engineered human life to be desk bound. They spread misinformation about what's healthy and what's not, so no one can truly know what's needed for a human body to sustain itself. They push us both to destroy the environment and fight for it. They distract and constrain, divide and conquer. But in their arrogance they allowed Di Blasio to push the boundaries of life expectancy, never expecting it to work. And ever since, have been sowing the seed that everything the company does is a lie, a conspiracy." She looks between them. "The people of the world are misguided then divided, while The Guardians live out whatever sick fantasies they want without fear of repercussion. They've engineered everything to work for them, and the masses plough on, bickering amongst themselves, not understanding the bigger picture."

"But why now? How come you and The Guardians are all here now?" Nige moves to poke Pete with his toe. "You. How did you know this was going to happen tonight?"

Pete looks up from the floor. Tears glint on his cheeks. "Dad just told us to come get Kenneth and—"

"Shut up." His brother elbows him in the ribs but he doesn't seem to have much enthusiasm for it anymore. "You'll get him in trouble."

Nige takes hold of Pete's arm and lifts him to his feet. Dave watches without taking a breath. "What did your dad say?"

"He just said that the angel –" his eyes swivel to the winged woman "– was to be avenged before Saturday. Kenneth and the whole of Di Blasio were in collusion with demons, and we had to kill him to make sure they didn't hurt anyone else."

Dave stands and brushes his robe down. "We were supposed to do it before Kenneth's birthday, to halt the sacrifice, but we couldn't even get that right."

"Angel," says Pete, not daring to look at Victoria, focusing on the ground instead, hands held in front of him like a chastised schoolboy. "We're sorry. We thought this was what you wanted."

Victoria sighs and cocks her head to one side. She doesn't look so intimidating anymore. "Kenneth is a good man. The company has an unbreakable hold on him and the others. If they breach their contracts, they lose everything. It happened to me. You hadn't heard of me but I was just like them." She smiles at Pete. "What your dad said about Di Blasio is right. But you can't stop them on your own. You'll need help."

"That's why we did the broadcast with the bomb. We were sending a message. Trying to start an uprising."

"Is it real?" Mac brushes a hand down the side of the boat, then rubs his fingers together. "The bomb."

Dave shakes his head. "It's just an old propane tank done up with cardboard to look like one."

There's a pause in which no one says anything.

"I think I need another cup of tea." Mac stands and moves towards the kettle.

Nige's mouth hangs slightly open. "I need to call my son."

He steps to the back of the room and dials Lewis's number. Each ring cuts deeper and deeper. It goes to answer phone. It's still early. The mornings are often busy for them. He texts: *Call me as soon as you get this*, then returns to the others.

"If people knew that there was so much more to life, that would change everything," says Victoria. "If they knew they could have more time, they wouldn't get so swept up in this hustle and bustle of modern life. We have to tell people."

"But how could that possibly work?" Mac says. "People would still need their jobs. They'd have to work to eat. Everyone would still be super depressed."

Victoria looks at him. "It's all a trap and hearing you say that proves that you don't even know you're caught in it. Why do you think The Guardians have created this society of depression? If you're depressed, you're lethargic. If you're lethargic, you can't resist."

"Not everyone's depressed." Nige shakes his head. At least he isn't.

Mac laughs. "Oh, says the guy who lives on his own in his boat shed."

"Shut it you." He shakes a fist.

Mac's mouth tightens into an apologetic smile. "Sorry, I've had a dreadful night. I'm tired."

Pete holds a finger up tentatively.

Nige ignores the cultist. He can't help but rise to Mac, letting his emotions get the better of him. "You think you've had a bad night? Two of my best mates were killed not five hours ago. Murdered by some world owning super power that no one's ever heard of. How the hell do I react to that?" His jaw aches. He's been grinding his teeth. He holds up his phone. "And now I'm shitting myself that some butterfly man is going to go after my grandkids."

Again, Pete stretches his hand, further into the air this time and clicks his tongue.

"But how does this help us?" Mac gestures with his hand, indicating the group. "If your Guardians know we know about Kenneth, then we're as good as dead already. I barely escaped them when I first saw them in the alley. And if it wasn't for these two demon slayers, then we'd have been sliced to bits back at the warehouse. What the hell can we do against a world order?"

Nige ponders for a moment. "I hate to say it, but might Stefan Di Blasio still be able to help us? If he finds out these Guardians are killing off his influencers, ruining his business, he might want to help us get the word out, and we know he has the means to do it."

Pete jiggles on the spot. "Um."

"But what if he's one of them? An evil overlord and Maggie is just his underling?" Mac says.

Nige contemplates that. "I don't see why he would risk everything he's built for a shot at longer life when he has the secret to it, anyway? That wouldn't make sense. I'm sure Maggie is doing this over Di Blasio's head."

"Guardians have familiars," says Victoria. "People who haven't yet gone through the metamorphosis who work for them. I have reason to believe some work within The Di Blasio corporation. Though, being a woman, they'd see Kenneth's manager die before she went through the change. But they could still make her life very comfortable in return for her attaching herself to Kenneth and keeping them abreast of how close he was to his transition."

Pete jiggles more violently. "Excuse—"

"What?" shouts Nige.

"Sorry, but shouldn't we do something about Kenneth's tracker? I don't like to bring it up while we're having such an interesting chat, but it's probably going to ping our location again soon."

Nige frowns. "What tracker?"

"The one you put on his arm. We followed it, the Di Blasio security probably followed it, and if the demons know about it, they'll follow it too."

Nige moves to the chrysalis and rolls it over, tracing a finger over the silk membrane. The join is seamless. He can't even feel the tracker inside where Kenneth's arm should be.

He looks to Victoria. "Can we cut him open? Get it out?"

She jerks her hand forward between Nige and Kenneth. "Oh, no no. You can't. Don't you know what happens to caterpillars?"

He shakes his head.

"He's basically soup in there. Sentient, but still soup. If you cut him open, he'll just seep out all over the floor and die."

"We could use an electro-magnetic pulse to break it," says Pete. "We have a couple at home."

"No." Dave shakes his head and folds his arms. "What are you doing? We can't take them all home to Dad. We'll lead those Guardians right to him."

"The tracker's pretty second rate, so it doesn't ping a location that often. If we go straight home and disable it, they won't know where we are."

Mac steps forward, clicking his fingers. "Wait a second. Wait a second." He points finger guns at Pete and Dave. "You went live on every single channel earlier tonight. How did you do that?"

"Dad did it. Why?"

Mac looks wide-eyed between everyone and turns his palms upward, waiting for them to get it.

Nige squints. "And?"

"When Kenneth's out we go live with him and Victoria on every channel. Put this thing out to the world. Millions of people will see it and know the truth. The Guardians can't kill everyone. It's our only chance of getting out of this. Or we'll be watching our backs forever."

"Of course we have the technology." Dave straightens. "But—"

"So that's settled. We tell the world about Victoria and The Guardians, and show them what's happened to Kenneth." Mac holds back a grin. "Then Nige and I can live out our days known as the heroes who saved the world."

Pete shrugs. "I'm sure that'd be fine."

Mac claps his hands together. "Well, that sounds like a pretty sweet plan I've just come up with." He winks and takes a cocky gulp of his very recently boiled tea, blinks, clearly trying to hide the instant, scorching regret, then heads for the door.

"I'll go hot wire us another truck," he says, with a slight burnt tongue lisp, then mimics pulling a truck horn. "Toot! Toot!"

The Church of The Fallen Angels

They park the truck in the only available spot two streets away from the cultists' home in Camden. Mac knows the area well. It's only a few roads from his office.

The rain has given up, and the sun slowly rises above short, fat blocks of flats.

A gentle breeze rustles the leaves of the sycamores planted every few metres along the pavement.

The streets are empty, and for a fragile moment this corner of the city is quiet.

The cultists lead the way. Nige follows in silence, lost in his own thoughts, with Kenneth flopped over his shoulder. He tried to call his son several more times but couldn't get through. He pushes the worry deep down, trying to ignore it, telling himself they are ok.

Victoria, wrapped in a cloak from wing tip to toe, walks behind with Mac. He batters her with questions much like a teenage boy asking an older friend about girls.

"What's it like?"

"I don't know how to describe it, really. The between time is like a dream, but you are fully aware and able to access all of your memories as if they are right there in front of you. Like picking them out of a box."

"And you can fly right? Those wings aren't just for show?"

"Oh yes."

The conversation peters out as they come to an old church. It stands, crushed awkwardly between two tower blocks that seem to lean away from it like anxious parents either side of their immaculately conceived antichrist child.

Despite the golden morning sunlight that trickles down from the vanilla skies above, the church is bathed in ominous shadow. Long, jagged grass pokes haphazardly through the surrounding rusted wrought-iron fence, and boarded-up windows stare at them like blind eyes.

In one corner of the front garden, a child's play kitchen lies dumped, forgotten. The once brightly coloured plastic is bleached pale, either by the sun or the caustic air which seems to permeate the area around the church.

"Home sweet home," says Pete with a smile. He pushes the gate open. It shrieks like a banshee. Cobwebs glisten with dew between the rusted spikes at its top.

Mac stands, his arms loose at his sides, staring up at the bent cross on the roof. He leans closer to Nige and says in a whisper. "I swear I've been down this road a hundred times before, and I've never seen a creepy abandoned church."

"Creepy church?" Pete frowns. He turns and glances up and down the road as if looking for a different building. Shrugs. "We should probably hurry. There's roughly fifteen minutes between each ping and the last one was on the way here. We have about five more to disable the tracker."

Dave takes a small ring of large keys out of a pocket in his robe, and approaches the door. It is thick, darkly varnished and reinforced with black iron studs. He unlocks it, but before he enters, turns back to the group. "Now, I don't know how Dad will react when he finds out that's Kenneth –" he nods towards Nige's shoulder "– so it might be best not to tell him for a bit."

Inside, the high ceilings echo every scrape of their feet. Tall stone columns make up pointed arches along the left and right side of the nave. Each topped with a stained-glass window boarded from the outside to stop stone throwing teenagers.

A tall golden statue of a winged saint stands to the side, covered in a thick layer of dust. The figure is in armour and clutching a fiery sword.

Wooden pews sit stacked against the right wall, and at the far end, beneath another panelled stained-glass window, and lit by a huge halogen lamp on an industrial base, is a white banner with a picture of an angel. In front is a bullet shaped propane tank painted to look like a warhead. The cultist's "bomb".

In the centre of the room, a large server bank hums quietly to itself. Green, blue, and red LEDs dance on its black surface. The only light is emitted by the halogen, the LEDs, and several computer monitors sitting on a desk next to the server. On the left wall, a few extra robes hang on pegs. Next to the servers is a large oak table. Four chairs occupy the space around its head. More are stacked to the side.

"Dad. We're back." The sound of Dave's voice reverberates around the high ceiling. There isn't a reply. "I'll go get him and we can prepare the initiation. Pete, you sort the EMP."

He hurries off towards an open door through which is a wooden staircase.

"I'm sorry what?" says Mac. "Initiation?"

Dave stops and looks back. Turns a palm to the ceiling and juts his chin as if to say 'of course'. "Like we're just going to let anyone use our tens of thousands of pounds worth of equipment. Only church members can use our stuff."

"And if we want to become church members we have to be initiated?" asks Mac.

"This is great." Pete claps his hands together. "Dad'll be so glad we've got some new recruits. Even more so when he finds out one of them's an actual angel." He swoons.

"Hold ya horses." Dave raises a placating palm and takes a step back towards them. "The initiation ceremony is not for the faint-hearted." Pete gulps audibly before his brother continues. "I can count on the fingers of one hand the amount of people that have gone through it and survived."

"Three you mean?" Nige folds his arms. "You two and your dad?"

"Yes, three." Dave smarms up his cheeks like an aggrieved teen. "But Dad didn't have to take it because he invented it, so shut up."

Nige waves a hand. "What ever it is I'll do it."

"You will," says Dave turning away and continuing through the doorway and up the stairs.

"Nice," says Pete pumping a fist. Then, referring to Kenneth. "We don't have a lot of time. Put him on there." He points to the table, then hurries off to a large transparent plastic box lying along one wall. It's filled with gadgets.

Nige puts Kenneth down.

"Pete, what does this initiation ceremony involve exactly?" he asks.

"I don't know how to tell you, really. It's very sacred." He sifts through the box, throwing assorted circuit boards and electronic bits over his shoulder. The clatters and bangs echo around the high ceiling. He looks up at Nige. "You must best Dad in a physical challenge."

"What, all three of us against him? Won't that be a tad unfair?"

Pete purses his lips and assesses Nige, Victoria and Mac in turn. Then shakes his head. "Not really."

Mac gives Nige a slightly worried eye. Nige doesn't usually get anxious when it comes to confrontation, but he feels a twinge of nerves somewhere deep in his stomach. What does this say about the cult leader? Who is he? And why do his sons think he has a chance against them?

"Disabling the tracker won't hurt him, will it?" Victoria's fingers fidget over the chrysalis as if of their own accord. She notices and moves her hands, gently resting them where Kenneth's shoulder should be.

"Shouldn't think so." Pete looks up. "It's not like a microwave. It won't fry him." He pulls out two black boxes, one small like a matchbox, and one larger, about the size of an iPad. Both have a red button in the centre and a thick coil of wire sticking out of one end. "We'll try the small one first, and if it doesn't work, we'll use the bigger one. It's more powerful," he says, making his way back over. "Can you find the tag?"

"It's in here somewhere." Nige squeezes around the left side of the chrysalis. Now that the scraps of Kenneth's clothing have fallen away, he can't tell whether he's facing up or down.

The tissue is a lot firmer than it was when he'd first found him, like fudge as opposed to caramel, and where he squeezes, he leaves dents which take some time to reform.

With Victoria's help, they quickly find the hard plastic strap. He feels a little sick when he realises the bracelet has floated to the surface and is no longer around an arm.

Pete presses the coil of the smaller EMP device to the fleshy mass and clicks the button a few times. Nothing seems to happen, but he checks another device in his pocket, then nods. "We're not picking him up anymore. That's either completely reset it, or fried a circuit." He puts both devices in an inner pocket of his robe.

Nige looks over the chrysalis. "Great, so we're safe here for now?"

"For now." Victoria places her hands on the table and leans over it like a general inspecting a war map. "But The Guardians are resourceful.

They'll have their familiars out searching for you by day, and then they'll be back on the hunt at night."

"Alright you lot?"

They look up at the sound of an unfamiliar voice.

A man wearing a thick pair of glasses that magnify a set of watery eyes, stands by a doorway at the far end of the room. He's holding a pot noodle and a fork, and wears a robe atop a pair of brown sandals. "I thought I heard voices."

"Alright Terry," says Pete. "What you doing up?"

"Oh, you know, just getting a snack. Your dad wanted me to wait for you to come back, then you didn't, so I've just been playing some games. Who's this? New members?" He moves towards them, stirring his pot as he shuffles along. He has the slow gait of a man that might turn into a sloth by the light of the full moon. His features are very plain. Forgettable. If he was on your opponent's card in a game of 'Guess Who?', you'd lose.

He smiles at Nige and Victoria as if they are old friends.

"Yeah, we're going to initiate them in a minute," says Pete. "Then we're going to do another broadcast."

"Brutal." Terry nods slowly. He pushes a large forkful of noodles into his mouth and chews methodically, eyes on Nige. "You think I can watch? I'd love to see what this big boy can do."

"Don't see why not." Pete shrugs, then holds up a hand. "Send me some noods."

"On yer 'ead." Terry flicks a snarl of noodles from his fork.

Pete catches it, then drops it into his mouth. "Nice one."

Dave enters the room and crosses to his brother. Whispers in his ear. They both look sheepishly at their guests.

"Terry, can you watch them for a moment?" Dave says. "We need to speak to Dad."

Terry nods.

Pete follows his brother back through the door.

Terry glances momentarily at Victoria. "Oh, you've got wings. Hm?" He purses his lips a moment then takes a sip of noodle juice. "Can I get anyone a pot noodle? I've got chicken and mushroom or spare rib."

Mac declines.

Nige raises an eyebrow. "I've always liked spare rib."

"Man after my own heart." Terry waves the hand holding the fork. "I'll brew up an assortment. BRB." He disappears back through the door that he came through.

Victoria moves nearer to Nige. It is the closest they've been and for a moment he is struck again by that strange feeling of knowledge once hidden, as if a pocket in his mind, one that he'd forgotten existed, has opened.

"Can we trust them?" she asks.

His first thought is 'can I trust you?' He checks to make sure Terry is out of earshot before replying. "I think they are as confused as I am. You saw the way they reacted to you. They think you're their god."

"Not that one though - he didn't seem bothered at all." She nods towards where Terry just disappeared.

"Well, he's clearly been huffing paint," says Mac.

Her eyes shift to the picture further down the hall illuminated by the bright halogen. It's not a great drawing, but it looks like a young woman with the usual angelic, feathery wings. "I'm definitely not their angel. Do you think that somehow they already knew the truth about what humans can become?"

Nige shakes his head. "Judging by their general level of intelligence, I think that would be pushing it. I presume it's a coincidence. Their angel isn't you, but they don't know it." He glances sideways at her thinking back to the moments in Kenneth's apartment and the shop. Though she does look a formidable opponent, with her height and wings, she doesn't look strong enough to have thrown Aidan. "What did you do to my friend in the shop and in Kenneth's apartment? You were going to do it again to the cultists in the boat shed." He pauses, not sure how to explain the buzzing sensation. "I felt it in my head."

"It's... a biological weapon."

"But The Guardians didn't use it?"

"Only females have it. It's why they don't want us to change." She sits on the table next to Kenneth's chrysalis and looks at her palm. Then turns it to Nige. In a line across the centre are three white pads that look a little like blisters. "It's like a blast of force. It pushes whatever living thing I aim my hands at back. And quite violently."

"Can you show us?" says Mac.

She looks away, almost shyly. "I wouldn't want to hurt anyone." She knocks her knuckles on the table. "To tell you the truth, I don't even know how to use it properly. I didn't finish my training."

"Training? Who trained you?"

"When I changed, I was on my own in the middle of nowhere. I thought I was dying. I got so hungry, ate everything I had, then woke up a few days later not knowing who or what I was anymore." She smiles. "And then someone found me. Abigail, her name was. This had happened to her, too. Years ago. They call it emergence. She found me the same way I found you at the boat shed. I could sense that Kenneth was with you." She taps her temple. "We women don't just have this weapon, we have a link to others like us, or to those going through the emergence."

"And what happened to her?" Nige feels a rising hope. "Are there others? Maybe they could help us."

Victoria looks down. She brushes her hand over Kenneth's chrysalis. "They were planning a rebellion, but The Guardians found out. They located us. I managed to get away when our home was attacked. And after, I waited and waited at our rendezvous point, but no one else showed."

It seems like every question she answers just invites another. "When did this happen?"

"A few years ago now. I've been watching Kenneth for a while. Waiting."

She sighs as the echo of her words die out.

Pete returns. "OK, Dad is very excited that we've got new recruits, and he's preparing for the initiation. He's so excited he says you don't even have to win." He beckons to them with one hand like an overeager game show host. "Come on down."

Before they have a chance to follow, Terry returns from the kitchen clutching a tray of steaming pots. "Are we starting?" he says. "Don't worry, I can microwave these when we're done." He lowers his head. The hood of his robe casts his face in ominous shadow. "If you survive." He puts the tray next to Kenneth and stops for a moment, as if only just taking in what's lying on the table. "Oh, what's that? A massive sausage?" He sniggers, then his attention snaps back to the others. He claps Nige on the back. "Come on, big boy, let's go. Not sure I've got a robe in your size, but I'll rustle something up."

They follow Pete past the stairs and down another set. They descend for quite some time. The passage is lit only by the occasional naked bulb hanging from the ceiling. After having descended one floor, untreated plasterboard replaces the stone wall of the church.

"Hold on," says Mac. "These stairs lead beneath the flats."

"Well spotted," says Terry from the rear. "The Church owns the block of flats above - nice little rental earner –" he waves an arm as he speaks, the way a flight attendant might indicate exits on a plane "– and over the last decade Alan has extended the church basement into an abandoned section of the Camden catacombs beneath the flats. Eventually this whole bit will be a secret underground training facility." He spreads his fingers in different directions to indicate the growth of the church's subterranean lair.

"Bit dingy, isn't it?" says Mac.

"Oh I don't know. I quite like being underground." Terry smiles happily, then leans forward and sniffs Mac's neck. "Oh, you've been in a bin. We've got showers. You should have one."

Mac wrinkles his nose. "Thanks?"

"No problemo!"

At the bottom of the stairs is a plain wooden door. Its ordinariness makes it feel ominous. Next to it, on the wall, is a metal box roughly fifteen centimetres square.

Pete turns as they reach it. He takes a deep, nervous breath. "Your initiation starts on the other side of this door. I won't lie to you, this will test your endurance like nothing you've ever faced. And," he looks up at Nige and Victoria, "some of you naturally stand a better chance than others." The corners of his mouth stretch out in an apologetic smile as he looks down at Mac. "Sorry. But the most important thing is to have fun and remember it's just an initiation. No one *has* to die. Once we've done this, we can get started on our broadcast."

"Isn't this just wasting time?" Nige says. "Shouldn't we just start? We need to tell the world about The Angel and The Guardians."

Pete leans in. So closely Nige can almost taste what he had for dinner on his breath. "It's the only way Dad will agree to help. We don't get many people over you see, and he likes everything to go through the official channels."

He opens the metal box and takes out a radio handset connected by a curly telephone wire. It fuzzes in his hand and he presses the button. "New initiates coming in, in three, two…" He pushes open the door to reveal a pitch-black room. A musty waft of stale air and waxed wood comes through. "…one."

The Initiation

Nige steps forward into the dark. Victoria and Mac follow reluctantly. Once inside, the door shuts behind them, cutting off all light. The sound of their breath echoes around the hard walls. Nige has the impression they are in a great chamber. And unlike the previous room, the floor has some give as if it is made of a soft wood or resin.

"Hello." He tests his voice. It bounces, returning twisted and warped. He raises his fists ready, but can't see a thing. The other two are close behind.

A deep voice, clearly Pete lowering his pitch, booms over a loudspeaker. "Welcome new initiates to the Church of The Fallen Angels. Are you ready to become The Followers of The New Way, Saviours of Earth's People, Destroyers of Corporate Greed?"

Nige is suddenly blinded as bright light fills the room. The opening riff of 'Twilight Zone' by 2Unlimited slams in at club volume.

"And Slaaaaam Dunk Record Holders of the Seventh Level of Heaven…" Pete's voice resonates around the high ceiling.

As the beat drops in the music, another set of doors at the other end of the room crash open. Dave enters, accompanied by a much older man dressed in baggy basketball shorts which display too much knobbly knee for Nige's liking. They wear team vests in the same burgundy as their robes and both dribble a basketball with each hand. Behind them, Pete enters and drops his robe to reveal a similar uniform. Dave passes a ball to him and he deftly catches it, then spins it on his finger.

Back where Nige entered the room, Terry leans against the wall bopping his head, watching as the three cultists surround the new initiates and perform a series of complicated and, if possible, slightly intimidating basketball tricks.

Nige takes stock of the room. It is an underground sports hall roughly ten metres in height and thirty long. At the far end, half buried in a wall of earth, is a JCB. Its long arm frozen out over the floor with a basketball net attached.

The ceiling is an arch of dirty brown brick.

The cultists break off and head for the net. Each shoots a three pointer with finesse. As they meet back at the penalty spot, the music fades, almost as if the whole thing has been choreographed and practiced to perfection. Dave and the old man stand back-to-back with their arms folded and Pete takes a knee in front of them with his chin rested on his fist. Mac starts a round of enthusiastic applause, which quickly dies when neither Nige nor Victoria join him.

The brothers move to stand side by side with their hands clasped behind their backs. The older man, their father Nige guesses, takes a step forward, looking slightly out of breath, but the deep-set lines around his eyes crinkle with unbridled joy.

"New initiates. Welcome to our church. I'm Alan," he says, removing his glasses to polish them on his vest, before replacing them. "We are proud that you have come to join us in our crusade against the dark forces that hold this world under their influence."

"You know about The Guardians?" says Victoria.

"The Guarda-who?" Alan squints at her, then over her shoulder at Terry, who shrugs. "No, Di Blasio and his devil worshipping influencers." He looks at his sons and scratches his balding head. "Well, I guess they could be seen as guardians of hell or something, maybe?" He beams at Victoria. "You must be the angel that my boys spoke about. Thank you for agreeing to join us. But first…" He takes a remote control out of his pocket and points it at a large blank screen on the wall. He clicks it and two zeros appear under the words 'home' and 'away'. "…Your initiation."

Nige glances at the others. Mac is visibly relieved. Mirroring Nige, Victoria is visibly annoyed.

Dave steps forward. "The rules are simple. Each basket is one point and we're going first to five. No walkin', no talkin'. Make it. Take it. Tezza calls fouls." He winks at Terry, who has started on a second pot noodle, then nods as if everything he has just said is crystal clear. He claps his hands. "Let's do this."

He returns to his brother and father and they place their hands in the middle. In another display of perfectly rehearsed union, they shout, "GooooOOOO The Church of The Fallen Angels," and do a little enthusiastic jump in the air.

Mac puts up a hand. "So the initiation is a basketball game? Do we have to win? Team sports aren't really my thing."

"No, no, no." The cult leader smiles wide. "It's just a bit of fun. Just get involved." Then his face flashes gravely. "But you better try. If you don't try…" He shakes his head, then smiles again. "Ooo. David, you didn't tell me they had a seven-foot ringer on the team as well as an angel." He bobs his head from side to side confrontationally. "Won't make a difference though."

Mac calls his team into a huddle. "Well, these guys are clearly a basket short of a picnic." He grins and waits.

Neither Victoria nor Nige give him the reaction he expects.

"I said these guys are clearly a bask—"

"Yeah, I heard you." Nige grits his teeth. All he can think about is the safety of his grandchildren and The Guardians' threats. "Why don't we just sod this off, nick their gear, and make the broadcast ourselves?"

"Oh, you know how to use all those whizz-bang servers and computery bits upstairs, do you?" Mac says.

"No." Nige glances back at the cultists. "What about live streaming it on social media or something?"

Mac lets out the biggest and most annoying raspberry shaped laugh of all time, which brings Nige within inches of squeezing the PI's head until it pops like a spot.

"Live stream it?" Mac snorts. "Yeah sure, Grandad. I'll just live stream it to my millions of followers. Unless you're being genuinely horrible to someone and calling it a prank, or a 19-year-old girl gifted with supernaturally good looks doing a dance or a glute heavy workout, who's going to watch?"

"I just want to get this done."

"It looks like the easiest way is to play their little game," says Victoria.

Mac shimmies his shoulders with a cocky jaunt. "We can take 'em. You're both good at basketball, right?" He scrunches his nose. "Tall. And er… Wings."

"I've never played," says Victoria.

"Me neither."

"Well, they never said we had to win. We just need to try."

"We can do that," Nige concedes. Arguing is just going to take more time.

They break the huddle and Terry blows a whistle.

Although a lot of effort is displayed – especially from Mac, who forgets himself completely and has a thoroughly lovely time running around and shouting old coaching slogans that his PE teacher had used at school such as "come on lads give it one hundred and ten" and "watch your man, WATCH YOUR MAN" – the home team win five to nothing.

The game doesn't take long.

Tell The World

The wings span fifteen feet wide and rise and fall listlessly on either side of Dawn's body. Covering them are a multitude of bright swirls and dots that remind Maggie of a hundred unblinking eyes. From the tips to the place they join her back, the colours fade and blend from red through crimson to black.

"What happened to her?" Maggie waits just inside the door of the lab, unsure about going any closer.

"Doesn't just looking at her tell you?" Stefan calls back across the room. "Come in. She won't bite."

Maggie approaches with caution. Dawn spots her and her eyes flutter. She crosses the room, moving like a low fog drifting across an open field, graceful yet mysterious.

She speaks, and when she does her voice is warm and deep. "Maggie, I'm so glad to see you. They've had me cooped up down here since yesterday morning." She winks at Stefan, surprisingly unbothered by her current state.

"You know I can't let you go anywhere until we go live with this Dawny. We just have to wait until Saturday. Can't risk the press getting a whiff of this before then," he says. He turns to Maggie. "I'm assuming when you say something's happened to Kenneth, you mean he's entered his chrysalis. The same thing happened to Dawn. We were going to cut her out, but luckily Dr Renham saw it for what it was." He beckons a red-haired scientist over with a hand. "Darcie, you're much better at explaining all this than me. Tell Maggie would you?"

The scientist smiles. "What's happened to Dawn is completely natural. A lot like puberty in terms of hormonal and bodily changes, but as you can see a lot more drastic a change. You know how we found those chemical triggers in each of the influencers roughly fifteen years back? The ones that appeared to be counting down?"

Maggie nods.

"This is what they've been leading to. Dawn went into her chrysalis at the start of this week. She came out yesterday morning, and here we are."

Stefan holds his arm up towards Dawn like a ring master introducing his next circus act. "Just live healthy enough, and we'd all get there. And Di Blasio was the first to rediscover it."

"Rediscover?" Warily Maggie steps closer as lab personnel flit around Dawn like moths to a flame.

"Well, we don't know for sure, but someone must have lived this long in the past. Every society has stories of winged humanoid creatures. Angels, demons, vampires."

"I prefer angels," says Dawn. Her wings ripple lazily as if they've always been there. Her relaxed mood is helping to relieve some of Maggie's anxiety.

"This is huge," she says, feeling the excitement build. The scope of the discovery forcing the night's earlier events to the back of her mind. "This is the biggest thing since… well, ever."

Stefan's grin widens. "And it's ours. We found it. We can market it however we want."

She thinks for a moment. Could everything be connected? The murders, the attack on Kenneth's apartment. "Does Lewis Davies know about this?"

"No. Just the scientists down here, and me and Ian. One or two of Jeff's guys helped get Dawn into the building, but I doubt they knew what they were seeing. I know what you're thinking, but Ian says there's a chance Lewis is just part of that Fallen Angels cult. None of this is linked."

Something about that doesn't feel right. The way the cultists had acted earlier didn't suggest they were capable of breaking into Kenneth's apartment or murdering any of the influencers. She'll talk to Ian as soon as possible, help him understand, but she knows there's no point in pushing Stefan when his focus is elsewhere.

"And in three nights this will happen to Kenneth?" she says.

Stefan laughs. "Maggie, this could happen to everyone."

Dr Renham looks up from her work. "You mean he's still alive?"

"Yes, but someone is after him." Maggie walks around Dawn. She has the urge to reach out and touch her wings. They almost sparkle. Each individual scale glints in the light of the lamps above. "And Stefan, it's not Korrigan and Davies, or those cultists. It doesn't sit right that it could be Nige's son either. Nige didn't even know his son had put him forward. He rescued Kenneth."

"Come on then, Maggie, what do you think's going on?" asks Stefan.

"It's the ones that attacked Jeff and his team in Kenneth's apartment. They must be the ones who killed The Twins. Trust me, I know you'd like to think it's as simple as a crazy cult on a murdering spree, but I met those boys. They couldn't have organised an ambush on The Twins or attacked Kenneth's apartment." She looks away, the answers suddenly falling into place in her mind. If The Tall Ninjas are taller than Nige, who in her opinion is pretty bloody tall, then the only likely explanation is... "The assassins must be people who've already gone through the change. They must be killing off anyone who it may happen to. They came for Kenneth. They'll be coming for Dawn. We're not safe here."

Stefan perches on a desk and folds his arms. "Even if you're right, we're three storeys underground with guards all over the building. There's no way in or out."

"We need to announce this sooner than Saturday," says Maggie. "Like now."

"You can't do that," Ian says as he enters the lab from the main corridor. He looks more worse for wear than any of them. She hopes Stefan hasn't given him too hard a time about their date. He looks at her and smiles. "Hello Maggie."

She smiles back. It's good to see him again. "Why can't we?" she says.

"The masses can't handle this." He holds up a hand to indicate Dawn. "Society is based upon this not being the case. People work hard for a living, economies grow, countries produce, and the world keeps turning. This changes everything. It halts everything. You can't change the world overnight and expect the cogs in the machine to keep turning. It just wouldn't work. For the good of the people, they can't know."

Stefan tuts and rolls his eyes. "I thought we'd gone through this." It's the first time Maggie has ever seen him annoyed with Ian before. He pauses and looks his second up and down. "You look dreadful. Why don't you go home?"

They've obviously discussed announcing Dawn's change already. Ian has a point. Can the masses handle this? Do they have a choice though? They aren't safe unless they put everything they have against The Tall Ninjas, and the only way to do that is to out them.

"I have a few loose ends to tie up down here first." Ian looks at her for a moment as if he's seeing her in a new light. "Where have you been all night?"

Her heart flutters. "I should have called. I've been at the docks with those bodyguards we hired. Kenneth's not safe out there, some people are after him."

"I told her Jeff and his boys are sorting it." Stefan looks at his watch. "It's been a while. Any news?"

Maggie can sense Ian observing her.

He nods. "They couldn't find him at the warehouse building."

As he speaks, his eyes don't leave her. She folds her arms. His lingering gaze isn't normal. It's starting to make her uncomfortable.

"They said they were going to take Kenneth somewhere safe," she says. "I was going to call after you'd promised to help them."

"Ian," Stefan says. "Where did you hear about this security company? Seems to me like they've run off with our influencer."

"Korrigan and Davies aren't the problem," he replies. "It's The Church of The Fallen Angels that we need to concentrate our efforts upon. The latest information from the police suggests they have a large underground following with links to Antifa and Anonymous. Some pretty creepy stuff."

"Hold on a minute," says Maggie. Whoever is giving Ian his information is obviously wrong. "Those morons in the burgundy robes couldn't organise a piss up in a brewery."

Ian turns to her. "Police reports say they can be quite deceptive. Either way, if Kenneth is with the security I hired last night, then he should be safe. But we need to get them all here ASAP, Davies included." He takes out his phone and passes it over to her. "Can you call him and get us a location? My phone will have signal down here. We'll get Jeff to pick them up."

She takes his phone and nods, indicating for him to step out of the lab with her. He follows, leaving Stefan to continue talking with Dr Renham.

Once they are out of earshot, she takes Ian's hand. "I'm sorry I ran out on you last night. Now you know why."

"I've been trying to call you. Why didn't you pick up?" He frowns. She can't tell if it's concern or anger.

"I didn't know what to say."

He gives her hand a squeeze. "Don't worry. We'll sort it." He smiles. "Call Davies now and we'll get them here safely."

She taps out the number from Nige's card into the phone. It only rings twice before he picks up.

Jeff?

"Maggie, is that you? Hold on." Nige holds up a finger and ducks away leaving Terry standing with a tape measure in one hand. The cultist shrugs and moves over to wrap it around Mac's chest.

"I don't think we've got a robe big enough for him anyway," Terry says to Mac, as Nige leaves the main room of the church to enter the vestibule where they are storing Kenneth.

"Robe? What are you doing?" says Maggie on the other end of the line.

"Oh nothing. Just joining a cult."

From the other room he hears Dave shout. "It's not a cult!"

Nige covers the phone. "Stop listening." He returns it to his ear. "Where are you? I was starting to worry."

"Sorry. It took me a while to get here. Stefan is going to help us. Where are you now?"

"We've left the docks. We're in Camden." He and Mac have already talked over their plan for when she calls. "There's an old office building there. I'll text you the address. We don't want to move until it's dark. We can meet you there tonight. Eight o'clock."

"We'll send Jeff and his team. Just stay safe until then."

Wait. What? If she's with Stefan Di Blasio now, how can she not know Jeff is dead? His ears start to itch. She's not safe. "Where are you?" He doesn't want to panic her. Maybe it's a miscommunication.

"I'm in the labs at Di Blasio. Under the main building. The thing that's happened to Ken—"

"Can you wait a moment?" He doesn't know what to say. Tries to buy a little time. "I'll just get the address of the office."

She says something but he doesn't hear it as he hurries back in to the main room. Terry is now standing behind Victoria looking at her wings, holding up a robe, and scratching his head.

Words tumble out of Nige's mouth. "Maggie says Jeff is going to come and pick us up." He looks at Mac. "But Jeff is dead. They are lying to her. She's not the one behind this and she's in trouble. I don't think she'll be able to get out if I tell her the truth. She's in the Di Blasio labs." He holds a hand to his forehead.

"We must help her," says Victoria batting Terry away. "Don't tell her. If she knows she's in danger it'll be too hard for her to hide it. They'll know."

"There's only two ways in and out of the Di Blasio labs?" says Terry. "Through the staff entrance or through Stefan Di Blasio's office."

"How do you know that?" says Mac.

"Oh, I work there as mail boy. It's how we get all our intel."

"Then how do we get her out?" says Nige. The phone in his hand is starting to feel heavy. He's been on hold too long.

"Tell her we won't show ourselves at the meet point unless she's there," says Mac. "Tell her we need an intermediary so we know we can trust them."

Nige nods. That could work.

He lifts the phone to his ear. "Can you come as well? It'd be good to have an intermediary. We won't show ourselves unless we see you."

"Sure, I'll be there," she says. "Until then can you make sure you look after Kenneth?"

"Sure thing. I'll text you the address." His heart pounds in his chest. Despite Victoria's suggestion, he has to warn her. Has to tell her to take any opportunity she gets to escape. He'll text it so there's no chance anyone else will over hear him tell her on the phone. "Make sure you read it all."

The Guardians

They end the call and she hands the phone back to Ian. Moments later it pings with a text. Ian raises an eyebrow when he reads it.

"Can you make sure you cancel the arrest warrant on them?" she says. "We can't have them getting caught before we pick them up."

"Sure." He rapidly types something into his phone as they step back into the lab.

"All sorted?" says Stefan.

"All sorted," Ian says as he tucks his phone into his chest pocket, then rubs his hands together. "Now, about those loose ends." He claps his hands together loudly so that the scientists stop working. "Dr Renham, can you and your team give us a moment?"

"Everybody take five," Darcie says, and leads the others out towards the break room. Dawn returns to her chair and reclines beneath the lamps.

What does he mean by loose ends? He's acting strangely. Maggie moves to stand closer to Dawn.

"What's going on, Stockwell?" Stefan folds his arms and squints at his second.

"Oh, just a little restructuring. Let me tell you something my father always used to say. He said it was better to be number two in the top company than number one in the second. You get most of the benefits, but avoid all the stress, all the scrutiny, of being top dog. He used to say that was the good life, and I'm going to be honest, I agree with him. But for quite a while I've known that The Di Blasio Corporation isn't, and in fact has never been, the top."

"I don't understand. Be more clear Stockwell." Stefan looks him up and down.

From out in the corridor, comes the ping that announces the arrival of the elevator. Someone screams.

Through the large oval window, dark shapes move through the scientists in their white coats, hacking and slashing. There is no time for them to run. It happens so quickly. Six butchered in the blink of an eye.

"What is the meaning of this?" Stefan backs away from the entrance.

Ian points at Dawn seemingly unfazed by what's going on outside. "I kept trying to tell you we couldn't let this out. You should have listened."

"I gave you everything." Stefan looks horrified as three tall figures enter the room. "What can you stand to gain?"

Maggie looks to Ian. This can't be true. He's with them? He's been with them all along. The date? It was just to get her out of the way.

A sly smile crosses his face as he sees the realisation on hers.

"I have everything money can buy. But some things, it can't. I've completed this life. It's my time to move on to something greater. What The Guardians can give me transcends money, the love of the people, it even transcends sex. I'm bored. I want more. No, I *need* more." His face is suddenly ugly to her. A spoilt and proud snarl. "Working for you can't give me anything that I haven't already experienced to the fullest a thousand times over. But helping them can."

Maggie scowls. "You're so deluded you have to lie to yourself. These monsters won't help you. They are murderers."

Ian laughs. "How do you think I've managed to own almost half of the biggest company in the world?"

"You own a third." Stefan lifts his chin proudly.

"And you only own what your father gave you. I threw everything away for this." He turns back to Maggie. "Where I'm going now, there will be pleasures that none of you can comprehend. And if I can help the world maintain equilibrium, then even better. If it's any consolation, Maggie, they were supposed to get Kenneth last night. I tried to make it so you weren't there."

She doesn't know what to say. She wants to spit venom, but her tongue is frozen.

"You backstabbing little weasel," says Stefan. "How long have you been working with them?"

"He has been working *for* us for over twenty years now, haven't you Stockwell?" A slithering voice drawls from the lab entrance. The accent is unmistakably old English, but every consonant drips with hissed poison, and every vowel so sickly sounding it makes Maggie want to clear her own throat in sympathy. "Although, judging by last night's absolute failure, his time may be up."

A figure stands in the doorway, clad in a matt black armoured bodysuit from neck to foot. His skin has the appearance of melted plastic in the way it hangs from the bones of his skull. His pale face is angled like Dawn's, but his eyes - a red so close to black you can hardly see the pupils - lack the warm shine of hers. He looms roughly a foot taller than Ian, who whimpers as he turns.

"It wasn't my fault, Isadore. Davies was more resourceful than we gave him credit for."

"We?" Isadore raises an eyebrow, although the lump of white flesh above his eye is hairless. "You let him slip through your grasp."

Ian scurries like a grovelling rat towards them and hands over his phone with the address Nige sent. "I have their location. They are going to meet here tonight at eight."

She hasn't told Ian that Nige will only show himself if he sees her. Maybe there's a chance he and the others can get away.

Isadore glances at the phone. "That is the investigator's address." He looks at Maggie. "I think the rest of this message was meant for you Miss Greaves." He reads aloud: "'*They killed Jeff. Get out if you can and come to this address. We'll find you.*' I guess you missed that."

Maggie opens her mouth but no sound comes out.

Isadore hands the phone to one of the two standing directly behind him. The pair are even taller. Their heads covered by blank faced helmets that look like shark eyes. They each hold long, bloodied swords.

"Might that mean Trent Macadamia and Davies are together?" Ian asks. His eyes look hopeful. Like he's trying to redeem himself for his mistakes.

"As always, the fates have aligned for us." Isadore smiles, his mouth a jumbled bookshelf of jagged, yellow teeth. "This little unfortunateness should be easy enough to get past. Tell me you at least have Davies' family."

Ian rubs the back of his neck. "They have eluded us. We've tried the son's home, schools, and the wife's place of work, but to no avail. It seems they upped sticks late last night. I can only think a last-minute holiday."

"You know they are our only bargaining chip. And there's no point in stopping Davies with them still alive." He nods to Maggie and Stefan, but continues talking to Ian. "Do you think either of them know where Davies' son is?"

Maggie steps back under his glare as Ian speaks. "There's no reason they would. Lewis is on my team."

Isadore looks unimpressed. He prods Ian in the chest. "If we don't cover our bases, this will get out of hand again. The higher council won't stand for another uprising on British soil. Before I leave I want you to know I'm taking this responsibility from you. Barthram will lead the hunt."

"Yes Isadore." Ian hangs his head.

"It was your idea to involve Davies as Kenneth's bodyguard. You said we needed a scapegoat." Isadore raises Ian's chin with a long-nailed hand. "Does he know what his grandfather started?"

"We don't know." Ian points accusingly at Maggie. "She's been with him all night."

The Guardian turns his baleful eyes on her. "What do you know about Nigel Davies's family history?"

Maggie looks to Ian for some sort of explanation, then back at Isadore. "Nothing."

Isadore runs his thumb up the face of his sword, then licks the blood from it. "It seems your plan has backfired, Stockwell," he says with obvious disappointment. "But it won't make a difference. The council will never know. This little unrest will be just as easy to quash as the last. And once we have the world under the spell of the new influencers, my position amongst the upper echelon will be assured."

The new influencers? The one's they were going to introduce to the world at Kenneth's birthday show. The main reason they were having the show altogether. Ian had been the one who'd had the final say on each of them. She'd always thought them strange. Did they work for The Guardians, too?

Isadore looks at Maggie and the others as happily as a hyena spotting an untouched buffalo carcass. "Now, for some fun. Mr Stockwell has requested we make this as painless as possible for each of you." He licks his lips. "But unfortunately for you, that's not really how we do things." Dawn steps back as his leer shifts to her. "The abomination will suffer most of all. But you must take comfort in knowing your bodies will not be wasted. They will go to the greater good. We will feed."

"Who are they, Maggie?" Dawn whispers.

"I don't know." She can hardly get the air in to speak.

Isadore moves to the side, allowing his henchmen to step forward into the room. "Lock the women in here for now," he says to them. "We'll have Di Blasio first."

The pair make a beeline for Stefan.

He puts his hands up. "Wait. I can pay you whatever you want."

Isadore laughs. "Don't be ridiculous. Money means nothing."

Stefan runs to the back of the room, upturning a desk on his way to block their approach. Isadore's men split and skirt around it, trapping him. In frantic dread, he tries to scramble back over the desk, but one of The Guardians catches him by the back of his shirt and pulls him back down. In his flailing panic, he falls awkwardly and cracks his head on the floor. They each grab a foot and drag him kicking, but clearly dazed, along the tiled floor.

"Wait," he shrieks as they pull him from the room. "Please."

Isadore follows.

"I'm sorry it has to be this way," says Ian, as he backs out of the door and seals it, cutting off the sound of the CEO's screams.

The Angels

Nige takes a shower. It's been forever since his last and his exhausted mind has been craving a moment alone. A moment to find himself. A moment to discover what he feels inside.

It's not often he cries. He loved his father, but even when his boat disappeared off the coast, tears didn't come. And when his mother had died a year before, his eyes had remained dry as bone.

The only time he can remember is the night after Fiona's funeral, when everyone had gone home and he was alone for the first time since she'd passed. The first time really since they'd met, because when you have someone who loves you, you're never truly alone. You always have something to go back to. He thinks of her now, and alone once again, the tears come, washed away by the clean, warm water before he can feel the emasculating shame of them on his face.

Where had it all gone wrong? They should have never taken the job. He'd told Korrigan. He'd told Aidan. Why had he let them bully him into it? Why had he rolled over and gone against his instinct?

He knew why. The money. And with it, the little shimmer of hope that life could be better. The feeling that something magic might come along and pluck you from your every day. That warm energy that makes you feel perhaps there are some peaks left in this tired, old life, and that you're not just on a downhill slog towards the inevitable.

Look where hope got you.

If he hadn't gone all weak-kneed for a bit of extra cash, the pair of them would still be alive, and he and his grandchildren wouldn't be in mortal danger.

He was supposed to be the sensible one. The dependable one. They'd have worked a nice normal shift at the club, come back for a cup of tea with some of the lads, talked about football or how much of a massive nob the prime minister was, then all gone home. Happy and alive.

It's funny. He's always fantasised about having to fight to avenge an innocent. If he ever read about a hate crime in the news, or if a friend got hurt, he'd dream about finding the attacker and giving them a good kicking. A beating they clearly deserved. He guesses a lot of men want to hit things when they're stressed, and a murderer or a rapist or a paedophile are justifiable targets. But it's not that simple. Now he's in the position to avenge, he hates it.

He never thought that stopping a crime happening in the first place was the ultimate aim. Stopping the pain before it occurred never feels as good. You need to hurt first to find the true value. Those lows followed by those vengeful highs made you feel alive. And that feeling was addictive.

He turns off the water and grabs a towel. It's used, but clean. If anything, these cultist boys know how to do laundry.

After the initiation, and after their obligatory robe fitting, Mac had gone downstairs with Terry for a post-match pot noodle. The brothers had headed off to bed.

While Alan was out of earshot, Dave reiterated that no one was to tell his father who was inside the cocoon in the nave. Alan currently believed Kenneth was a shrink-wrapped rug.

They'd each been offered beds, and Nige plans to sleep. Although, with his brain worrying at light speed, he doesn't know how easy that will be. He slips his underwear back on, enters his dormitory, and lies down on the springy mattress hoping to catch a few hours before his meeting with Maggie.

He doesn't know what's going to happen later. Will she come? Will he be able to get her away? What if she isn't there? He hopes she got his message. But she hasn't replied. He knows he has to try to help her. Almost feels like she's his only link to sanity. The only one that can vouch for his innocence if Kenneth doesn't emerge as Victoria says he will.

He stares at the ceiling, allowing his thoughts to coalesce in to pictures. He and Mac would go to meet her. If she's there, he'll do his best to get her away. At least they know no help is coming from Di Blasio.

He checks his phone for a sign from his son. There's a missed call and an answerphone message.

"Hey Dad, it's Lewis." It's so good to hear his voice. The kids' laughter in the background. His body sinks in relief. "I saw your picture on the TV. They had your name and everything. We started getting calls from the press. A few turned up outside the house this morning. We managed to get away and have gone to stay at Nan and Grandad's old place. Come find us if you can. No one knows we're here."

He closes his eyes and holds the phone to his chest. Could he get down to Port Isaac without his car? He tries Lewis again but it goes straight to answer phone. The signal at his parent's old house was always bad.

But they're safe. Thank God.

He places the phone back on the table next to the bed.

Three other beds occupy the room, each of them made up and untouched. The Church of The Fallen Angels have been a little presumptuous in how many people might be interested in signing up to their cause. But despite their initial encounter, he likes the devoted optimism of Alan and his boys; it touches Nige as a sweet pain in his heart.

It's like when terrible unsigned bands think everyone is going to be as in love with their music as they are. He's seen a lot of young musicians playing noisy guitars to empty rooms. It's endearing to see people enthusiastic to succeed in something which is clearly never, ever going to happen.

As expected, his thoughts won't let him sleep, so he decides to find Victoria and see what else she knows. He swings his legs out of bed and dresses.

As he passes the second dormitory where the brothers doze, he looks in. With the tranquillity of sleep on their faces, he can see now how young they are. Barely out of their teens.

He slips past and heads downstairs.

In the vestry, Mac and Terry are sitting at the table, chatting like old friends. Several plastic pots are strewn between them.

"Oi Mac, where's Victoria?" he asks.

"I think she left."

"To go where?"

"I don't know. Haven't seen her for a while and she's not with Ke—" Mac stops himself and glances warily at Terry who is inspecting a freeze-dried pea on the end of his fork. They haven't told him yet. "She's not with the rug."

"Oh, bloody hell. How are we supposed to tell the world what's going on when our proof is off gallivanting around London?"

With Victoria out of the picture, Nige wonders whether he can find a bit more out about the church and what it is exactly they have just joined.

Alan sits on a swivel chair by the bank of servers. Nige approaches. He is no longer wearing his basketball kit, having traded it for a set of burgundy dungarees and a white shirt with the sleeves pushed up to his elbows. His tired, wrinkled eyes, covered by a large pair of high magnification goggles that gleam in the light of the blue and white LEDs, squint in concentration as he tinkers with a complex circuit board.

Though a little older than Nige, it's clear the cult leader has always been of smaller stature. A man who has given more time to working on his mind than his body.

"There was a lot of pushback last night during the broadcast, so we've blown a few parts here and there." He doesn't look up. "Yeesh. All burnt out. Look at that." He holds the board up to Nige. It's charred and melted up one side. "We don't have spares for all of them, so I've had to order some in. I'm hoping they'll arrive the day after tomorrow. Maybe Saturday." He glances up to see how Nige takes the news.

"That might work in our favour. More people will be watching if Kenneth's birthday show is on." He leans forward. "We're safe here though, right? For the time being."

"As houses. It'd be sooner, but I have to get the parts from a few different places so it doesn't seem so suspicious." As he speaks, his bushy moustache twitches beneath his large gnome-like nose.

"Anything I can do?" Nige moves to lean on the rack, which holds several flat black boxes that whir quietly.

"You can not touch that for a start." Alan points at the units. "One of those alone cost us ten grand."

Nige jerks his arm away. And looks at the bank of servers. They are sleek and modern. As far as he can tell, very high tech. "Where are you getting all the money to fund this? The beds, the building, all this equipment, it must have cost you a bomb."

Alan places the circuit board back inside one of the black boxes, tightens a few screws and then drops his screwdriver into a front pocket of his overalls. He removes his glasses, and places them carefully on the desk. "Terry has covered some. Don't know where the boy came from, but he definitely made something of himself before we found him."

Nige raises an eyebrow. "Terry?"

Alan looks over towards Terry who in that moment is laughing heartily at something Mac said, and spitting a fountain of noodles onto the table. "Most is covered by an out of court settlement."

"Must have been a big settlement." Nige pulls over a chair and sits.

"Not big enough." Alan stares coldly for a moment. "Coffee? I've just made a cafetière." He chuckles and fills a mug. Holds it out. Nige takes it as Alan begins to fill another. "Cafetière. That's a funny word, isn't it?"

"I think it's French."

"I don't expect the boys offered you any refreshments when you arrived. We don't really get company." He sighs, and Nige can see something behind his eyes. It could be regret. "It's lovely to see them making new friends. And bringing home an angel." He blows air through pursed lips, then leans forward and pats Nige on the knee. "I'm so pleased you've come to join our cause. If we've got three new initiates in just one night, imagine how many we'll get after our next broadcast."

"You do know we're only broadcasting to tell the world about Victoria, right? About the bastards who killed my friends. It's not a recruitment drive." Nige shifts uncomfortably on his chair. He knows these guys hold the key to his, and possibly his family's, survival.

Alan waves a hand. "Pfft. We'll see. Anyway, I saw you guys on the news. That's what swung it for me, why I let you into the Church. Where have you got the demon stashed?" He raises his eyebrows and leans closer. "I'm fairly certain the boys didn't manage to do what I asked."

"Kenneth is somewhere safe. Why do you hate him and Di Blasio so much?"

Every trace of joy leaves Alan's face, and he looks down. His gaze tracks quickly over the ground, as if searching for something. By the fresh gleam in his eye, Nige can guess he's looking back on painful memories.

"Are you married, Nige?"

"I was. My wife passed a few months ago."

"Sorry to hear that." Alan nods knowingly. "And offspring?"

"A son."

Alan's gaze returns to the floor. His posture loosens. "It wasn't always just me, Peter, and David. The boys had a mother. Well, that stands to reason – all boys do somewhere along the line. But they also had a sister. My Sophie. My sweet angel. She was our first." He pushes his goggles up to the top of his head. "For a long time it was just the three of us. Me, Cassie, and Sophie." His eyes flick quickly to meet Nige's, then back down once more. "She'd be 33 now. Back then, she was like any teenage girl. Kenneth this, Terrence that. 'Oh Dawn's wearing such-and-such a dress, can I get it Daddy?' And I'd say, yes just as long as it wasn't too revealing, you know?" He laughs.

"I'm sure you quickly grow out of that." Nige smiles, if only to try to instil some joy back into Alan.

Alan returns the smile, but it looks forced. "Do you?"

"They are their own people after all."

"Aren't they just?" He rubs his forearm absentmindedly. "She wanted to be just like them. Then when she found out they were looking for new influencers, she jumped at the chance. She auditioned and was one of the thirty to get access to the schedule. Spent a month's wages from working at that clothes store she hated and bought those terrible pastes and shakes they sell." His lips tighten into a snarl. "Di Blasio didn't even fund their own experiments. I told her, 'Sophie, you need to eat real food'. But all she could say was, 'Dad, look at them, look at Kenneth, he's a hundred and twenty, and this is all he eats'."

He rubs his eyes with weathered hands. Nige holds his breath, not sure if he should speak.

"I couldn't stop her. We'd cook for her, but she wouldn't eat. I just remember her getting smaller and smaller. As if she wasn't already tiny. Then I suppose you always think of your little ones as tiny no matter how big they get, don't you?"

Nige tries to make a noise in agreement, but something catches in his throat.

"We could both see what was happening, me and Cassie. The boys were young, they didn't really understand. But she was so adamant. So sure she could be one of them if only she followed their schedule. She just had to push through. Influencers." He almost spits the word. "How many young women have ruined their faces with surgery, or drunk their body weight in laxative teas, just to try to compete with a photoshopped image on a phone? How many men have worked their lives away in the gym, or thrown away their life savings, just for the latest gadget to impress someone who either doesn't care or is not worth caring about?"

"What happened?" Nige grits his teeth. Feels an unfamiliar tingle behind his eyes.

"Turns out those perfectly calculated diet and exercise plans were calibrated wrong. I tried to tell her. I really tried, but when they've got their mind set on something…" He shakes his head. "And her mother. She couldn't face the reality of life without our baby. I always thought it was crazy to think someone could die of a broken heart. Then when it happened to her I nearly followed, but I needed to stay for the boys."

Nige sniffs. Clears his throat. "Alan, I'm sorry. I had no idea."

He shrugs. "Why would you? You only just got here."

The two men sit for a moment in silent thought as the servers hum. The dots connect for Nige.

"That out of caught settlement." He nods at the bank of servers. "You're using Di Blasio's money against them?"

"It is profoundly insulting to be paid for silence over your daughter's death. Money is just dust in the wind to them, and so was my Sophie. They took our world, so the only fair thing to do is take theirs." Alan's eyes are hard. He holds his mug firm in two hands. "We may have been silent, but we will never forgive and we will never forget."

"Couldn't what happened to Sophie just be a terrible accident?" If he's learnt anything working security, it's that people in high-stress situations make mistakes. And no one is infallible.

"How could it have been? A company like that. They have quality control. No, they did this on purpose, for their own gain. It's the only thing that makes sense."

"Why don't you just, I don't know, use your equipment to broadcast your story? You could reach every home around the world."

Alan sits back in his chair and nods. "Don't think I haven't thought about that. But you know what happens when small fries like us take on behemoths like Di Blasio. Even though we have justice on our side, everyone loves those influencers. They trust Di Blasio. To them, we're just hoaxers, lunatics who need to be locked up. Do you know how much crazy stuff there is out there on the internet? It doesn't leave much room for the truth." He leans forward as if telling a secret. "You got to ask yourself, what do Di Blasio stand to gain from hurting people? They already have all the money in the world. How much more do they need? Why risk people's lives for something they've already got?" He makes a face as if he already knows the answer.

Nige considers this. "Not everyone thinks the same way you and I do. It's a bit like some of the real big guys in the gym. Being functionally fit and not getting fat is fine for most people. But then there're some guys, they just want to grow and grow, push the boundaries, find out how big they can really get."

Alan shakes his head. "That's not it. Believe me, I've done my research. When their mother died, the boys were three and six. I spent a lot of late nights with little Peter until he slept. I did a lot of surfing on the internet while I held him. You've heard of The Illuminati, right? The secret group of people out there who run the world. They sacrifice the innocent for their demonic pleasures. And often they do it as publicly as possible without giving the game away, just to rub it in. Terrible bunch."

Until last night, Nige had believed most theories regarding all powerful groups gave the government way more credit when it came to competence than he'd ever seen them earn. But things changed. "That sounds a lot like The Guardians who are after us and Kenneth, don't you think?"

"Perhaps, they are the same." Alan takes his screwdriver from his front pocket and points it into the air, as if trying to work something out. "Maybe they go by different names. And even if they were trying to kill Kenneth too, it doesn't mean it's not all devil worshipping hell stuff. I can't pretend to know all the ins and outs of the mind of The Illuminati, but Kenneth would make one hell of a public sacrifice wouldn't he?" He picks up a circuit board from the table and attaches a pair of wires to it.

"What do you mean?"

"It harks back to the time of the druids. Of public sacrifices to the gods. This still goes on, only now society frowns upon it. So The Illuminati have to do it a different way. They've been bumping off pop stars and actors for the last hundred years. Jimi Hendrix, John Lennon, even Marilyn Monroe. Sacrifices, the lot of them. Everyone knows it deep down. And the more faces they can rub this in – in the most public way – the better."

Nige holds his breath, not sure what to say. He's heard this sort of thing before and it's not usually possible to bring someone back from the bottom of the rabbit hole. Though it is strange how close Alan can be whilst totally missing the mark.

"It's like an illusion," Alan continues. "You show someone something they never thought they'd see, and sometimes they don't see it. If you sacrificed Kenneth, and the whole world kind of knew about it, but said nothing, that'd probably get you a mansion in Satan's own private gated community."

"So you tried to kill Kenneth to stop him being sacrificed?"

"We know something's going to happen this weekend at his birthday show. All the signs are there. So, yes. If he's dead, they can't use him."

"What signs are there?"

"You first have to open your eyes, and then your mind. They are there. You've seen the mark on your screens? The sickle and the flail on each of the new influencers' hands? Hidden, but certainly there."

"I don't really watch TV." Nige scratches his head. He has seen this sign, but can't quite remember where.

The Hunters

"I get it now," says Mac as he and Nige skirt through the noisy streets of Camden. He has his collar up and his hat down. Nige is equally obvious in a cap and pair of Alan's old glasses which have had the lenses poked out.

When they left the church, Alan did his best to get them to wear the robes. "You always wear the robes on missions."

They declined, but Alan made them promise that all seven of them, including Victoria wherever she was, would get a picture wearing them when they came back.

It's only a five-minute walk to Mac's office, but Nige was keen to get there a couple of hours early so they could scope it out from all angles. He said that if Maggie had managed to get away, she could arrive at any time.

"Yeah, it's sad," Nige continues. He's been filling Mac in on the conversation with Alan. "It must have really sent him off the rails, and Pete and Dave had no choice but to follow. They were pretty young when their mum died." Ahead of them is St Martin's Gardens. The park across the street from Mac's office.

"It seems a bit extra, though, you know? Forming a whole religious cult just to get back at a corporation that accidentally killed your daughter."

Nige wrinkles his nose. "Don't have kids, do you?"

The pavement becomes less crowded as they approach the park. They use the entrance on the side furthest from the office. Under the large groupings of oak and ash, a pervasive mist hangs in the air. Mac welcomes it. It means they'll be harder to spot from the office and the surrounding road.

"We should be careful. There are a lot of muggings around this block," he says, his eyes darting warily around the shadowy haze as they move deeper.

"I'm sure we'll be ok."

They cross the park diagonally, cutting across the dewy grass. As far as Mac can tell, the area is deserted, not even a pigeon out for a night-time stroll.

"Last night they were hiding behind the bins over there," says Mac as he returns to the same spot where he'd felt so cocky the previous evening.

The alley behind the bins is visible. It's empty. "We could hide in there." He points towards the place where he'd seen ferret face. "That's the best place to watch anyone approaching the building."

"And what if they plan to hide in the same place again?" Nige says.

Mac guesses he's right. It's not wise to be trapped in a dead-end alley. Here in the dark they can see the office and the road leading up to it.

"We'll stay here," Nige says. "This park has four exits." He points each of them out. "If this thing goes south, which – if we're both honest – we think it will, then we head out the one furthest from danger." He taps his temple. "One thing you learn working clubs, always be on the lookout. Always have an exit plan."

Mac steps ahead, glimpsing the telephone pole he came to know intimately the night before. "Wish I'd thought about that last night." He rubs his still tender groin. "How are we going to get Maggie out if she is here?" He looks back, but Nige isn't there.

Someone else is.

"Macadamia, standing in the park late at night playing with his balls," says a female voice. "Now, why am I not surprised to see that?"

"We knew you'd come back at some point," says another.

"Red, Blue." The pair of bounty hunters stand under a large oak tree roughly ten metres away. Mac turns on his winning salesman's smile. "And why would that matter to two lovely ladies such as yourselves?" He starts to back away as they converge on his position. In each of their hands are bracelets, ready to cuff him.

"Oh, I'm sure you know Mac."

"How about, just this one time, you show a little compassion? You know me. What about the bounty hunter code?"

"Bounty hunter code?" Blue shakes her head. "I ain't heard of anything like that. Have you Red?"

"Nah, don't think so. Have you, Bobby?" Red flicks her head up at someone behind Mac.

He turns and sees another figure step out of the shadow under a nearby tree.

"Good evening, ladies," he says. "Leave this one to me. He's dangerous."

Mac squeezes his eyes shut. This is bad.

London's most notorious bounty hunter pulls a wooden staff from a holster on his back. He is wearing a long dark green jacket over dark green trousers, and a dark green Alice band that pulls his dark greasy hair back from his dark greedy eyes. He's got this whole 'dark gree—' thing going that gives him a strong sense of consistency, and authority.

Mac *hates* him.

He stretches his hand out towards Red and Blue, fingers, covered in tip-less, padded (dark green) gloves. The two women don't look overly impressed either. "Leave now." He draws his fist inward dramatically. "Macadamia's mine."

Red and Blue simultaneously puff air through pursed lips and stay exactly where they are.

"I am nobody's. Least of all yours, Bobby flippin' Feta," says Mac. "Still going on hunts with a pocketful of sausages?"

Bobby pats his left pocket. "When you're as successful as me Macadamia, you need your energy on the move."

"Yeah, but sausages?" Mac would usually have smelled Bobby Feta coming, but his nose is still thoroughly blocked from last night's chill.

He looks between the three of them. He's only just realising now that they all seem to have some sort of colour coding. Did he miss the memo? He raises his hands. "I'm being framed, guys. You have to believe me."

"That's for the law to decide." Bobby Feta swings his staff around like a majorette. He dips his other hand in his pocket and pulls out a bracelet, then springs into action. As one, Red and Blue dart forward too.

All Mac can think to do is fall to the ground, curl up into a ball, and tuck any body part that's slim enough to wrap a bracelet around beneath himself. So he does in the hope that eventually the hunters will just give up and walk away.

The trio pounce. They grab at his arms and try to pull them free, but he holds tight. The hard plastic of the bracelets dig into his flesh, but they can't get them around his wrists or ankles.

"Nige." He doesn't want to shout. He doesn't want to alert any would-be watchers outside the park. There's the chance of being braceleted, and hounded by the police, or there's the chance of a grisly, stabby death if The Guardians are nearby. He knows which he'd prefer. "Niiiige." He hisses the word. Where can he be?

To his left through wide spread fingers he sees a set of blue jeans move quickly towards them. The weight of the bounty hunters is wrenched away as Nige crashes into the trio, tackling them to the ground. Mac stands quickly and brushes himself down, looking for a way to either escape or help - he hasn't quite decided which is in his best interest yet.

Deciding on the latter, he picks up a large branch from the floor, but the damp wood crumbles in his hands.

Nige grabs Bobby by the arm and locks it behind his back. Grips the bounty hunter's collar and pulls him between himself and Mac, and Red and Blue.

"Friends of yours, Mac?" he says as Bobby struggles in his grip.

"They're bounty hunters. You know what those bracelets do, right? You can't get them off."

Red pulls out her phone, scrolls for a second, then shows Blue. "The big guy's number two. We're going to be quids in if we get them both." They gaze at Nige and Mac with hungry eyes.

"You ain't getting no one," says Nige, twisting Bobby's arm up further.

"It's too late for you old man," Bobby says, as a bracelet clicks shut over Nige's wrist, the one holding Bobby's collar. Mac can hear the familiar whir as the bracelet pulls tightly to Nige's bare skin.

"Uh oh!" His mouth gapes in horror. "Nige, we gotta get out of here. With the price on our heads, the cops'll be coming quicker than you can say cops, which is a super short word." He starts to sprint across the park. "Come on!"

Mac looks back. Nige shoves the bounty hunter hard into Red and Blue, knocking them all over in a tangle of arms and legs, then gives chase. He inspects his wrist as he runs. The black bangle flashes with a green light. He pulls at it, but it's too tight to fit over his large hand.

"Don't tamper with it. It'll poison you if you do. We need to get back. Alan might be able to help. If not, we're on the run."

"What about you?" Nige calls as Mac flees through the gates of the park in the direction of the Church.

"Those idiots weren't quick enough for old Trent Macadami—," he shouts back, but is distracted by the flashing light that moves in time with his own stride. He looks down to see his trouser leg pulled up to his knee and a black bracelet wrapped around his left ankle just above his sock. He skids to a stop. "Balls, balls, bugger, balls." His hands screw into little fists and he shakes them petulantly at the sky.

He grabs Nige's lapels. "You know what this means." Stares wildly into Nige's face. "This is it. Game over. We might as well just sit here and wait for our deaths to come rolling around the corner." He sits on the floor cross-legged and folds his arms. All those times he'd whacked one of these on a criminal in the past, not once had he considered this was how he'd go down. "Buggering hell."

"You said Alan might be able to fix this." Nige shakes his own bracelet in Mac's face.

"I was just trying to get you to follow me so they wouldn't band me too. There's no hope. If you tamper with it, it injects you with a poison which makes you vomit up your intestines. The only hope is severing your arm." He kicks his leg out straight and indicates it with two open hands. "Or your bloody leg."

"Well, what can we do?"

"We can hack bits off. Or I suppose we could at least see what Alan says. He does seem pretty technical. But we'll have to be quick, otherwise the old bill will find The Church."

"What if he can't help?"

"Then we'll find a chainsaw, and you can do me and I'll do you."

Cut Up

As Mac slams through the front door, the cultists are sitting at their table eating something that looks like stew and mash.

Alan waves. "Mac, Nige. Welcome back. Fancy some st-"

"No time for that," says Mac as he runs down the centre aisle, and smacks his leg up on the table, almost knocking Dave's stew on to his lap. "Can any of you help with this?"

Alan pulls a pair of glasses down from the top of his head and leans closer. "What am I looking at here? Those aren't real converse."

"No." Mac pulls up his trouser leg. "Look."

Pete stands and leans closer. "Oh. You've been caught by a bounty hunter. When did that happen?"

"About five minutes ago," says Nige.

"Pete, do you think we have enough time?" says Alan.

"Yeah, I can do it."

"Then there's no time to lose." Alan sweeps Mac's leg from the table, then turns and points to the far end of the room as if mobilising an elite squad of marines. "To the workshop. Davey fetch the kitchen hacksaw, quickly."

Dave rolls his eyes. "Oh Dad, not the kitchen hacksaw again." He gives a petulant huff.

"David," says Mac, with all the fury of a secondary school maths teacher at breaking point. "If your father asks you to get the kitchen hacksaw, then you damn right bloody well get the kitchen hacksaw."

Dave tuts. "Fine." He runs off toward the kitchen.

Mac suddenly shrinks. Kitchen hacksaw? To cut the bracelet, right? "Forgive me, Alan, but why do we need the kitchen hacksaw?"

"No time to explain," Alan says and then races up the length of the church, rolling his shirtsleeves up to his elbows as he does so.

Mac and Nige exchange worried looks.

"Nige has one too," Mac says as they follow the cultists to the back of the room.

"Sorry Alan. We've put you in danger by coming here," Nige says. Ever since Mac told him what the bracelets did, he's been supporting his arm as if moving it in the wrong way will release the poison.

"Not to worry. Followers of the Church are welcome here any time." Alan pulls back a long heavy drape and leads them into a darker, closed off part of the church. The rest follow close behind.

"I'll need to freeze the trackers, then remove them without releasing the poison," says Pete. "It's actually a lot easier than it used to be."

Alan flicks a switch, lighting the workshop with several bright fluorescent tubes. The room is a gear head's paradise, expertly organised. Shelves of boxes full of bits and pieces line the walls. Lengths of wire, circuit boards and electrical components poke out of every available space.

Despite their predicament, neither Mac nor Nige can help but 'ooh' in manly appreciation.

"Mac, I'll do you first." Pete moves around the workshop swiftly, picking up little odds and ends, putting them into the huge front pocket of his robe. "Get your leg up on that bench."

Mac hesitantly does this while Pete pulls over a bar stool. He sits, then pulls Mac's ankle closer, rolls up the leg of his trousers, and opens a vice by the side of the workbench. He stuffs his calf in, just above the bracelet, and twists the vice shut.

"Is this really necessary?" Mac says, while hopping a little to keep balance.

"Can't have you moving around during the procedure," says Alan as he inspects the bracelet.

Pete reaches for a bright light on a posable arm and swivels it towards the ankle. "Dad's the expert."

Nervousness starts to bubble in Mac's tummy. He looks at the cult leader. "Well, maybe Alan should do it then?"

Alan waves a hand and folds his arms. "No, no, no. Peter needs the practice."

"I've done it before," Pete reassures him. "In fact, that's how we met Terry." He leans back and presses his fingers together. "It's quite a funny story act—"

"Pete!" Mac's voice almost jumps an octave. "Focus!"

"Sorry, I get side-tracked. Shouldn't be tricky." He gets to work immediately, removing a small, almost undetectable panel next to the LED on the bracelet.

"You're lucky," says Terry as Pete works in silence. "These things used to explode when you did this."

Mac gulps.

"Gulp indeed," says Alan. "If you really didn't want to get caught, the only way to get them off was to lop off the arm or leg and shove it out of a car window whilst speeding along the motorway. That way you were out of reach by the time it blew up."

Mac looks between Alan and Pete. His mouth works wordlessly. Then Dave steps in, hacksaw in hand, and he almost faints. The only thing that stops him from flopping to the ground like an elderly Victorian women who's been out in the sun too long is his leg in the vice.

The saw drips with a congealing red goo.

Alan looks at it and tuts. "Oh David, you could have at least cleaned it. Have you got a screw loose or something?" He looks at Nige and rolls his eyes as if to say 'kids.'

"Ring pull snapped on a tin of beans," Dave mutters.

Mac can't take his eyes from the saw.

Alan flicks his fingers at his eldest. "Take it back to the kitchen and clean it. Use fairy liquid; we don't want it covered in germs, do we?"

Dave leaves the room.

They sit in silence as Pete continues to probe the inner workings of the bracelet. He then removes the device he used to disable Kenneth's tracker from his pocket and presses the button next to Mac's ankle.

"That's the tracker frozen for a few minutes, just got to sort out the poison," he says.

"We need the saw just in case he messes it up," says Alan.

"If I do, we'll have about thirty seconds to get the leg off," Pete says seriously. "The vice should slow the poison a little, but we'll probably have to take it off at the knee to be safe. We'll wait for Dave." He puts down his screwdriver.

Terry leans on the workbench. "Anyone see the match on Tuesday?"

"Um… I think I'd like to get down now," says Mac, starting to sweat. He tries to wriggle his leg free, but it's stuck fast."

"Oh, nonsense." Alan waves a hand. "The boys are always getting into little scrapes with bounty hunters. Pete's never botched it. What was I saying? Oh yeah, highways England were a little miffed at all the motorway explosions. Caused a fair few potholes on the M25. And of course, it made more sense to change the entire bounty hunter banding system than fill them in. So now here we are with the intestine liquidating poison. And—" Dave enters once again with the saw still dripping with water. "Ah, David. And you used dish soap, didn't you?"

"Guh, yes Dad." He rolls his eyes, drops the hacksaw on the table in front of Alan and strides back out.

Alan holds the saw out. "You be ready with that, won't you Nige?"

Nige takes the saw as if in a dream. Looks at it, then at Mac's leg. He nods slowly. Mission accepted. Mac feels like he might throw up.

Pete picks up his tools and continues working. "I'm going to need for you to hold still for a moment. One slip and it's chop chop." He fiddles with the bracelet for what seems like an eternity until they hear a tiny click.

"What was that?" Mac's eyes are wide. "Was that it? Am I going to die?"

Pete holds up the bracelet. It dangles in two parts. "Not today. Ok, Nige next."

The cultist frees him from the vice, and he jumps down out of the way. He reaches down and rubs his ankle. "Thank God," he sighs. "I tell you what, my heart was going like the clappers. Duh dum! Duh dum!" He smiles and wipes the sweat from his brow.

"My go then." Nige takes a deep breath and leans forward, pulling up his sleeve and presenting his thick forearm to Pete.

"Should have this off in a jiffy." Pete quickly fastens his arm in the vice and picks up his tools.

"What, the arm or the bracelet?" says Mac as he leans in to get a better look.

Nige glares. "Oh, it's all fun and games now, isn't it?"

Pete goes through the same process as before, and removes the panel on the bracelet. Then uses the EMP device. "That's the tracker taken care of. They have a back-up, so it'll only be down for a few minutes. Now, the tricky bit." He leans back, lets out a breath, and shakes his arms above his head before moving back into position.

A silent moment. Then the bracelet clicks.

"Is that it?" says Nige.

Pete looks at him with open mouth and staring eyes. A look that doesn't fill one with confidence. Mac's heart leaps to his throat. "I didn't get the needle out of the skin!" He grabs for the saw. "The poison has been released."

"What?" Forgetting his arm is trapped in the vice, Nige leans back, trying to get as far away from his own wrist as possible.

The hacksaw is pushed into Mac's unwilling hands. "What?" he says. "No. No! I don't want to."

"You have to." Alan points. "Above the elbow. You have to do it now."

Nige takes several deep breaths and looks Mac in the eye. "Do it," he says, nodding towards his arm.

"Can't someone else—"

"Do it, Mac! I don't want to vomit out my own intestines."

He skirts around Pete. The saw shakes in his hands. He places the blade on the flesh of Nige's large bicep. "I'm scared."

"You're scared? Just bloody do it!"

He clasps both hands on the handle of the hacksaw. Nige squeezes his eyes shut and turns his face away.

Mac also closes his eyes, and, preparing himself to saw, screams.

He pushes down. Continues screaming.

The blade snaps out of its frame, leaving little more than an indentation in the doorman's arm.

A pause.

Then Pete hums in quiet delight. "Got ya!"

Mac's scream stops dead. "Wh—?"

"Paaah!" An exhale leaves Terry's mouth, the sound of a tyre stabbed with a screwdriver.

Alan laughs, wiping a tear from his eye. "Hook, line, and sinker lads." He points at Mac. "You should have seen your face. Now you, Nige, were very brave."

"Very brave," confirms Terry, watching Nige with a small smile on his lips. "The bravest."

"And it was lovely to see you were up for the chop, Mac," continues Alan, "but flip. Ping. Heck, I've never heard such a scream." He laughs again and slaps his leg. "Oh, we do like to have fun here."

Pete flips the vice handle, freeing Nige's arm and pulls the bracelet off in two pieces just as he did with Mac's.

Mac clears his throat and places the saw down carefully on the workbench. He closes his eyes. "That was—"

"That was bloody brilliant!" Nige palms his forehead and smiles. "Me and the lads used to do stuff like that all the time. Bloody love it. Classic prank." He claps Pete on the back, then points at Mac. "Alan's right, you should have seen your face."

Mac raises his nose. "Yes, very funny."

"No one keeps their good hacksaw in the kitchen," says Alan. "Remember we got you the same Terry. That'll teach you boys to come in here with a bloody tracker on your leg. Jeez." He picks up the bracelets from the workbench and hands them to Pete. "Nice work, son. Now, go and tape these to a taxi or something before they start tracking again. Don't want any uninvited guests."

At that, Pete disappears out of the door.

"Yes. Quite," Mac says haughtily, then turns away and hurries from the room. "Find me when it's time for the broadcast," he calls back. "Until then I shall be in my dormitory crying."

Food or Wallow?

Mac's hands shake as he lies on the bed. He can still feel the grip of the saw in his hand. When it broke, he thought it had cut directly through Nige's arm, so sharp it had gone clean through in one stroke, as if he was cutting through a moist Victoria sponge. He rubs his fingers frantically against the mattress, trying to grate the feeling away.

Despite having the cover pulled tight to his chin and all of his clothes on beneath, he still feels cold. His teeth chatter and his head is light.

Why do people always think jokes like that are funny?

They aren't.

Back in school, he could never understand the other boys and their incessant plague of jovial ribbing. He always felt he was missing something. Was it their tone of voice that gave it away? A hidden inflection that suggested that they were actually joking? When they called you the weakest boy in the year, or took the mick out of your enjoyment of drama, or said that no girl was ever going to fancy you, was it all just a joke?

He could never get his head around it.

Come to think about it, he never really liked any of his friends from school anyway. They were always telling him what he could and couldn't like. That his favourite band was lame. He always questioned himself because of them. Could never settle on who he was. Instead he just put up a shield of over the top masculinity and hid behind it. And though he didn't overly like the person he presented to others, he was stuck behind that veneer. The real him forever enclosed.

Once again, he contemplates running and joining the thousands of unnamed homeless that sleep the streets of London.

But he knows he's dead if he runs. Is he dead if he stays? The best thing to do is lie in bed and hope that he'll wake with all this having been a dream.

He pulls the cover up over his face and closes his eyes.

Footsteps outside. A soft knock on the door. He keeps quiet. The door opens a crack.

"Mac, it's Nige."

Mac pulls the covers back, and with eyes accustomed to the dark of the dormitory, sees the man's large hand reach blindly in, and slap the wall either side of the light switch. With a hand that big, how can he keep missing it?

"I'll get it," he says, pushing himself up. He turns on a small reading light above the bed.

Nige pushes the door open. "They're serving up stew and mash downstairs. Do you want some?"

"No, thanks." He moves his pillows so he can sit up comfortably.

Nige's lips tighten into a sympathetic smile. "Are you alright?"

"Yeah, why wouldn't I be?" Mac says, wriggling from one position to another. In his twenty-six years, he has never found a way of sitting up comfortably in bed. He doubts anyone has. And if they say they have, they are lying.

Nige clears his throat. "Well, you know," he says. "It's all been a bit go since yesterday. And with the whole hacksaw arm chopping thing..." He rubs the back of his neck and shrugs, clearly embarrassed to be confessing. "I admit, I'm feeling a little bit shaky."

"Shaky?" Mac sits up straight. "Two of your best friends were killed last night, we've joined a religious cult, and found out the biggest secret on the whole planet in the space of twenty-four hours, and you're feeling, in your own words, 'a little bit shaky'?" He holds his palms up and looks about the room as if begging an unseen studio audience to agree with him. "Jesus Christ Nige, I don't know what sort of training you've done to become a bouncer, but you must have nerves of bloody steel."

"Well, you do see a lot of stuff on the job. It kind of desensitises you a bit."

"What have you seen that even comes close to this?"

Nige scratches his chin. The fresh stubble rasps like sand paper on glass. "I don't really like to talk about it."

"No, really, what?" Mac folds his arms.

Nige looks at his hands. "There was this one time in this club. This girl was hit with a bottle. She didn't even have anything to do with it. Just the wrong place at the wrong time, really. This drunken twat swung a bottle at another drunken twat, missed, and hit this girl in the head. She can't have been much older than twenty. The bottle fractured her skull. I spent the best part of an hour holding her head together, promising to her she was going to be alright." He grits his teeth.

"And?"

"And what?"

"Was she alright?"

"Not really."

Mac swings his legs out of the bed. Sits there for a full moment in silence. "That's tough. I guessed paramedics saw stuff like that, the police, fire service too, but I had no idea door staff got that sort of thing as well. And people give you so much aggro."

Nige shrugs. "It's just part of the job. I guess that's why we learn to laugh at stuff." He taps his temple. "Like security for your mind."

Mac bobs his head. "I can see that. I'm sorry I stormed off. I'm just…"

Nige shrugs again. "Don't worry about it. I like pranks. You don't. We're all different. That's what makes this place so interesting." He points at the bed opposite as if to say 'do you mind?'

Mac nods and raises an inviting hand.

Nige settles on the end of the bed. "Here's an example. My girl Fiona, she absolutely loved roller coasters. Couldn't go to a theme park without spending the day running between the biggest rides. She screamed her head off, loving every minute. Me, on the other hand, I'd rather pull out me insides than get on one of those things."

Mac frowns, taken aback. "What? A big guy like you scared of roller coasters?"

"Hey, if you were a big guy like me, you'd be scared of roller coasters too. Always thinking the next time you go racing round a bend that a tree is going to whack your head off."

"You know that's completely irrational, right? If they are letting someone as tall as you on, then there's no way a tree is going to come close to smacking your head off."

"Yeah. Fiona always said that too. And deep down, I knew it. But my point is, we would both be doing the exact same thing with completely different experiences. You don't think a joke about chopping my arm off is funny, but I do. It doesn't make you or me any less – just different. It's what makes us who we are."

"That's not really why I left."

"I know."

They sit in silence for a moment. Nige looks down at his hands and spins the ring on his wedding finger.

"You have to feel a little more than just shaky, though," Mac continues. "I'm falling apart. This is madness."

"Well, maybe I do." Nige looks up and points a finger between them. "But you know us lads, we don't really let that stuff out. We build a wall in front of it and keep our mouths shut. Squash it down until one day it comes out as an aneurism or a heart attack."

"Do we?" Mac appraises the man at least 35 years his senior as if he's from another time. He guesses he is.

"Of course. We deal with it in our own time, if at all. For now, I've put all that away. I'll pick up how I feel about Korrigan and Aidan another day." He pauses. Shrugs, a solitary shoulder this time. "Or, maybe I won't."

"And what about everything else? The Guardians, Kenneth, winged angels?" Mac can feel the weight of it all pressing down on him. Always present behind every thought.

"That too."

"How do you do it?"

Nige stands. "I dunno. I've always done it. If I can't control something, I move on to the next thing before I let it bother me. No point in worrying about stuff you can't do anything about when there's stuff that you can. Now, do you want to come and have some food or do you just want to wallow?" He moves to the door.

Mac sits rigid for a moment. Wallowing is addictive. It takes a lot of strength, a lot of will power, to pull yourself out.

"Have you ever heard the story about the dog on the nail?" Nige stops in the doorway. Turns back.

Mac shakes his head. An all-encompassing lethargy is pinning him down. He's not really up for another story.

Nige ploughs on anyway. This is the most he's talked since they met.

"My dad had all these stories that made no sense when I was younger, but as I grew up, they seemed to fit life exactly." He pauses for a moment, thinking of how best to start. "So there's this dog on a nail right, but he's lying by a fire. He's all lovely and warm and relaxed by the fire, but there's this nail digging into his guts. It's not that bad, but it's annoying. All he has to do is get up off the nail, kick it away, then he can lie down again. But he's too snug to do it, and the nail doesn't hurt that much. But it is annoying..."

Mac makes a pained face at Nige. "It must have been nice to have a father around to tell you confusing stories."

"I'm not telling it right," Nige says. "The point is, you lying there in your bed thinking about everything that's going on, it's not going to help this situation. You gotta get up and get rid of the pain. Then you can go to bed again without all this crap floating around in your head. You either lie there because it's comfy, but always have the problem, or get up and fix the problem, then you can come back and really enjoy lying there."

"Um… I think I know what you mean, but I'd… I'd just prefer it if none of this ever happened."

"But it has."

How can he be so calm? Knife wielding ninjas want their heads. "You realise we're probably all going to die?"

Nige raises a hand and knocks on the wall as if testing whether it's hollow. "Probably, but all I can do is what I can do. And maybe it'll help and maybe it won't, but whatever I do will get me further along than I am now. I just do things inch by inch. One step at a time."

"You're lucky," Mac says. "A big lad like you can probably punch his way out of most scrapes."

"A big lad like me has probably had more than my fair share of scrapes because of it. Either way, what's next for Trent Macadamia PI? Food or wallow?"

Mac sets his jaw before replying. "Food." He spits out the word, hoping it'll help galvanise his lead-like limbs into action.

Nige jerks his head. "Good lad. Come on then."

The Prisoner

"If it's any consolation I really did fancy you, you know."

Maggie swallows back the vomit that is slowly rising in her throat as Ian leers at her through the locked door of the lab.

Consolation?

Well, that really is a consolation. Thank you, Ian.

Oh sorry Maggie, that you didn't get to live out your full and happy life, and sorry you had to spend the last thirty hours before you were murdered locked up on your own with no food or water, but some guy, who is the sole reason you're here and who – by the way – now owns the biggest company in the world, really did fancy you.

Brilliant!

Run out of consolation prize branded mugs, did you, you prick?

Of course, she doesn't reward him with an answer.

His voice chimes in over the lab's speakers. "It's just a shame their society doesn't value women otherwise you could join me. Seems a little strange, but this is the life I've chosen."

She doesn't know what has happened to either Dawn or Stefan, and can only fear the worst. Shortly after they locked her in, several men in Di Blasio security uniforms – normal men, not eight-foot-tall winged beasts – pulled Dawn out, leaving Maggie on her own.

A thin trail of blood from the back of Stefan's poor head stains the floor. In the clinically sanitised environment of the lab, she swears she can smell its iron tang.

It makes her feel queasy.

Her mouth aches for water. She's weak. Hasn't slept. But she doesn't want to give them the satisfaction of seeing her scared. Doesn't want to show she's terrified.

According to Ian, Nige and Kenneth weren't at the meeting point, and The Guardians are still looking for them. She's glad of that at least. But for some reason they think she knows more about Kenneth's location. She's told them that she doesn't, so why are they keeping her here?

Her stomach rumbles. She has little body fat – Di Blasio's forward facing staff requirements being what they are – and the day without food has taken its toll. Who knew there was a reason your body stored fat and that it wasn't actually a punishment for eating all your favourite foods?

As if sensing her thoughts, Ian clicks the intercom again. "I can get you something to eat. Would you like that?"

She doesn't answer. What's the point?

"They'll hurt you, Maggie," he says with what sounds like a hint of remorse.

Butterflies squirm in her stomach. Fucking butterflies. A laugh escapes. It ends as a sob. She clears her throat and sets her jaw, hoping he didn't hear.

Behind her, she hears the sizzle of the door sliding open, the click of his tongue and a short inhale as he opens his mouth to say something. Then silence. The door slides shut again.

She listens, then glances up over the parapet of the desk. He's gone.

Careful not to step in Stefan's blood, she shuffles towards the door. Pressing her face right up against the window, she tries to look further down the corridor, but the angles are all wrong. All she can see are the bodies of the dead scientists piled up outside. She turns away quickly and fights the urge to throw up.

Her heel clicks on something on the floor. She looks down. Stefan's lanyard and key card. Her heart jumps. It must have fallen from his pocket when they dragged him away. It should have clearance to enter any room in the building. Suppressing her hopes, she bends to pick it up. Maybe it'll still work?

She investigates the corners of the lab. No cameras that she can see. Slowly, and with rising hope, she casts her eyes to the keycard scan point. Would they have bothered to revoke his security clearance?

With a shuddering breath, she steps towards the door. Closes her eyes and holds out the security card. There's a little peep. A particularly underwhelming fanfare for the magnitude of the moment. And the door slides open. Her breath catches in her throat. She pinches herself. Could this be real?

She steps slowly through the door and hides behind the pillar which rings the large viewing window. The corridor down to the elevator and beyond is clear.

If Dawn and Stefan are alive, they'll be in one of the underground lab rooms. With the building as busy as it always is, it would have been too much of a risk to take them up and out.

She tiptoes down the hall, her every step squeaking on the metal floor. Why is it that whenever you have to move quietly, your shoes decide it's the perfect time to serenade you with the song of their people?

She ducks into the recess of each window. Peers inside every one. Each room is dark and empty, but as she nears the lift, she can see a light coming from the room at the far end of the corridor.

For a drawn-out moment she stops at the lift. It calls to her. If Ian or anyone returns while she's down here, they'll have her trapped. But she can't leave Dawn or Stefan behind. She couldn't live with herself knowing she hadn't tried. What if it was her?

She nods to herself and accepts the consequences of her decision, then moves, now with a little more speed, towards the end of the corridor. She doesn't look into the other labs as she runs, knowing that her best chance is the illuminated room at the far end.

She slows as she approaches. The door is closed. Looks through the window. On a table in the centre of the room lies Stefan. Pale. Drained. Eyes closed. She wretches, gripping the sill of the window for support, but there's nothing inside her stomach to come up. She can tell he's dead. Several large bottles stand on a trolley next to him. They appear to contain what must be most, if not all, of his blood.

With gritted teeth, she swipes his keycard at the door. It opens. She steps in and moves to his side. There's nothing she can do. She should just leave, but she can't take her eyes away. Forces herself to look. To remember what they did. So that someone at least knows what happened to him.

She's never seen a dead person before. Not even at her grandparent's funerals. He seems so small. Hollow cheeks. Hands curled inward on his chest, like the life, the personality, the immaterial stuff that made him who he was, had actually added volume to his living body.

A movement in the corner makes her jump. But when she looks up and sees who it is, she relaxes. At the far side of the room, Dawn sits on the floor with her knees pulled up to her chest. From here, Maggie can see the cuts on her arms and legs. Straight bloody lines.

Dawn looks at her through hair that falls limply across her face. "They killed him." Her shoulders shake. "Oh, Maggie."

Maggie passes Stefan's body and holds out her hand. "What have they done to you?"

As Dawn rises, the full extent of her injuries becomes clear. Cuts all over her arms and legs. Made with a sharp blade, evenly spaced.

"They were just hurting me. They didn't even ask me any questions." She looks around as if she doesn't know where she is. "They said they were tenderising me." She looks to Maggie, hoping for an answer.

"We have to go. I found Stefan's key card." She pulls Dawn towards the doorway, stealing one last look back at Stefan. They have to make it, for his sake.

The way back to the elevator is clear. Maggie begins running, but with a single flutter of her wings, Dawn gathers her up and powers them down the corridor. They land at the elevator. Maggie hits the button.

Her heart drums in her chest as the lift descends from Stefan's office.

"What if someone's in there?" Dawn says. With her angular eyebrows drawn together, she looks nervous.

"We'll just have to hope they're not." The only thing Maggie can think to do is raise her fists. For the last few moments of the lift's descent, she can hardly breathe.

The doors open.

Empty.

They hop inside. Maggie presses the button and they ascend.

Dawn looks her over. "Did they cut you too?"

"No. They didn't hurt me. They want to know where Kenneth is." She leans against the wall. Where will they go now? How will they find him and Nige?

"Why Kenneth?"

"Kenneth entered his chrysalis the night before I arrived." The words that come out of her mouth seem almost unreal. "Whatever these things are, they want to stop people finding out what's happened to you. The Twins are dead. So is Terrence." She bites her lip. Knows she should have tempered her words. The influencers are almost like family to each other. But she just doesn't have the energy for sensitivity. "I'm sorry," she adds when Dawn's face falls further.

"I had no idea. And now poor Stefan. He was still awake when they…" She lifts a bloodied hand to her brow. "All my closest friends. Oh Maggie, how could this happen?"

"Ian must have told them. He told them all about where the influencers were going to be, what they were doing. Betrayed us all." Maggie glances nervously at the display at the top of the lift doors. They are nearing the top. If they can just get out of Stefan's office, they'll be safe.

The doors open to an empty office. The room is dark save for the night-time glow of the city that shines in through the windows. The light glints on the metal trinkets on Stefan's desk.

She rushes towards the doors, hoping Stefan's PA, Duncan, will still be there at his desk.

"We shouldn't go out through the main building," says Dawn, and before Maggie can respond, she has grabbed a large paper weight from Stefan's desk and launched it through the nearest window. The glass shatters.

Maggie looks through the window and down at the snaking lines of headlights way down below. She presses her back to the opposite wall. "No. I can't go out there." She points at Dawn's wings. "Have you even tried using those yet?"

"I've had some practice up and down the corridor. I'm sure I can do it. I'll just guide our fall to the ground. How hard can it be?"

"As hard as a seventy storey fall on to tarmac." With her mind set, Maggie turns and opens the door to leave through the building.

But something is in the doorway. Like an eel emerging from its shadowy hole between sea rocks, an eight-foot-tall figure steps through. Its head covered with an opaque black visor. Maggie backs away, but already two more figures have appeared behind Dawn, silhouetted in the lights of the city.

The two women stand back-to-back in the centre of the room as the figures move in on them.

She hears a dark brooding chuckle from over by the fireplace, and a fourth figure steps out of the shadows. "Going somewhere?"

In the pale light from outside Isadore's ashen face stands out like a ghost. "You found Stefan's security card. Who left that lying around?" Another sneering laugh.

Maggie feels like she's left her body behind. Like she's floating on the cold night breeze outside the window.

"There is one true way of reaching and sustaining perfection." Isadore grins and licks his lips as if appreciating a delicious meal before him. "It's a delicate practice passed down from father to son over centuries."

Maggie can't speak. Her words are blocked by her heart in her throat.

"It's like a cocktail. Part fear, part pain, a little despair, a sprinkling of hope." He rubs his first finger and thumb together before him as if salting a dish. "Shaken, not stirred." He laughs and inches forward like a hungry ghoul. The others remain completely silent, statue still. "I should be interested to try a female who has been through the emergence. We usually just kill you. I expect I shall be one of the first in, what, a thousand years, maybe more." He holds his arms out towards them, then addresses his comrades. "Take them down and start the bleed."

Something grabs Maggie from behind and Dawn yelps as they are both dragged back towards the elevator. She fights with everything she has, but it's like battling a current in a raging sea. It takes all of your strength, but the ocean doesn't even notice.

How could she be so naïve to think they would have just left Stefan's card there in plain sight?

They are thrown into the lift.

Dawn clutches her arm, shaking violently. Maggie wants to tell her it'll be ok.

But she knows it won't.

As the doors begin to close, she can see glass twinkling by the broken window. Another silhouette appears, casting a shadow across the room.

"Leave them," it says. A female voice.

The four men look up.

Isadore looks at the others and then releases a disappointed sigh. "Don't mess around. Just kill her."

The new figure braces herself as Isadore and his men approach. The lift doors come together, blocking Maggie's view of the office, just as she feels a strange and deep pulse throb through the air.

Several moments later, the doors open again. Maggie steps forward and peers around the office. The men have been blasted around the room. Two are tangled up in Stefan's now-broken upturned desk, another has been dashed against the far wall. She can't see the fourth, but it is dark, so she suspects he is here somewhere.

The newcomer steps forward. She wears a red polka-dot dress under a large, black rain mac. She holds out a hand. "Come with me, now."

Maggie takes it and is instantly drawn up under the newcomer's arm like a rugby ball.

"And you Dawny," the newcomer says as she sprints towards the window. "Don't think about it. You know how to use your wings. Just feel it."

Maggie knows what's going to happen. There's only time for one deep breath before the three of them plunge out of the window and into the chill of rushing night.

Stakeout

Unlike most of London's bounty hunters, Bobby Feta always safeguards his investments. Especially the high-profile ones. He's lost out before on a few big marks. Danny 'The Biscuit' Portensteiner, The Baker of Bedford, who cooked his victims into cookies, lost him over eight grand, when instead of allowing himself to get caught, he lopped off his arm on the M25 before disappearing into obscurity. And there was Penelope Topato, a knife wielding gang leader from Clapham, who lost him upwards of two grand when she went and got herself drunk and drowned in the Thames.

Maybe he's a little too careful. But then maybe that's why he's one of the highest paid bounty hunters in the country, why – he expects – his name is spoken in hushed, frightened whispers in the alleyways and dive bars around town, and also why he's been sitting in his car for two days outside a dilapidated church in Camden. Watching. Waiting.

Using a well-worn spatula, he presses down on the four apple cider sausages he has heating on a gas stove on his passenger seat, and regards the building with a careful eye. If he were a dirty, murderous criminal hiding out, then somewhere like this would be perfect. And if his brilliant detective's mind is correct, then it is not a coincidence that a) Mac and his compatriot, both wanted in connection with the disappearance of Kenneth and The Twins, are hiding in a church, and b) a religious sect threatened the lives of said influencers on the same night.

If his sagacious mind is correct, and it's rarely wrong, this is the very place where said religious sect is hiding too.

He hasn't seen Mac or Davies leave, not since he caught up with them running to the church, and he hasn't had a notification indicating that the police have picked them up. This alone suggests something is wrong. The police never take this long to catch up with high-profile bounties.

He checks his watch for the thousandth time in two days. Where are the cops? Surely Di Blasio should be paying through the nose for any leads on their top influencers.

Something better happen soon. The parking charges alone are quickly sending his bank account spiralling towards the red. Though few, living in your car does have its downsides.

He flips his sausages. They're done, so he pulls them off the grill. Waves one in the air to cool it down. Takes a bite.

He nods to himself. It's time, he decides. Time for this industrious entrepreneur to take life by the macadamias and see what's going on inside. He shovels the other three sausages into his front pocket - nothing like a mid-fight snack - then pulls his staff from the back seat.

He tiptoes up to the front door, and with what in usual circumstances would be considered great forward thinking, seals his fate by slapping a tracker on the wall. Usually a device used to instruct the police of criminal hideouts, it might also alert anyone else who knows how to listen to the whereabouts of its occupants.

Using his phone, he groups Nige, Mac, and the two members of The Church of The Fallen Angels, under the tracker so the police know who they'll find.

He rubs his hands together. With the tracker up, the police shouldn't be long. Although, he'll get a little bit of cash for everyone arrested within the building thanks to the tracker, every weird little religious psycho he can stick a bracelet on before then will give him a tasty bonus.

He wonders how many are holed up in there.

He smiles. By the end of the night, he's going to be dead rich.

Why A Sausage?

It's nice. The church is homely. The last two days with just the six lads – seven if you include Kenneth – have been a strange oasis of calm. Like the outside world isn't even there anymore.

The whole alpha-beta vibe doesn't seem to have stretched further than the cultist's bracelet prank. Mac likes it. He doesn't get to spend much time with other people. Nige seems happier too. Apparently his son and his grandkids are safe down in Cornwall.

He's come to know the others well in their short time together. Each evening they share a meal expertly cooked by Terry, who it turns out used to be head chef at The Savoy before he, like so many in high-power, high-stress positions, began experimenting with instant noodle snack foods and fell on hard times.

The cultists have grown on him.

Despite their vengeful thirst for Di Blasio blood, Mac enjoys each of them in their own way. Pete's slow but methodical mind, Dave's short temper yet warm love towards his father, Terry's upbeat positivity – and the food he makes – and, having watched Alan with his sons, he knows that the man is just a father trying to do his best in a world that hurt them.

Victoria still hasn't returned. She's officially been AWOL for over twenty-four hours now. They've not heard from Kenneth's manager, Maggie, either. Once the bracelets were off, Nige had suggested they return to the office to see if she would meet them. Although the trackers had been removed, the police would still be scouring the area so Mac had suggested it wasn't the best of ideas.

Nige keeps saying how he hopes Victoria will return soon. And Mac gets it. They need to go live as soon as the broadcasting equipment is ready. Alan says it won't be long.

Knowing they'll only get in the way while the more technically minded cultist's wire and solder, Mac and Nige spend most of their time battling it out on the court. Nige has picked the game up quickly. Mac still sucks.

Occasionally Terry joins them, but for most of the day he goes out to work, leaving the church through the tunnel behind the JCB at the back of the sports hall. This leads to an underground storage area that used to operate beneath Camden Market and by Regent's Canal.

"What do you think will happen once we've broadcast," says Mac as they play a quick game before dinner. The question has been bugging him since he came up with the idea. To tell the truth he hadn't expected anyone to agree with him. But now here they are. "Do you think just telling everyone in the world will be enough?"

Nige holds the ball for a moment considering this. "There's got to be groups all over the world. People like the ones Victoria met who have gone through the change. Maybe in hiding. They'll know they aren't the only ones. We could unite against The Guardians. Call for a resistance." He shoots. He scores. The ball bounces to Mac. "Maybe the military could get involved too?"

"Maybe." Mac doesn't like to think of Nige as naive but there's an innocence there. An ignorance as to how the world actually is beneath the surface. There will be repercussions. Maybe with the world in upheaval after the broadcast he'll be able to disappear into obscurity.

Something beeps, and Terry, who's joined them this evening pulls a small gadget out of his pocket. "Oh," he says. "Oh dear."

The gadget beeps again and flashes a red LED.

They both turn to face him.

"What is it?" Nige picks up a towel draped over Kenneth, who has been propped up by the door. Wipes it over his face.

"That's the alarm." He runs for the stairs back up to the church. "Intruders in the church."

"That's not good." Nige heaves Kenneth's chrysalis on to his shoulder and follows. Mac hurries after.

"Intruders in the church," Terry says again as he leaps up the stairs two at a time. When they near the top, he sweeps his robe aside, bringing out a nasty looking automatic rifle seemingly from nowhere.

"Where did you get that?" says Mac.

"Where did I get what?" he says as he eases the door open at the top of the stairs.

Beyond, they can hear karate style shouts, followed by the slow meandering voice of Pete. "Calm down, mate. You'll have someone's eye out with that stick if you keep wah-charring it all about."

"Criminal underling, it is time for you to meet justice by my swift hand." Shouts a voice from beyond.

"Bobby flippin' Feta," Mac says, recognising the voice. He taps Terry on the shoulder. "We've got to stop him or he'll bring the entire police force down on us."

"Leave it to me." Terry kicks open the door and runs out with his rifle. Mac follows.

Nige creeps after them, hampered by the cumbersome weight of Kenneth. He catches up just as they enter the nave of the church. To their left, Alan and the boys are sitting at the table surrounded by little gadgets and bits of wire. Bobby Feta, poses at the far end of the nave with his staff held off to his side.

As Terry enters the room, brandishing his rifle, Bobby dives for cover behind a stone pillar.

"Bobby," shouts Mac. "You're in over your head, mate."

"Not for long." Though not the slimmest of chaps, Bobby manages to hide himself completely behind the pillar. "The police are on their way. I'm just here for bracelet bonuses. You're all going to get picked up. Might as well give in."

Mac slaps a palm to his forehead. "Come on…" His fists shake in frustration. "Why did you have to do that?"

Bobby's hand shoots out from behind the pillar and two small white balls bounce out into the open. They explode into dense clouds of green smoke. The sound of scurrying footsteps carry through the mist towards the front door, which is now completely obscured.

Hoping to head him off before he can escape, Mac darts into the smoke, trips over a step, and lands sprawling on the hardwood floor. Rolling on to his back, he pushes himself up to seated. He can't see more than a foot in front of his face. Waves his arm to clear his view.

Something swishes, then someone gurgles. The green cloud lifts a little, revealing the outline of two figures, one tall and one Bobby Feta sized. They stand between Mac and the door.

The tall figure has Bobby by the throat. Bobby Feta reaches into his pocket and appears to pull out a sausage, with which he repeatedly strikes the wrist of his assailant. But it's misty, and Mac can't really tell what's going on.

For a second's brief naivety he hopes that it is Nige who has stopped Bobby. But even big ol' Nige isn't that tall.

Or dark.

And he's definitely not that skinny.

As the cloud dissipates, the power cuts out. The only source of light now comes from the streetlights outside, shining through the cracks in the boarded up windows at the front of the church. The orange corona reflects off Bobby's sweaty skin as he is dropped to the floor, unmoving.

Like long black spider legs appearing from a darkened hole, The Guardians step out of the vestibule and into the church proper. Mac counts eight of them, but there may be more in the shadows beyond. He crawls backwards on his hands and feet, hoping they haven't seen him through the smoke and darkness, until he comes to one of the legs of the dining table.

"Begone foul demons!" shouts Terry, who stands in a wide stance on the table with his rifle at his hip. He sprays a volley of bullets towards The Guardians. With ultra-fast reflexes, some dart for cover behind pews and pillars. Others leap into the air, their wings carrying them up to the rafters. The bullets leave nothing more than crumbling holes in the church's brickwork.

Terry leaps from the table and Alan flips it over, leaving Mac out in the open, with the four cultists behind.

"Mac," hisses Nige. "Quick!" He motions for him to come away from the centre of the room.

But Mac can't move. He's frozen to the spot, staring up into the rafters where shadowy figures leer down at him.

There's a knock on the table. "Are you on the other side, Mac?" It's Pete. "Don't you want to come back here?"

Mac doesn't really hear him. All he can think about is one thing. The twitching blades glinting twenty feet above him in the orange streetlight. And the dark figures skulking in the extremities of his peripheral vision. And Bobby Feta lying motionless on the cold, hard floor. And also, for a moment, like the sprinkles on the top of a three-scoop ice cream sundae of thoughts, the question of why Bobby had been striking his attacker with a sausage?

So, actually more than one thing, but it's understandable as to why he doesn't hear Pete suggesting he move to safety. In his ice-cream sundae of thoughts, Pete suggesting he move would be that little bit of chocolate sauce you can't quite reach because your spoon is too fat and your tongue is too short.

This is it. He's done for. No hope for it. He lies down, closes his eyes, and waits for death.

"What are you doing?" Nige hisses.

The sound of his voice reminds Mac of Nige's earlier advice.

"All I can do is what I can do."

Well, what can he do? Right now he can move his arms and legs. So he does, and like a weird little crab person, he skitters sideways and around to the other side of the table where the four cultists have secreted a small arsenal.

Guns, knives, clips, and pipe bombs are all strapped to the bottom of the table.

"How many of them are there?" says Alan as he loads a magazine into a pistol.

"I counted eight. But think there's more." He remains in his crab pose, too scared to even consider finding a more comfortable position.

"Well, those demons came to the wrong church," Terry says. He crouches, ready to fire over the top of the table.

"Which church were they looking for then?" says Pete.

"Shut up, Pete."

Alan gives Dave a look. "Don't talk to your brother like that." Then to his other son. "It doesn't mean they physically came to the wrong church. It's a saying, you know, like 'make an entrance'."

"A-hah." Pete nods in understanding. "Meaning enter with pizzazz." He does a jazz hand with the hand not holding his shotgun.

The cult leader nods with warmth. "Exactly. Now, let's get out of here."

Mac shakes his head. He feels a little like someone has popped his brain in a blender with a couple of ice cubes. He can't think straight through the fear.

Terry stands and fires another volley at the ceiling as The Guardians drop to the floor and scatter to the corners of the room. They are hidden in shadow, but Mac can sense them creeping in from all sides like the unwanted, hugging arms of a drunken stranger.

Alan flicks on the two LED mag-lights attached to the bottom of his pistols, then starts firing at the shadows. Sparks and ricochets in the darkness suggest the bullets aren't quite cutting it. Terry joins him with more suppressive fire, and Mac makes a run for it towards Nige, who is still holding Kenneth. He stumbles past and back down the stairs into the near pitch-black darkness followed by Nige and the other cultists.

"Everyone get to the JCB," Alan shouts after them as he shuts and locks the door at the top of the stairs.

At the bottom Mac waits in darkness unsure of where to go. When the others reach him, Alan holsters his weapons and takes a thick piece of paper from his pocket. He passes it to Dave as the others gather around. "Take care of your brother for me."

Dave slides it into the pocket of his robe. "Why are you giving me this?"

"To inspire you." He places a hand on his son's shoulders. "Now, lead Peter and our new initiates to the underground tunnel. It will take you into the catacombs, then up near the market. I'll cover the retreat."

"No, Dad…"

Alan touches his face. "One of us needs to move the JCB back into place once you're through, otherwise they'll just keep coming for you. I want you and your brother safe. If I don't get out, I need you to spread our word. It's up to you now. You must avenge the fallen angels."

Dave nods.

"I'll stay with you, boss," says Terry. His face is lit by the torch on the end of his rifle. "Someone needs to cover you while you move the digger."

"That's very kind, Terry. Thank you. Though, maybe point your gun away from your face."

Together they cross the echoing space, using only the light from the torches on their guns to guide them.

A splintering crunch at the top of the stairs suggests The Guardians are coming.

Alan beeps a key fob and all the lights on the JCB flash. The cockpit illuminates, and he clambers up. "Watch the stairs, Terry. Don't let anything through."

The engine roars to life and the digger jumps forward a metre or so. Terry clambers up on to the roof, training his gun at the doorway. As The Guardians pour like cockroaches out of the opening he fires short controlled bursts. They disappear out of the arc of light from the JCB headlamps and into shadow, taking to the air with great thrusts of their wings to cross the court.

Pete leads the rest of them behind the digger. When Mac reaches him, he sees an archway cut into the naked soil, previously hidden behind the JCB.

Once they are all inside the tunnel, Dave looks up to his father still sat in the digger's driving seat. "Come with us, Dad. We can lose them in the catacombs."

"You know they'll catch us," Alan shouts as he wrangles the digger into reverse. "This is the only way, son."

Dave presses his lips together. The lights of the JCB shine in his eyes. "I swear we won't let you down."

"You never have. Love you, boy." Alan looks around for his other son, but Pete has already gone ahead to lead the way. "Tell your brother." He takes a large cylinder out of the pocket in his dungarees. "Now get." He pauses. "Terry, I won't tell you twice, off you go."

"Good luck, Alan," Terry says as he jumps from the roof and dives through the gap.

"Thank you, Alan," says Nige.

"Come on we've got to go," says Mac grabbing his arm. He can hear those same feathery footfalls that he'd heard in the alley outside the club.

"Keep my boys safe." At this, Alan's attention returns to the bucket at the front of the digger as a black shape lands on it.

They sprint into the tunnel and the JCB chunks backwards across the hole, barring the exit and sealing them inside.

The engine dies soon after and so does the light.

As they make their way down the tunnel, they can all hear the last sounds of combat: Alan firing his pistol, his battle cry, "Die foul spawn of Satan!" and then the inevitable detonation of the cylinder he was holding. A scorching heat presses against their backs, pushing them on as the mouth of the tunnel comes crashing down around the JCB.

The Catacombs

There is no light in the catacombs apart from Terry's gun which Pete, who is guarding the rear, now carries. He occasionally looks back leaving the rest of them in darkness. Dave leads the group, storming ahead, confidently turning corners left and right as if he's followed this route a hundred times before.

The surrounding brick walls are caked in brown flaky silt, which comes up to around head height. Nige has to stoop to avoid the low filthy ceiling.

Mac breaks the silence. "Where are we going?" He waddles along, carrying one end of Kenneth. Terry carries the other.

"Go wherever you want," Dave calls back, voice gruff, as he leads them in to an open underground space. To either side, rows of unlit arches gape like toothless, black mouths.

"Hold on a second," Nige stops, as do the others. Dave pauses up ahead. "We need to think of a plan. We can't just let it all fall apart." He looks to Mac for support.

Mac drops the chrysalis to the ground. Terry continues to drag the other end for a moment before realising. Placing both hands in the small of his back, Mac stretches, releasing a relieving crack. He leans against a pillar, but is immediately plagued by a cloud of crumbling silt.

"I don't know about you Nige," he says rubbing dirt from his eyes, "but I've just about had it with this. Two days it took them to find us and we only got away because Alan—" He cuts off and looks to the brothers. "I'm sorry, fellas." He slides to a heap on the ground. "They must have followed Bobby's tracker. This is going to keep happening as long as we're wanted men."

Dave stalks back towards the group. "We don't care what you two do, but The Church of the Fallen Angels is going to do what we've always done. Get revenge." He motions to his brother. "Pete, we're going straight to the Di Blasio building now. Terry, you with us?" Then he taps his pocket. "I've got all the C4. We'll see how much of a hole we can make."

"That won't solve anything." Nige moves between the brothers. "It's not Di Blasio that's doing this. We need to get our story out. It's the only way."

"And how the hell are you going to do that with no broadcasting equipment? In case you hadn't noticed everything is back at the church." Dave looks like he wants to spit. "Unless you managed to sneak out a giant rack of servers while my dad was blowing himself up so we could escape."

Nige looks down. "We have to try. We know too much. And if we don't, they'll never stop hunting us. Our family's lives are in danger. We need to figure a way to out The Guardians."

"Then what? You out them and then they just forgive you? Move on?"

"I don't know. They threatened my grandkids. We have to try something." Nige is shaking. Covered in a cold, terrified sweat.

Dave maintains a long stare with him, which he cannot hold.

"Mac, it was your idea?"

Mac doesn't look up.

Nige draws in a long breath. "I have to try. For my family."

Dave shakes his head. "Your family?" He steps right up to Nige and prods him in the chest. Even though his forehead comes to an inch beneath Nige's chin, Dave doesn't look at all intimidated. "You're worried about losing your family? That must be really hard on you."

"Dave, don't be cruel." Pete tries to grab his brother's shoulder to turn him around, but he shrugs it off.

"Do you know what happened to ours?" The muscles in Dave's jaw twitch. He doesn't blink as he stares into Nige's eyes.

He nods.

"Told you, did he?"

Nige nods again.

Pete leans in to get his brother's attention, but Dave pays him none. "Dave, what happened to our family?" he asks.

"Why don't you tell him," says Dave, not taking his eyes from Nige. "Go on. Tell everyone."

Nige opens his mouth, then closes it. "It's not my place to."

"Dave, tell me, please."

Dave turns to face his brother. His lip curls. He snatches himself away and stalks ahead, disappearing inside an archway to the right.

"Nige, please tell me."

Pete's eyes are lost. The desperate look on the lad's face opens up a wound Nige thought he'd long since closed. A deep ache in his heart caused by his own father's mysterious disappearance.

He doesn't know how to start.

"Your sister wanted to be an influencer," he says quietly, trying to find the right words. "She signed up to a programme nearly fifteen years ago."

Pete's attention shifts momentarily to Terry, then Mac, then back to Nige. "My sister?" He shakes his head. "We don't have a sister."

Nige nods. "You and Dave were young. The programme wasn't set up right or something. She died. And I think so did your Mum."

Pete's eyes glaze over as he looks away, trying to remember.

From Dave's arch comes a muffled sob.

"I'm sorry, mate." Nige places a hand on Pete's shoulder.

"And now the demons have killed Dad," says Pete.

At this, Dave steps back into view, eyes on his brother. The glint of tears are visible on his cheeks in the torchlight.

Nige lets out a sigh. "What did Alan give you in the Church?"

Dave pats himself down, then pulls out the piece of card. It's folded in two. With slow, careful movements, he opens it. His lip trembles as he smiles. "I've never seen this."

"What is it?" Pete leans over.

"It's us." Dave's smile falters. It's a photograph. He points at the people one by one and says, "That's you and me. Dad. And that's Mum and Sophie."

"Wow, look at them. We look so happy." Pete's eyes shine. "We were a family."

Dave puts an arm around his brother's shoulders. "We still are." He hands the photo to Pete, who studies it in delighted awe. Dave's gaze flicks to Nige. "I'm sorry. Family is important and if yours are in danger, then we will help as best we can." He tightens the rope that secures his robe. "But I don't know what we can do. All our equipment was in the church, and I don't see us getting back in there anytime soon. The place will be crawling with demons."

There's a silence for a moment, broken only by the rumble of a train somewhere below them, and the seemingly constant mouth breathing from Terry, who simply stares ahead into nothing.

"Can you hear that?" he says eventually. "Or is it just my tinnitus?"

Nige moves to the front of the group and strains his hearing. There's definitely something there. A faint crunch or rustle. Then it hits him.

Wide-eyed, he looks back at the others. "Someone's coming. Hide," he hisses. "Pete, hit the light."

Nige grabs Terry and Kenneth and drags them both into the nearest archway. Here, the ground slopes away from the main path, and the crumbling mud beneath their feet gets softer. It smells of sour, stagnant water and mould.

Pete's light winks out. All vision goes with it.

The crunching rustle comes closer. Definitely footsteps. A few people. And the muffled words of someone speaking. Nige leans forward so that he can peer around the brickwork and down the corridor. Two tall thin figures, silhouetted in a faint white light and hunched due to the low ceiling, make their way towards them.

He clenches his fists and rolls his shoulders. He's tired and his body aches, but there's still some fight left in him.

The Chosen Few

"I thought I saw light ahead, but it's gone," says Maggie. She lifts her phone to look further down the deserted tunnel. It illuminates the path between the rows of arches, throwing long shadows from every hump and irregularity in the dirt floor. It's muddy and horrible. This can't be where they are.

"He's near," says Victoria. "Can you feel him, Dawny?"

"I think I know what you mean. A faint buzzing, but it's got a Kenneth quality to it. I can't explain it."

"It quickly becomes second nature."

"I don't get why they'd be down here in the dark," says Maggie, as she steps through something sludgy and brown. "They said they were in Camden, but this isn't what I expected."

"Maggie?" comes a voice from up ahead. Her heart jumps into her throat at the sound of her own name. "Victoria?"

Nige steps from one of the archways ahead. He raises a hand to shield his eyes. "Where have you been— Oh?" His eyes widen as he sees Dawn.

A little further along the two cultists step out of the shadow. They all look like they are together. But there's no Aidan. No Korrigan. She's about to ask where they are when a man in a trench coat appears from the same archway.

"Woah! That's Dawn," he says pointing. "And Victoria. How did you find us? We don't even know where we are."

She recognises him from somewhere.

"They have some sort of link, Mac." Nige looks at Victoria. "Is that right? You used it to find Kenneth here. Does that mean he's close to coming out?"

"I think so," she says and then gives him a remorseful look. "You have my sincerest apologies for leaving without saying anything. I heard Dawn and knew she was in trouble. I just had to go." Victoria looks around. "Where is Kenneth?"

"Oh." Nige ducks back into the archway. "You can come out Terry. It's safe," he says from within, before heaving Kenneth's chrysalis into view. A third man in a cultist robe follows him out and stands watching. "Once he's up and out of this bloody thing, we'll see how he likes carrying me everywhere we go." Nige gives it a pat. "Anyway, where have you been, and how are you guys all together?"

Maggie recounts the story of her last few days. All the while she watches Nige carefully, recalling what The Guardians had said about him. Does he know they are after him specifically? What does he know about his grandfather?

Suddenly he catches her gaze. "Why are you looking at me like that?" he asks.

"Who are you?" Maggie holds her light up one more time to look at his face.

"What do you mean? I'm the security guard you hired in to look after matey boy," he points at Kenneth, "while you headed off on a date with, and this is probably a bit of an understatement, Mr Wrong."

She smiles, but does he really have no idea? "No. I mean, who are you? Why are you so important to them? They knew you. The Guardians, Ian, they knew who you were. They asked about your grandfather. They said he'd stood up against them."

Nige shakes his head. "Don't think so." Then he frowns as realisation meets his eyes. "Are you telling me I'm mixed up in all this because of some case of mistaken identity? My grandad didn't know anything about this. My grandad died over thirty years ago."

Victoria takes a sharp intake of breath and steps forward to look at his face.

He takes a step back.

She says nothing, but raises a hand to cover his chin. She studies his eyes intently. "My goodness. Your grandfather is Samson. Samson Davies. Abigail, the one who told me what had happened to me, the one who showed me that what I am is perfectly normal, she's your great aunt."

"Aunt Abi? But they never…" Nige looks down. "They're dead. I was at their funerals."

Victoria shakes her head. "They went through the emergence. They changed to become like me. Before he died, not five years ago, your grandfather was going to lead the revolution against The Guardians. He was one of the lucky ones. One of those with a genetic disposition. And that means so are you, Nigel. You have it in your blood."

"That's ridiculous. This is all ridiculous. Five years ago? Why wouldn't he try to contact me? Grandad Sam wasn't…" Nige points an accusing finger at Victoria. "You're making this up." Then he turns to Maggie. "You said Lewis put us forward for this job. It's just a coincidence… Right?"

She thinks back to exactly what Ian had told her. That someone in the office had put forward a suggestion for the security. There had been no reason to check.

"Ian just told me what to do. He must have already known who you were. Maybe he even employed your son to keep your family close."

In the light of her phone Nige's face turns pale. He leans against the wall. "Do they have them? Do they have Lewis and the kids?"

"No, but they are looking." She rests a hand on his shoulder.

"They've gone to Cornwall," says Nige. "I need to go."

"Wait a second here." Mac, who has remained quiet since they arrived, steps to the middle of the group. "So what, does this make Nige some sort of chosen one?" He folds his arms and raises an eyebrow.

"What's a ch—" begins Nige.

"Like he's Harry flippin' Potter or something?" Mac's other eyebrow rises to join the first. "Seems a little…" he rubs his forefinger and thumb together as he searches for the word, "…convenient to me."

"I always thought you had a chosen one vibe about you, Nige," says Terry, touching him lightly on the arm. "You've quite the presence."

"That is true." Mac taps a finger on his chin. "But I find it very hard to believe. It's all too coincidental."

"It was all Ian," says Maggie, everything becoming clear in her mind. "He booked him so they could use him as a scapegoat for Kenneth's disappearance. They were planning to pin all the murders on him. It's hard to make the biggest celeb in the world just up and disappear, but if you get some random guy to murder him, then it's not hard to make that random guy disappear, especially if it kills two birds with one stone."

"You know what that means though… Person-I've-Never-Met?" says Mac, rounding on her.

"Maggie." She looks him over. He really does look like he's had a tough couple of days.

Mac nods politely and holds out his hand to shake. She obliges. "Trent Macadamia PI. But, you know what that means, Maggie?"

She shakes her head and the others wait for his conclusion with somewhat bated, and in Terry's case phlegmy, breath.

"It means while I'm here, with you, I'm never going to be safe." He moves his finger in a circle, gesturing to the group. "The lot of us aren't going to start some sort of uprising, even if we find another way to broadcast what's happened to Kenneth and Dawn." He paces across the tunnel, fingers spread in his hair. Dark eyes widening in fear. "In fact, this is worse. They aren't just going to let us go now if they think you are the grandson of the person who started this resistance against them. I need to get as far away from you, and this, as possible." He pauses for a moment, studying the others, thinking. "And for that reason, I'm out." He strides past and disappears around the next corner.

Nige stands and calls after him. Maggie recognises desperation in his eyes. "Wait, Mac. You can't."

Mac returns. "You're right. It's too dark. My phone ran out of battery ages ago and I have no idea where I'm going. But," he points a warning finger at them all, "as soon as we're out of these wretched catacombs, I'm leaving."

"No, I mean we all have to stick together."

"You're as crazy as they are if you think we're getting out of this." He points to the brothers, but continues directing his words at Nige. "Oh, it's been lovely sitting around the church and playing basketball, but we only managed to lie low for *two days* before those things came in with murder on their minds." He holds up two fingers. "Two days! You must really have a high impression of yourself if you think we can fight this. Even if you are going to magically change into a butterfly man in thirty years, it doesn't change our situation now, does it? Our only hope is to hide – for the rest of our lives! I have a better chance if I'm nowhere near you."

"We can go to Port Isaac," Nige suggests. "My family is safe down there at my dad's old place. We can take some time, maybe even find any others that have changed, try and start this uprising again."

Maggie really hopes he's right.

Mac screws up his nose and folds his arms. "Nah. I'll just go back and live with my mum. Become a postman or something. Live out my days in peaceful small village bliss." He pauses for a moment, as if weighing up his options, then, speaking almost to himself, says, "Those early mornings are going to be a bit of a struggle, but at least I'll be alive." He looks back at the group and nods, then moves to stand several feet behind them, lurking in the shadows like Gollum in a trench coat. "Nobody talk to me. You're to pretend I've stormed off, which I would have done if it wasn't so bloody dark." He folds his arms in finality.

Nige sighs and looks at Victoria. "Where was the uprising based before? Maybe we could go there. Find out what happened."

"Well, it's funny you mentioned Port Isaac. We weren't far from there. Near Tintagel Castle."

"Do you think you could find it if we went?" says Maggie. After what she's been through she's more than happy to get away from the city.

"I'll never forget that place. I can take us. Though there won't be much left."

"Perhaps there's something there we can use. But first, we should find somewhere we can get some rest tonight and then leave in the morning." Nige looks to the cultists. "I know you'd like to go and put a hole in the Di Blasio building, but this might be a better use of your time."

The brothers barely look at each other before saying in unison, "We're in."

Terry repeats it a moment later.

Nige smiles and looks back towards Mac.

"Don't talk to me," he says before Nige can open his mouth. "I said not to talk to me." He hums to himself and looks about the ceiling and walls, anywhere but at Nige.

It's clear Nige wants him to stay. There's an awkward pause and he opens his mouth long before speaking. "But you're the best guy I know at stealing trucks, and my car's stuck at Kenneth's apartment building."

"I'm going to be honest with you, Nige," says Mac, arms still tightly folded over his chest. "I'm jealous. I always thought I'd be the chosen one. Bullied at school, excellent powers of deduction, but not that good at anything else. It was my destiny."

"Oh man," Pete chimes in. "I thought I was going to be the chosen one. Motherless, different from all the other kids, but with a unique grasp of technology."

"Everyone did," says Dave. "At least until they grew up to find they were nothing special."

"I didn't." Nige looks between the three of them.

"It is those who want it least, that deserve it most," Terry says, waving his hand as if he is a Jedi doing a mind trick, then bows his head sagely.

"And those who want it most, deserve it least. Which is why you always get a total nob for a prime minister," says Mac.

"Either way," says Nige. "Are you coming or not?"

One half of Mac's mouth creeps up into a smile. "Well, I do hate early mornings, so maybe a postal career isn't right for me. And I do love a road trip. Oh, bloody hell." He mimics pulling a truck horn. "Toot! Toot! Boys and girls on tour!"

The Sleepover

Unsurprisingly, the truck is no longer where they left it.

"Guh," says Mac. "How'd they tow something so big?"

It's still a few hours until morning.

"Perhaps we could stay at mine. Get some sleep. I've got a food delivery coming later." He grins and rubs his hands together. "It won't be comfortable, but one of those big chiller vans could probably carry those of us who can't fly down to Cornwall. And we'll have snacks for days. I went to town on chips and dips."

"How big is your place? Can it fit us all?" Maggie asks.

Mac does a quick head count. "If I'm honest, probably not. But we don't have any other options, do we?"

"Isn't that the first place they'd look to find you? They had someone at your office. They'll be watching your house." Nige transfers Kenneth to his other shoulder. The chrysalis isn't any heavier, but it's become longer, stiffer, and more cumbersome, a lot like a melting canoe.

The PI taps the side of his nose. "I had to put my name down on my office so people knew where to find me for work. But I used a pseudonym on the lease for my apartment. Didn't want anyone I'd whacked a bounty on coming to find me where I slept."

The crowds on the back streets of Camden are thinning as the eight of them wander towards Mac's apartment. Duos and trios of drunken club goers singing and waddling their ways home don't pay them much regard. Nige expects three guys in hooded robes, a small man in a dirty-looking trench coat, two giants, and a tall, 60-year-old carrying what could possibly be a shrink wrapped corpse on his shoulder, don't look like the most approachable bunch.

The tall, brown bricked building that Mac leads them to sits right on the side of the road. Small yellowing balconies, some with washing out to dry, mark each room. Loose white net curtains hang at most windows.

"Here we are." Mac smiles and points up. "My balcony is on the third floor, second from right. Might be best if you two fly up there," he says to Dawn and Victoria.

"We won't need to sleep much," says Victoria. "If you don't have much room, perhaps I'll spend the night watching from the roof. Dawn, it would be an idea for you to take watch from the balcony. Just in case."

"Good plan," says Nige.

Victoria and Dawn fly to the roof and balcony respectively as Mac leads the rest inside.

"I don't bother with the lift. Either someone's pooped in it or it breaks down between floors. Or both." For a moment he stares with blank eyes, and behind them Nige can see only unfathomable horror.

They follow him up to a cramped apartment. Inside, one worn looking upholstered armchair, setup at a dining table with a lace doily place mat, faces a small television that stands on the floor.

"Anyone want a drink?" asks Mac.

"Oh yes please," says Terry. The other three men nod.

"I'm good, thanks," says Maggie. "But do you have a bathroom?"

Mac points her to it, then returns his attention to the gang in the living room. "Make yourself comfortable," he says, then heads to the kitchen.

The cultists and Nige stand in the lounge looking at the one chair.

It's a tale as old as time.

Four proud Englishmen.
One chair.
No one sits.
The end.

"You take it," says Dave. "You're old, aren't you?"

Nige lowers Kenneth to the floor, but although his legs ache after carrying him up the three storeys of stairs, doesn't move towards the chair. "I'm alright thanks."

A few quiet moments later, Mac returns carrying a large recipe book with five assorted vessels balanced precariously on it. "Sorry, I've just realised I've only got one mug." He smiles and holds out his makeshift tray.

Nige takes a peanut butter jar filled with tea. "Thanks."

Terry takes a vase, Pete a bunged up salt shaker, and Dave gets the mug.

Mac swirls his pint glass of tea. "How-"

"This-"

"Sorry."

"This is nice." Nige indicates the flat with a motion of his jar.

"Thanks. I don't get many guests."

"Mm." Nige nods and takes a sip, then removes something from the tip of his tongue with a finger.

"I suppose we better all get some sleep ready for our road trip. I'm sorry I only have one sleeping bag," says Mac.

"That's alright. I've slept outside hundreds of times with nothing," says Terry, removing his robe, lying down, and balling it behind his head. "This is a luxury."

The other cultists do the same.

Maggie returns from the bathroom and makes a beeline for the chair.

"Great. I'll get the sleeping bag." Mac leaves the room, then returns with a kid's GI-Joe sleeping bag, which looks set to come up to around Nige's waist. "Sorry, might be a bit short."

"Don't worry," says Nige. "Maggie, you take this. I'll just make do on the floor." He passes the sleeping bag to her, and she snuggles in as best she can.

"The shop's coming at ten." Mac checks his phone for the time. "We should wait downstairs. When he brings the food up, the van'll be unattended. We'll nick it then."

Wake Up Kenneth

Despite the events of the last few days, Nige wakes feeling some relief knowing that by tonight he will be with his grandchildren and Lewis.

He sits up and gives his neck its morning crack. The three cultists seem to have migrated towards each other during the night. Illuminated by the soft morning sunlight that squeezes through the dirty net curtains, they snuggle together on the floor, underneath the makeshift blanket of their burgundy robes. They look like kids at a sleepover, and once again it strikes him how young they are and how many troubles they've faced. They are outsiders, alone in the world.

Nige gets it. Ever since Fiona passed, he hasn't belonged anywhere either.

When you've got someone, it's ok to never leave the house, to stay in and play board games just the two of you, to spend all your evenings together watching TV, or to just not go out because people get on your nerves.

But that all gets a bit sad when you're on your own. And now that he's lost the two people he called his best friends, he's more alone than ever. He realises how precious the moments with them were, how much of a ball he and Korrigan used to have on a night out, or how much he and Aidan enjoyed poking fun at each other the few times they'd hit the gym together.

He should have done more. Spent more time with them.

And right here, lying on the floor of Mac's apartment, with its one chair, one mug and one bed, he can finally understand why Mac is the way he is. How many other young people lived like this? With social media, streamed video, and working from home, leaving the house has become redundant. Did people have friends any more or was everyone just destined to drift further and further apart? Bubbles of one, staring into their own private windows.

He turns and freezes. Last night, when he finally quelled the rebellious tick-tock of his overactive brain and nodded off, Kenneth had been lying in the hall under Mac's empty coat hooks. Now, he isn't. But there is something there. A shedding. A cracked, withered husk, dry and flaking. But no Kenneth.

He pushes himself up. The others remain asleep.

Sticky footprints lead from the chrysalis into the unlit kitchen. Now he's focusing his attention that way, he can hear a faint papery rustle, a low muttering, and the soft opening and closing of cupboards.

He looks to where Maggie sleeps soundly in the chair. Should he wake her? No. Who knows what Kenneth might look like.

With one hand on the wall to steady himself, hoping to minimise the weight of his steps on the old floorboards, he creeps toward the kitchen. He clings to his breath, letting it out in slow, quiet exhales. What does he fear? He knows what he's going to see - Kenneth. Only changed. With wings, an angular face, taller. But it'll still be Kenneth. Right?

He wasn't scared of Victoria when he saw her for the first time. But the thought doesn't slow the rapid hammering of his heart. He knows why. What if Kenneth doesn't recognise him? Will he know what's happened? What if he remembers the cultists from their broadcast, from the shop where they attacked him? What will he do in response? What might he be capable of when angry or scared?

A floorboard creaks under foot. The rustling stops.

"Hello." Nige's voice comes out without breath. A click of the tongue. A movement of the lips. "Kenneth."

Silence from the kitchen.

He edges further. Peers around the door frame. He can just about see Kenneth's tall form glistening in the shadows.

"Where am I? Is this some sort of soirée?"

"Hey Kenneth," he says, gently raising his hands. "How are you doing?"

"Excuse my French, but my mouth tastes like a badger's arse and I've this blasted headache. Did we get a bit merry last night?" Movement in the dark. The sound of another cupboard opening and closing. "There are no glasses in this infernal kitchen."

"I'm going to turn the light on. Close your eyes." Nige reaches for the switch on the wall outside the kitchen. Hesitates. "Whatever happens, I don't want you to panic."

"Panic?" says Kenneth just as the light comes on.

He is naked. Head nearly touching the ceiling.

"No, don't turn ar— Oh." Nige covers his eyes. Some of his previous, internally logged questions regarding how much the body might change are answered, and along a similar thread, at least one sizeable rumour he's heard about the influencer appears to be true.

He doesn't want to look, but at the same time can't tear his eyes away. It's difficult to describe. (Before you get any ideas, we've moved on from the subject of the sizeable rumour.) Kenneth's body hasn't changed extensively. The skeletal structure is the same only longer. He's slimmer. His musculature stretches over his bones in the same way, but as if the same physical mass has just been pulled tighter.

The wings are two sets of two rather than one large set, as Nige had assumed when he first saw Victoria. The first pairing connects to Kenneth's body from arm to mid lat, and the second from where the others finish to just below his kidneys. They are mainly blue with long black lines that run from the outer edges in towards where they connect to his torso. Covering each wing, and twinkling like sequins in the light of the kitchen's solitary naked bulb, are thousands of tiny scales.

Kenneth moves a hand to cover himself. "Sorry, didn't realise I was starkers. Sticky and naked - not a good way to start the day. Though I suppose that does depend upon who you wake up next to - woof!" He leans his head back, and crinkles his nose in thought. "Is it my birthday?" He rubs the back of his head, his hand touching one wing briefly. Cranes his neck to look over his shoulder. "What the dickens?" Turns quickly around as he catches sight of the four new appendages on his back, and steps backwards towards Nige, trying to get away from them.

Nige raises his hands to catch him as they stumble through the hallway and into Mac's bedroom opposite.

Mac leaps out of bed immediately, as if on guard, dressed in a pair of boxer shorts so old that the main trunk appears to be trying to flee the elastic waistband. He raises half a pool cue and a small pin hammer from somewhere beneath the sheets. "I was just doing my job." Flails them about with eyes half closed.

"It's us, Mac," says Nige, untangling himself from wing and limb. "Kenneth, Jesus Christ, I said not to panic."

"Not to panic? Not to panic? You try not panicking when you awake in some filthy bedsit, lying in a pool of god knows what, only to find out you're naked and have wings." He rolls over and backs away on all fours. Bumping into the wall. He grabs a discarded T-shirt and covers himself. "What the heck is going on? Who are you both? Kidnappers? What have you done to me?"

Mac, eyes now open and fully awake, looks at Nige and slowly lowers his weapons. "Has it happened? Is he out?"

"No," Nige says, exasperated. "I just opened the window and a really big moth flew in."

Mac shoves his tongue into his bottom lip and makes a face. "Sarcasm is the lowest form of wit."

"Has what happened?" Kenneth says from his cramped position in the corner. His eyes dart between them. "What's happened to me?"

"Kenneth," comes Maggie's voice from the other room. The sound of her hurried footsteps approaching, and then she's in the room, flying towards him. Her hand covers her mouth as she sees him, and she takes a tentative step back.

"Maggie?" he says. "Do we know these people? What's happened to me?" His voice rises unsteadily.

She holds out her palms, trying to calm him. "We're ok, Kenneth. These people are friends."

"Do you remember me at all?" says Nige.

Kenneth looks like he wants to shake his head, then blinks a few times. His cheeks rise as he squints. "I want to say Nigel."

Nige smiles. "That's right. I was hired as your bodyguard. Do you remember the intruder in your room?"

Kenneth shakes his head.

"This is going to sound strange to begin with, but Victoria Desdemona came to visit you."

Kenneth's mouth hangs loose. His whole body seems to relax. "Victoria?"

"We thought she was an assassin, so we got you out. There were others trying to kill you, but we managed to get you away."

Kenneth holds up his arms and looks at them as if he's never seen them before. "That doesn't explain what's happened to me." He pauses, flexing his fingers. "But, it…"

"It seems right?" says Nige.

Kenneth nods.

"This happened to Victoria, and Dawn, too," Maggie says. "They're on the roof. I'll get them." She leaves the room.

"My Victoria? She's still alive?" He frowns slightly, but Nige can see the joy beneath.

The panic over, Mac tucks his hammer and pool cue back into bed. "She has wings like you," he says.

"And who might you be?" Kenneth pushes himself up to stand, keeping Mac's T-shirt in place.

Mac doesn't move. "Trent Macadamia PI," he says automatically.

"And what's your involvement?"

"I was hired to find out what happened to someone who worked for Terrence. He disappeared last week. I think the people that were after you may have killed Terrence and his security. The Twins as well." Nige notices that Mac looks at Kenneth the same way Aidan did, completely starstruck. It causes a soft ache to swell in his heart.

"Weren't you bigger? With a beard?" says Kenneth as he moves a hand in a circular motion over his chin to elucidate.

The words come like a kick to the stomach. Nige senses the turn of Mac's head towards him. He chews the corner of his mouth. For the first time, the question of blame bubbles in his mind. Clears his throat. "That was Aidan. They killed him. He was trying to save you."

Kenneth's face falls. "Oh, Nigel. I'm sorry. I remember now, the lad with the cereal." His eyes wander across the ceiling, as if he's searching through unpleasant memories. "It's tough to lose someone in battle. At the whims of someone else. It can be so needless. So thankless. I'm sorry. You have my word that I will do my utmost to help you right this wrong."

Mac starts to rummage through a wonky wardrobe and pulls out a pair of shorts. He throws them to Kenneth. "You can start by putting these on."

Kenneth catches them and pulls them up, knotting the drawstring tightly around his waist. "Do you have any idea who it was?" he says.

"We do." Nige folds his arms.

"Then we must go to the police at once."

"We can't. We think…" He swallows. "We think whoever did this is bigger than that. If we go to the police, we'll just find ourselves back in hot water."

"Indeed." Kenneth rolls his shoulders. His wings twitch. "I have so many questions. I don't know what to ask first."

"'I'll put the kettle on," says Mac. "Shoe of coffee, anyone?"

A text comes to Nige's phone as he and Kenneth follow Mac out of the room. The phone doesn't get much use, and when Mac sees him pull it from his pocket, he snorts.

"Bit big, isn't it?" he laughs.

"What, like your house Richie Rich?" Nige bites back.

"Touché," Mac says with a wiggle of the head.

Before Nige can read the message, a shadow falls over the room. A figure lands on the balcony outside, swiftly followed by another.

"Is that them?" says Kenneth, stepping forward. A hopeful look of wonder on his face.

"Victoria and Dawn," says Maggie.

"Oh, I really should have bought more chairs," Mac says as he leans out of the kitchen doorway. "And more cups." He disappears back into the kitchen and begins a frantic search for extra vessels.

Kenneth hurries forward into the main room, then stops, throwing a confused look at the cultists who are sprawled under their robes on the floor, like a three-headed beast.

The balcony door cracks open from the outside and his face softens. "Victoria?" he says as the two-winged women step into the confines of the living room. His eyes sparkle. "Is it really you? And Dawn too?" He takes her by the hand. "What is the world coming to?"

"Oh Kenneth, it's always been this way," says Victoria, stepping closer. Her smile takes up her entire face. "Happy birthday Kenneth."

He beams. "You remembered? I can't believe you're here. I thought you'd left me." He holds his hand up and she twirls beneath it. He watches her in awe as her wings brush his bare chest.

"I wanted to come back, but I couldn't," she says, for a moment her eyes flick to the floor and she sighs. "I tried to find you before this happened. I didn't want you going through it alone."

Nige smiles. A warm glow fills him. He's always been a sucker for a reunion.

And for a moment he feels everything might one day be ok again.

Then he glances at his phone. And all the good feelings evaporate like spit on a hotplate. In the time it takes to read a text his whole world crumbles.

Mac steps out of the kitchen with a concerned frown. "What is it?"

Nige's mouth is dry. Doesn't know if he can speak the words. With a shaking hand, he passes the phone.

Everybody in the living room watches him as he falls apart.

Mac reads the text out loud. "If you ever want to see your grandkids again, then be at Television Centre for the start of tonight's show, and bring Kenneth's chrysalis." His arm drops to his side. "Nige, I'm—"

The room blurs into silence as Nige sinks further into his own thoughts. Frantic talk starts up around him, but he can't hear the words. He takes shallow breaths. Fights the crushing grey that threatens to overwhelm him. "What… what time does it start?" His eyes lift to Mac's.

"Seven." Mac's face is pale.

"Fuck!" He slams his fist into the bathroom door, then again. The wooden veneer crumples. He clutches his head in his hands. "You don't know what they said they'd do to them." The sting of tears in his eyes. "They're just little kids."

He is powerless. All he has is his strength, and what good is that? This problem can't be fixed with force. There's no one to hit. He squeezes his useless hands into fists and leans his head against the wall.

Mac bends down to look him in the eye. "This isn't the end, Nige," he says, holding up the phone. "They've been cocky. This is a weakness. We can use this. This message means we can do something."

"Whatever they want, I'll do it. I don't care about anything else." He feels dizzy. The room and its occupants spin around him. This can't be happening.

"But they won't let any of you go," says Victoria. "It's not going to be a trade. I'm sorry Nige, but if you are what they think you are, they will want your whole family."

"What can we do then?" Nige takes a step backwards towards the front door. "I don't care what you say, I'm going."

Mac tries to stand in his way. "If we do what they want, they win. We need to come up with a plan."

"But if we don't go, I lose everything." His stomach lurches at the thought that those two innocent children are somewhere now captive. Probably separated from their parents, scared and alone. And what of Lewis? Is he still alive?

"Let's think." Mac begins to pace the room, though in the cramped hallway it looks a little more like he's just turning in circles. He starts to mumble to himself. His facial expressions becoming more animated at every turn. He suddenly stops and looks at Nige. "So they want us to arrive at 7pm, right? That gives us a while. They can't know we're all together. They can't know Kenneth's out. They think they've got us on the back foot after the attack at the church. I say let's do something they wouldn't expect. Let's storm the gates. Let's take the fight to them! What have we got to lose? We know they won't let us go if we go in for a trade." Mac looks at Nige. "Let's just do something."

"Just last night you wanted to leave." A little flicker of flame lights in Nige's belly at Mac's words. "Why would you risk anything for me?"

"Who was I kidding? We're all in the same boat. Our fates were smooshed together the moment I hopped in that bin."

"But what can we do?"

"All we can do is what we can do, Nige. Isn't that right?"

Nige nods.

"Can any of you think of a way to get in to Television Centre before tonight?" Mac looks around.

"There's a studio audience," says Maggie. "I have a friend that could get us some passes. But that'd be later on."

"Right, and we can't all go in through the front door," says Mac. He points between himself and Nige. "We're wanted men. And these three are giant butterfly people!"

Nige puts his hands on either side of his head and squeezes. He needs to think. "I know a guy who's done security at the BBC before. He might know the place. Could get me a key card for backstage or something, but..." he shakes his head. "... he's a bit of a liability."

"Sounds like that's the best we've got," says Mac.

Nige looks at each of them in turn. "I appreciate it, but you don't all have to come. I don't expect I'll survive."

"If we don't end this tonight," says Victoria. "Then all of us will be on the run for the rest of our lives."

Mac nods. "We'll put a rain check on the road trip."

Dave squeezes his fist as if crushing a plastic cup in anger. "If it involves obliterating The Guardian hell spawn, then you have the warriors of The Church of The Fallen Angels by your side."

A loud buzz comes from Mac's door, causing them all to jump. He hits the intercom.

"Tesco delivery."

He releases the button. "Looks like our ride's arrived." Then holds the button down again. "Ok mate, be right there."

Recruitment Drive

The Tesco delivery driver doesn't look overly surprised when all nine of them come barrelling out of Mac's apartment building, storm straight up to his van, and in unplanned yet semi-tuneful chorus, demand he hand over the keys.

The young man takes one look at Terry's rifle and rolls his eyes. "I always knew this area was rough," he says. Without protest he takes a box of cornflakes from the back of the van, goes to sit on the kerb, and begins snacking. "The keys are in the ignition," he sighs. "I should go work for Ocado. I bet they never get their vans nicked."

The winged members of the group take to the skies, and Mac climbs into the driver's seat, with the cultists squeezed next to him up front. Maggie and Nige are crammed in the small space between the food deliveries.

Once they are on the road, Nige makes a call.

A voice like gravel finally answers the phone. "Alright boss."

"Spoony."

"Mate, fuck's going on?" says Spoony Phil. "Ain't heard from Korrigan in days. Almost missed my shift last night. Was just settling in for a night on that Light A Penny Candle you gave me, and Dick Kicker Kath rings to see where I am." He sounds annoyed. As unlikely as it may sound, Spoony Phil has been churning through the Maeve Binchy novels as fast as Nige can lend them to him.

Nige covers his eyes with his hand. "Have you not seen the wanted posters?"

"What wanted posters?"

"Look Phil, we've worked together a long time. You know I'm of pretty sound mind, right?"

"As sound as any of us." A snorting chuckle escapes from him.

"I need you to listen to me and trust what I've got to say."

A short grunt on the other end of the line is the only indication that Spoony Phil's ears are open and willing to receive.

He fills him in on the last few days.

"You what? Who the fuck—" comes the reply.

"I need your help, mate."

"You got it, mate."

Nige could say a lot of things about Spoony Phil, but his loyalty is always without question.

"I need to get backstage at BBC television centre tonight. You've worked there, right? Can you get us in? Maybe get a keycard?"

"Yeah. Been up there a few times. I'll give Tommy the Wizard a ring. He should be able to sort a copy of the card I nicked, make sure it still works with their system." He pauses. "What are you up to?"

"It's hard to explain over the phone. How long do you think it'll take to get the card and meet us there?"

"I'll get on it now. Two hours, I reckon. There's a little cafe round the corner. The Penguin. All you can eat breakfast. Muchos delicious. I can meet you there."

Nige confirms and finishes the call.

"All sorted?" asks Maggie, already off hers.

He nods. "Did you have much luck?"

"Got four passes for the studio audience."

"I should have a way in backstage." He shouts to Mac at the front. "What are we going to do once we're there?"

"Let's pool what we know," says Mac. "Terry, grab that clipboard and pen. Time to put this detective's brain to work."

Brunch

They arrive early. Maggie gets a table in the corner and the others enter separately in a bid not to draw too much attention.

They needn't have bothered. The place is nearly empty, and the waiter doesn't look at them twice before throwing menus down and disappearing back behind the counter.

The carpet under the table pulls at their soles. Years of cooking greasy, all day breakfast gives the air a soupy quality.

Mac looks down his nose at the menu, which has several dry tomato ketchup blotches on the cover.

"Don't they ever wipe these down," he hisses.

A dead fly falls out when he opens it. He gags.

Nige doesn't look up. Keeps reading the text on his phone, searching for a hidden meaning. Some clue to tell them they are doing the right thing. His thumb hovers over the call button. He wants to give them a piece of his mind, but what would he even say?

"Well, I'm famished," says Maggie. She calls the waiter over and orders. "You should eat something, Nige. You'll need your strength."

"I'm not hungry. I'll just have whatever you're having." He looks back at his phone.

Mac orders a single black coffee, and in a show of boyish competitiveness, the cultists order enough cholesterol to clog up a blue whale's aorta.

Spoony Phil arrives as the first plates are being brought to the table. He's not as tall as Nige, but he's broad. Dark-haired, heavy greying stubble, and a thick, red neck that disappears into his chin, giving his head the appearance of a thumb. A long pink bottle scar that he received in a fight outside a club runs along one cheek. He removes his moleskin coat, revealing his usual hi-vis vest and black windbreaker.

"Jimmy, my usual please," he says, before he's even sat down. The waiter nods.

Nige stands and holds out a hand. "Thanks for coming."

Phil shakes it. "I won't hear it. Anything I can do to get back at the punks who did this, I'm here for it." He scooches a chair over from an occupied table. Sits before the occupying woman, who's husband has just popped to the bathroom, can protest. "Now, who's this we plannin' to fuck up?"

Nige tells him.

"Sounds like you called the right guy," he says as he shovels a whole fried egg dripping in ketchup into his mouth. "You got a plan?"

"Mac?" says Nige, hopeful.

Mac hasn't spoken since Phil arrived. He's spent the entire time with his nose in a notepad, jotting things down. He finishes his coffee and carefully places the cup on its saucer with both hands. "I have something." He turns to Phil. "Mr Spoon, do you know the layout inside?" Spoony Phil nods. "Would you be able to get Nige to the roof, and Maggie and I to the room where they control the broadcast?"

Phil bobs his head. "Yeah, sure. Last time I worked there was only a couple of weeks ago. I know the layout pretty well."

"And Katy and Charlie? Would they recognise you?"

"We've met a few times," says Phil.

Nige nods in confirmation. "They know who he is."

Mac pauses, his eyes flicking from side to side for a moment. Finally, he nods. "Then here's what we'll do…"

The Plan

Mac drives the Tesco truck right up to the main gate with Nige and Maggie, once again, stuffed in the back. The cultists are already waiting out front of television centre, ready to meet up with Spoony Phil once he's helped the rest in backstage.

A bored security guard in a small wooden tollbooth style box bars their way.

He looks over his list and shakes his head. "I haven't got you down. You're going to have to leave."

This is expected, and something Mac has planned for.

Spoony Phil rocks up from nowhere with a confident swagger, dressed almost identically to the man in the booth. He knocks on the glass. "Sorry, Doug," he says. "I ain't updated the list yet. This Tesco van needs to go round back to Studio One. These fuckin' influencers are banging off demands like no one's business. You know the sort." He adopts a posh English accent and waggles a little finger by his chin. "I need four thousand Pringles smashed into my arse, or I'm not going on stage tonight. Bunch o' twats."

The guy in the booth shakes his head. "Course they are," then to Mac, "sorry to keep you waiting."

He hands them an A4 map with limited directions to Studio One then buzzes them in.

The back lot is quiet, a ghost town. Nothing like Nige expected, what with the year's biggest show happening tonight.

They park up in a small car park and wait.

It doesn't take long for Spoony Phil to catch up with them.

He leads them towards the back door. Hands Mac, Maggie, and Nige a keycard each. Holds the last one aloft. "Now, Tommy the Wizard said he's made these skeleton keys. They should get you through most doors in the building."

He steps towards a set of blacked out double doors that lead inside and holds the card next to the reader. It beeps and the door clicks. "Bingo."

He ushers them into a long corridor lined with open flight cases and cables. Two techs wearing headsets hurry past without giving them a second look.

Nige feels some relief at finally being inside, near where he thinks his grandkids might be, but there's still the worry of what might lie in their way. The place must be crawling with security. They'll need to move carefully.

"So, two locations," says Mac, holding up two fingers. "Nige to the roof to meet the others. Me and Maggie to the control room." He turns to Phil. "What's the best way to get there without being stopped? If anyone working here today has been paying attention to the news, then they're likely to recognise us. And we can't afford that."

"The control room is one floor up," Phil explains while he leads them. "There's a stairway near the main entrance that'll take you there and also to the roof. Last time I was here there weren't many people hanging around the main entrance. It's generally pretty quiet until the audience comes in."

"And I need to know where the new influencers are likely to be," says Nige. "If the kids are here, they'll probably be there. Somewhere with security."

"That's backstage," says Phil. "As long as you can find the main stage area, you'll see it. Look for those laminated signs on the doors."

As they arrive at the stairwell, Nige places a hand on Phil's shoulder. "We couldn't have done this without you."

"Thank me when you got those kiddies safe," he says. He slaps Nige on the arm and heads out the main entrance to meet up with what remains of The Church of The Fallen Angels. The plan is for the four of them to come in as studio audience. Phil, dressed in his guard uniform, will help them get by security.

Nige goes up the stairs, closely followed by Mac and Maggie. At the first floor landing, when they are due to part, they stop. Neither Mac nor

Nige know what to say.

Maggie looks between them.

"Thanks for—"

"Good lu—"

They say simultaneously.

"Thanks for being here, Mac." Nige scratches the back of his head.

"I don't know where else I could be. You really give them what for."

"Will do. Will do."

Mac holds out a fist.

"Um?" Nige looks unsure.

"Isn't this something you old people do? I think you're supposed to bop it."

"I know," says Nige. He scratches his chin then pulls a startled Mac in for a hug. It's the first time he's ever hugged another man. Not even his own father. "Be careful."

Mac closes his eyes. Nige suspects it's also the first time he's ever hugged another man. The impression he got from Mac in the church was that he never knew his Dad. "You too."

With that out of the way, they give solemn nods and split.

The Control Room Heist

Mac feels sick. Physically. And he can't stop yawning.

He touches Terry's rifle which is secreted beneath his trench coat. Taking over the control room is crucial to his plan. He knows, but can't stop questioning why he put himself forward for this role and not someone more imposing.

His primary concern is what to do if one of the crew tries to be a hero. Does he shoot? Does he pistol whip that fool? Is it still called a pistol whip or is that all very nineties? Do you even pistol whip with a rifle? Rifle whip starts to sound like a creamy pudding. He really should have googled a few movie quotes before they arrived. But there's been no time.

'Everybody get down!' was a classic gun wielding maniac catchphrase.

'Nobody move or I'll blow your bloody brains out!' Another strong contender.

"There it is," says Maggie, pointing to a door with a small circular window.

From outside, Mac can see the room houses two rows of five monitors hanging above a desk covered in buttons, faders, and tiny LEDs. Three people, two men and a woman, attend to them.

Maggie takes her phone out and points the camera at Mac. "Recording," she says.

He pulls the rifle out and takes a few quick breaths. Then he kicks the door. It doesn't move. Doesn't even shudder. A jarring pain screams up his leg and into his hip. The crew inside turn to look.

"I think it's a pull," Maggie says and reaches for the handle.

"I was just getting their attention," says Mac. "But you can probably cut that bit." With one last breath for luck, he charges in, brandishing the gun. "Everybloody blow or I'll down... um... your brains," he shouts. Ah, balls. Messed that up.

Understanding the implication more than the words themselves, the crew dive to the ground. At the sight of the gun, one of the men starts to cry.

"What's going on? What do you want?" says the other, then pauses as he looks at them. "Maggie Greaves, is that you?"

"Quiet you," says Mac. "We're taking over the show. The Church of The Fallen Angels will be heard."

Maggie lowers the phone. "Ok, I think that's enough." She turns towards the man that recognised her and holds her hand out. "George, I'm so sorry. Please let me explain."

The man takes her hand, and stands with his other still held to his head. Sweat gleams on his brow. "Is this some sort of prank?"

"No. I just needed it to look like we'd taken over the control centre here. We need your help."

"I'm sorry I don't understand." He turns towards the monitors and massages the top of his head. "Look, we're really behind with the show. Stockwell's changed everything around, and now he wants to add a birthday message for some kid's grandad too. We're up to our arses here."

"Listen to me. Ian Stockwell isn't who we think he is," she says. "He's working for a secret agency that has murdered The Twins, Stefan Di Blasio, and Terrence. They tried to kill me and Kenneth." She nods to Mac. "And they've tried to frame Mac here for it." She looks to the monitors. "I'm guessing that grandad is Nige Davies; he's reported to have kidnapped Kenneth. He's been all over the news."

"Have you got any proof?"

"I was there when they killed Stefan."

"And I have these." Mac hands him his phone already set to show the pictures he took of The Twins in the alley. "Before you ask, I didn't do it."

"Pictures of bodies doesn't exonerate you," says the other man. He wipes his cheeks and peers over George's shoulder to see.

"No, but perhaps a call from Kenneth and Dawn might?" says Maggie, holding out her phone.

"Kenneth?" says Maggie into the phone. "George is listening."

"Old boy, long time no speak," comes Kenneth's voice on speaker phone. "Maggie's telling the truth. These blaggards have been hounding me since Wednesday. We need your help to tell the world. You in?"

"I guess." George frowns.

"What do you want us to do?" says the woman.

"When the time comes, you just need to make sure the show keeps running," says Mac. "Make sure the cameras stay on us."

"If that's all, then why did you pretend to take us hostage?"

Mac takes one of his two remaining bounty bracelets from his pocket and slaps it on his own wrist. "Police protection."

The Roof

Nige steps through the door at the top of the stairs that leads to the roof. The air is cool, and in the distance he can see the faint darkening of the sky. The odd twinkle of an early star marks the oncoming and gradual end to the day.

So much has happened since he last looked at the London skyline four nights ago in Kenneth's apartment. So much he knew as fact has turned out to be fiction. He's lost and tired, but most of all, he is angry. His lip curls. He will get his chance to get back at those who have hurt him.

He squeezes his fists and scans the rooftops of the surrounding buildings. Despite the stunning backdrop of the sunset and city, all he can see in his mind are Charlie and Katy. He doesn't know what he'll do if The Guardians hurt them.

He phones Dawn.

"Where are you?" he says.

"To your right. We're coming."

He spots them take off from the top of a building across the road.

He takes the bounty bracelet Mac gave him and slaps it on his wrist. Apparently, the police usually respond within around five hours, but for London's most wanted, it could be as little as two. If they are lucky, the police will get here after the show starts, when the audience is in. If not, it means the cultists and Phil will be stuck outside and they won't have reinforcements.

Nige doesn't care either way. He's no longer worried about clearing his name. He just needs to get his family out. He cracks his knuckles.

It's not in Mac's plan, but with or without anyone's help, Nige has decided he's going straight for the cordoned-off area where the new Di

Blasio influencers are. And if the kids aren't there, he's going to hit someone until either his fist liquidates or they tell him where they are.

Victoria and Dawn land first with poise and grace, followed by Kenneth. He flies the way a newborn giraffe walks, ending his flight with a crash landing into the side of the little outbuilding that holds the door back downstairs.

"Not as easy as it looks this flying business," he says upon recovery.

"There's been a change of plan," Nige says. "Spoony says the kids are likely to be with the new influencers in the artist's area behind the stage, and us four are going straight for it." There's no reason why they wouldn't believe his lie.

"Really?" says Victoria.

"It's the only way to guarantee their safety," he says, leading them back down to the level below. He doesn't look back, afraid his face might give him away.

Victoria grips Nige's shoulder. "This all seems a bit hasty. Is this what everyone has agreed?"

Nige doesn't meet her gaze. It's not in Mac's plan. But he can't stand the thought of the kids on their own.

"We don't want to rush in," says Kenneth. "If we've got this wrong, they'll have everything they want."

"But we don't know what hell they are putting Katy and Charlie through. Jesus Kenneth, they're just kids. They don't deserve this."

"But if we fail, Nigel, or if they aren't there, then we might lose them. I know you want to go in guns blazing, but we need to wait. Wait and make sure."

Nige brushes both hands over his head, pulling the skin of his forehead taught, then throws a fist through the nearest wall, smashing it into powdered plaster.

"Does that mean you agree with me?" says Kenneth.

Nige wipes the wall from his hand onto his trousers, leaving a white powder mark. "It does."

"Then we wait?" says Kenneth.

He sighs in resignation. "We wait for Mac's signal."

The Show Begins

They find a small canteen area with a TV on the wall and a coffee machine. The place is empty. Nige guesses most of the workers are busy with show prep.

They lock themselves in and wait for what seems like forever. When the show finally begins, the studio audience's screams and cheers rattle through the walls like thunder.

They watch as the show opens with a thought-provoking rendition of Candle in The Wind by Elton John Two, followed by an introduction by the night's host, Cara Montega. Her skin, teeth, and hair are flawless. She smiles as the audience quietens.

"Thanks for joining us for this special Kenneth Bailey memorial show. We were all terribly saddened this week when the news came that our favourite influencer was taken from his home." She looks down and shakes her head, then looks defiantly into the camera. "But as the proud British people that we are, we will not let acts of terrorism and the threat of violence make us change how we live our lives. We cannot let them win. We refuse to let that happen." She holds her hands up to the applause of the audience before continuing.

"Kenneth Bailey was a brave man who fought for this country in two world wars. He would not want us moping about as our enemies try to threaten our freedom."

"Bloody would," says Kenneth, folding his arms. "Just look at them. None of them knew me, and they're using my death as an excuse to party."

No one else says anything.

"Tonight we are going to celebrate the life of a great, great man. We've got loads more live music coming up, as well as a few other special guests." A short video of each of the different acts runs. "And later, at 9 o'clock, the moment we've all been waiting for, the first interview with the five new Di Blasio influencers." She smiles, and the audience goes wild.

"But first, we have a special little girl, who, like Kenneth, is celebrating her birthday today."

Nige's breath catches in his throat. Although it's nowhere near Katy's birthday, he knows it's her that Cara is talking about. Please let her be here in the studio.

The camera pans across the audience. Then the shot zooms in on a little face he knows so well, surrounded by others he doesn't. Except one. Sitting right next to Katy is the doorman he and Korrigan hired to work at the club the night The Twins were murdered. The man smiles into the camera. Mac was right. He does look like a ferret.

As far as he can see, Lewis, Charlie, and Nikki aren't there.

"This is Katy," says the host. It's clear she is reading from a teleprompter. "A few weeks before we lost Kenneth, Katy sent a letter asking him for help. She told him that the only thing she wanted for her birthday was to see her grandaddy again. You see, he's been missing for months." She turns to the audience with a grin. "And what better way to find a missing person than with a show that everyone in the world watches."

The ferret-faced man puts his arm around Katy's shoulders as if to make a show of comforting her, and it takes everything for Nige not to storm into the main studio.

"So of course, Kenneth, being the kind and generous soul that he was, promised he'd do all he could to help. We told Katy we'd do our best tonight to find her granddad for her birthday. So if you're watching Nigel, then we want to hear from you. If you can get to the show within the next hour, before she has to head home to go to sleep," Cara smiles, "then we would love to reunite you with your family. Please come and make your granddaughter's birthday a real dream come true."

Although he can tell the show host is only reading what she's been told to, Nige can sense the element of threat in the words.

The Kids

Last night's shift had been a late one and Phil is shattered. He and Dick Kicker Kath had been on the door at Aqua Lounge, and he stayed afterwards to have a chat and a drink with some of the girls.

Despite it being a Saturday, he had no plans to go out tonight. He hoped to catch up on the time he missed last night, and chill out with a cup of chamomile and smash through the rest of Nige's copy of 'Light a Penny Candle'. The old fella was right. Maeve Binchy was pretty bloody good.

But instead of his pre-planned me-time, he finds himself trailing the three biggest nerds in history into some glitzy celeb kiss-arse party. He looks around at the assorted audience members as they take their seats and tuts. Bunch o' sycophantic bell ends.

He takes a bottle of Newcastle Brown that he's brought from home from inside his coat, and cracks it open on the back of the chair in front. The man sitting there turns and gives him the evil eye. Phil doesn't react.

"Do you boys want a beer? Got enough for a cheeky one each."

All three cultists turn him down, which to be fair he's quite happy about. More for him. If he has to sit through this bollocks, at least he can do it with a beer or four.

An usher in a luminous attendant's waist coat notices him take a swig and moves towards them. Phil folds his arms and shakes his head to let him know that he's about to come up against an immovable object. The usher, clearly realising he himself is not a particularly unstoppable force, focuses ahead, and walks straight past.

As he scans the stage and audience, Phil leans over to the cultist on his right, the taller of the three. Pete, he thinks he's called. He nudges him with his elbow. "So what we doin'? Where're these pricks that offed my boys and got Nige's grandkids?"

Dave leans over his brother. "We have to wait for the fire alarm," he hisses. "We must do nothing until the signal."

Phil holds up a palm. "Alright mate, I know the plan." He gives Pete a look as if to say what's his problem.

Usually when people don't answer your question, it's because they don't know the answer themselves. He decides not to press it, but marks Dave down in his mental little black book of muppets.

"Then why did you ask?"

Maybe they got off on the wrong foot. While he and the lads were chatting outside, he complimented their evening wear. People could wear what they liked. He didn't care. But they hadn't seemed too happy about it. Apparently they were robes not dresses. Like he gave a fuck.

Nevertheless, he moves Dave from the little black book of muppets to the big black book of pricks.

The show begins with the hologram Elton John singing that song about candles. What a load of old shit. And as the rest of the audience gawps, Phil scans them for any familiar faces. It doesn't take long for him to spot one. The ferret bastard. The one Korrigan hired in as a backup doorman only last week. He'd been working the Electric Ballroom on Wednesday when Phil had been manning the door. And now here he is sitting in the section to the right, near the stage.

There's a nipper sitting next to him.

Phil doesn't have kids, and if anyone ever bothered to ask, he'd say he never wanted any, or that he never found the right woman. But deep down, he's always wanted one or two. Boys or girls. Doesn't matter.

Bit late in the day now though.

Still, he knows kids are a lot of work, and sometimes people who had them question whether it was a good idea. So, when Nige shows off the latest picture or video of his two grandkids, Phil always responds with as much enthusiasm as he can. Not nonce level, or anything. Just enough to show he cares without getting too maudlin.

He recognises Katy instantly.

"That's her." He stands.

"Wait." Pete grips his wrist tightly. Pulls him back down.

Surprisingly strong for a bean pole.

Dave leans across. "We can't do anything now. If we can see her, she's safe. As soon as the alarm goes, we intercept."

Phil shakes his head. His blood boils. The beer affects his forearms like Popeye's spinach. He cracks his knuckles and the man sitting in front of him turns around. "What?" he spits, to which the man doesn't respond, quickly turning away again.

His gaze returns to the guy next to Katy. He snarls as the prick puts his arm around her. A little too friendly-like. He decides as soon as he gets his chance, that same arm is coming off at the shoulder, only to be unceremoniously shoved right up its owner's arse.

A video reel of Kenneth Bailey's best bits starts and the audience begins to chat amongst themselves.

As soon as the fire alarm sounds, Phil is up like a bull at a rodeo.

The attendants at the front of the stands raise their hands for calm and start instructing the panicking audience towards the fire exits on either side of the studio. Ferret-face pulls Katy from her seat and drags her across the front.

Phil pushes through the flow of people as they rush against him.

"Excuse me, sir," says the same attendant that had noticed his beer. "The fire exits are the other way."

He doesn't hear. All he can see is Katy being led away. "Move," he roars, and a path clears like the red sea.

He runs through the opening, the three cultists close behind. With his carefully honed doorman senses, he realises that his shouted order, even above the chattering hiss of the excited audience, has drawn the attention of several Di Blasio security guards dotted around the room. They move to block his path, but he lowers his head and pushes on, bowling over any audience members unlucky enough to be in his way.

Police Protection

About ruddy time.

Mac stands in a room across the hall from the control room. From here, through the wall of windows, he can see both ends of the road that runs across the front of the building.

At the far end, a line of police cars – the most he's ever seen in his life – suddenly smash around the corner, lighting the whole of the street blue. They scream up to the front of the television centre and spew out a legion of officers who quickly blockade the road, moving pedestrians away from the area.

Mac crosses the room. With the heel of his hand, he cracks the glass on the fire alarm and presses the button. A wailing klaxon blares out of the ceiling. He puts his hands over his ears and returns to the window.

A black truck pulls up outside, and a SWAT team 'hut' their way out and up to a small gazebo that is being erected by the front door. For a moment he's a little proud of himself for being awarded such a strong police presence, but then he remembers that he hasn't actually committed any crimes.

He calls Nige. "The police are here. SWAT and everything. Time to see if I can get through to them."

"Make sure they stay outside. Be ruthless."

"I will."

Mac calls 999. Tells them who he is. Asks to be put through to the head officer outside. After a few minutes, and with a hiss of static, they are connected.

"Trent Macadamia? This is Officer Torrence of the metropolitan police. I'm in charge of this situation."

Mac has had a little more time to google classic terrorist lines now so he tries one.

"No, you're not Officer Torrence. I am." He pauses. Feels maybe he put the emphasis in the wrong place. "I mean um… I'm in charge of this situation. You're still Officer Torrence…" he says. This is already going badly. "Either way, I've selected twenty hostages at random from the studio audience. They all have guns to their heads."

"What do you want, Trent?" says Officer Torrence.

Ah, trying to use first name's to build a rapport, huh? Oldest trick in the negotiators hand book.

"Tonight's show is to be broadcast no matter what. We will release a hostage every twenty minutes until the show ends and then the rest once it has. If you cut the show, we'll know and we'll kill them all."

"There's four hundred members of the studio audience inside. Let the rest out and we'll know you're serious."

"Oh I'm serious, alright. They should be coming out right about…" Mac looks towards Studio One as the side door opens and the studio audience flows out into the street. "…now."

"Jesus." Officer Torrence begins to shout orders to his team. "Somebody get them out of here. OK, Trent. Anything else?"

"Yes. No one comes in or out of this building until we've finished. Again, we will know."

"If someone comes out, we aren't going to stop them."

"You will if you know what's good for the remaining hostages."

"Ok. Ok. I'll see what we can do. Can you tell me what this is about?"

"This is about vengeance for the fallen angels," says Mac, hoping he sounds unhinged. "We will execute our first hostage in twenty minutes if we don't have confirmation that our demands have been met."

He hangs up. That's what real terrorists do to make sure no one messes with them. A nice dramatic hang up. He hopes it works.

He casts a glance up to the roof opposite. Prays they'll send snipers. If not, this will all be for nothing. They need eyes on the skies. He doesn't want any uninvited guests coming in from the air.

Admit This

As soon as the fire alarm starts shrieking Nige is on his feet. He's been teetering on the edge ever since he saw Katy.

Now is the time.

Flanked by the three winged ones, he leaves the canteen.

With purpose, he strides through the empty corridor that leads to the backstage area, tensing his fingers as the anger surges through him. For him, the rage is a generator. It gives him power.

He has to trust that Spoony Phil and the cultists have his granddaughter safe. The focus now is Lewis, Nikki, and Charlie. If they are in the building, they must be backstage.

They approach a set of doors on which a laminated sign reads 'Di Blasio Influencers - No admittance'.

Kenneth catches his arm. "You saved my life, and I'm with you 'til the bitter end, but there may be guards on the other side of that door. Don't go in there with anger. If you do, then they'll only reciprocate. Recall my words from the night we met. It's good to be strong, it's good to be trained, but it's better to be underestimated."

Nige nods, a grim determination on his face.

Pulls the door open.

He strides towards two squat, but broad men in Di Blasio security uniforms. Good or bad, they are in his way. They are going down.

"Hey fellas, is there a bathroom up here?" he says as he approaches.

The first speaks before looking up. "No admittance."

"Admit this," says Nige, and throws a hammer-like fist into the guard's face. His nose bursts. Nige skirts around, pulling him into a sleeper hold. The man jerks and thrusts with his legs, throwing Nige back into the wall.

But there's nothing that will make him let go. The pain of the plaster digging into his back only makes him grip tighter.

The other guard reaches for his pistol, but Kenneth hurries in and sends a roundhouse kick into his stomach. He bends double. Kenneth grabs his assault vest with both hands and rams him, teeth first, into the edge of a table with a satisfying crunch. "Eat this," he says, looking mighty proud of himself.

In his hands, Nige's guard goes limp, and he pushes him on top of his unconscious comrade. "Hey, you can't go stealing a man's one liner," he says.

"The influencer has become the influenced," says Kenneth, doffing his invisible cap.

"Victoria, we're going to be counting on you in there," says Nige.

She stretches her fingers. "Just like I showed you Dawn."

"Why? What are you going to do?" says Kenneth.

"It's a weapon," says Victoria. "I don't quite know how to aim it yet, so if I say get down, you get down."

"It's what she used on Aidan and the cultists when we first met them in the store," says Nige.

Victoria looks at Dawn. "I have a feeling, with both of us, it'll be even more powerful."

Follow That Ferret

Ferret features picks Katy up and steals her away across the stage, like a rat finding a chip in a bin. They disappear out of sight past a large LED covered screen.

Ignoring the plea of another attendant, Phil cuts across the stage. Three Di Blasio guards block his way. They draw batons. He spreads his arms wide and approaches.

"Come on then," he shouts. "Who's first?"

They all come forward at once.

"Fine by me," he says. He's had worse odds. He feints to the left so that rather than coming at him all at once they are now in an orderly queue. Pulls out one of his bottles of Newcastle Brown, holding it by the neck.

The first guard swings a baton and Phil catches it under his arm. But before he can swing the bottle, the other two are on him. He doesn't quite know how it happens, but within seconds he's on his back having ten bales of shit kicked out of him.

"That the best you got," he says as something cracks in his ribs. He holds his hands over his head and looks for an opening, but the kicks are perfectly timed to leave none.

In a flurry of burgundy, the cultists are on the attackers, flinging their robes over each of their heads. The guards stumble back, trying to untangle themselves. But that's all the time Phil needs. With all his might, which is rather a lot, he rises and smacks his bottle into the chin of the nearest guard. The bottle doesn't break, but something gives, and the guard face plants into the ground.

Pete stands behind the other two guards, holding one of the coolest looking shotguns Phil has ever seen. He flips it around and gun butts the guard on the left in the back of the head, sending him sprawling across the floor.

The other cultist he doesn't know the name of, the little mouth-breather with the glasses, catches Phil's eye conspiratorially, then ducks to the ground behind the last guard's legs. Phil gives the guard a good hard shove, and he flies into the back screen like a cannonball, smashing hundreds of tiny LEDs and releasing a cascade of sparks.

"Nice one, lads," he says, then gives the guard he bottled a kick for good measure.

They run towards the backstage area. It is quiet. Phil assumes everyone left when the fire alarm went off. But at the back, a door still swings. It leads to an exit to the main road out of the complex.

"There."

He sprints for it. Every step burns his left flank. The guards kicked him in good.

They emerge into a well-lit corridor. Ferret-face is at the other end dragging Katy along behind him. Her little legs barely scrape the floor. She wails, red faced.

"You, stop now," shouts Phil, lurching after them, the cultists in hot pursuit.

Ferret-face grins and shakes his head as they disappear through another door that opens out on to a street. He can't lose them.

He growls, putting everything into his legs. His frame is not one built for running, but he'll never forgive himself if he lets her go.

Two of the cultists overtake him on the stretch. As they sprint past he is surprised to see, that now they've disrobed, they both wear identical basketball kits and hi-tops.

Phil huffs after them as best he can.

Through the door is a short alleyway cut off by a raisable barrier. Ferret-face ducks under it, and pulls Katy towards a waiting car. He fumbles the boot open and lift her up.

"Give me that." Dave pulls the ale bottle out of Phil's hand, draws his arm back, and lets it fly.

It's gonna hit the kid. Phil puts his hands to his head.

"Watch ou— oh," he says as the bottle comes clunking down on Ferret-face's head. He stumbles and falls. Katy drops to the floor, apparently unharmed. Phil raises his eyebrows, clearly impressed. Swiftly crosses Dave's name off the prick list and runs toward the little girl.

She looks so small and lost.

"Katy, remember me?" he calls to her. "Your grandaddy sent us." He beckons her to him as he ducks under the barrier. Scoops her up into his bearlike arms and checks her over. She's so light. She clings to his neck, but remains silent. He checks her over carefully. No cuts or bruises that he can see.

The driver of the car starts to climb out so Phil boots the door back into him, crushing one of his knees in the frame. He shouts in pain and crumples to the ground.

Phil passes Katy over to Pete, who takes her hand. "This nice man will look after you, darlin'. Take you back to Grandad." He nods at Pete, then turns back towards Ferret-face and the driver. Slips a knuckle duster out of his pocket. A gift from his mother - God rest her. It reads 'PHIL' in big, bold letters. He slides it snugly over his fist. "Get her inside," he says over his shoulder. "Probably best she don't see what happens to this pair of nonces."

He's a Maniac

From what Mac can see, everything is going to plan. Well, the show is still running at least. Hoping to buy them some time before they need to cut back to the studio, the control room workers have managed to cobble together a few old interviews of Kenneth and interspersed them with some footage from previous years' influencer events. They have about five minutes before everyone needs to be back in position on stage.

He hasn't heard from Nige since the police arrived.

But in a way, that's part of the plan.

Once again, he leaves the control room to survey the scene outside. A huge crowd, made up of ousted audience members and other bystanders, has congregated on the other side of the police barricade.

Parked behind the crowd are three large vans, each with a huge satellite dish, and next to each is a reporter standing in front of a camera. He'd wished for more. Every eye, every camera focused on the building, is another plate in their armour.

With his hands cupped to the glass, he squints at the rooftop opposite. Three snipers peak over the parapet. Their helmeted heads give them away. Hopefully, there are more marksmen on the other surrounding buildings, but he can't see them. He casts his fearful eyes to the night sky. Assuming The Guardians are as all powerful as Victoria says, they will need all the guns they can get.

He closes his eyes and prays he hasn't doomed them all by surrounding them with police. If this goes wrong, if they don't change people's minds, if The Guardians get in and prevent them from getting Kenneth and the others on camera, then there's no way out. They're trapped.

A blur of movement at the top of the building opposite catches his eye. For a moment he thinks it's perhaps another sniper. But it's moving too fast.

They're here.

He fumbles for his phone. Calls the police. They transfer him quicker this time. "Officer Torrence." He can't keep the desperation from his voice. "Your guys on the roof of the apartment building are in danger."

"Is that a threat?" Mac can see Torrence down below. He's wearing a high vis jacket and shirt combo. He looks to the sniper's position.

"Someone's on the roof with them. You need to warn them."

As he speaks, the dark blur reaches the first of the snipers. It hardly stops before continuing towards the second, but the tell-tale helmeted head has gone.

Though he can't hear him, he can see Officer Torrence barking orders and pointing up towards the roof.

Below, several officers sprint towards the building.

Back to the rooftop and the blur is already upon the second marksman. They're so quick.

The third sniper, standing tall and out of cover now, begins firing. Another dark shape drops out of the sky, and as quickly as the firing started, it stops.

"What the hell are you doing, Macadamia? This wasn't part of our deal," Torrence growls over the radio.

He thought the snipers would have been more of a match for the Guardians, but they got through them too fast. If The Guardians get in, it'll be carnage. He has to stop them. He glances at the rifle in his hands. It won't be enough.

Think Macadamia!

Something comes to him. Something stupid that might just work. A change in plan that will test his acting abilities to the absolute limits.

He focuses back on the phone call.

"Snipers wasn't part of the deal, Torrence. You've smoked your last popsicle stand," he says. That sounds like something someone might say at such a crucial juncture. "I'm gonna kill all the hostages, and there's nothing you can do to stop me. The Church of The Fallen Angels will not be made a mockery… of!"

Bugger. At school, English was one of his stronger subjects, and he feels he's really let himself down by ending such a crushing line with a preposition.

Embarrassed, he cuts off communication once more, a la terrorist, and wipes his brow. This is quite the hole he's dug himself. Even that peaceful village postman job seems out of the picture now.

With crossed fingers, he looks down towards the little gazebo where the special forces team are gathered. Torrence marches over and points to the main building. Mac's prayers are answered when the men in black make their way towards the entrance to Studio One, armed to the teeth.

He sprints back to the control room, and throws open the door. "We're going to have company real soon," he says to Maggie, George, and the other two control room operatives.

"What's happened?" says Maggie.

"Guardians on the roof opposite, and I might have just called in SWAT to deal with it."

"Guardians?" says George.

"The guys who really killed The Twins and Terrence," says Mac.

"Well, that's not your only problem." George points to a rapidly falling countdown. "In about thirty seconds, my hack job of a VT is going to end. Cara's done a runner, so everyone watching at home is going to come back to an empty stage. I give you two minutes max before people switch off and head to Netflix." He sits down and looks to Mac for instructions.

"Ok, plan B. Maggie, you're going down there. Keep the viewers interested until Nige and the others arrive."

Maggie crinkles her nose. She looks less than keen. "Er… I guess I could tell a joke or something."

Mac snaps his fingers. "That's the spirit." He steps out into the corridor with Maggie close behind.

"What about you?" she asks. "Aren't you coming?"

"I may not be the chosen one, but that doesn't mean I can't go and do something amazingly, and possibly stupidly, heroic." He runs his hand quickly up and down the barrel of the rifle as if cocking a shotgun. It not being a shotgun, means he doesn't receive the expected *chik-chuk*. He gives it a disappointed look, saddened by its unwillingness to cooperate with his attempts to look cool in his big moment.

"Twenty seconds," shouts the tech from inside the control room.

"Just buy us enough time. Nige and the others will be there as soon as they find his grandson." He holds his breath, willing her to change his mind, to say something to stop him from having to do what he is about to. Even though they've just met, perhaps they could run away together. Move to Mexico. Start a family. Grow old with each other. Live long lives filled with happiness and love and cocktails on the beach in the sun. Forget that this whole damned, stupid thing ever happened.

In that moment a life time flashes before his eyes.

Her beautiful brown eyes gaze into his own. She says, "bye then," and legs it down the corridor.

"Oh. Ok. You too," he calls.

She's already rounded the corner.

"I'll just…"

To be honest, he doesn't know which job he'd prefer. Making up jokes on the spot in front of a live home audience of billions. Or – as is his only option for keeping the wolf from the door – acting as live bait, putting himself in between a bunch of highly trained special forces officers who want to kill him and another bunch of highly trained ninja butterfly-men who want to kill him.

In terms of anxiety induction, he guesses they are about the same. But at least no one will know if he messes this up, because he'll be… He shakes his head before he falls too far down that little rabbit hole.

All he can do is what he can do.

He sprints up the corridor towards the staircase Nige previously took to the roof. Next to the stairs is a map of the building. The SWAT team were heading for the main door. They'll probably be going straight to the studio. He needs to cut them off before they leave the reception area, then lead them away and up towards the roof where The Guardians will be.

He plummets down the stairs as fast as his legs can carry him. Nerves a jangle. The only thing that stops him from turning back and finding somewhere to cry is the momentum gathered from flying down the steps.

Back in the day, while getting ready for a night out with the lads, he used to listen to loud music. It got him pumped up, excited, and ready for the night's shenanigans. So, thinking it might help him now, he sings one of his mother's favourites as he descends the steps. An eighties classic about a girl in a steel town.

At the bottom of the stairs, he thumps a fist on his chest and kicks open the door that leads to the foyer. As soon as he pops his head into the reception area, roughly ten laser sights converge on his forehead.

"Freeze Macadamia," comes an order.

So he does the only sensible thing and pops his head back out again.

Standing with his back to the wall behind the door, he shouts. "We've got them all on the roof. And we're going to blow their brains out!" Tries an evil laugh. Cuts it short at the sound of the rapid approach of ten pairs of boots.

He grips his rifle and fires a few rounds into the floor. Having never fired a gun before, he is more than a little surprised by the excessive volume. Every shot is a kick to the eardrum, and the recoil nearly pulls his arm off. Surely nothing needs to be that loud. So much for movie heroes firing machine guns one handed.

Hoping the special forces team are perturbed, he legs it up the stairs.

"You'll never stop me. I'm a maniac!" he cries, but with his hearing destroyed, he can barely hear himself.

When he reaches the second floor, he looks down. The police are in hot pursuit. He glances up, and to his absolute horror, sees exactly what he expected coming the other way.

Two storeys above, a pale white face glares down over the bannister.

Mac looks down into the light of several torches aiming straight up. This is what a general must feel like when sending troops into battle. It makes him giddy. It's all for the greater good though, right?

"That's it, my minions," he shouts to The Guardians, but really, it's for the benefit of the boys in blue. He wants to make sure his voice carries downwards. Give them a warning, so at least they know it's not just him. "The metropolitan's finest are right behind me. Go get 'em." He tries that laugh again.

With that, he ducks out of the stairwell, through a side door, and back on to the floor with the control room. Sprints up the corridor. Stops briefly to shout a warning to George, but the control room crew is no longer there. On the screens he can see Maggie, standing centre stage. She is holding a mic, talking into the camera, but Nige and the others aren't with her.

Time is running out. Where can they be?

He looks back. Beyond the doorway comes the rustle of leathery wings. He crouches. Raises the rifle to his shoulder, not knowing what he'll do when the time comes to fire.

Then come the first shots from the floor below.

Bright muzzle flashes light up tall, slim figures that rush past. The screams of men tell Mac he shouldn't hang about, so he turns and runs. He is useless here.

He needs to find Nige and the others and get them on stage immediately.

The Inner Sanctum of BBC Television Centre

With its breeze block walls and untiled ceiling that reveals a trail of pipes and wires overhead, the corridor isn't as pretty as the one they just left behind. Someone with less vengeance on their mind might even consider it a little spooky.

But Nige and the angels are on a mission and they creep down the dim corridor undeterred. At the far end, the orange glow from candle flames around the corner pulses and wavers.

There's a strange sound. A low chant. One clear voice singing low. A baritone drone. With every change in note, the melody darkens. It's almost hypnotising in its slow simplicity. Painful, but somehow placating. It drains the energy and life from his muscles.

Nige pinches himself to shake away the sleepiness and edges forward with the others in tow. When they reach the corner, he peers around, not knowing what to expect.

The room beyond is square, about half the length of a tennis court, with a black curtain pulled halfway across. Five hooded figures, kneel in a semi-circle in the centre of the room. For a moment Nige thinks it's the cultists, but these five are broader at the shoulder, and the robes are a slightly different colour. Three tall shapes move in circles around them. In the flickering candlelight, The Guardians are black skeletons of smoke that seem to flit in and out of existence.

As the low chant rises to a crescendo, The Guardians form a line in front of the hooded figures. With some unseen signal, the singing stops dead. The Guardian in the centre draws its blade as those in the semi-circle sit up and remove their hoods. A slight intake of breath from Dawn. Nige glances at her.

She mouths, "the new influencers."

The Guardian takes the hand of the influencer on the right and cuts a line across his palm. A long black tongue emerges from its white, puckered face, and it licks the blood from the wound.

"Your gift has been received," it says and the hair on Nige's neck prickles.

The influencer bows its head and stands as The Guardian moves on to the next.

Nige moves back out of sight.

"Do you think they know what's happened in the studio?" whispers Kenneth.

"They must have heard the fire alarm," says Nige.

"Now feast on the sacrifice we present to you."

The sound of a child crying cuts through the air.

Another hooded figure enters from behind the curtain. He carries Nige's three-year-old grandson, Charlie, towards the semi-circle. The boy wails and struggles, trying his best to escape the arms of his captor, his little face red with effort. Seeing him pushes Nige over the edge.

"Charlie!" He steps out, not knowing if the others will follow. Instinct propels him. "Put him down." He growls and stalks across the room with his baton held ready by his side.

He watches the influencers and Guardians in his peripheral vision, but does not take his eyes from the one carrying his grandson. Speeds up to a jog as Dawn, Kenneth, and Victoria follow him into the centre of the room.

"Be ready," shouts Victoria as The Guardians creep forward, knives drawn.

Nige doesn't wait to see what happens. The man holding Charlie holds the boy up like a shield as he closes in. Coward.

Nige is taller and reaches over, pulling the hood over his opponent's eyes. Stamps on his knee, then pulls Charlie from his arms. The boy buries himself in his shoulder.

He wheels around with Charlie in one arm and his baton drawn. The five influencers block his exit. They shrug off their robes. Beneath, sharp suits cover their solid looking frames. This isn't a fight he can win.

"Get down," shouts Victoria, and Nige can sense that pressure well up inside him like a migraine. As if someone has placed a vice over his head and tightened. He jumps to the floor and slides towards the curtain with his grandson wrapped in his arms.

Kenneth shoves The Guardian he is grappling with away, and dives to the ground too.

Nige's gut twitches as the influencers approach. Senses their outstretched fingers reaching for him. He closes his eyes.

And nothing happens.

Charlie continues to sob in his arms.

"Why didn't it work?" says Victoria. She stares at her hands then flexes them. Still nothing.

Two sets of rough hands grab Nige and pull him up. He pushes the child as far away as possible. "Run, boy."

He grabs one of the influencer's hands and twists a finger. He is rewarded with a snap and a scream, but the rest are on him before he can scramble away. Though he fights as hard as he ever has, they pin him to the ground. They weigh down on his back and he feels a sharp kick in his ribs.

From his position, nose down in the rough carpet, Nige can see Kenneth, Dawn, and Victoria also being subdued by The Guardians and influencers.

"Did you think we wouldn't have a plan in place in case you showed up?" says one Guardian, as he twirls his knife around his fingertips. "It's easy to drown out the pulse with some technological know how." His pasty white lips crack into a wide smile, revealing teeth like the sweepings from a china shop accident. He looks at Nige. "We used it on your grandfather's pathetic little band too. Your paltry uprising will be as unsuccessful as his. Isadore and our brothers are on their way."

"How did you do it?" Victoria stops her struggling and scowls.

"I couldn't pretend to know." The Guardian shrugs. His mouth turns into a grotesque frown. "Something to do with waves." He places a clawed hand on a tall rack-mounted box that whirs and hums quietly, then rubs his fingers together. "It's warm. You must have been prepping for quite the blast. Best I apply something more local."

He opens a padded attaché case next to the rack and takes out two sets of intricate bracelets. He moves towards Victoria. She recoils. The two influencers that are holding her force her hands forward. Taking great care, the Guardian clicks the bracelets around her wrists. It tightens much like the bounty bracelet. He does the same to Dawn.

"What are you going to do with us?" says Kenneth. The Guardian holding him has its knife pressed so close to his throat, a rivulet of blood starts to drip down his neck.

The Guardian points at the three angels, one at a time. "Dead, dead, dead." Then at Nige and Charlie. "Dinner, dessert."

"You harm a hair on his head and I'll rip every bone from your body," shouts Nige, his voice muffled by the carpet and the weight on his back. He bucks but only throws one of the three influencers pinning him off. "Where's my son?" From his position he can't see Charlie. He hopes he managed to get away.

"Stockwell, you worm, bring the little one here then fetch the others. I think it's time for a family reunion."

The man that had been carrying Charlie removes his hood.

"Stockwell," Kenneth says. "I wondered when we'd see you writhe out of the dirt."

Stockwell looks pale and haggard. Like he hasn't slept in days. He stares daggers at Kenneth, then responds to the Guardian. "Certainly Barthram," he says, then grabs Charlie.

Barthram beckons him over with a long white finger. Ian hands the boy over then retreats behind the curtain.

"There, there, little one. Don't cry." The Guardian makes eye contact with Nige as the child's sobbing slows. He sneers in condescension. "All these nasty people are a bit scary, aren't they?"

The boy looks so tired. He rests his chin innocently on Barthram's shoulder as The Guardian pats him gently on the back.

Barthram glances at the other Guardians with a hidden, baleful meaning. "For centuries we've toiled for the good of humanity. What made you think you could ever stop us?"

"The good?" says Victoria. She barks out a laugh.

Barthram's lip curls. "You think you know so much, don't you? You see us feeding on children, and holding blood rituals, and you think you've got us pegged."

"It does all give off a bit of a skulls on the uniform vibe," says Kenneth. He stands defiant with his chin raised.

"We do what needs to be done to save you from yourselves. What do you think would happen if we just let you sheep do what you want? If we let everyone go through the emergence?" He raises his eyebrows. "You think overpopulation is bad now? How do you think it would look if everyone born in the last five hundred years was still alive?" He pauses and shakes his head. "Imagine seas empty of fish, the lands and forests buried by grey, barren concrete, wars fought over oil, fertile land, water. The planet would not sustain us. Everything would die." He rubs the front of his neck. Several large flakes of dead skin fall to the ground. "You can't control yourselves. You think you have ethics and freedom, but it stops you from making the right decisions. Even now, even with our aid, the planet is dying and your politicians, your chosen ones, are too slow, pompous, or greedy to do anything about it. Culling you is for your own good."

The curtain ruffles and Stockwell returns with Lewis and Nikki. Hands bound. Both are gagged. Lewis's gag is red with blood and he has bruises across both eyes. The state of his knuckles suggests he put up a fight. Nige can't help but feel proud. It was never a fight he could win.

"Isn't this nice?" says Barthram. "Lovely to see your son and his beautiful wife again. We know it's been a while. You see, you've been on our radar for quite some time." He grins and draws his knife. "So, which one should I kill first?"

Put Your Whole Self In

The building is deserted. On his way to the studio Mac doesn't see a soul.

As he enters the back of the studio, he spots the three cultists. They stand in a ring, holding hands with a small girl of about five. She is wearing a robe. Terry's or Dave's, as Pete is the only one still in his. Suddenly they let go of each other and put their right legs in. Then their right legs out. Then they shake them all about.

"Woahoah guys!" says Mac, waving an arm to get their attention. "We're gonna have company real soon."

Pete holds a hand out. "Did you want to join in? It's left legs next."

"Maybe another time. Here." He passes Terry his rifle. "Don't ever make me hold one of those again. Are Nige and the others in there with Maggie?"

"We don't know where they are," says Dave. "Maggie's running out of things to say. I'm pretty sure she's been through 'Do Not Stand At My Grave and Weep' twice already."

"Oh god. That bad?" He strides past them, aiming for an opening between two large LED panels that leads on to the stage. "The press are here, so by now anyone watching knows what's going on. I guess I should just try to tell the people why we're really here." He turns and looks back. "Keep an eye out."

As he makes his way towards her, Maggie looks over, and with a frantic waving of her arm, beckons him closer.

She covers the mic with her hand and hisses. "Where are they? I don't know what I'm doing."

"I think we just start, and hope Nige and the rest get here."

The cultists wander on to the stage as well. Pete carries Katy on his back.

Mac takes the mic from Maggie and turns to face the camera.

He was wrong. This is way more nerve-racking than leading a group of people who want to kill him towards another group of people who want to kill him. With that, all he really had to do was run around and convince people he was crazy, which was easy considering the way he looked.

He glances down at himself. Yellowing shirt, stained coat, loose crumpled tie. At some point, he's lost his hat and his belt. His eyes sag with fatigue and bruises cover his face. He looks a million times worse than when he emerged from that alleyway in Camden screaming bloody murder.

And no one had listened to him then.

Now, he has to figure out how to convince a planet full of people that he's completely sane, and that everything their parents, teachers, and governments have told them about their own species is wrong.

He stares wide eyed into the camera, knowing billions of people are watching at home. Worst of all, his mum never misses the show.

He readies himself, opens his mouth, and all the lights in the room go dark.

Familiar feathery footfalls fill the surrounding stage.

"You've come a long way, Macadamia," says a voice right by his ear. He can sense a tall figure standing close on his right. "And in doing so, you've already done a lot of our work for us."

"How so?" he says, as if he and the owner of the voice are the only two people in the room.

"When someone finds out about us, we usually either silence them immediately, or, if it gets a little too far like this has, we convince the public that that person is insane." There's a short pause in which Mac hears an amused hum. "Your little stunt couldn't have done it better if we had planned it ourselves. You, Davies, even Miss Greaves here, everyone watching at home thinks you've joined a deranged religious cult, and they know you murdered the influencers and Stefan Di Blasio. You've almost made it too easy."

Nearby, he can hear Katy crying softly.

Dim emergency lighting clanks on in the roof, revealing the menagerie of fiends that surround them. Five winged, stick-thin devils of the sort he'd seen at Korrigan and Davies's warehouse, several hooded familiars, and three Di Blasio guards.

Standing slightly separate from the rest are a pair of gnarled and haggard things that he can't help but look at with horrified fascination. One leers at him from bulbous eyes that rest either side of its face. Its pale visage more like a fish than a man. The other, with a head that's almost all mouth, sits upon the ground in some sort of bag pulled tight around its neck. It chatters its teeth at him hungrily when he catches its eye.

The Guardian standing at his shoulder is pale and haggard. Almost decaying.

"Isadore," spits Maggie.

He looks to the Di Blasio guards. "Send for the others. I want them all here." The flutter of Isadore's breath tickles Mac's ear as he whispers, "we're going to make such a mess of your friends, that by the end of the night you're going to beg me to kill you."

Mac looks him in the eye. Struggles to breathe.

The Guardian grins wide. "But I won't."

Bracelet For Impact

Two Di Blasio guards enter the room and approach Barthram. "Isadore has arrived," says one. "He wants everyone brought to the main studio."

Barthram rolls his eyes. "Just as we were about to have a little fun." He slots his knife back into the sheath on his belt and points at Nige. "Get him up."

They tug him to his feet and shove him back towards the main corridor. He tries to turn to see where Charlie is, but something thin and sharp digs into the back of his neck.

"Keep moving."

The Guardians lead them all towards the studio. The lights in the main corridor are dead. Only the fire exit signs illuminate their way.

The first thing he sees is Katy surrounded by monsters. What little hope he had drains away to nothing.

"Ah, the ever resourceful Nigel Davies," says The Guardian in the centre. "We finally meet."

Mac stands to his left, his head lowered, staring at the floor. Hands hanging loose by his sides. His body shudders with each breath. The poor lad looks utterly defeated. He glances up towards Nige, then quickly looks down again.

"And Kenneth, Victoria, and Dawn. All in one place. I love it." The Guardian claps his hands. "Barthram, bravo on the bracelets. You said they might all come gallivanting in after we sent the message and you were right."

Barthram bows his head and smiles. "It wasn't worth taking any chances. They tried to use the weapon."

"Fabulous forward planning." Isadore raises an arm, ushering his retinue to move all prisoners to the space between the stands and the stage. "Let's not waste any more time. I'm sure London's finest are formulating a new strategy and will be with us any moment."

Nige and the others are pushed to their knees. Three of the hooded men force Terry, Dave, and Maggie to join them.

One of the Di Blasio guards takes hold of Mac's arm, but Isadore places a hand on his shoulder.

"He stays with me." He then clicks his fingers at Pete, who remains with Katy by the interviewer's sofa on the stage. His hood leaves his face in shadow, and in the pale emergency lighting, his robe looks almost identical to The Guardian familiars. "You with the girl. Place the child with the others."

Pete starts, then carries Katy down from the stage. He places her next to Lewis, who hugs her as best as he can with his arms bound. Pete then moves to stand behind Dawn and Victoria. He begins to rummage in his pockets.

"Well, isn't this wonderful? All together at last. I—"

The thing in the bag interrupts Isadore with an agitated chattering. Its black, little eyes scan over the prisoners hungrily. The thing with the fish-like face leans in closer to it, listens, then approaches and whispers to Isadore. Mac can't look away from its pale, dead eyes.

Isadore looks back at the creature in the bag with a placating, if somewhat impatient, smile, and says, "Soon Father, we will feed soon."

He then turns back to his congregation. "This was never going to go well for you. Any of you. And I'm afraid it ends now. No more games. As we have told countless others, what we do…" He closes his eyes as if needing to convince himself more than anyone else. "What we do is for the greater good. You must understand that by silencing you, the world shall remain in blissful ignorance. It's not personal."

"But surely there has to be another way." Nige pushes himself to his feet. He's never felt more weary. His bones ache. But he has to try something. "None of you are stupid. You must see this is wrong. Hurting children? Murdering families? The ends can't justify the means."

For the tiniest of moments, Nige senses a sadness behind Isadore's eyes.

"You are more like your grandfather than I gave you credit. He tried a similar tact." Whatever sadness was there quickly turns to anger. "You think you're superior just because you are genetically predisposed to the emergence."

He grips Mac's shoulder causing him to wince.

"Not everyone has been afforded that gift. Some of us had to sell our souls for the fountain of youth. And if we hadn't, where would we be? Your sort never suffered for anything, never knew hardship, never knew what it took to make the right decisions. You pussyfoot around and call it compassion. If we'd left it up to you, then we'd all be dead. Skeletons floating through space on an arid husk."

"But—"

"Let me pose a question, Davies. How many children would die if we did not do what we do?" He leans his head to one side. "If I save five billion by killing five thousand, am I wrong?"

Nige struggles to speak. Can't give an answer because there isn't one. This was never his fight. But then, when has any fight ever been his?

"There's got to be another way. Think of all we could achieve if we just worked together for a solution."

"I won't hear it," says Isadore.

He flicks his hand, and each Guardian unsheathes their blade.

The sound of someone stepping through the entrance from the backstage area causes the Guardians to pause.

"Oi, oi, saveloy. What's going on here then?"

Spoony Phil stops and takes in the scene. Isadore turns to face him, and for a moment there's silence.

Mac frowns, then his eyes widen as if an idea has come to him. His hand slowly slips into his front pocket. He pulls something out wrapped in a clenched fist, whips it around Isadore's wrist, and then immediately tears it away. He dives to the floor in what has become his trademark forward roll, but misjudges the landing and falls off the stage into Kenneth's lap.

"What was that?" says Isadore, rubbing his wrist and moving to the edge of the stage to look down on the others.

"Something I learnt from Bobby Feta," says Mac rising to his feet.

A look of agony crosses Isadore's face and he bends double, clutching his stomach. "What did you do to me?" He gags.

"Prepare to vomit up your own molten intestines." Mac throws a broken bounty bracelet up on to the stage.

Shortly after, four similar, yet more intricate, bracelets land next to it along with Pete's screwdriver.

"Oops, didn't mean to throw that as well," he says, stepping forward awkwardly to retrieve it.

Nige looks back at Victoria and Dawn, now rubbing their freed wrists. Victoria smiles and raises her hands.

A buzzing in his head warns him of what's about to happen. He tackles Lewis, Nikki, and the kids to the ground, covering them as best he can just before the whole room explodes.

Through the maelstrom of flung bodies, he glances up. Both Victoria and Dawn stand hands raised, as waves of force pour forth from their palms.

"You wanna go some, you fuckin' prick?" shouts Phil from on stage.

He strides out of the darkness carrying a pole and lumps Isadore in the stomach. A gout of dark red ichor spouts out of his pale mouth, splatting the thing in the bag, who, on his backswing, Spoony Phil manages to decapitate.

"The fuck was that in the bag?"

Isadore continues to vomit out molten intestines as Spoony Phil moves on to batter the fish looking guy.

"No one messes with Korrigan and Davies security, least of all you cod-chops."

Nige lurches for the nearest influencer and tackles him to the ground. Beating him about the face with his fists until he's nothing more than a bloody pulp. He looks for his next target, but Victoria and Dawn have already blown most away.

Kenneth is deftly striking out at anyone that comes close.

With The Guardians distracted, Nige pulls the gag from Lewis's face and moves around to untie his hands.

"Dad, who are these people?"

"No time to talk," says Nige. "Pick up the kids. We're going."

Once Lewis is free, Nige moves on to help Nikki. Lewis pulls the kids towards him, hugging them close.

They follow him towards the main exit between the stalls. Maggie hurries after them. Behind, the sound of the fray intensifies as Terry picks up his assault rifle and begins blasting.

When they reach the main foyer Nige doesn't slow. The doors to the outside world are the surface of the sea, and he's drowning in its depths. He bursts through, family in tow.

"Freeze," shouts a voice over a megaphone, and Nige is blinded by three sun-like spotlights trained on the group.

He puts his hand to his brow. "It's me, Nige Davies. Let my kids through."

The police stare wordlessly at the group. Beyond, he can hear voices in the crowd.

Spoony Phil catches up to them, barging the group forward through the door, causing Nige to trip out into the open space in front of the barricade of police cars and officers.

The hubbub of the crowd builds to an excited crescendo. Phones are raised and the press cameras over by the vans are turned their way.

"What is that?" says a nearby officer. Her mouth is open in shock.

"It looks like Kenneth and Dawn!" says another.

Air rushes overhead as Kenneth takes to the skies and then rests, hovering a few feet above them.

"Yes, it is I, Kenneth Bailey," he says. "Former Di Blasio influencer, current… er…" He looks back down to Victoria who remains on the ground and hisses, "What exactly am I now?"

She rolls her eyes and joins him in the air.

With the world watching through the hundreds of cameras now trained on them, she begins to tell their story.

Her voice becomes background noise as Nige kneels and pulls his grandchildren towards him. He holds them close. Lewis and Nikki wrap their arms around them too. And in the comfort of their embrace, his tears come, unashamedly and unrestrained.

The Change

Mac spends the next five days in police custody answering all sorts of nasty questions, but in the end, they let him go.

He has no access to the news while he's inside, so it surprises him to discover the affect Victoria's story has had on the world.

People are divided. Some believe absolutely in what has happened to the Di Blasio influencers. Others are convinced the whole thing is a hoax - a classic case of a Big Food corporation spouting lies to sell more product.

The internet is lit up with arguments from both sides. And people fight bitterly on social media. There's not a lot of talk about The Guardians.

He can't help but think that is all very intentional. That every ludicrous conspiracy theory dreamt up and spat out has groomed people to distrust everything they see. As if someone high up - higher than he'd ever thought possible - has built a fail safe into society ready for that day when their secret was finally revealed.

He returns to his office after those three days to find it freshly trashed. Graffiti covers the walls. "LIAR!" Unfortunately it is those who are scared or angry who are easiest to manipulate into believing lies, and it is those who are scared or angry that shout the loudest, and behave the worst.

Mac decides to leave London and move back in with his mum. At least until things cool down. But before he heads home with his tail between his legs, he has something he needs to do. One loose end to tie up.

It takes him another forty eight hours to pluck up the courage to go, and when he finally reaches Suzy's door he just stands there, hand over the doorbell.

He looks back up the garden path to the road. He could leave. This is not a conversation he ever thought he would have. It was the real police who gave people the sort of news he is about to give.

But it's his duty to tell her. Every time he looks at the big wodge of cash she gave him, he is reminded.

He pushes the bell. Moments later a boy of around eight or nine inches the door open, still on the chain. This is going to be harder than he thought.

"Yes," the boy says, eyeing Mac cautiously.

"Is your mother in?"

Without another word or look, the boy turns around and shouts, "Mum!" Then disappears out of sight.

A few seconds later, Suzy's face appears through the crack in the door. When she sees Mac, she quickly closes it. The chain rattles, then the door opens again.

"Do you have news?" She stands there in a dressing gown, her face puffy. She's clearly been crying.

Mac feels the tug of his breath in his lungs. "I'm sorry," he says.

She nods slowly. By the look on her face he's only confirming what she already knows to be true. She stands back and opens the door wider. "Come in."

He tells her what he knows. Everything. She takes it better than he thought someone could.

"I saw you on TV," she says once he reaches the end of his story.

He nods. He doesn't know what to say. So far today he's been spat at, cheered, threatened, and shaken a total strangers hand. And that was just on the tube ride over. Which side of the fence does she sit?

"It was convincing," she says, her face passive.

"I expect you'd rather be with your children than with a stranger at a time like this." He stands placing his untouched mug of tea on the table. It's best not to get into an argument. "I should go."

She holds up a hand before he can leave. "I believe you, Mac. Lots of people do. Enough people. But you know what people are like - if something doesn't affect them directly, they forget. I can't forget what happened to my Harry. I won't let it go."

She looks at him with hope in her eyes. What does she expect from him? "But what can we do?" he says.

"Harry always said you only had to fight a little bit harder, a little bit longer, than those who oppose you and you'll win. We just have to persevere."

"It's not my job to make people change."

She reaches out and takes his hand. "You're not the man I thought you were back in your office, Mac. I thought I'd never see you again. Thought you'd take every excuse and disappear with the money I gave you." She nods to the cash lying between them on the table. "But you didn't. You're a nice guy. And if nice guys like you don't do anything, bad guys like them win."

A fire stokes in his belly. A mixture of hatred for The Guardians, of what they have done, but also pride. Pride at what he himself has already achieved. He still has nothing to lose. Maybe that's a strength.

He smiles. "I suppose all I can do is what I can do."

THE OPEN SEAS

Nige considers moving to Manchester to be nearer to Lewis and the kids, but in the end he decides he's had enough of city life. He always promised Fiona they'd get away, so why not start now? A clean break. A new start.

He sets up camp in his parent's old house in Cornwall. An old B&B on the side of a rugged hill that leads down to the bay. He hides away for some time. Right now, the world is a more confusing place than it's ever been, and he doesn't want to be a part of it.

He likes to think that they've helped. Done something good, but knows they've barely scratched the surface.

He doesn't like the idea that The Guardians are still out there. He hopes, despite what he and the others have done, that they'll perhaps leave them alone for now. He's spoken to Mac a few times. The lad seems to think, for the time being at least, while the world's eye is on them, that they have some sort of immunity. That if they were to end up dead it would seem too suspect. He hopes this is the case. Not just for his sake, but for his family.

But how long can that last?

He transports the boat from the shed in the industrial estate and moors it at his dad's old sailing club. It's a five-minute walk from the house down the little coastal path. It takes two months to get it seaworthy again. And about a week longer for him to realise that what he at first thought was a glitch in the GPS is in fact a destination.

Mark, the electronics guy from the club, points it out when Nige asks him to take a look.

"It's not a defect. Looks like a location hardwired in or something. Can't delete it. Can't edit it," he says as he screws the unit back in place. "If you want, I can get you a new one."

Nige shakes his head. He'll probably just ignore it.

"The spot's not very far off the coast," says Mark, pulling a large wooly hat down over his ears and climbing back over to the dock. "In fact, it's not far from the spot we found the old girl after… you know." He clears his throat.

"Yeah?" Nige says. Something about that peaks his interest.

Though he and Nige are of a similar age, Mark was a friend of his father's, and one of those manning the rescue boat that had found The Pathfinder abandoned on the waves.

"I reckon you should have a look. Might be cathartic. Give you some closure with your old man. There are a few little islands out there." Mark bobs his head from side to side. "Well, not really islands, more like underwater mountains. They peek up out of the water in a few spots. Probably just a load of guano. But might be an interesting trip."

Nige strokes his beard. He's let it grow in. Thinks it adds to his salty sea-dog look. The kids are coming down with Lewis and Nikki for Christmas and he's been thinking about taking them out on the boat so this could be perfect. "Might be."

Christmas comes, and on the second day of their stay, he takes Lewis and the kids out with the promise of adventure on the high seas.

With life vests on, and enough story books and crayons to keep them entertained if they get bored, they set sail for the destination locked in his father's GPS.

He lets the boat do its thing, turning the steering a few degrees at a time. The chill of the wind and the fine salt spray take his breath away, hitting him like a refreshing slap in the face from a well-trained masseuse. The hairs stand on the back of his neck and he smiles at ease. He always enjoyed the silent sway of a calm ocean.

He and Lewis talk very little on the way. But what they say is enough. Nige is just happy they're together enjoying each other's company.

The location is somewhere in the Bristol channel, not far off the Cornish shore. They set up on deck and eat peanut butter sandwiches, with Nige telling the kids stories of his times working the clubs. He leaves some of the more risky bits out, which doesn't leave much, but the kids seem entertained.

After lunch, he checks the GPS. The marker is roughly a mile or so to the west. He takes his binoculars from a little pouch by one of the jammers to see what he can. Mark was right. There are a few small islands out here. They show up as little dark lumps surrounded by foamy surf. A few white gulls float in the water nearby.

"There we are kids. What we've been looking for!" He points out the islands and lets them both have a go on the binoculars.

"What's that blue light?" asks Lewis.

Nige looks to where he is pointing. Sure enough, on the nearest of the three little islands, a blue lamp hangs from a tall post. It's difficult to see in the light of day against the clear blue skies. Nige takes the binoculars back and looks again. The post stands at the end of a short wooden pier.

"Not sure." He surveys the horizon. There are no other man-made landmarks.

He checks the GPS again. The coordinates lead them directly to it.

"Grandad, the blue light up here's come on too," says Katy.

He looks to his own lamp that hangs beneath the boom. For the first time since he's had the boat, it's on.

Something clicks in the steering wheel and it turns ever so slightly. Nige takes hold and applies some pressure, but it doesn't move. He pushes harder, but it still won't budge. It shifts, bringing them on a collision course with the pier.

"Lewis, take them downstairs. Something's not right here." He wrestles with the wheel as Lewis leads the kids into the cabin.

After getting them settled, Lewis pokes his head back up. "What's going on?"

"The wheel's stuck. We're heading straight for the island."

With a flick of the wrist, he un-jams the mainsheet, and when the main sail begins to flap, he lets the halyard go taking all power out of the boat. It quickly comes to a stop, leaving them bobbing on the waves.

He takes hold of the wheel again but it still won't turn. He picks up the radio. Mark might know what to do, and if not they can hopefully send out a rib or something to tow them back. But as he does, the engine at the back of the boat splutters into life. He frowns and looks at the controls by the wheel, convinced for a moment he's accidentally turned it on himself. But there's nothing there that could.

At a much slower pace than before, they begin heading for the short pier again. It's less than fifty metres away now and closing.

"Balls on parade," he says as he climbs to the back of the boat. He scratches his ears and looks at the engine. He hits the kill switch but it doesn't stop. They are definitely going to hit the pier. He races back up the boat throwing the fenders over the side in the hope that they will dampen the impact.

As they approach, the sound of the engine quiets, and the speed of the boat slows. What is going on?

Despite its remote location, the pier looks to be in a good state of repair.

When the prow of the boat passes the blue light, it clicks off and so does the engine. They slow and come to a gradual stop next to the dock.

Nige jumps out and wraps a rope around a cleat. He notices it is placed in exactly the right position for the size of his boat. At the other end, Lewis does the same.

"It's like this boat was made for this pier?" says Lewis. He hops back aboard and ducks into the cabin to check on the kids.

Nige scans the island. A craggy outcrop of near black rock in the middle of an endless sea. Deserted save for the pier. But there has to be electricity, otherwise what's powering the light? And who's maintaining a pier in the middle of nowhere? If Dad's old boat is anything to go by, things left in water degrade very quickly.

Lewis hands Charlie over the side of the boat, and Nige places him safely on the pier. They do the same with Katy. He takes both their hands. He shouldn't have brought them. This was reckless.

"Grandad," says Katy, pointing once more, this time to the end of the pier. "Who's that?"

Nige looks up. A tall but slightly crooked man stands there, wrapped in a thick waterproof coat. His head is decked with a large bobble hat that wags with the sea breeze. He is alone. Despite his obvious age, his stance is strong. The man smiles, and lines, like the crags of the island, crease at his eyes and mouth.

Lewis joins them. "Dad, that's…"

Nige smiles back. A strange mix of emotions washes over him.

It's been so long.

"Dad?"

"I wondered how long it would take you." Nige's father holds out a welcoming arm. "Come on in. It's cold out here, and there's work to be done."

Hello!

Thank you for reading my book 'A More Perfect Human'. I hope you enjoyed it. I'd be eternally grateful if you could take two minutes to leave a review on Amazon. When you leave one it helps other people find my book. It would really make my day!

For updates on new releases, freebies, and offers on other books please sign up to my mailing list at my website - https://cjpowellauthor.com/amph When you sign up you'll receive a playlist of songs that helped influence me in the writing of this book. Music I used as a soundtrack while sitting in the dark sipping chamomile tea and tapping at my laptop. They are all total bangers so worth signing up for! And don't worry I won't spam you.

Please get in touch to let me know if you enjoyed the book - I'd love to hear your feedback. And feel free to recommend it to some friends!!

You can also find me on Instagram and Facebook by searching C J Powell Author.

Thanks again!!

Chris x

Use your phone camera on this QR code to go straight to my website.

Also By

A More Perfect Human is my debut novel. This won't be the only book in the Chrysalis series. Wouldn't be much of a series if it was. And I've commited now with a bit of a cliffhanger ending and writing 'Chrysalis series' on the cover. I have another novel on the way plus several other stories in the pipeline. The best way to find out about new releases is to sign-up to my mailing list here...

https://cjpowellauthor.com

About The Author

Hi, I'm Chris. I'm a wedding band musician from the south of the UK. I write in my spare time and am hoping to become a full time author once I'm no longer cool enough to play at weddings... ideally before, so there's not a sort of weird lull between where I become a total layabout.

I live with my wife and daughter and enjoy retro computer games, sci-fi movies, and, if I ever get the opportunity, rock climbing.

I'd like to thank my lovely wife for reading the first disgusting draft of this book and telling me it was ok, and also giving me the time to work on it. I'd also like to thank my mum, dad, Jess and Mole for having a look and giving me the confidence to continue. Also Pedro, the first person to ever give one of my novels a go. And Emily my editor who gave me some awesome advice. Wouldn't have been able to finish this without you guys.

Printed in Great Britain
by Amazon